ZADRUGA

ZADRUGA

MARGARET PEMBERTON

BANTAM PRESS

LONDON · NEW YORK · TORONTO · SYDNEY · AUCKLAND

TRANSWORLD PUBLISHERS LTD
61–63 Uxbridge Road, London W5 5SA

TRANSWORLD PUBLISHERS (AUSTRALIA) PTY LTD
15–25 Helles Avenue, Moorebank, NSW 2170

TRANSWORLD PUBLISHERS (NZ) LTD
3 William Pickering Drive, Albany, Auckland

Published 1994 by Bantam Press
a division of Transworld Publishers Ltd
Copyright © Margaret Pemberton 1994

A catalogue record for this book is available from the British Library.
ISBN 0593 027922

Printed in Great Britain by
Biddles Ltd, Guildford and King's Lynn.

For my son, Michael Carl.
With love.

May 1914–August 1919

Chapter One

Although the distance from the Vassilovich residence to the Royal Palace was a mere hundred yards and although Belgrade's pleasant early summer heat was tempered by a cooling breeze, protocol dictated that the Vassilovich sisters travelled the distance in an open landau.

As the horses turned out into Prince Milan Street, Natalie Vassilovich wrinkled her pretty nose in distaste.

'Why do we have to endure living on a street named after an Obrenovich? Why hasn't it been renamed after King Alexander or King Peter, or even after Sandro?'

Katerina Vassilovich regarded her seventeen-year-old younger sister with amusement.

'If Belgrade's street names had changed every time an Obrenovich had replaced a Karageorgevich on the throne and every time a Karageorgevich had regained the throne from an Obrenovich, the population would be dizzy,' she said, revealing a streak of common sense so prosaic Natalie found it almost unintelligible.

'How can you be so *dispassionate*?' she asked in disbelief. 'You have just as much Karageorgevich blood in your veins as Uncle Peter or Sandro, and yet you behave as if you were *all* Vassilovich.'

'I *feel* as if I am all Vassilovich,' Katerina said, her grey-green eyes darkening slightly.

'Well, *I* don't!' Natalie's eyes, flecked gold where her sister's were grey, flashed fire.

Katerina adjusted the mother-of-pearl handle of her

parasol a little more comfortably against her shoulder, a slight frown creasing her brow. That Natalie had inherited their maternal great-grandfather's legendary temper and passionate hotheadedness had been obvious ever since their nursery days. And she knew that their mother, as well as their father, heartily regretted it.

As the Vassilovich landau bowled past the Russian Legation and towards the palace gates she wondered why it was that the Karageorgevichs were so self-destructive; not her mother, of course. The Karegeorgevich temper and passion was as alien to her mother as it was to herself, but it had resulted in violent death for their great-grandfather and for innumerable cousins and uncles and great-uncles.

'It is a great pity I am not to marry Sandro,' Natalie said wistfully, dismissing the annoyance of the inappropriately named street and alighting on another, far more important grievance. 'Why should it matter that we are cousins? Royalty has always intermarried and I would make a *wonderful* queen.'

At the thought of Sandro and Natalie's unstable Karegeorgevich blood uniting in marriage Katerina shuddered, not remotely surprised that her sensible father had vetoed the idea the instant it had first been suggested.

'Aunt Zorka would also have made a wonderful queen,' she said divertingly as ceremonially dressed guards opened the high, wide gates and their landau rolled between them and into the palace park.

It was a moment or two before Natalie answered her. Zorka had died long before either she or Katerina had been born but their mother, who had acted as her companion during the years of Zorka's marriage to their uncle, had brought them up on stories of her brooding Slavic beauty and of how she had passionately longed for the day when her husband would oust the Obrenoviches from the Serbian throne and retake the Karageorgevich crown. Fourteen years after her death he had finally done so; but he had not remarried. There was no Queen of Serbia and there would not be one until Sandro ascended the throne and made the girl he had yet to marry, queen.

'Yes,' Natalie said slowly, 'but I doubt that Zorka would have been content being Queen of Serbia. She would have wanted to be queen of all the Slavs – Serbians, Montenegrins, Bosnians, Herzegovinians . . .'

Her face had taken on a rapt expression and Katerina stared at her, filled with a sudden sense of foreboding. Though Montenegro, like Serbia, was an independent kingdom and no longer part of the Ottoman Empire, Bosnia and Herzegovina enjoyed no such independence. Once Turkish possessions, they had been annexed by Austria-Hungary six years earlier, becoming part of the massive and unwieldy Habsburg empire. In Belgrade the cafés were full of young fanatics scheming of a way to liberate their fellow Slavs from the Habsburg yoke and Katerina had no desire to see her idealistic and impressionable young sister becoming one of their number.

'For goodness sake, stop filling your head with impossible dreams,' she said with uncharacteristic sharpness as the landau rocked to a halt. 'And don't start discussing Slav unity with Sandro. We're here to talk about his visit to St Petersburg and which of the grand-duchesses it is Uncle Peter has arranged for him to marry, not to indulge in contentious street talk.'

Natalie didn't trouble to reply. Katerina had been exercising her two-year seniority, trying to curb and restrain her, for as long as she could remember and she had long since ceased taking the slightest notice. As she stood up in the landau, smoothing the ankle-length skirt of her yellow-silk Parisian day-gown she marvelled yet again at how different Katerina was from herself in both looks and personality. Katerina took after their father's family. All the Vassilovichs were tall and slender, the men possessing an air of nonchalant elegance the women serene and graceful, cool and calm whatever the crisis.

As she stepped from the landau Natalie pondered, not for the first time, on the mystery as to why all Vassilovich characteristics were so absent in her own physique and character. When she had said that she was all Karageorge she had been speaking the utter truth. Like all Karageorgevich women she was short, only a smidgeon over five foot two, with hair as night-black and curly as a gypsy's and a nature recklessly passionate and impulsive.

It was her great-grandfather, George Petrovich, who had given her family the name by which it had been known for the last hundred years. A peasant farmer turned guerilla fighter he had been nicknamed Kara, meaning black. As Black George he had led the Serbian people in an uprising against their Turkish masters. Capturing Belgrade, putting the Turkish garrison to the sword and proclaiming himself Prince of Serbia, he temporarily ended the darkness of three and half centuries of Ottoman rule.

'And his temper lost him it all,' her father had said to her wearily when, as a small girl, she had questioned him about her mother's family. 'When there were no Turks to fight he fought with his supporters and when the Turks attempted to reoccupy Serbia, many Serbs gave their loyalty to another guerilla leader, Milos Obrenovich.'

'And was that when great-grandfather was forced to leave Serbia?' she had asked, her little hands clenching into fists at the thought of the wicked upstart, Milos Obrenovich.

'Yes,' her father had said gently, sliding his arm around her shoulders. 'And what you must remember, Natalie, is that Milos Obrenovich would never have been able to style himself Prince of Serbia if your great-grandfather had been able to control his temper. Because he constantly failed to do so he lost his family the undisputed right to the Serbian throne.'

As an eight-year-old child she had been impressed, but not in the way her father had intended. In her eyes, great-grandfather Black George was a hero and it was his traitorous followers and the villainous Obrenovichs who were the cause of her family's subsequent, intermittent exclusion from the Serbian throne.

As she stepped down from the landau in Katerina's wake she wondered which of the four Russian grand-duchesses was to be her cousin's bride and Serbia's next queen. At eighteen, Olga was the eldest and the likeliest candidate. She looked up at the walls of the newly built palace, seeing it as the Tsar's eldest daughter would see it, mortification flooding through her.

What on earth would Olga think of it? Known simply as the *Konak* it was new because the last Obrenovich king, together with his queen, had been savagely murdered in the old palace and in an attempt to obliterate the memory of their violent deaths it had been torn down. In its place had been built a palace that resembled not so much a royal residence as a stolid French provincial chateau. To Olga, accustomed to the gigantic Winter Palace in St Petersburg and the sumptuous splendour of the Romanov palaces in the Crimea and the Baltic, the *Konak* was going to appear devastatingly provincial.

'I wish Uncle Peter would live a little more ceremoniously,' she said exasperatedly as they stepped into the modestly-sized entrance vestibule. 'One day he will not merely be King of Serbia but Tsar of all the Slavs and then he will *have* to live in great state and . . .'

'I do wish you would get that particular bee out of your bonnet,' Katerina said, her earlier flicker of anxiety deepening. 'Can't you think about the wedding instead? We shall both be bridesmaids and every crowned head in Europe will be in attendance.'

It was a heady thought, but so was the vision of a great Slav empire ruled over by a Karageorgevich. As a footman led them down a mirror-hung corridor towards the main drawing-room Natalie was both bewildered and irritated by Katerina's lack of enthusiasm for what had always been the great Karageorgevich dream. She frowned slightly. It meant she couldn't possibly confide in Katerina as she had intended. And she couldn't confide in Sandro. Her new-found friends had been quite adamant about that.

Footmen opened the drawing-room's double portières and a black and white spaniel bitch puppy tumbled out of the room and into the corridor, distracting her completely.

'Oh, you *darling*!' she cried, bending down and scooping her up in her arms, Slav unity and her exciting new friends temporarily forgotten. 'Oh, just look at her, Katerina! Isn't she adorable?'

Katerina's anxiety faded. With the puppy in her arms Natalie looked little more than a child and her disquiet of the last ten minutes or so suddenly seemed ludicrous. It was perfectly natural that Natalie should echo popular sentiment and day-dream of the day when all Slavs, Catholic, Orthodox and Moslem, would live in unity no longer owing unwilling allegiance to the Habsburgs, and it had been crassly stupid of her to have imagined that Natalie had even heard of the Belgrade-based organization committed to bringing that end about by violent means.

Amused by her foolishness she walked across the sun-filled room to where her elderly uncle was standing with her father, and curtsied deeply.

Lean and slightly built, with grey hair rapidly turning to

silver and a bristly handlebar moustache, Peter Karageorgevich was not a particularly kingly figure. Only his
eyes revealed his ancestry. Dark and piercing, they were
the eyes of Black George and they commanded instant
respect.

'You've come to hear all the St Petersburg gossip, have
you, eh?' he said to her affectionately.

Sandro was standing a little to his left, dressed in
ceremonial army uniform and looking extremely pleased
with himself. Further to the left was her mother, surrounded by a coterie of aunts and great-aunts and on the
periphery of her vision she could see a throng of cousins
and second-cousins and a small, élite group of foreign
diplomats.

'Yes, sir,' she said, amused by her family's unabashed
impatience for the latest news on the long hoped-for
marriage between Sandro and a Romanov.

Behind her she could hear Natalie regretfully lowering
the puppy to the floor as she prepared to make her curtsey.
She felt a stab of relief. Though Natalie complained
bitterly about lack of ceremony in the *Konak*, it would
have been quite typical of her to have attempted the
curtsey, the puppy still in her arms.

'The puppy was a present from the Tsaravich,' Sandro
said, reading her thoughts as she stepped away from his
father and towards him. 'She's from the same litter as
his own spaniel, Joy.'

The puppy tumbled over Katerina's neatly shod feet
and then lay on her back, waiting to be tickled. Sandro
obliged with the toe of a glossily booted foot.

Impatience was foreign to Katerina's nature but she felt
a twinge of it as she waited for her cousin to return his
attention to her and to indicate whether or not one of the
Tsar's daughters was to be his bride.

'How was St Petersburg?' she prompted meaningfully.

He removed his attention from the puppy. 'As grandiose as ever,' he said, grinning.

Katerina refused to be provoked. Although Sandro's demeanour was usually serious, as befitted the heir to the throne, he was never solemn when Natalie was in the vicinity. Despite the difference in their ages they were very close. So close that, if it hadn't been for the blood-tie between them and the political necessity of Sandro marrying into a strong royal house such as the Romanovs, their marrying would have surprised no-one.

They would certainly have made a handsome couple. Sandro was not particularly tall but he was pleasingly built. He had good shoulders which showed to advantage in uniform and despite his short-sightedness, which necessitated his wearing gold framed pince-nez, he moved with athletic strength and confidence. His black-lashed eyes were almost as dark as his father's and when he smiled the lines running from nose to mouth deepened attractively. Like his father he sported a moustache, but whereas his father's moustache was steely-grey and flamboyantly waxed and curled, Sandro's moustache was trim and neat and glossily black.

His eyes held hers teasingly. 'As for the gossip, Hélène has adapted wonderfully to Russia and the baby is thriving.'

Hélène was his sister. Two years ago she had married the son of the Russian Grand-Duke Constantine and the official reason for Sandro's visit to St Petersburg had been his attendance at the christening of Hélène's first-born son in the Cathedral of Our Lady of Kazan.

Katerina smiled serenely, knowing she was being baited and refusing to rise to it. Afternoon tea at the *Konak* was a weekly social event at which all female members of the Karageorgevich clan were welcome. Her aunts and great-aunts did not, however, usually turn out in such numbers and they had certainly not done so in order to hear news of Hélène and her baby. If Sandro was being annoyingly unforthcoming about what had taken place in St Petersburg it was because he didn't want to pre-empt the announcement that was about to be made.

She looked across to the small group of foreign diplomats and her certainty grew. It was highly unusual for anyone other than the Prime Minister to be in attendance at a family afternoon tea-party and she recognized representatives from both the French and British Legations.

The young Englishman exchanging words with his French counterpart, sensing her eyes on him, turned his head slightly. As their eyes met in friendly recognition he quirked an eyebrow. Katerina circumspectly made no response but as she allowed her glance to travel further around the vast room, her smile deepened. She knew very well what Julian Fielding was silently asking. He was wanting to know whether her uncle and Sandro had pulled off the coup of the decade and secured a marital alliance with the mighty Romanovs.

Natalie was now chattering to Sandro, the puppy once more in her arms and Katerina moved away and towards the cluster of female relations grouped around her mother.

'. . . and apparently the Empress allows Rasputin into her presence at all hours of the day and relies on his advice utterly,' her Great-Aunt Eudocia was saying in tones of shocked disapproval.

'Then let us hope Sandro found favour with him,' her Great-Aunt Elena responded with acerbity. 'I'd hate us to lose the Romanov alliance because of a monk who apparently never washes.'

Eudocia sucked in her breath, her ample bosoms rising until her many necklaces were almost horizontal. 'Don't be ridiculous, Elena! Of course I wasn't inferring that

Rasputin would have a say in anything as important as a royal marriage! I was simply informing you of the Empress's extraordinary behaviour where he is concerned. It is the talk not only of the court, but of the entire country . . .'

Her mother stepped away from their fractious relatives and towards her.

'I was beginning to think you weren't going to be here in time,' she said, kissing her lovingly on the cheek. 'It's quite obvious the visit to Petersburg was a success and that a family announcement is to be made. I only hope it won't prove to be premature.'

Katerina's eyes were once more on the young diplomats standing on the far side of the gold-papered, chandelier-hung drawing-room.

'Premature?' she asked vaguely, her thoughts elsewhere. 'How could be it premature, Mama?'

Her mother slid her arm lightly in hers and began to walk with her down the room. 'The Tsar is a great equivocator,' she said dryly. 'He hates to hurt anyone's feelings and Papa thinks it quite possible that he has agreed to Olga marrying Alexander without having the slightest intention that she will, in fact, ever do so.'

Julian Fielding was again in conversation with the French diplomat, his brows drawn together in a slight frown. Katerina dragged her eyes reluctantly away from him.

'I'm sorry, Mama. What did you say? That the Tsar doesn't truly want an alliance with us?'

'He already has one,' her mother retorted dryly, 'and he doesn't need to marry his eldest daughter to Alexander in order to maintain it.' Beneath her high-piled chignon her fine-boned face was perturbed. 'King Carol has high hopes of Olga marrying Prince Carol, who is his nephew and heir, and it has already been agreed that the imperial family will visit Romania early next month in order that Carol and Olga can meet.'

Katerina looked across to Sandro and Natalie. The puppy was back in Natalie's arms and Sandro was laughing and tickling it behind its ears. If Sandro believed he was unofficially engaged to the Tsar's eldest daughter, and if she then married Prince Carol, he would feel himself to have been monstrously insulted.

'And you're worried because you think Sandro is going to be hurt?'

Her mother didn't immediately answer her. They were strolling past a cluster of cousins and Vitza, Eudocia's twenty-year-old granddaughter, was saying authoritatively, 'The Empress's favourite colour is mauve and she is bound to wear mauve at the wedding. Grandmama will wear Serbian-blue and thinks that I should wear pink . . .'

Katerina felt a flash of amusement. If her mother's prediction was correct, disappointment among their female relatives was going to be vast.

'No,' her mother said in answer to her last question when there was no longer a chance of being overheard. 'My concern isn't for Alexander. It is for Serbia.'

Katerina stared at her. Her mother rarely spoke of national issues, regarding politics as her husband's province. That she should do so now, and in the *Konak*'s grand drawing-room, meant that something was seriously troubling her.

'Why would it be so important if the Tsar reneged on a promise that Alexander marry Olga?' she asked, struggling for understanding.

Her mother came to a halt in order not to come within hearing distance of the next group of cousins and second-cousins.

'It would be serious because of the bad feeling that would arise. Your uncle has so far contained the impatience

19

of the hotheads who want to help Bosnia and Herzegovina free themselves of Habsburg rule. He's been able to do so because he has had Russia's promise that when the time is right she will give us all the support she can in such a struggle. But the time isn't now. For the first time in our history, thanks to your uncle, we are enjoying stability. We need to consolidate it, not plunge into armed struggle against the Austro-Hungarian empire.'

Though her mother had continued to speak quietly there was no mistaking her depth of feeling. They had reached the far end of the drawing-room and were now beginning to walk across its breadth. At the top end of the room the King was in conversation with Elena and her daughter. Natalie, Sandro and Bella had gravitated to Vitza's circle and the doors leading on to the terrace had been opened, revealing a dozen white-naperied tea tables laden with plates of delicately cut sandwiches.

'And if there was bad feeling against Russia, you think the hot-heads would gain popular support and plunge us into war?'

Julian Fielding was still in conversation with the French diplomat. She wondered what their subject of conversation was. She wondered how she could engage him in conversation herself without appearing too forward.

Her mother lowered her voice, saying with startling frankness, 'Papa has long had a contact in South Slav. The group is made up of army officers and parliamentary officials and though their avowed aim is to restore Serbia's boundaries to those she enjoyed in the Middle Ages, they have always been law-abiding. The new organization,' she added darkly as they began to near Julian Fielding and his companion, 'is not.'

Katerina felt her tummy muscles tightening in nervous anticipation. Her mother hadn't chosen to join any of the previous cliques and groups they had passed in their circuit of the room but she might very well make an exception when she drew abreast of Julian Fielding. Tall and broad-shouldered, he was dressed with British reticence in a black tail-coat and pin-striped trousers; his only visible jewellery was the watch-chain looped across his waistcoat. The French envoy was dressed with far more panache, his ceremonial diplomatic uniform awash with gold braid, an emerald sparkling on the index finger of one hand, a diamond on the other.

Katerina was barely aware of him. Sunlight was streaming into the room through the long windows and open doors, burnishing Julian's hair a dull gold. He wore it longer than other Englishmen she had met. Thick and springy as a Greek god's, it curled low over his waxed shirt collar, giving him an air of almost Slavic flamboyance.

With great effort she returned her attention to her mother. It was extraordinary that their conversation should have veered on to the subject that had been causing her so much disquiet only a little while earlier. She wondered if she should speak to her mother about Natalie's disturbing new enthusiasm for Slav unity. In ordinary circumstances it would have been a natural preoccupation that would have given no cause for concern. As it was, however, the new organization working for Slav unity was doing so by very dangerous methods, methods that Natalie was reckless enough to find attractive.

'Mama,' she began hesitantly, 'this new organization Papa spoke of the other day. Is it trying to gain Karageorgevich support?'

'The Black Hand would *love* Karageorgevich support,' her mother replied tartly, 'but it certainly won't receive it. Your uncle's main aim is to maintain Serbia's new found stability, not put it at risk indulging in meaningless acts of violence.'

Katerina had been plunged so deep in thought she had

been unaware of how rapidly they were approaching Julian Fielding and his companion.

'Mama . . .' she began again, but it was too late.

'Good afternoon, Mr Fielding. Good afternoon, Monsieur Quesnai,' her mother was saying pleasantly. 'How nice to see you at what is usually only a family occasion.'

Aware she was letting him know that she knew the reason for his presence, Julian Fielding's brown eyes gleamed with amusement. He enjoyed conversation with the Vassilovichs. Alexis and Zita Vassilovich both spoke excellent English and Katerina and Natalie had been educated from early childhood by an English tutor and spoke it flawlessly. 'It is an honour to be here,' he said truthfully as he took her proffered hand, bowing slightly over it.

As her mother turned her attention to Monsieur Quesnai, allowing him to raise her hand a hair's breadth from his lips, Katerina was able to enjoy a moment or two of Julian Fielding's undivided attention.

'I take it you are as much in ignorance as the rest of us,' he said in the easy, friendly manner she found so attractive.

There was no need for her to ask to what he was referring.

'I think we shall be put out of our misery very shortly,' she said with a slight, suitably restrained smile.

Inwardly she felt anything but restrained. Her heart was beating in sharp, slamming little strokes she could feel even in her fingertips, the happiness she had felt on entering the room and seeing him, deepening and intensifying until she wondered how on earth she was going to prevent it from becoming embarrassingly obvious.

'If the announcement is the one everyone is expecting, it will be Serbia's gain and Britain's loss,' he said gallantly.

'It's no secret King George would very much have liked a Romanov bride for the Prince of Wales.'

'Even after Olga is married there will still be three grand-duchesses available,' she said impishly, her usual shyness wonderfully absent.

Beneath his narrow blond moustache his mouth tugged into a smile. 'Maybe so, but it's always the eldest daughter who is regarded as the real prize.'

She looked away from him quickly, the blood rushing to her cheeks, wondering if he was aware of how his remark could be interpreted.

When she trusted herself to once more look towards him he wasn't looking at her, but across the room at Natalie.

'His Royal Highness will be lucky if he retains ownership of that dog,' he said, amused. 'She and your sister seem to have adopted each other.'

It was true. Natalie was no longer with Sandro, but the puppy was gambolling around her feet as she moved away from one group of cousins and towards another.

Katerina regarded her sister indulgently. No other member of the family would have been able to appropriate the Tsarevich's gift in such a guileless manner. At seventeen there was still something winsomely child-like about her. Although she had persuaded their mother to allow her to wear her smoke-dark hair in a sophisticated chignon, feathery tendrils had escaped and lay waywardly against her cheeks and another one curled provocatively in the nape of her neck. She was laughing now at something someone had said to her, her green cat-eyes dancing, her zest for life tangible and infectious.

'I doubt if the King will allow it to leave the *Konak*,' she said a trifle regretfully. 'It would be too insulting if word got back to Petersburg that the Tsarevich's gift had been given away.'

'But only to a family member,' Julian said with diplomatic

23

expediency. He looked around the room. 'And talking of family members, I had no idea the Karageorgevich family was so vast.'

'Our interpretation of the word family is a little different from the British interpretation,' Katerina said, hardly able to believe her good fortune at having such a long, uninterrupted conversation with him. 'Family in Serbia means extended family. Traditionally we all live together in what you would call a clan, and we call a *zadruga*. The strongest male member acts as the *zadruga*'s chief and loyalty to him, and to every other member of the *zadruga*, is absolute. It is only in Belgrade, where life is sophisticated, that families no longer live communally under a patriarchal chief.'

The smile that had tugged at the corner of his mouth when he had looked across at Natalie, deepened. He had heard Belgrade described as many things, but never before as sophisticated.

'Family and country are very important to Slavs,' Katerina was saying, touchingly serious. 'I cannot imagine how the Russian grand-duchesses must feel, knowing that when they marry foreign princes, they will have to leave their homeland.'

'They are brought up to it,' he said gently. 'As princesses it is their fate and always has been.'

On the far side of the drawing-room, among the aunts' grey and purple ensembles, Natalie's yellow-silk dress was a vivid slash of colour.

'And you and Natalie,' he asked, his eyes darkening slightly as they remained on Natalie. 'Would either of you ever contemplate leaving Serbia?'

Katerina felt the blood beginning to drum in her ears. The conversation had taken a heart-stoppingly intimate turn and she wasn't sure she could trust herself to answer without her voice betraying her hopes.

'Perhaps . . .' she said, struggling to sound indifferent, 'if marriage made it necessary.'

On the terrace, teapots had been set on the exquisitely laid tables. A little to their left, her father had joined her mother and Monsieur Quesnai. In the centre of the room her uncle was taking up a position in front of the marble fireplace, obviously intending to make his announcement.

'And Natalie?' he prompted. 'Would she feel the same?'

The reply to his question was easy. Natalie would certainly not feel the same. When they had been children, living in exile with their parents and her uncle in Geneva, she had said like a mantra every evening after they had said their prayers: 'When we return to Serbia I will never leave it. Never, never, *never!*'

A slight smile touched her lips. 'Natalie . . .' she began, and was silenced by her uncle clearing his throat.

'This is not, of course, an official announcement,' he said to his suddenly hushed female relatives, his rheumatically-afflicted legs slightly apart, his hands clasped behind his back. 'That will come later, when all the negotiations attendant to such an announcement have been completed.' He rocked back on his heels a little. 'This is a strictly family announcement,' he continued, as if the diplomats he had so assiduously invited were not present, 'and one that I know is going to give great joy.' He paused and not even the rustle of a skirt or the tinkle of a bracelet broke the tense silence. He was not a man who relished speech-making and he put an end to the suspense swiftly. 'It is my happy task to inform you that an engagement between Grand-Duchess Olga, eldest daughter of the Emperor of Russia, and Alexander, Crown Prince of Serbia, will be announced in the early months of next year.'

A buzz of elation rippled around the drawing-room. A

Romanov bride for Serbia! It was wonderful news. Glorious news.

'This is not, of course, to be discussed outside the *Konak*,' King Peter concluded, knowing very well that the British and French governments would be appraised of the news within hours.

With immense and obvious satisfaction he began to lead the way out on to the terrace. He had scored a triumph. He, and everyone present, knew it, and soon the whole world would know it.

'When we free Bosnia and Herzegovina from Habsburg rule, Grand-Duchess Olga will become not merely a queen but Tsarina of the whole South Slav peoples,' a know-all voice was saying as they filed out of the drawing-room in the King's wake. 'That is why the Tsar has agreed to the union. It is because he knows his daughter's influence and glory will one day stretch over the entire Balkan peninsula.'

It was an echo of the sentiments Natalie had expressed a little earlier.

As she seated herself at one of the tea tables Katerina wondered if the French and British governments were aware of just how impatient her countrymen and women were becoming in their desire for unity with their fellow, Habsburg ruled Slavs, and if they knew of the existence of the supposedly secret Black Hand.

Certainly if Julian Fielding was not aware of Black Hand's existence he would be grateful to her if she informed him of it. She looked around to see where he was sitting and saw, with a surge of pleasure, that he was at her father's table.

'Please like him, Papa,' she whispered beneath her breath, looking away quickly as, with a rustle of royal-blue taffeta, Vitza seated herself next to her.

'You Vassilovich girls really do enjoy an unconscionable

amount of freedom,' she said enviably. 'Max saw Natalie in a Belgrade *kafana* yesterday afternoon with a host of students.'

Katerina's face froze. When she could trust herself to speak, she said rebuffingly, 'We enjoy a *reasonable* amount of freedom, Vitza, not an unconscionable amount, and it certainly doesn't extend to frequenting cafés.'

'It did yesterday,' Vitza retorted, unfazed. 'Max was quite concerned about it. He thinks Natalie too *avant-garde* for her own good.'

Avant-garde was not the word Katerina would have chosen. The word she would have chosen was stupid. Criminally, crassly, *unbelievably* stupid.

'Max was mistaken,' she said, knowing full well that he hadn't been; knowing that her earlier sense of unease had been entirely justified. 'It couldn't possibly have been Natalie. Natalie has music lessons on Tuesday afternoons.'

Vitza arched an amused eyebrow. 'And where does she have her lessons? At home or at the Conservatoire?'

'At the Conservatoire,' Katerina replied icily. 'And there's no need to look so foolishly knowing, Vitza. That was exactly where Natalie was yesterday afternoon. At the Conservatoire. She was certainly not in a café.'

All around them the conversation was of the engagement that would be taking place next year. At a distant table Katerina could see Natalie chattering to Monsieur Quesnai, her eyes shining, her smile radiant.

Vitza grinned. 'Believe what you want,' she said with infuriating complacency, 'but Max is telling the truth. It would be impossible for him to have mistaken someone else for Natalie.'

Katerina didn't doubt it. She curled her fingers into her palms, itching to seize hold of her younger sister and shake a modicum of sense into her.

'Did Max recognize any of the students in the café?' she

asked, hating herself for prolonging the conversation yet knowing it was a question that had to be asked.

'No, why should he?' Vitza was affronted. 'They were *students* for goodness sake, not cavalry officers.'

Katerina's eyes were still on Natalie. Unknown to the great-aunts sitting at her table she obviously had Bella on her lap, for she kept surreptitiously lowering sandwiches beneath the overhang of the tablecloth where they instantly disappeared.

'Except one,' Vitza added. 'He knew the name of one of them, a Bosnian.'

'And what was it?' Katerina asked, wondering what she was going to do about the situation; wondering if it could be resolved without her parents learning of it.

'Princip,' Vitza said, losing interest in the conversation now that Katerina no longer seemed perturbed by it. 'Gavrilo Princip.'

Chapter Two

'Princip? Princip?' Natalie said vaguely, stalling for time. 'I'm not sure I recall the name.'

'Of course you do,' Katerina said exasperatedly. 'You were *seen* with him for goodness sake!'

It was early evening and still warm and they were in the garden of their home. Katerina had judged it to be the safest place in which to speak to Natalie. In the garden they would not be overheard by her parents or by servants.

Natalie plucked a petal off a *Belle de Crécy* rose. She had never been any good at telling lies or prevaricating and though she knew it would make life enormously easier if she did so now, she was unable to summon the necessary guile.

'Vitza Karageorgevich is a despicable busybody,' she said crossly. 'Why should it matter to her where I go and who I meet? And what was she doing in the *Golden Sturgeon* anyway?'

Katerina mentally filed away the name of the café, saying with as much patience as she could muster, 'It wasn't Vitza who saw you. It was Max.'

'Oh, *Max*.' Natalie's voice was heavy with irritation. 'I might have known it would be Max Karageorgevich. He's never liked me. Do you remember the time when we were children and he . . .'

'I'm not going to be side-tracked, Natalie,' Katerina said firmly. 'Max liking you, or not liking you, doesn't alter the fact that he saw you.'

'Oh, I dare say he saw me,' Natalie admitted with bad grace. 'I just don't see why he has to make such a big thing of it. Goodness knows who else he's told and . . .'

'Of course he would make a big thing of it!' Katerina never lost her temper but she was coming close to doing so now. 'You're only seventeen! Mama and Papa may give us a lot of freedom, but even they would draw the line at your wandering around Belgrade unaccompanied. Why wasn't Miss Benson with you? As your governess she should chaperone you to your music lessons. If they knew you had gone into a student *kafana* they would have ten fits!'

Natalie began to shred the rose petal with short, pearl-buffed nails. Despite all her rebelliousness she loved her parents dearly and had no desire to cause them hurt. 'You don't intend telling them, do you?' she asked, her winged eyebrows pulling together in a slight frown.

'I don't *want* to tell them,' Katerina said truthfully, 'but unless you explain to me just why you were there, and unless you promise never to do such a thing again, I shall *have* to tell them.'

They had been strolling aimlessly, too involved in their conversation to care where their route was taking them. Natalie paused now, knowing that she would have to tell Katerina something about her involvement with Gavrilo and his friends and knowing that she would have to be very careful not to reveal too much.

'Gavrilo and Nedjelko attended the Conservatoire earlier this year and . . .'

She had come to a halt near one of their mother's much-loved rose bowers. A garden seat was carefully positioned so that her mother could enjoy the fragrance and Katerina sat down on it, her alarm growing. Until now, she had imagined that Natalie's foray into the *kafana* had been a single, isolated, incident. Now it was beginning to seem as if she had been there before, perhaps several times.

'. . . we became friends when they accidentally walked into my classroom and . . .'

'But your classes are private!' Katerina protested, appalled at the thought of the city's riff-raff having such easy access to a member of the ruling house. 'Where was your tutor?'

'Monsieur Lasalle was late. He's often late. Sometimes he doesn't even arrive for my class at all.'

Katerina blanched. What if the person in the empty classroom had been Sandro? It would have been a heaven-sent opportunity for an assassin. She wondered how accidental Gavrilo and Nedjelko's walking in on Natalie had been. If they were young Bosnians, in Serbia in order to gain support for a revolt against Habsburg rule, then waylaying a Karageorgevich would make a great deal of sense. Through such a contact they would have the ear of the heir to the throne, perhaps even of King Peter himself.

'And are Gavrilo and Nedjelko political activists?' she asked, already sure of what the answer would be.

Natalie remained standing, a spray of delicate pink *Belle Isis* almost touching her hair, a thick truss of parched-gold *Jeanne d'Arc* brushing her skirt. She couldn't lie to Katerina and yet she didn't want her to know the depth and seriousness of Gavrilo and Nedjelko's commitment to Slav unity; or of her own.

'They are students,' she said prevaricatingly; 'all students are politically aware. Did you know that the new editor of the *Serbian Literary Herald* was Paris educated? He is exactly the kind of cultured intellectual Papa would enjoy meeting and . . .'

'Stop trying to change the subject,' Katerina said, no nearer to knowing what she was going to do about Natalie's escapade than she had been before they had begun talking. A new thought struck her, striking real fear

31

into her heart. 'They aren't members of the Bosnia Youth Movement, are they?'

Members of the revolutionary Bosnian Youth Movement were notorious for their recklessness and violence. Only four years previously one of their members had tried to kill the Governor of Bosnia. If they had succeeded Habsburg wrath might well have resulted in such repressive retaliation that a full scale uprising might have been provoked.

'No, silly,' Natalie said emphatically, deeply relieved at being able to speak the truth unequivocally for once. 'Of course they aren't.'

She didn't add that Gavrilo and Nedjelko were not members of Young Bosnia for the simple reason that they had come to the conclusion that Young Bosnia was pathetically ineffective and that they were, instead, members of a much more militantly orientated organization.

Katerina sighed with relief. The scent of the roses was heavy as a drug, the air thick with the zoom of bees and she could feel herself beginning to relax. Natalie had behaved foolishly but no serious damage had been done. She hadn't become embroiled in Bosnia's fanatical revolutionary youth movement and it was quite obvious from the way she had spoken of Princip and his friend, that she hadn't fallen in love with either of them. Her visits to the *Golden Sturgeon* had not been prompted by either nationalistic extremism or infatuation. All that now remained was for Natalie to promise her that she wouldn't visit the café, or any other café, ever again.

'It was crassly stupid of you,' she said, feeling more like a governess than a sister. 'It was a betrayal of Papa and Mama's trust and Monsieur Lasalle's . . .'

Natalie was aware she had behaved badly where her parents' trust in her was concerned and had no wish to be reminded of it, especially as it was a trust she had no choice but to continue betraying. Trying to exonerate herself of the guilt she felt, she said spiritedly, 'If Monsieur Lasalle had not been so negligent about tutoring me it would never have happened. I would never have met Gavrilo and Nedjelko in the first place and I would never have been able to meet them again. I only ever went to the café when he failed to arrive for my music lesson.'

Silently cursing Monsieur Lasalle for his negligence Katerina said, striving to be understanding, 'I suppose it was exciting for you to be out without a chaperone and among people of your own age, but it mustn't happen again, Natalie. It was an extremely dangerous thing to do. Anything could have happened to you.'

Natalie was sorely tempted to ask for an example, but restrained herself. She loved Katerina dearly, but her temperament was so different from her own there were times when she found communication with her almost impossible. Why, for instance, was she so unexcited by the thought of a federated South Slav state incorporating Serbia, Bosnia, Croatia and even, perhaps, parts of Macedonia? Belgrade would be its capital and a Karageorgevich its king and it would be just like medieval times when the kings of Serbia had been known as Tsars, the empire they ruled stretching from Belgrade to the Aegean and taking in most of the Adriatic and Ionian coasts as well.

Containing her irritation at Katerina's lack of vision she said sincerely, 'I'm sorry, Katerina. I didn't mean to cause you anxiety.'

'Then don't cause me anxiety again,' Katerina scolded, too happy the difficulty had been resolved for there to be any real censure in her voice.

Natalie's relief was absolute. Katerina hadn't asked her to promise never to see Gavrilo or Nedjelko again or to visit the *Golden Sturgeon* again. She had simply assumed she would not do so.

'Did you know that Mama has invited every member of the British and French Legation to the Summer Ball?' she asked, knowing that she would have to be much more careful in future and changing the subject before Katerina realized her carelessness. '*And* the Russian minister is to be in attendance and a party of Cossack officers. I do think Cossacks are handsome, don't you?'

Indulgently allowing Natalie to prattle on about their mother's Summer Ball and the officers who would be in attendance and with whom she could innocently flirt, Katerina rose to her feet. She had her own romantic hopes for the Summer Ball and they didn't centre on exotic Cossacks. For the hundredth time she wondered if Julian Fielding had meant her to interpret his remark about the eldest sister being the prize, personally. And if he had?

Her heart began to beat faster. If he asked her to marry him, and if she accepted his proposal, it would mean her eventually leaving Serbia. Young diplomats never remained long in a posting. In a year or so, perhaps even less, Julian would be posted to Vienna or Paris or perhaps even St Petersburg.

Natalie was chattering about Bella now. Sandro had said that, if her father didn't object, he would give her to her.

'And I spoke to Papa this morning and he said as long as Bella didn't get under his feet or into his study, then I could have her. Do you think she could sleep in our bedroom, Katerina? She's too tiny to sleep all alone.'

Trying not to imagine the damage Bella would do to her clothes and shoes, Katerina said tolerantly, 'Of course I don't mind.'

She wondered how hard she would find it to leave home. They were a very close-knit family and she would miss her parents and Natalie terribly. She thought of the pleasurable excitements of Vienna and Paris and St Petersburg and knew she would be able to adapt.

Until her uncle had returned to Serbia as king, ten years ago, he and many other Karageorgevichs had lived in exile in Geneva and it was in Geneva that she and Natalie had been born. Whereas Natalie had loathed Switzerland on principle, vociferously claiming that it was far inferior to the homeland she had never seen, she had been happy there. She had liked the neatness of the country and the sensible level-headedness of the Swiss. There would be very little level-headedness in a Slavic capital such as St Petersburg, but she imagined that Vienna and Paris and other European capitals to which Julian might be posted would be very similar to Geneva.

They had reached the house now and Natalie was saying, 'I'm going to ask Mama if I can go to the *Konak* to collect Bella. Miss Benson can accompany me.'

Their mother was sitting on the terrace with Eudocia and after Natalie had asked and received permission to go to the *Konak* accompanied by her long-suffering governess, Katerina joined them.

'I thought both you and Natalie looked extremely elegant at the wedding announcement this afternoon,' her great-aunt said to her generously. 'Of course, yellow is a very *ingénue* colour and Natalie will soon have to stop favouring it. Blue would be a suitable alternative. Did you notice Vitza's gown? It was a most wonderful shade of royal blue but royal blue would not, perhaps, be the right shade for Natalie. It requires a great deal of stylishness if it is to be worn successfully and I'm sure your mama will agree with me that though dear Natalie possesses many commendable qualities stylishness is not, as yet, one of them.'

Katerina's eyes fleetingly met her mother's, their amusement mutual. It was quite true that Natalie's

35

kittenish exuberance could hardly be described as stylish but Vitza, who was showing incipient signs of one day becoming as stout as her grandmother, was hardly an example of it, nor was royal blue particularly flattering to her.

'Vitza's gown was stunningly head-turning,' her mother said resourcefully. 'Parisian dressmaking always shows.'

The gown had been made by a local dressmaker as both Katerina and her mother well knew, but Eudocia didn't trouble to correct her.

Highly gratified she turned to Katerina saying, 'I was just remarking to your mother that I really cannot understand why there have been so few court balls this year. There has been only once since Christmas. Can you imagine? Only *one*! It really isn't good enough. I am sure that in London and St Petersburg there are balls every night of the week.'

Aware of the British king's introverted personality and the Russian empress's dislike of socializing outside of her immediate family circle, Zita doubted it, but kept her doubts to herself.

'I don't think Peter is very well,' she said with a slight frown, laying aside her embroidery. 'He's sixty-nine now and he tires very easily.'

'Then he shouldn't do,' Eudocia said tartly. 'I'm seventy-two and *I* don't tire!'

Katerina kept her eyes from meeting her mother's with difficulty.

'The last few years have been extremely stressful for him,' her mother said patiently. 'The military are constantly pressuring him to take a more aggressive stance towards Austria.'

'Quite rightly,' Eudocia said hawkishly. 'She should never have annexed Bosnia and Herzegovina. They are predominantly Slav and should be part of a great federated

South Slav state. Serbia would then have a window on the Adriatic again and . . .'

'We should have nothing if we went to war with Austria,' Zita said with unusual sharpness. 'She has German backing, both countries have been arming Bulgaria and you don't need me to point out how uneasy our relationship with Bulgaria is. If it came to war, we would be overrun within days.'

Eudocia's heavy jowls trembled indignantly at the very thought. 'Not if we had Russian support. With Russian support we would soon rid the Balkans of Habsburg rule.'

'And if Russia engaged in war against Austria-Hungary and Germany and Bulgaria, where would it all end?' Zita's cameo-like features were taut. 'France has reciprocal agreements with Russia that if either are attacked, the other will come to her aid. And if France is involved in the fighting, it won't be long before countries with which she has alliances are involved as well.'

For the first time since the conversation had begun, Eudocia looked uncertain. She soon rallied. 'Nonsense,' she said robustly. 'Once faced with the might of Russia, Austria-Hungary will back down and abandon her occupation of Bosnia and Herzegovina. It will all be over within days.'

Realizing that her aunt was not going to change her views Zita said merely, 'If some foolishness triggers off a war then I only hope you are proved right.'

The atmosphere had become sombre and it was Eudocia who lightened it. Changing the subject she said garrulously, 'Did you notice the attention Monsieur Quesnai was paying Vitza this afternoon? It isn't to be encouraged, of course. Vitza will marry into the Romanovs as dear Hélène did and as Alexander is so splendidly to do. The Grand-Duke Dimitri has three eligible sons and it has long been understood . . .'

Katerina ceased to listen. She had found her mother's prognosis of what might happen if Serbia declared war on Austria, or if Austria was provoked into declaring war on Serbia, profoundly depressing. Her head had begun to ache and she rose to her feet, excusing herself. When she next saw Julian Fielding she would not only tell him all she knew of the Black Hand, she would also find out if his assessment of the dangers of Slav nationalism was the same as her father's.

It was two weeks before her opportunity came. The Vassilovich Summer Ball was customarily held in August but because of the dearth of parties and balls at the *Konak*, her mother had decided to hold it early.

'At least the roses are in full bloom,' she said as she surveyed the marble-floored ballroom, its dozens of french windows open to the terrace and the garden beyond, 'and roses in moonlight are so romantic.'

Katerina, her thoughts full of Julian Fielding, agreed wholeheartedly. She knew that he would dance with her that evening and she knew that when she discreetly mentioned the Black Hand, she would have his undivided attention. Would he ask her out into the garden so that they could talk undisturbed? And when they had finished discussing things that were of professional interest to him, would the conversation take a more intimate turn?

She was wearing a ballgown of white tulle, the heart-shaped neckline and bodice encrusted with seed-pearls, the skirt swirling behind her in a delicious demi-train. Her lustrous, copper-highlighted hair was piled high in a glorious confection of deep waves and curls and orna-mented with fresh gardenias. Without being the least immodest she knew she looked lovely and she was yearning to see acknowledgement of the fact reflected back at her in Julian Fielding's golden-brown eyes.

'Guests will be arriving in a few minutes, Mama,' she said, butterflies beginning to flutter in the pit of her stomach. 'Shall I go and tell Natalie we are ready to receive?'

Her mother nodded, casting a final look around the ballroom. The coffered-gold ceiling gleamed richly in the brilliant light of the chandeliers; huge crystal vases of orchids decorated every alcove; the orchestra was in position; the footmen were at the ready. Satisfied that there wasn't a ballroom east of Vienna that could match it for splendour she turned on a satin-slippered heel and walked to the grand entrance hall where, with her family around her, she would formally receive her two hundred guests.

Katerina slid the loop of her demi-train over her little finger and hurried up the crimson-carpeted stairs towards the room she shared with Natalie. When she had left the room fifteen minutes earlier Natalie had still not decided which of her ballgowns to wear and both she and her harassed German maid had been knee-deep in discarded confections of tulle and silk. On entering the room, the first thing that was obvious was that Natalie still hadn't made up her mind.

'Mama is ready to receive!' she said, aghast. 'You've only got five minutes at the very most!'

Natalie, clad only in her camisole and lace-trimmed bloomers, made an unladylike grimace. 'I want to wear the mauve but Helga is being annoying. She thinks it unsuitable and is refusing to fasten me into it.'

Helga, who had been in service with the family for fifteen years, said without the least trace of apology in her voice, 'The gown is unsuitable for a seventeen-year-old child. I said so when it was first bought and I still say so.'

Katerina looked at the gown spread across the bed. It was made of embroidered brocade, had a hideous bunch of silk violets on the shoulder and was plungingly *décolleté*.

'You're quite right, Helga,' she said supportingly. 'It's hideous. Natalie would be mistaken for the Tsarina in it.'

At the thought of being mistaken for the forty-two-year-old Tsarina Natalie giggled, her crossness forgotten. 'All right, I give in. But do I *have* to wear white? White is so *boring.*'

'It may be boring,' Helga said phlegmatically, 'but it is suitable.'

'And you must *hurry,*' Katerina remonstrated as the sound of carriages could be heard rattling into the courtyard. 'I can't wait for you any longer. I'll see you downstairs.'

Guests were already filing into the entrance hall as she descended the stairs. Julian Fielding wasn't among them, but then she didn't expect him to be. Only family arrived unsophisticatedly early. She took her place next to her parents as Vitza entered in yet another royal-blue creation, this time the silk unflatteringly ruched and draped. Katerina forgave her cousin her appalling dress sense. No word of Natalie's escapade had reached anyone's ears but her own. Vitza was being discreet and Katerina was profoundly grateful.

As Vitza and her mother made their way towards the ballroom, Natalie breathlessly joined the family receiving line. With relief Katerina saw that Helga had won the day. Although off-the-shoulder, Natalie's gown was demurely white with pink rosebuds embroidered on the bodice and a matching pink silk sash emphasizing her tiny waist.

'Good evening, Great-Aunt Eudocia,' she said dutifully as the rest of Vitza's family made their way along the short receiving line. 'Good evening, Max.'

A smile touched the corners of Katerina's mouth. Natalie's voice was all sweetness and light and without a hint of the irritation it had held when she had spoken of

40

Max earlier. Her amusement at Natalie's short memory vanished as Julian Fielding was announced. In full evening dress, he looked more handsome than ever. And not only was he handsome; there was an inner strength about him that was almost palpable. As he shook hands with her father she was intuitively sure that he was that rarest of all creatures, a man who, once he gave his heart, would be utterly faithful.

She could tell by the way her father greeted him that he, too, liked Julian Fielding immensely and suddenly she knew that what she felt for him was far, far more than liking. Far more, even, than infatuation. She was in love with him. Utterly and irrevocably and head over heels in love.

Her mother was greeting him now. He was so near that she could smell the cleanness of his starched linen and the faint tang of his cologne. Panic flooded through her. What if she had misread the attentions he had given her? What if he had merely been being polite and nothing more? She remembered his remark about the elder sister being the first prize and clung to it with fierce hope. Surely he would not have made such a comment if he had not intended her to interpret it personally? And surely his eyes would not have sought her out whenever they were both at the same social event, the expression in them almost colluding, if he were not as attracted to her as she was to him?

When he took hold of her hand it took every ounce of her considerable self-composure to be able to meet his eyes.

He flashed her a dazzling, down-slanting smile. 'Would it be premature of me to ask now if you would have the first dance with me?'

Her fears vanished. 'It wouldn't be at all premature,' she said, her heart feeling as if it would burst with happiness. 'Of course I will have the first dance with you.'

For the next half hour, as guests made their way down the Vassilovich receiving line, Katerina smiled and murmured greetings, her eyes glowing, her face radiant. Julian would not have asked her to have the first dance with him unless he was on the verge of declaring his feelings for her. She had been too overwhelmed by his request to have paid much heed to his short, subsequent conversation with Natalie, but she had been aware of Natalie's gurgle of laughter and knew that Natalie liked him just as her father liked him.

'Please, please, *please*, fall in love with me,' she whispered to herself as her father decided that any further guests would have to enter the house without benefit of being formally received.

It would all be so perfect. Julian had already shown patience and kindness in his dealings with Natalie and would be an ideal brother-in-law for her. His political knowledge would make him an equally ideal son-in-law, for her father would be able to have long, stimulating conversations with him and her mother would surely be gratified by his English good manners and sensible level-headedness.

As she followed her parents into the ballroom she was sure that the next few hours were going to be hours she would always remember; hours that would live in her heart for ever.

It was tradition for Vassilovich balls to begin with a waltz and for that waltz to be the 'The Blue Danube'. As the music began, and as her father led her mother out on to the ballroom floor, Katerina had never been happier. Cousins and second cousins were politely converging on her in order that she could fill her dance card with their names, but the first gentleman to reach her side was Julian. Ignoring her prospective dance-partners she allowed him to lead her on to the dance floor and as her parents completed their solo circuit of the ballroom, Julian took her lightly in his arms and began to waltz with her to Strauss's timeless masterpiece.

'Are Vassilovich balls always so illustriously attended?' he asked as Prince Paul, the son of King Peter's only brother, danced past, a Montenegrin princess in his arms.

'Always.'

The room was mirrored and she could see their reflections as they danced. Julian, tall and broad-shouldered in his exquisitely-fitted tailcoat, his sun-bleached hair brushed to a high sheen; herself, her pearl-embroidered white tulle dress looking almost bridal, her mahogany hair an unswept cloud of deep, gardenia-decorated waves and curls. Other dancers swirled around them. White glacé dance gloves gleamed, tiaras glittered, medals shone. As they waltzed past the orchestra the fragrance of the flowers banking the rostrum was headily intoxicating. More flowers cascaded from lavishly placed wall vases. Through the many french windows opening on to the terrace her mother's roses could be seen, milkily pale in the moonlight.

Natalie danced past them in the arms of an elderly Karageorgevich uncle and Julian's brows pulled together in a slight frown as he said, 'Isn't Natalie's partner a little old for her?'

'Her partner isn't a suitor,' Katerina said, amused by his concern and not wanting him to think Natalie unseemingly precocious. 'He is both her great-uncle and her godfather.'

'A Karageorgevich uncle?' Julian asked, an eyebrow quirking interestedly. 'An offspring of your great-grandfather? The legendary Black George?'

'Not directly,' Katerina said, unable to remember exactly her great-uncle's paterfamilias. 'I think he is descended from one of great-grandfather's brothers.'

They waltzed past a sea of seated aunts and great-aunts and Katerina was aware of several raised eyebrows. She wondered if it was because she and Julian made an extraordinarily handsome couple or if it was because it was obvious they were dancing together for reasons other than social politeness.

'I find your family history extremely intriguing,' Julian was saying. 'To have regained a throne after losing it once is unusual enough, but to regain it after losing it twice is remarkable.'

'If great-grandfather had regained the throne himself it would never have happened,' Katerina said, happy to tell him all he wanted to know about her family. 'He was on the point of doing so when Milos Obrenovich, who had usurped him, had him murdered and sent his head to Istanbul as a present to the sultan. After that the Obrenovichs ruled in collusion with the Turks until great-grandfather's eldest son regained the throne in 1842.'

'And lost it again sixteen years later?'

If there was a hint of amusement in his voice Katerina was unaware of it. 'The Obrenovichs never ceased plotting and trying to overthrow him,' she explained, wanting him to understand that losing the throne a second time had not been mere Karageorgevich carelessness. 'They created such unrest in the country and such distrust that eventually they succeeded, but they didn't do so with popular support. Eleven years ago Alexander Obrenovich and his queen were murdered and parliament invited Uncle Peter to return from exile as king.'

It was a bizarre, bloody story, made all the more bizarre because of the sumptuous surroundings in which it had been told and the Mona Lisa-like beauty and grace of the story-teller.

As he held her lightly and securely in the curve of his arm, Julian wondered if she had heard any other version of her family's history. Before he had left London he had been given a far more graphic and much less biased account of the Karageorgevich saga.

'Bloody barbarians,' his foreign service officer had said to him succinctly. 'Not the present king perhaps, but certainly the whole previous tribe of Karageorgevichs and Obrenovichs. Black George would have killed his mother if it had been to his advantage and all the Obrenovichs ever did was quarrel over women.'

When he had arrived in Belgrade his minister had been even more scathing. 'London may have decided to recognize King Peter's legitimacy, but it only did so after three years of haggling. Not surprising when you consider the hideous manner of Alexander Obrenovich's death.'

'But the present king wasn't responsible, was he?' he had asked, baffled. 'I thought Peter Karageorgevich was in Geneva when Alexander and Draga were murdered.'

'So he was. And he certainly didn't personally plan the murders. That was done by Captain Dragutin Dimitrievich. What you have to bear in mind, however, is that instead of being executed as a regicide Dimitrievich was promoted to colonel and is now head of Serbian Army Intelligence. His nickname is Apis and my advice to you is to give him a wide berth. He's a ruthless man and a dangerous one.'

As the strains of 'The Blue Danube' began to come to a close Julian wondered if Katerina had ever heard of Apis, or of the suggestion that her uncle had condoned the assassination of King Alexander and Queen Draga. Whether she had or not, her family was certainly volatile and had often been notorious and he wondered if he was right in his head, wanting to marry into it.

As the waltz came to an end Katerina said hesitantly, 'I wonder, sometimes, if diplomats ever really know all they should about the countries in which they serve.'

He had been scanning the glittering room and it was a second or so before sharp-edged diplomatic intuition surged into life. 'They probably don't,' he said frankly, immediately giving her his full attention. 'I certainly wish I knew more about Serbia and about Serbian aspirations.'

People were leaving the dance floor. Out of the corner of his eye he could see Natalie being escorted by her elderly kinsman. The Montenegrin princess swept past, the jewel-secured plumes in her hair quivering and swaying.

Katerina's cheeks were flushed. Now that it had come to it she did not see how she could possibly suggest to him that they talk further on the subject and in relative privacy. The suggestion would have to come from him.

He said perceptively, 'Let me mark your card for the supper dance. We can walk on the terrace instead of going in to supper. It will be easier to talk there.'

She nodded agreement, overcome at how easy it had been. As he escorted her back to where her father was standing she smiled to herself. It had been easy because they intuitively understood one another. They were in mental accord, just as her parents had always been in mental accord.

'The French minister is quite a Lothario,' her father was saying in easy informality to Julian as he watched the gentleman in question sweep yet another pretty girl on to the dance floor.

Julian, knowing better than to make an indiscreet remark in return, merely murmured, 'A niece I think, sir.'

'Ah, of course.' Beneath Alexis Vassilovich's waxed moustaches was a hint of a smile. 'Some senior diplomats have so many nieces and god-daughters that I quite lose count.'

Julian, mindful of Katerina's description of Natalie's aged dance partner, scanned the thronged ballroom once again in the hope of catching sight of her.

She was with Vitza Karageorgevich and heading towards him. Everything about her shone; her hair, her eyes, her wide dazzling smile. She exuded health and vitality and every head turned as she passed, relations and foreign dignitaries alike gazing after her with appreciative eyes.

'Papa!' she exclaimed with almost child-like pleasure as she approached, 'You'll never believe it but both the French minister *and* the Russian minister have asked for my dance card.'

'They would be fools not to have done,' her father said with amusement. 'I trust you still have some dances free?'

'Not many,' Natalie said with immodest truthfulness. 'I can't remember a ball being so much fun before. Mama said I was not to dance with any Cossack officer without her permission, but I keep losing sight of her and it's very aggravating. Can I have your permission to accept the next time I am asked, Papa? I feel quite *juvenile* having to refuse.'

'No, you may not,' her father said, having no desire to see his younger daughter's head turned by Russian military glamour. 'You can, however, allow me to mark your dance card. If you can endure dancing with both the French and the Russian ministers you can surely endure a dance with your father.'

From where Katerina was standing she could see Vitza's dance card and it was pathetically barren of names. Julian had obviously also seen it and he now said chivalrously, 'Would you allow me to mark your card, Mademoiselle Karageorgevich?'

Vitza flushed and rather clumsily handed him her card.

'And if you can spare a dance for me, Vitza,' her father said with equal gallantry, 'I would much appreciate it.'

After doing his duty where Vitza was concerned, Julian turned towards Natalie.

'Not being a Cossack, perhaps you could dance with me without having to seek your mother's permission first,' he said teasingly.

Natalie flashed him her wide, generous smile. 'I have very few dances left, Mr Fielding. I do, however, have this next dance free.'

Together, watched indulgently by her father and Katerina, Natalie and Julian stepped out on to the marble dance floor.

'I like that young man,' her father said, grateful that Katerina was not yearning for Cossacks and that he had no need to promise her a dance in order to protect her from unsuitable partners. 'He has a nice manner, easier than the majority of Englishmen and yet not overly familiar.'

'I like him too, Papa,' Katerina said, her eyes on Julian's barley-gold hair as he whirled Natalie around the room to a tune from Franz Lehár's 'The Merry Widow'. Never before, in any situation, had she behaved impulsively or rashly and she did not believe she was doing so now. He was as swashbuckling in looks as a Slav and yet as dependable in character as the most archetypical Englishman. It was a rare combination and it suited her romantic, yet fundamentally sensible personality, perfectly.

For the next few dances she caught only brief glimpses of him. Max Karageorgevich danced with her and had the good sense not to mention Natalie's foray to the *Golden Sturgeon*. The French minister, determined to dance with every pretty girl in the room, also danced with her as did the Russian minister, the Russian *chargé d'affaires* and Monsieur Quesnai.

Her attention was held by none of her partners. After Julian's waltz with Natalie he danced with Vitza, and then with the Russian minister's wife, and then with Natalie again.

Katerina, mindful of the Cossacks, was grateful. Her

parents' long years of exile in the heart of Europe had given them a Bohemian attitude towards life and it showed in the unusual amount of freedom they allowed both Natalie and herself. Because Natalie had thought it adventurous to attend the Conservatoire rather than to have her music lessons at home, they had allowed her to do so and, unknown to them, it had proved almost catastrophic. What would happen if Natalie were to become infatuated with a Cossack was anyone's guess and Katerina was glad that her father, usually so lenient, had upheld her mother's decision that Natalie must ask permission first before dancing with any of them.

When it was the supper dance she stood discreetly near one of the french windows until Julian approached her.

'Let's go outside,' he said without preamble. 'It's unbearably hot in here. I can't imagine what it must be like when the ball is held in August.'

As the orchestra began to play and the ballroom floor began to fill, they stepped unobtrusively outside on to the terrace. The moon was full, the garden silvery-pale, the scent of the roses thick as smoke. Excitement spiralled through her as he led the way across the terrace and down the shallow stone steps leading to the lawn. He was ensuring that no-one from the ballroom would be able to see them; that they would have the maximum privacy.

'I had the feeling you wanted to talk to me without being overheard,' he said as they stepped on to the gravelled pathway leading to the rose garden.

'Yes.' Her mouth was so dry she could hardly force the word past her lips. When they had finished talking about the Black Hand would he propose to her in her mother's rose garden? When she re-entered the ballroom would it be as his unofficial fiancée?

'It occurred to me, at the *Konak* tea-party, that there were aspects of Slav nationalism of which you might be

49

ignorant,' she said, forcing herself to concentrate on the pretext for their being together. 'There is a new nationalistic organization, for instance, that is causing Papa and his friends a lot of concern. It is supposed to be secret but Papa says the more people who become aware of it, the less harm it will be able to do.'

Although they were still walking she was aware of his sudden inner tension.

'Is this organization on the lines of the Bosnia Youth Movement?' he asked with a slight frown.

'Papa thinks it is potentially much more dangerous than the Bosnia Youth Movement. Its official title is "Unification or Death", but it is commonly referred to as the Black Hand.'

'And its aims are the same?'

'Its aims are to free all Slavs living under Habsburg domination.'

'There's nothing new about that,' he said wryly. 'There must be a score of Balkan revolutionary groups all with that aim.'

'Yes, but not all are committed to the use of violence.'

Julian thought differently but didn't trouble to correct her. If the new organization was one that was perturbing Alexis Vassilovich, then it was one the British government should certainly know about.

He said thoughtfully, 'Would your father mind if I were to speak to him about what you have told me?'

She paused for a moment and then said slowly, 'No, I don't think so. He likes you and he has always said that Serbia should maintain the closest links possible with Great Britain.'

He stopped walking and turned to face her, his good-humoured face unusually solemn. 'I'm glad your father likes me and I'm glad you asked to speak to me in privacy this evening, Katerina. There's something I've wanted to ask you for a long time and there's never before been a suitable opportunity . . .'

Katerina stood very still, so still she could hear her racing heartbeats.

'Katerina, I . . .'

It was Max Karageorgevich who interrupted them. He came tramping along the pathway, a lighted cigarette in his hand. 'Sorry,' he said gracelessly as he approached them, 'am I interrupting a romantic *tête-à-tête*?'

'No,' Katerina lied, wishing him a million miles away. 'We simply wanted some air. As you apparently do.'

Max dropped his cigarette to the ground. 'If you also want some supper you'd better hurry back for it.'

'Thank you for your advice,' Julian said dryly, 'but we're not in need of it.'

'Then here's some advice you might be in need of,' Max said with the same infuriating complacency his sister often displayed. 'Uncle Alexis is looking for Katerina. He might not like it if he found her out here.'

It was true and both Katerina and Julian knew it.

'We'd better go back inside,' he said to her regretfully. 'We can continue our conversation later.'

'Yes.' Her voice was oddly abrupt and Max looked across at her, frowning slightly.

'I'll walk back with you,' he said, uncaring that his presence was very obviously not wanted. 'You're not coming down with a cold, are you, Trina? Your voice sounds suspicously hoarse. Perhaps you should make an early evening of it and dose yourself with a lemon powder.'

Katerina remained silent only with the greatest difficulty. He had spoiled what would have been the most beautiful moment of her life with his crass oafishness and she doubted if she would ever forgive him.

When they returned to the ballroom Julian escorted her to her father and then dutifully went in search of Vitza.

'So that's where you were,' her father said when Julian was safely out of earshot, 'with young Fielding. I thought he'd been paying our family rather a lot of attention recently and now I know why.'

Katerina blushed. 'You don't mind, Papa, do you?'

His eyebrows shot upwards. He had been merely teasing when he had suggested Fielding was a prospective suitor. Now, realizing he had inadvertently hit on a momentous truth he said, suddenly serious, 'I shall want him to speak to me before this goes any further, Katerina.'

She took hold of his arm lovingly. 'He hasn't actually said anything to me yet, Papa.'

He patted her hand thoughtfully, sure that if the look in her eyes was anything to go by Julian Fielding would be doing so very soon.

His premonition was correct. Half an hour later Julian was declaring himself ardently. He had wanted to speak to Katerina before he did so, in order to find out if he was likely to meet with any success. Max Karageorgevich's untimely arrival had prevented him from doing so but she had told him that her father liked him and the information had given him courage.

He was in the Italian drawing-room. It was the smallest drawing-room in the Vassilovich house and its unconventional blue and lemon décor gave it a summery atmosphere even when the curtains were drawn and it was lit only by candlelight.

He was down on one knee before the sofa and he didn't feel even slightly ridiculous. All he felt was terror in case she rejected him.

'I want you to marry me,' he said thickly. 'I love you, and I shall always love you. Only you. For ever.'

Chapter Three

Natalie stared at him in stunned amazement. She had accompanied him into the Italian drawing-room because she had wanted to put her feet up for a minute or two, because he was amusing and diverting company and because leaving the ballroom with a young man was such a daring, *moderne* thing to do. Never had it remotely occurred to her that he would take advantage of the situation in order to declare undying love for her, still less that he would actually propose marriage to her.

'You can't mean it,' she said, suddenly sure that it was a joke, a typical example of obscure British humour. 'You're teasing me, aren't you?'

'I've never felt less like teasing in all my life,' Julian said, his voice slightly unsteady. 'You must have guessed how I feel about you, Natalie. I love you with all my heart and I can't imagine life without you. Please say you care for me, at least a little.'

'I do,' Natalie said truthfully. 'I like you an awful lot. But I'm not in love with you. I can't imagine being in love with anyone, or at least not with just one person for the rest of my life.'

Despite the terrible gravity of the situation Julian felt a tremor of amusement at her guilessness. 'That's because you're only seventeen,' he said, still clinging to fierce hope. 'I know we would be happy, Natalie. I know you would soon stop only liking me and learn to love me. I may not be a Serbian prince but I come from impeccable family, my forebears landed on the coast of England with William the Conqueror in 1066. I have a brilliant future and . . .'

With horror Natalie realized that he was in deadly earnest. 'Please stop,' she begged, before he could go any further. 'Your asking me to marry you is the sweetest thing that has ever happened to me. I feel so flattered I can hardly believe it . . .'

It was true. Now that she had recovered from her amazement, she was overwhelmingly flattered. It wasn't as if Julian Fielding was a callow, impressionable youth. He was in his late twenties, a handsome, mature, sophisticated diplomat. And he was in love with her. So much in love that he wanted to marry her. It was incredible. Euphoria engulfed her. She wondered what her mother would say when she told her. What Katerina would say.

Julian saw the successive emotions chasing across her face and cursed himself for a fool. He should have realized that at seventeen she was too young to have responded to him as he needed her to respond. The freedom she was allowed had fooled him into believing that Serbian girls matured early. Certainly Katerina was sensibly mature and she was only two years Natalie's senior, but he wasn't in love with Katerina. He was in love, God help him, with the fairytale vision sitting before him on the sofa.

In a sea of misery he rose to his feet, saying with a stiffness totally alien to him, 'I'm sorry if I took you by surprise.'

'Oh, please don't apologize!' Natalie's horror was genuine. Even though she wasn't in love with him his proposal had been the most wonderful thing that had ever happened to her and she didn't want the memory of it to be spoiled by apologies. 'I shall always remember this moment,' she said with a carefree sentimentality that almost destroyed him, 'the candlelight and the scent of the flowers and the music . . .'

From the distant ballroom could be heard the faint strains of a mazurka.

'And can we still be friends?' With luck he had at least another year to serve in Belgrade. A lot could happen in a year. In a year Natalie could grow from liking him to loving him.

She rose from the sofa and slid her arm affectionately through his. Until now it had never occurred to her that they *had* been friends. She had always thought of him as being more Katerina's friend, or even of his being her father's friend.

'Of *course* we will still be friends,' she said, highly gratified at all the new, grown-up things that were beginning to happen to her. As he began to walk with her out of the room she said effervescently, 'Have I told you that Prince Alexander has given me Bella? She's absolutely adorable. I'm teaching her to sit and to stay and she's very, very good.'

Julian couldn't have cared less about Bella. He felt unbelievably exhausted, both emotionally and physically. For once in his life he had grossly miscalculated. As they neared the ballroom he assessed his feelings, wondering if rejection had altered them.

The assessment took the merest fraction of a second. If his feelings had altered at all, it was only that he was more determined than ever that one day she would be his wife. At twenty-eight he had been lightly in love many times and had enjoyed many affairs. What he had never been previously was totally and irrevocably in love and that was because he had never before been bewitched. Natalie, with her dark brilliant eyes and her irresistibly infectious gaiety, had bewitched him at their very first meeting. Since then he had done everything in his power to ensure

55

that their paths converged on every conceivable occasion. Fortunately in a capital city as provincial as Belgrade, such connivance was relatively easy.

He genuinely liked the entire Vassilovich family. Alexis Vassilovich was that rare thing in the Balkans, an enlightened liberal. Zita Vassilovich was refreshingly intelligent with as sure a grasp of the current political situation as any diplomat. Katerina Vassilovich possessed the grace, beauty and calm composure of a Renaissance madonna and a man would be a fool not to be grateful at the thought of having her as a sister-in-law. And Natalie . . . Natalie had become an obsession.

She said now, smiling guilelessly at up him, 'I've promised this next dance to Monsieur Quesnai and he'll be looking for me.'

Wishing Phillippe Quesnai at the far ends of the earth Julian watched her hurry lightly into the ballroom. He also had dances promised but he didn't have the heart to seek his partners out. As unobtrusively as possible he made his way round the back of the room until he came to the first french window and then, once again, he stepped outside.

It was after midnight now and there was the hint of a chill in the night air. Lighting a cigarette he inhaled deeply and crossed the terrace. There were a half dozen couples, walking modestly together, heads as close as propriety permitted. Julian ignored them and taking the steps two at a time descended to the gravel pathway and the lawns.

If Max Karageorgevich hadn't interrupted his conversation with Katerina, would she have warned him that his proposal would be in vain? And if she had, would he have heeded her warning and not made his proposal? He walked quickly, head down, shoulders hunched, towards the rose garden. Probably not. And in an odd way he was beginning to think his proposal, and Natalie's rejection of it, had been no bad thing. At least now she knew what his feelings for her were and when she had time to reflect on them she might very well discover that her own feelings were not quite so fraternal as she had supposed.

He sat down on a rustic bench strategically placed in a rose-bower, ground the remains of his cigarette out beneath his heel and lit another one. He no longer felt as if he had made a fool of himself and he no longer felt that he had acted imprudently. At seventeen it had obviously never occurred to Natalie that she was old enough to fall in love or old enough to have anyone fall in love with her. He had just disabused her of that belief and now that she realized she was a child no longer, and that he loved her, reciprocation would soon follow. It was bound to if he courted her assiduously enough.

He rose to his feet feeling a whole lot better. The future was once again hopeful. He had suffered a setback, nothing more. Full of renewed optimism he began to make his way back towards the ballroom. No prize was worth the having if winning it didn't necessitate a long, hard struggle. And he was determined to win Natalie. Winning was his style.

Katerina saw him as he entered the ballroom from the terrace and her first thought was that he had been outside hopefully waiting for her.

'My dance, I think?' Max was saying to her.

'Oh Max, must we? It's too hot in here and I feel quite faint . . .'

Out of the corner of her eye she could see Julian approaching Princess Xenia of Montenegro. Princess Xenia checked her dance card and then with a smile allowed him to lead her on to the dance floor.

Katerina's heart plummeted. There was no chance now of discreetly approaching him and of him being able to

57

invite her once more out into the garden so that their interrupted conversation could be continued.

'You don't look at all faint,' Max said unhelpfully. 'All you look is anxious and I want you to tell me why,' and with one hand beneath her arm he propelled her mercilessly out on to the thronged floor.

Katerina didn't desist. With Julian now dancing with Xenia there was very little point. The dance was a waltz and it felt distinctly strange going through the same movements as she had with Julian only an hour or so earlier, and with such different effect. Max was as tall as Julian, but much more ruggedly built. His large hands held her far too proprietorily and he didn't smell deliciously of lemon-scented cologne. He smelled of riding leather and, very faintly, of brandy.

'Why the anxiety?' he persisted as the orchestra blazed into a new coda. 'And why were you in the garden taking a breath of air with an Englishman? Don't you know they're all degenerate?'

Katerina treated his remark with the contempt it deserved. 'With whom I choose to walk on the terrace is my affair, not anyone else's,' she retorted frostily, trying to catch a glimpse of Xenia's magnificent plumed headdress and Julian's thick thatch of fair hair.

Max negotiated her past the orchestra's dais with all the grace of a hippopotamus, saying, 'It was the garden, not the terrace, and if he knew of it your father would think it very much his affair. I imagine he would also regard Natalie's excursions into *kafanas* as being his affair as well. Or he would if he knew about them.'

'One *kafana*,' Katerina corrected, wondering why on earth she had allowed him to mark her dance card. 'And there are no blackmail opportunities in it for you. Natalie realizes how foolish she was and it isn't an incident that will be repeated.'

The waltz was reaching its climax. Julian and Xenia were nowhere in sight and were presumably at the far end of the room.

Max's dark eyebrows rose slightly. 'Blackmail? Why should I want to blackmail anyone? All I'm doing is warning you to keep an eye on Natalie. She's all Karageorgevich and it's bound to mean trouble some day.'

'You're full of unwanted advice, Max,' she said dismissively as the music came to an end. 'And don't bother approaching me for another dance. I shall be unavailable.'

A strange, shuttered look came down over his face and she spun on her heel, hoping that she would be able to meet with Julian before the next dance began.

She saw him almost immediately. He was on the opposite side of the ballroom, speaking to her parents. Incredibly she saw him inclining his head as if he were thanking them for the evening and saying goodbye. With rising consternation she picked up her demi-train, crossing the ballroom floor as quickly as her skirts and dignity would allow.

She was too late. He was shaking her father's hand and when she was still a good ten yards away he walked from the room, making what was unmistakably a final exit.

She stood still. Should she follow him? For a rash, reckless moment she almost succumbed to the temptation and then good sense prevailed and she remained where she was, looking towards the now empty double doorway, her sense of excitement and expectancy draining from her.

Had he left so precipitately because he was crushed with disappointment at not being able to talk to her in privacy and because he believed there would be no future opportunity that evening to do so? Or was she simply letting her imagination run away with her? Was she reading into his behaviour motives she ardently wished were true but which might, in reality, be very far from the truth?

A distant Vassilovich cousin approached her. 'My dance, I think,' he said genially.

She felt suddenly very tired but to excuse herself before the last waltz would draw comment and after the short conversation she had had with her father earlier, he might even think she was leaving in order to keep a romantic assignation with Julian Fielding.

Forcing a smile she agreed that it was, indeed, his promised dance and allowed him to lead her on to the floor for what she realized with a heavy heart was an energetic cotillion.

Natalie had never felt more full of life. She was fizzing with *joie de vivre*. Her dance card had been crammed with names all evening and the names had not been merely family names, uncles and cousins doing their duty. Every minister present had asked for a dance, some of them more than once. Prince Danilo of Montenegro, who was in Belgrade for private talks with her Uncle Peter, had also asked her to dance as had a Russian Grand Duke and the most wonderfully handsome Cossack officer it was possible to imagine. And to top it all, she had received her very first proposal of marriage.

Even now, an hour later, she could scarcely believe it. And it hadn't been just any old, mundane proposal. It had been heart-stoppingly serious; unutterably romantic.

She smiled dazzlingly at her partner as he whirled her exhilaratingly round and round. Once her immediate shock at Julian's proposal had worn off she had found herself reflecting that it was a great pity he was an Englishman and not a Slav. If he had been a Slav she might, just might, have been tempted to accept. To be engaged at seventeen would be a triumph. Katerina would have to stop taking such a heavy-handed attitude with her, Vitza would be green with envy and a magnificent engagement ring of diamonds and emeralds would look simply *stunning* on her left hand.

The music gained momentum. Or would diamonds and rubies be more sensational? Or just one magnificent diamond? As the music reached a crescendo and her silver-slippered feet seemed barely to touch the ground, she decided that a solitaire diamond would be far more elegant than a diamond with emeralds or rubies.

She could almost feel the ring on her finger and then she remembered again that Julian Fielding was not a Slav and that even if he were Britain's heir to the throne she couldn't possibly marry him. Her decision as to whom she could or could not marry had been made long ago when she was a small child living in exile in horribly boring Geneva. She had vowed then she would never marry any man who would expect her to live anywhere else but the country she longed for with such fierce passion.

Regretfully abandoning all thoughts of diamond solitaires she reflected on other pleasant things. Katerina had not mentioned the affair of the *Golden Sturgeon* again and so she had wriggled out of that difficulty without having to promise never to go there again. Consequently she had all the excitement of future meetings with Gavrilo and his friends to look forward to as well as the thrill of telling Katerina and Vitza about Julian Fielding's proposal.

The music came to a thunderous end. Her partner was laughing breathlessly down at her. With sheer animal high spirits she laughed back. Life was wonderful and if it was so wonderful at seventeen how much more wonderful was it going to be when she was eighteen? Nineteen?

As her partner escorted her from the ballroom floor she was struck by another thought, not quite so exhilarating. If her mother and father were to know of Julian Fielding's proposal, they might assume it had been occasioned because they had allowed her an inordinate amount of freedom. Her hard-won lessons at the Conservatoire might come to a speedy end and she might find herself once again having music lessons at home. If she did there would be no more easy opportunities for sitting in smoke-filled cafés with her friends, discussing all that was wrong with the world and how they were going to put it right. It was a risk that wasn't worth running. The heady pleasure of telling Katerina and Vitza about Julian's proposal was one she would have to forgo.

The next morning, as she ate an exceedingly late and light breakfast that had been brought to her in bed, Natalie was too preoccupied in thinking about the meeting she was to have that afternoon with Gavrilo to notice that Katerina was also unusually quiet. Her music lesson was scheduled for three o'clock and she thought it best that she didn't mention it to Katerina. She didn't want Katerina suddenly demanding good behaviour and a promise that she wouldn't abscond if Monsieur Lasalle was so lax as not to turn up on time, or didn't turn up at all.

And he wouldn't turn up. At their last meeting she had intimated to him that today was her grandmother's birthday and that consequently a lesson would not be possible. She had not been telling a lie. It *was* one of her grandmothers' birthdays, but the grandmother in question had been dead for over five years. She knew that Monsieur Lasalle would be too pleased at having an unexpectedly free afternoon ever to think of checking up on her story, or of mentioning the missed lesson to her father.

'I'm going to spend time training Bella today,' she said, pushing the breakfast tray from her knees and swinging her feet to the floor.

Katerina, who had already had two pairs of shoes and a

hat ruined by Bella's habit of playing and chewing with any and every available object, didn't attempt to dissuade her. She was wondering if Julian Fielding would call at the house later in the day to ask for an appointment with her father in order to discuss with him the significance the Black Hand might have on British/Serbian relations. If so, and if they should meet in the hall or the garden, then something might be said that would put an end to her uncertainty as to what his feelings for her were.

Natalie, grateful for Katerina's lack of talkativeness, began to wash and dress without ringing for Helga to help her. She put on a sensible white and mulberry striped piqué dress that would not look too out of place among the poverty-stricken students in the *Golden Sturgeon*, and tamed her riotously curling hair as best she could before securing it in an uncomplicated and undecorated chignon.

Looking at herself in the cheval-glass she was pleased with the effect she had created. She might be a Karageorgevich but she looked as restrained in appearance as if she were the daughter of a doctor or a lawyer. With the addition of a pair of plain lensed glasses she might even be taken for a student herself.

The *Golden Sturgeon* was down a narrow cobbled street in an area thick with coffee-houses. There was the *Acorn Garland*, the *Green Garland* and the *Moruna*, all within a stone's throw of each other. To Natalie, her first expedition there in the company of Gavrilo and Nedjelko had been a dizzying adventure. Never before had she met with people from a different social class from her own; never before had she walked through the city's teeming, claustrophobic back streets.

Once inside the *kafana*, she had found the atmosphere and the conversation even more of an adventure. Nearly all the clientele were young, with only an occasional middle-aged nationalist joining them in order to offer them the benefit of his experience. Nearly all of them were students and those who had fled to Serbia from Bosnia or Herzegovina or Croatia were poor in a way that was almost inconceivable to her. They didn't seem to mind their poverty. All of them were sure that at any moment some great happening would wonderfully transform their lives.

It was this sense of camaraderie and of being part of the vanguard of a whole new, exciting future, that Natalie found irresistible. Unlike her parents' generation, who merely talked of there being a great united South Slav state one day, Gavrilo and his friends were actively plotting and planning for one. It was unbelievably thrilling. Utterly intoxicating.

Gavrilo no longer met her at the Conservatoire and walked with her to the café. His doing so had become far too conspicuous. Instead, when the family coachman set her down at the Conservatoire's gates she walked through them and into the Conservatoire, leaving almost immediately by a discreet side-door.

Her only regret as she walked across first one tree-shaded square and then another, was that Bella wasn't scampering at her heels. The temptation to bring the dog with her had been almost overpowering but she was still too small to be safe on the street and besides, if Katerina had seen her leave the house with Bella, she would have known that she wasn't truly going to a music lesson.

She turned left at the far side of the square, walking into the maze of streets that formed the Bohemian Quarter. Although it was still only early summer the heat was fierce and she wished she had brought a parasol with her. As a man passed her wearing the shabby baggy trousers of a peasant she changed her mind. A parasol would only have made her look even more out of place in an area where loose Zouave jackets were more common than western clothes.

With a surge of excitement she drew abreast of the café. Here, for the price of a coffee, she could sit all afternoon listening to the thrilling talk of how, one day very soon, all southern Slavs would be united in a powerful empire which would be known as Yugoslavia, the Kingdom of the South Slavs.

With a euphoric sense of destiny she opened the door and stepped into an aromatic fug of coffee aroma, tobacco smoke and plum brandy.

'Here she is!' Nedjelko Cabrinovich called out to his companions as he saw her enter the room. 'Pull out a chair someone. Order another cup of coffee.'

She walked across the crowded room to her friends' discreetly positioned corner table and smiled sunnily, unaware of the quick, meaningful glances that were exchanged between them before she sat down.

'I'm glad you could make it today,' Gavrilo said, rising to his feet. 'I'm going away for a few days with Nedjelko and Trifko and I wanted to be able to let you know.'

Trifko Grabez gave her a slight, acknowledging nod. He was a slightly built, serious young man and she had never felt completely comfortable with him. Though nothing had ever been said she was sure he disapproved of her.

'Trifko disapproves of all women,' Nedjelko had once said to her with a grin. 'He thinks they distract from the great crusade of freeing Bosnia from Habsburg rule.'

'Where are you going?' she said to Gavrilo as she sat down. 'Is it an assignment? Are you going on a mission?'

He gave her his quiet, almost shy smile. 'It's just a training exercise,' he said, and then turned away quickly from her as he began to cough.

Natalie frowned. Both Gavrilo and Trifko had chronic coughs and on her last visit to the *Golden Sturgeon* she had brought with her all the cough pastilles she could find. She said now, 'You really should get that cough seen to, Gavrilo.'

'And how would he pay the doctor's bill?' Trifko asked, an edge of sarcasm in his voice.

Natalie flushed. She hated it when the difference in her circumstances and those of her friends was so brutally pointed out. She was immensely proud of being a Karageorgevich but there were times when her comfortable lifestyle was also an embarrassment.

'Don't mind Trifko,' Nedjelko said with a grin. 'Tell us if you've managed to speak to Prince Alexander yet.'

Both Trifko and Gavrilo adjusted their chairs, bringing them in closer to the marble-topped table, looking towards her intently.

Natalie forgot her discomfiture and said with quiet triumph: 'Prince Alexander is with us heart, mind and soul.'

'And deeds?' Trifko asked, cynically. 'Is he with us when it comes to deeds?'

'Be quiet,' Gavrilo said to him abruptly. He gave Natalie his slight, endearing smile. 'What Trifko wants to know is, will he meet with us?'

Natalie shifted uncomfortably on her chair. Alexander had said that she could tell her student friends that if they were working for the unity of all southern Slavs, irrespective of religion, then they had his whole-hearted support. He could not, however, meet with them.

'In a *kafana*?' he had asked disbelievingly. 'Don't be ridiculous, Natalie. Think of the attention I would attract if I stepped into a *kafana*.'

'A meeting would be difficult,' she said prevaricatingly. 'He would be recognized and . . .'

'I knew it!' Trifko slammed his fist down exasperatedly on the table. 'Prince Alexander has no intention of coming out in the open and supporting us! When it comes to

66

talking militant action for the creation of a united South Slav state he and his father are just as supine as Alexander Obrenovich was!'

'No, they're not,' Gavrilo said, his annoyance obvious.

Trifko folded his arms and pursed his lips and there was a short, uncomfortable silence.

Gavrilo smiled at Natalie again, this time apologetically. 'Ignore Trifko. He has a hangover and he's not happy at the thought of going back to Bosnia on a training mission.'

Natalie remained stonily silent. Trifko hadn't apologized to her himself for his ridiculous outburst and she had not the slightest intention of saying that she forgave him.

'Bloody Habsburgs,' Nedjelko said cheerily, changing the subject, 'here's to their downfall!' He raised his coffee cup high in a toast, as if it were a glass of plum brandy.

Everyone laughed, even Trifko, and Natalie's crossness with him ebbed. Happy that the atmosphere was again relaxed and friendly, she said to the table at large, 'Will you all be seeing your families when you return to Bosnia?'

The laughter drained from Nedjelko's face. 'Gavrilo and Trifko might see theirs,' he said, looking suddenly very young and very vulnerable, 'but I doubt if I will see mine.'

'But why not?' Natalie was bewildered. She couldn't imagine being away from home for months and months and not taking advantage of any opportunity for being reunited, however briefly, with her family.

'Nedjelko's father is an Austrian police spy,' Trifko said dryly.

'I'm sorry.' Natalie's eyes were wide with shock. 'I hadn't realized . . .'

'No reason why you should have.' Nedjelko shrugged his narrow shoulders philosophically. 'The old ba . . .'

Gavrilo cleared his throat.

'. . . the old devil once locked me up for three days for being rude to him. God knows what he would do if he knew I was a member of . . .'

Gavrilo cleared his throat again, this time loudly.

'. . . a South Slav nationalist organization.'

'I doubt if I shall visit my father either,' Trifko said sombrely.

No-one made any comment. Trifko's father was an Orthodox priest and there had been no contact between them since Trifko had been expelled from school for striking a teacher who had been trying to indoctrinate his class with Austro-Hungarian sympathies.

'I'd visit my family if it were possible,' Gavrilo said to her quietly, an odd expression in his voice, 'but I don't think it will be.' He was silent for a moment or two and then he said, 'Will you approach Prince Alexander again, Natalie? Will you tell him that there are things he needs to be told? Things that can't be put down on paper.'

She nodded, determined to be useful to them, determined to play an active part in the dream of building a federated South Slav state.

The conversation moved on. Both Gavrilo and Trifko were high-school students, studying hard in order to graduate and they began to talk of their studies and of the differences between the Serbian and the Bosnian education system. As they began to argue whether there was less Latin and Greek taught in Serbian schools than Bosnian schools Natalie, who had never come to grips with either subject, glanced at her watch.

It was nearly half past three. In five more minutes the family coachman would be waiting for her outside the front entrance of the Conservatoire. Reluctantly she rose to her feet.

'I must be going,' she said regretfully. 'I'll do as you ask and speak to Prince Alexander again.'

'And King Peter,' Trifko said suddenly. 'He's the one who should really be supporting us.'

'And King Peter,' she said, trying to keep doubt out of her voice.

She still hadn't told Alexander that her friends were members of a militant organization so secret she hadn't yet been told the name of it and she couldn't quite see herself having the nerve to tell her uncle. It would be foolish, however, to make such an admittance to Trifko. If she did, she would lose all credibility.

They had all three risen to their feet with her.

'See you when we return from Bosnia,' Nedjelko said with his usual cheeriness.

Trifko merely shook her hand. Only Gavrilo walked with her to the door.

'I can't come with you back to the Conservatoire,' he said with genuine regret. 'There's a lot of things to be discussed before we leave for Bosnia.'

'When do you leave?' For the first time she realized that she hadn't asked him exactly what they were going to do in Bosnia. He had said their trip was a training exercise, but a training exercise for what? It was too late now to ask.

'Tomorrow,' he said, as they stepped out on to the cobbles. He began to cough again and then said, 'We leave in the morning.'

'Goodbye.' She determined that next time they met she would bring him some more cough pastilles. 'Good luck.'

As she walked away up the narrow alley he stood watching her, a troubled expression on his olive-skinned, high cheek-boned face.

When he returned to the table Trifko said bluntly, 'You're too fond of that girl. If you weren't, you would see that she's never going to be of any real use to us.'

Gavrilo frowned slightly. He was renowned for being too committed to the nationalist cause to have time for girls. If there was a lady-killer in the group it was Nedjelko, not him.

Unaware of the role Gavrilo was mentally allotting him, Nedjelko grinned. 'Trifko's right. You are too fond of her.' He began to chuckle. 'You'd make a damned odd pair! The son of Bosnian peasants and the daughter of a Vassilovich and a Karageorgevich! Can you imagine the wedding. There would be . . .'

'Shut up.' A faint flush of embarrassed colour had heightened Gavrilo's cheeks. 'I'm always happy to see Natalie because I believe she can be invaluable to us. With royal support there's nothing we couldn't achieve.'

'I still don't believe she will gain us that support,' Trifko said obstinately. 'I think she's going to be far more of a liability than an asset.'

'Trifko could be right.' There was a slight frown on Nedjelko's usually cheery face. 'It was rash of you to mention our going to Bosnia. What if after our mission is completed she puts two and two together and comes up with four?'

'She won't.' Gavrilo's voice was sharply abrupt. He already knew he shouldn't have told Natalie of the trip to Bosnia and he wasn't enjoying having it pointed out to him by Nedjelko. 'We're going to be in Bosnia a month before we carry out our mission. I'll make sure she believes we're back in Belgrade long before then. She won't connect us with what happens in Sarajevo. No-one will.'

Chapter Four

It was three weeks before Julian had a satisfactory pretext on which to visit the Vassilovich residence. Rumours had reached the British minister that King Peter was considering abdicating in favour of Crown Prince Alexander and as no confirmation was forthcoming from official channels the minister had decided on an unofficial approach.

'Alexis Vassilovich will know,' he had said to Julian. 'The King relies heavily on him for advice. Be open with him. Tell him we've heard the rumours and that His Majesty's Government is anxious to know whether or not there is any substance to them. Any such change at the moment could have far-reaching consequences. We know where we are politically with Peter Karageorgevich. His son may not be such an open book. Especially where the Austrians are concerned.'

Only too glad for a legitimate excuse to meet with Alexis and perhaps bring up the intriguing subject of the Black Hand, Julian wasted no time. Five minutes later he was striding through the hot narrow streets towards the Vassilovichs' white-walled Belgrade home.

Alexis greeted him urbanely. He saw no reason why the British shouldn't be told the truth about King Peter's intentions, especially as there was to be an official announcement later that week.

'King Peter has not been well for some time,' he said, handing Julian a glass of *slivovitz* pungently distilled with juniper berries. 'He needs to take a long and much-needed rest. While he does so, Crown Prince Alexander will take over his duties and govern in his name.'

'As Regent?'

Alexis nodded, sipped at his plum brandy and said, 'Yes, as Regent.'

There were a lot more questions Julian would have liked to have asked but Alexis's tone of voice indicated he had said all he wished to on the subject.

Julian swirled the *slivovitz* around in his glass. What he really wanted to talk to Alexis about was the Black Hand. He wondered how to go about it and decided that frankness was the best course. Taking a deep breath he said as casually as possible, 'There's something else I would like to ask you about, sir. I wonder if you could give me any information on an organization of which I've recently heard rumours. It's nationalistic in spirit and goes by the name of the Black Hand.'

Alexis Vassilovich's reaction was almost comic. He dropped his glass. It rolled on the Bokhara rug, the *slivovitz* seeping into it and staining it. He was oblivious. 'Where the devil did you hear of the Black Hand?' he asked hoarsely, his normally imperturable face ashen.

Julian's mind raced. The Black Hand was obviously of far more importance than he had realized or, from the way she had spoken of it, than Katerina had realized. If he answered her father's question truthfully it might make things very awkward for her. And if he didn't, and if she guilelessly mentioned the organization to anyone else, then it might make things more than awkward for her. It might cause her very serious trouble.

Mindful of the relationship he hoped to one day have with Alexis Vassilovich and knowing that Alexis would be the best person to protect Katerina if she should have talked carelessly to anyone else, he trusted well-honed instinct and said, 'It was Katerina, sir. She thought you wouldn't mind my knowing about it . . .'

'Holy God!' Alexis Vassilovich's face had gone whiter than ever.

'. . . she quite obviously didn't regard it as a forbidden subject . . .'

'Stay here.' Alexis Vassilovich collected himself with an effort and began to stride towards the door. 'I shall be back in a few minutes. Whatever you do, don't leave until we've spoken further.'

'No, sir. Of course not . . .'

The door slammed and he was alone, wondering what on earth was so terrible about the Gothically-named Black Hand that it would cause a sophisticated, seasoned politician such consternation.

'Where did you hear of it, Katerina?' Alexis was again in control and in command but the tension in his voice was unmistakable.

Katerina looked at him in faint surprise. She was in the sunny Italian drawing-room, reading *Madame Bovary*.

'From you, Papa. You were talking to Mama and . . .'

'And who else have you mentioned it to?' He could spend time cursing himself for a fool later. What he had to do now was to ascertain the extent of the damage.

'I've spoken about it to Mama. No-one else.' She slid her book off her knee and on to the sofa and stood up, her face troubled. 'Was I wrong to talk about it to Julian Fielding?'

He didn't answer her. He said abruptly, 'No-one else? No-one at all?'

She shook her head.

He breathed an unsteady sigh of relief and then said, 'It *was* wrong to talk about it, but you weren't to know. I've always talked to you quite openly about politics and the

73

problems facing your uncle and if I was so careless to talk about the Black Hand in your hearing, there's no reason why you should have thought it a taboo subject.'

'You said that the less secrecy there was about the Black Hand, the better it would be . . .'

Alexis groaned and passed a hand across his eyes.

Katerina slid her hand into his free hand, saying urgently, 'Have I done something very terrible, Papa? Is my having spoken about the Black Hand going to cause you immense problems?'

He lowered his hand from his face. 'Not necessarily,' he said, praying to God that Fielding hadn't already spoken carelessly and in public of it. 'What I'm more concerned about is your safety.'

'My safety?' She looked at him in bewilderment. 'I'm sorry. I don't understand.'

'Then I shall have to make you understand,' he said heavily. 'And I shall have to make Fielding understand too. He's waiting for me in my study. Come with me and I'll speak to the two of you together.'

She had day-dreamed about such a meeting between the three of them, but in her day-dream the subject under discussion had been a very different one. With strongly conflicting emotions she accompanied him down the corridor. She was fiercely looking forward to seeing Julian again but she didn't want to look foolish in his eyes, and having inadvertently spoken of something she should not have spoken about, she was afraid she might.

When they entered the room he shot her a warm, reassuring smile, instantly allaying her fears. She smiled back at him gratefully and then her father closed the door behind them.

'It seems I've been very careless,' he said, turning towards them both. 'As a consequence I'm going to have to be very frank and I'm going to have to ask you to give me your word that what I am about to say will go no further than these four walls.'

'But of course, Papa!' Katerina was stung at the very idea of again being indiscreet.

Her father merely nodded. He hadn't been worried by the prospect of Katerina again talking carelessly. It was Julian Fielding who concerned him.

'As a servant of the British government my situation is rather difficult,' Julian began cautiously.

'As a father, my position is even more so,' Alexis retorted crisply.

Julian flushed. 'I would never do anything that would compromise the safety of any member of this family, sir,' he said with palpable sincerity.

Remembering the hints Katerina had given him regarding their burgeoning relationship, Alexis was satisfied of his trustworthiness.

'The Black Hand is a secret society,' he said, determining to keep his explanation as brief as possible. 'So secret that its initiates vow death to anyone who reveals its secrets.'

Julian waited for him to smile dryly and to begin talking seriously. When he didn't do so he said hesitantly, 'You are joking, sir?'

'It's no joke,' Alexis replied grimly, retreating behind his massive Biedermeir desk and sitting down. 'That is why I had to have your promise that you wouldn't speak of it outside this room. If it should come to certain ears that Katerina had been talking of the Black Hand to a British diplomat her life would most certainly be in danger.'

'I still don't understand . . .' Fierce excitement and utter horror battled for supremacy in him. Excitement at being privy to knowledge of an organization of which his fellow diplomats were ignorant. Horror at the promise he had given that he wouldn't reveal what was said to him to

75

anyone, not even his minister. 'I still don't understand,' he said again. 'If you are a member of the Black Hand, surely you can secure Katerina's safety . . .'

Alexis's hard-won control momentarily slipped. 'God in heaven, I'm not a member of it!' he exploded, rising to his feet as precipitately as he had sat down and striding across the room to the long windows that looked out over the courtyard. 'I know about it because it's my business to know such things.'

He didn't add that as the organization had been illicitly formed and was illicitly led by the Chief of Army Intelligence he would have been extremely negligent if he hadn't known about it. He stared broodingly down into the courtyard where Natalie and Bella were playing zestfully with a ball and then said abruptly, 'Did Katerina tell you its aims?'

'I told him its aims were to free all Slavs living under Habsburg domination, Papa,' Katerina said, relieved that he hadn't made her look foolish and thankful that she truthfully knew very little else.

'And that violence was sanctioned in order that those aims could be achieved,' Julian added, knowing that it was the sanction of violence which was the crux of the matter.

'And that's all?'

'Except that you had said the less secret the Black Hand was, the healthier it would be,' Katerina said, knowing that the statement absolved her of the least accusation of indiscretion.

'And so it would be,' her father said tersely, 'but indiscretions need to come from inside the organization in order to damage it and lessen its power. An indiscretion from elsewhere would result with the person in question merely being murdered . . .'

'But why?'

'To stop them continuing to disclose Black Hand secrets

76

and to serve as a warning to other Black Hand initiates not to talk.'

Julian stared at him. If Black Hand members were prepared to kill rather than have the acts they committed becoming public knowledge, then those acts had to be truly terrible. He racked his brains to think of the crimes for which they had probably been responsible.

Had it been Black Hand members who had attempted to assassinate Emperor Franz Josef three years ago? And had it been Black Hand members who had attempted to gun down the governor of Croatia and who had missed and killed a bystander and a policeman instead? And then there had been the attempted murder of the governor of Bosnia. Again the attempt had failed but the young would-be assassin had been fanatical enough to turn his gun on himself and to commit suicide. If all those crimes had been perpetrated by the Black Hand then no wonder its members were vowed to utter secrecy.

Despite his revulsion for the methods used he felt a surge of admiration for whoever had formed the organiz-ation. Habsburg officialdom was being attacked from within the countries it governed and without any blame being laid at Serbia's door. It was damned clever and, as far as the prospects of continued uneasy peace in the Balkans was concerned, it was damned dangerous.

'Does the Black Hand have official sanction?' he asked, well aware of the enormity of his question.

Alexis's face tightened. 'No,' he said shortly. 'Absol-utely and emphatically not.'

It wasn't a lie. Julian, with a diplomat's ear for the nuances in speech revealing lies and subterfuge, would have known if it had been, but he sensed that it came very close to being one. He was intrigued. If neither King Peter nor his government were sanctioning Black Hand activi-ties who, dangerously close to be being able to do so officially, *was* sanctioning them? The answer came with such suddenness that he gasped aloud.

Apis. It was Apis who had masterminded the assassination of King Alexander and Queen Draga. Apis who had put the elderly Peter on the throne in the hope that he would pursue an aggressive policy against Austria-Hungary. And Peter had not done so. Instead he had concentrated on building a stable economy for Serbia and so Apis, thwarted, had taken matters into his own hands and in a way he hoped would never lead back to him, or to Serbia.

Knowing that no matter what the cost and despite the promise he had just made, he couldn't possibly keep such information to himself he said, not trusting himself to look in Katerina's direction, 'I'm going to have to renege on the promise I made to you, sir. As a servant of His Majesty's Government I am honour bound to inform my minister of the Black Hand's existence and its aims.'

'And Katerina?' Alexis's nostrils were pinched and white.

'There will be no danger to Katerina, sir. I promise. I will explain the situation fully to my minister and no-one else in the British Legation will know of it. The British government, however, *has* to know of it and the minister is the proper person to pass on such information.'

Alexis remained silent, deep in thought. It was just possible that a beneficial situation had arisen out of a difficult one. It would be no bad thing if the British government was informed as to the existence of the Black Hand from an impeccable Serbian government source and was also informed that King Peter and his ministers disassociated themselves utterly from it. Then, if Apis perpetrated a crime that scandalized Britain and if it became known that the crime had originated in Serbia, there would be a chance for the Serbian government to escape any blame for it.

He said slowly, 'I appreciate your position but I must have your promise before God that no-one else in Belgrade, apart from your minister, hears a word of what we have just discussed.'

'You have my promise, sir.'

It was a far less theatrical promise of secrecy than the promise made by Black Hand initiates who made their vow in a room lit only by a candle and at a table covered by a black cloth on which were displayed a dagger, a revolver, and a crucifix. As he thought of all he had been told of Black Hand initiation ceremonies he was grateful he hadn't had to detail them to an Englishman who would have regarded them all as being the most ridiculous Slav mumbo-jumbo.

'Then the subject is closed,' he said, walking across the room and opening the door.

Katerina remained standing in the centre of the room. Julian looked across at her and smiled. It was a smile of caring complicity and it warmed and reassured her as he had intended it should.

'Goodbye,' he said, wishing he could have stayed and talked to her without her father's presence; wishing he could have spoken to her about Natalie.

'Goodbye.' She could hear the regret in his voice and she knew that at the earliest opportunity he would seek her out and talk to her again in private.

Happily confident of the future she watched him as he left the room and then crossed to the window, hoping to catch a glimpse of him as he walked outside into the courtyard.

Alexis escorted Julian down to the circular, rococo entrance hall. He would have to inform the Prime Minister of what he had done, but he was sure Pasich would see the wisdom of his action, especially if anything untoward happened next week in Bosnia.

Bosnia. He still hadn't told Natalie and Katerina that they were to accompany him on his unofficial visit there. He would tell them that evening at dinner. And he would write again to Bosnia's governor, stressing the need for vigilance and tight security.

'*Bosnia?*' Natalie stared at him across the lavishly laden dinner table in startled surprise. 'But why, Papa?'

Alexis crumpled his napkin and laid it by the side of his plate. He had deferred the announcement until now because he had known what Natalie's reaction would be when she was told and he hated scenes, however minor.

'Archduke Franz Ferdinand is visiting Sarajevo to oversee the manoeuvres of the Fifteenth and Sixteenth Army Corps. There hasn't been a Habsburg royal visit since Emperor Franz Josef visited four years ago and . . .'

'No, Papa!' Natalie's face was white. 'Uncle Peter can't possibly expect you to represent Serbia on such an occasion! It's unthinkable!'

Privately Alexis agreed with her. He had used the exact same words to Pasich when Pasich had informed him that the heir to the Austrian throne was to visit Sarajevo and that it had been decided it would be politically beneficial if Serbia was represented in some way.

He said now, 'It isn't unthinkable, Natalie. Such gestures between states which are at odds with each other keep the doors of political negotiation open and . . .'

'Negotiation?' Natalie pushed her chair away from the table almost in tears. '*Negotiation?* We should be at war with the Austrians, Papa, not negotiating with them!'

If only Serbia were strong enough for war he would have been in agreement with her. As it was he said patiently, 'All countries make such outward shows of goodwill even when no goodwill exists. Think of the Kaiser's many visits to Britain.'

Natalie didn't care about the Kaiser. She was thinking about Gavrilo and Nedjelko and Trifko and wondering what on earth they would say when they heard of the visit and of her family's participation in it.

'I can't go, Papa,' she said unsteadily as Bella skittered around her ankles. 'I understand that you have to go, but I can't.'

'We all have to go,' her mother interposed. 'Our presence there isn't to be official but your uncle regards it as being important.'

'How long will we be there?' Katerina asked, concerned. She hadn't seen Julian Fielding since the interview in her father's study and she had been hoping to see him within the next few days.

'Four days, possibly five.'

'And when do we leave?'

'At the end of the week.'

Natalie grasped hold of the back of her chair. 'Please make an excuse for me not to have to go, Papa. Vitza has chicken-pox and you could say that I have . . .'

'No.' It was said without anger but Natalie knew that it was utterly final.

In despair she turned away, tears stinging her eyes. If Gavrilo ever got to hear of it he would never speak to her again. Even worse, he might think she was an informer.

Bella was running in circles around her and she picked her up, hugging her close. Her father had said that their visit wasn't to be an official one which meant it might not be reported in the Belgrade papers. Perhaps, with luck, no-one in Belgrade would learn of it.

It meant she wouldn't be able to go to the *Golden Sturgeon* later in the week as she had planned. A friend of Gavrilo's had told her that Gavrilo and Nedjelko and

Trifko were all back from their training manoeuvres in Bosnia and they would, no doubt, be full of stories of what had happened to them while they had been there. To sit with them, knowing that she was going to Bosnia herself within a few days and that she couldn't possibly let them find out, would be deceit on too grand a scale, even for her.

Two days later Gavrilo's friend, the Vassilovichs' butcher-boy, solved her immediate problem.

'Gavrilo won't be at the *Golden Sturgeon* tomorrow,' he said as she waylaid him at the kitchen door. 'He and Nedjelko and Trifko all caught bad chills when they were away.'

'How?' she asked, nonplussed. It was the middle of June and the weather was scorching.

He grinned. 'Something about falling into the Drina,' he said, hitching his basket higher on to his hip.

Natalie frowned. The Drina river served as a border between Serbia and Bosnia. For the first time she wondered just how her friends had entered and left their homeland.

'Thank you,' she said, knowing that she couldn't keep him talking any longer without someone seeing them. 'Tell Gavrilo I won't be at the *Golden Sturgeon* for a week or two. Tell him I'll see him in July.'

As she watched him hoist his basket on to his bicycle and pedal away towards the street she was vastly relieved. She didn't have to worry now about not going to meet Gavrilo and with luck, by the time they did meet again, she would be in the happy position of knowing that nothing about her family's trip had appeared in any Belgrade paper.

The night before they were due to leave for Sarajevo she

knocked on her father's study door. He called out for her to enter and as she did so, she said, 'I need to talk to you, Papa.'

He put down his pen, saying gently, 'About tomorrow?'

She nodded, sitting down on the leather chair opposite his desk. 'Yes. I don't understand why you should have agreed to pay your respects to an ogre like Archduke Franz Ferdinand . . .'

Alexis suppressed a smile. 'Franz Ferdinand isn't an ogre, Natalie. In fact, for a Habsburg, he's extraordinarily radical.'

He seldom spoke about politics to Natalie as he did to Katerina but now he said, trying to make a complex subject simple, 'When he becomes Emperor he intends taking drastic steps in order to silence Slav discontent within Austria-Hungary.'

'How can he do that? Slavs don't *want* to live within the horrid Habsburg empire, they want . . .'

'He intends forming a separate state for them.'

She stared at him, not understanding.

'Instead of two states in the empire, Austrian and Hungarian, there would be three, Austrian and Hungarian and Slav. Power would be shared equally by all three states, there would be joint foreign policy, joint armed forces, a joint economy. It would be very similar to the American system where . . .'

She understood now. And she understood what the consequences would be. 'But that would be terrible!' she whispered, hardly able to believe he was telling her such things.

'Why? It would remove all grounds for discontent. Given such freedoms Slavs would live quite happily beneath Habsburg rule . . .'

'And they would no longer want to leave the empire!' Her eyes were wide and dark and horrified. 'They would

83

no longer want to join with Serbia in a united South Slav State!'

'Exactly,' he said, highly pleased with the speed with which she had grasped the nub of the matter. 'There would be no more talk of engaging in a war to liberate them because Franz Ferdinand would have liberated them himself.'

The enormity of what he was saying made her feel faint. Unsteadily she rose to her feet, saying hoarsely: 'But if Franz Ferdinand's plans for reform are ever implemented there will never be a Yugoslavia! There will never be a Kingdom of the South Slavs with Belgrade its capital and Sandro its king!'

His eyebrows lifted sharply. Because he wasn't in the habit of talking politics with her he hadn't realized quite how much of a Slav unionist she had become. With great gentleness he said, 'Extremists may dream mystically of a great confederation uniting all the scattered remnants of our race, irrespective of religion, but it isn't a realistic dream, my dear.'

'It is, Papa,' she said with fierce stubbornness. 'It will just be harder to achieve it if Franz Ferdinand becomes emperor and I hope he never does.'

A spasm crossed his face. She had merely meant that she hoped the middle-aged Archduke would die of natural causes, but there were other people who would not be particular about what causes Franz Ferdinand died of as long as he did not become Emperor and put his plans into action.

He thought of Apis and shuddered. Apis wouldn't scruple to assassinate an archduke, not if it meant keeping Slav discontent alive.

'Good night, my pet,' he said tiredly, hoping to God that Bosnia's governor had done as he had advised him and put all his security forces on the alert. 'Don't forget we have an early start tomorrow. You need to be up early.'

It took Natalie a long time to fall asleep. The more she thought about Archduke Franz Ferdinand's plans for reform, the more horrifying she found them. What if union within a Austro-Hungarian-Slav federation appealed to Slavs outside the empire as well as within? What if it appealed to Serbians? What would happen then? Would it be the end of the Karageorgevich dynasty? The end of Serbia as an independent kingdom?

A few yards away from her, Katerina also lay awake in the darkness. Julian had paid no further visits to the house, nor had he been at the weekly afternoon tea party at the *Konak*. Despite all the fierceness of her wishful thinking, underlying common sense was beginning to raise its ugly head. If he had intended proposing to her at the Summer Ball surely by now he would have manipulated another occasion on which he could do so?

A surge of hope overcame doubt. How could he have done? There had been no parties at which they had both been invited; no court functions. Wishing she wasn't going to be away from Belgrade for the best part of a week she closed her eyes and tried, unsuccessfully, to sleep.

'And so we are staying at the Hotel Bosna, in Ilidze,' Alexis said to his family as their private train sped west. 'It's a small resort town near to Sarajevo. We shall be there in time to greet the Archduke and Duchess on their arrival. Tomorrow and the day after I shall talk with the Archduke's aides while the Archduke attends the army manoeuvres. Your duties will be to accompany the Duchess on her visits to hospitals and orphanages in the area.'

'I'd rather watch army manoeuvres,' Natalie said darkly.

Alexis's straight handsome mouth crooked into a smile. 'Young ladies do *not* attend mock battles and you will enjoy yourself much more with the Duchess. She is an extremely likeable woman . . . and a maligned one.'

Natalie's interest was immediately caught, as he had intended it to be. 'Why?' she asked as their train steamed towards the Bosnian border. 'Because the ogre is cruel to her?'

'I've told you before, Natalie, Archduke Franz Ferdinand is not an ogre.'

'Papa describes her as maligned because of the treatment she has received from the Emperor and the rest of her husband's family,' Zita interposed before tempers grew frayed. 'Although she is of noble birth she isn't of royal birth. When she married the Archduke the Emperor insisted that the marriage be morganatic, consequently she doesn't receive the same deference her husband does. She isn't allowed to accompany him in the royal carriage or sit by his side at the theatre in the royal box. At court dinners the youngest archduchess is placed above her at table and at court balls, though Franz Ferdinand might lead the procession, Sophie has to leave his side and appear behind the last princess of royal blood.'

'That's outrageous!' Katerina was appalled. 'If she's his wife, she should be treated as his wife.'

'Ogre!' Natalie said again vehemently.

'I shan't tell you again, Natalie,' Alexis chided. 'The Archduke is not a . . .'

'I wasn't referring to the Archduke,' Natalie said succinctly. 'I was referring to the Emperor.'

This time no-one disagreed with her. Her mother said: 'Even worse than the social slights is the fact that no child of the marriage can succeed to the Habsburg throne. Franz Ferdinand sacrificed a lot in order to marry Sophie and it would seem he has never regretted it. Friends in Vienna tell me he is as devoted to her now as he was fourteen years ago, when they married.'

'I think that's terribly romantic,' Katerina said dreamily, staring out of the carriage window at a wild landscape of mountains and forests and rushing rivers and thinking of Julian.

'I quite agree,' her mother said, opening her bag to take out some embroidery. 'It's a love story that would make a wonderful novel.'

For the rest of the journey Natalie imagined the Duchess as a fatally beautiful, ethereal heroine. The reality did not live up to her expectations.

'My daughter, Natalie,' her father said, introducing her to a middle-aged motherly looking woman with a cloud of superbly coiffed soft dark hair and a warm smile.

There were other introductions. To the Archduke, who was just as stiff and formidable as she had imagined he would be; to the Governor of Bosnia, General Potiorek; to the Moslem mayor, Fehim Curcic; to Colonel von Bardolff, the head of the Archduke's military chancellery, and to Countess Lanjus, the Duchess's lady-in-waiting.

When all the introductions had been completed and when refreshments had been served in the hotel dining-room, the Duchess said to Natalie, 'We have received some very pleasant news today. My eldest son, Maximilian, has passed all his high-school examinations with distinction.'

Natalie was genuinely pleased for her. It would have been very hard not to have liked the Duchess and as the Duchess was not a Habsburg, she saw no reason why she should even try.

'After we have rested, we are going to drive into Sarajevo to visit the Oriental bazaar,' the Duchess said confidingly. 'Would you like to join us? I do so love shopping, don't you?'

'I *adore* shopping,' Natalie said truthfully, deciding that the Duchess was very much her sort of person. 'Will there be dresses at the bazaar as well as *objets d'art?*'

'I imagine so. There will certainly be silks and I'm hoping there will be some inlay and metal work and that I can buy something for Maximilian, as a reward for his having worked so hard at his lessons.'

Paul Nikitsch-Boulles, the Archduke's private secretary, arranged that the Archduke and Duchess would travel with General Potiorek and that other members of the Archduke's retinue who wished to shop, including the Vassilovich girls, would travel in another car.

Natalie was beginning to enjoy herself. Much she hated all that Archduke Franz Ferdinand stood for it was impossible to brood continually on that hate when she was amid countryside she had never seen before and when she was about to visit Sarajevo's fabled Oriental bazaar.

The city lay in a bowl, surrounded by mountains, and the journey down from Ilidze did not take long. Everywhere there were flags and bunting in readiness for the official start of the visit the next day. As their Daimler sped across a bridge fording a mud-green river and headed towards the centre of the town, Natalie felt light-headed with happiness. There would be an exceedingly grand dinner that evening at the hotel and no doubt there would be shoals of handsome young army officers present.

She forgot all about her distress at being forced to be part of the hated Archduke's retinue. None of her new friends would ever know. The visit was turning into an intriguing, exciting experience and she was determined to enjoy every minute of it.

Within seconds of their Daimlers drawing up outside

the bazaar word spread of their arrival. Well-wishers came running from all directions and even before they had reached the first of the stalls a crowd had gathered. Officers in the Archduke's entourage slowly paved a way through the crush and Natalie laughed across at Katerina, revelling in the noise and the colour and the sensation of being in an exotic, medieval Eastern market. It was then, as a shaft of late afternoon sunlight dazzled her eyes, that she saw him.

She blinked, her smile vanishing, certain she must have make a mistake. Like everyone else his eyes were on the Archduke and as she stared, still disbelieving, he moved slightly to try and see better over the heads in front of him.

She hadn't made a mistake. The sun was no longer in her eyes and he was barely three yards from her. Horror engulfed her. What on earth would he think when he saw her? How could she possibly convince him that her family's inclusion in the Archduke's retinue was a matter of political expediency and that none of them truly wished to be there?

As the Archduke's party moved with difficulty deeper and deeper into the bazaar she remained standing absolutely still, staring at Gavrilo. Her initial horror was beginning to ebb and bewilderment was replacing it. What on earth was he doing in Sarajevo? The butcher's boy had told her that he and Nedjelko and Trifko had all returned from Bosnia a week ago, and that they were all suffering from severe chills and in bed, ill.

An eager stallholder, seeing that she had become separated from her companions, thrust a roll of crimson silk into her arms and was grinning toothlessly at her as he urged her to buy. She ignored him, still staring at Gavrilo. As if sensing her eyes on him he turned his head suddenly, too suddenly for her to swing round and pray he wouldn't recognize her from the rear.

His eyes widened and she saw in them all her own emotions of disbelief, horror, and stunned amazement. He began to struggle through the crush towards her and as he broke free of the crowd surrounding them he grasped hold of her arm as if to steady himself, saying dazedly, 'Natalie . . . for the love of God . . . what the devil are you doing here?'

Chapter Five

The roll of silk spilled from her arms, streaming over the dusty ground like a river of blood.

'I . . . I . . .' She tried to think of a plausible explanation and failed. 'What are *you* doing here?' she countered, deciding that attack was the best form of defence. 'Your friend told me you left Bosnia a week ago and that you were sick.'

It was Gavrilo's turn to flounder in search of an explanation. 'I was due to return to Belgrade last week when Trifko and Nedjelko returned, but there was a hitch.'

The crowd had closed in around them and the Archducal party was now too deep within the bazaar to be seen.

'And you're not sick?' Natalie demanded as the stallholder scrambled on the ground to retrieve his precious silk.

'Sick?' Gavrilo looked blank for a moment and then said, 'No. I'm not sick.'

He looked it. Never robust he now looked positively feverish. He looked around quickly as if nervous of being seen, and then said quickly, 'I'm not supposed to be here and I'd appreciate it if you didn't tell a single soul we've met up like this . . .'

Over his shoulder Natalie could see a member of the Archduke's entourage pushing his way through the throng, obviously searching for her.

'. . . I can't explain but I'm sure you understand, Natalie. It's all part of the training exercise and . . .'

Natalie didn't understand but was too relieved at his not pursuing his questioning as to why she was in Sarajevo, to care.

'. . . you must just forget this meeting. You haven't seen me. I'm not here.'

The uniformed member of the Archduke's staff was looking straight at her. She saw recognition flare through his eyes and then relief followed almost immediately by annoyance.

'Then if I haven't seen you, the sooner we finish talking together the better,' she said, anxiety returning in full flood as the uniformed figure began to bear down on them. 'We'll talk later, Gavrilo. At the *Golden Sturgeon* . . .'

Gavrilo was still holding her arm. 'You do understand, Natalie, don't you?' he asked, his hazel eyes urgent. 'For your own sake it really is vitally important . . .'

What was vitally important to Natalie was that Gavrilo didn't realize she was a member of the Archduke's shopping party.

'I understand,' she said, stepping away from him, praying that the officer who had come in search of her would not ask her to accompany him in Gavrilo's presence. 'And now I must go, Gavrilo.'

She didn't wait for him to say goodbye. His hand was no longer fraternally on her arm and she turned on her heel, forging her way through a mass of Sarajevans towards the formdiable looking Austrian officer who had come to retrieve her.

'What on earth happened to you?' Katerina asked her later in the privacy of their bedroom at the hotel. 'One minute you were by my side and the next you were gone.'

'It was the crowd,' Natalie said, wishing she could be more truthful. 'The crush was terrible. I just couldn't keep up.'

She pretended to be deeply intent on choosing which of the gowns she had brought with her to wear to dinner. When she had first embarked on her meeting with Gavrilo and his friends at the *Golden Sturgeon* she had felt a *frisson* of excitement every time secrecy and subterfuge had been called for. She did so no longer. A secret it was impossible to talk about had drawbacks and she longed for the thrill of being able to share it with Katerina.

'I'd save the hyacinth-blue for tomorrow night,' Katerina said, looking across at her as she continued to gaze at a Paris-coutoured gown Helga was holding up for her inspection. 'It's only going to be a quiet dinner tonight. I don't think Papa is looking forward to it. Count Conrad von Hötzendorf, Chief of the Imperial General Staff, is to dine with us. Papa says he is a terrible old warmonger who has been urging Emperor Franz Josef to crush Serbia for years.'

Natalie's eyes blazed with patriotic fervour. 'Just let him try! It would be the exact excuse we need finally to rout the Austrians from Bosnia and Herzegovina . . .'

Katerina's eyes darkened. Despite all her expectations she was quite enjoying the trip and she didn't want it spoiled by reminders of how tense the political situation was between Serbia and Austria and of how difficult a position her father was in, representing the Serbian government on Habsburg-ruled soil and in the presence of the heir to the Habsburg throne.

'Don't let's talk about freeing Bosnia,' she said, fastening a white rose to the neckline of her gown. 'We might be overheard. It might cause terrible trouble for Papa.'

'And what if von Hötzendorf or nasty old Franz Ferdinand talk about Bosnia?' Natalie persisted belligerently. 'Am I not to say anything then?'

'*No!*' Katerina went cold at the very idea. 'You are not

to say *one word* about the present political situation. It shoudn't be difficult. No-one else is going to bring up such an emotive subject.'

She was wrong. Count Conrad von Hötzendorf brought up the subject almost immediately.

'You must make your government understand that the Habsburg empire will tolerate no trouble from Slav nationalists, either beyond its borders or within,' he said cholericly to her father as drinks were served before dinner.

Katerina shuddered and looked towards Natalie to see if she had overheard. Natalie hadn't. She was chattering to Countess Lanjus and Katerina joined them, leaving her father to the difficult task of both upholding his govern-ment's stance towards fellow Slavs in Bosnia and dis-associating it from any illegal, terrorist activity.

Despite the pleasant conversation she was having with the Duchess's lady-in-waiting, Natalie was no longer truly enjoying herself. Sarajevo's heat and humidity, coupled with the shopping trip to the bazaar, had tired her. There were no shoals of dashing young officers present and even if they had been, they would all have been Austrian, a fact which had not earlier occurred to her. The Duchess was now very firmly at her husband's side and so there was no opportunity for further cosy chats about her children.

As Katerina and the Countess began to talk of silks and dressmakers she looked around the room, seeking for diversion. The Archduke and Duchess were deep in conversation with Sarajevo's mayor. Natalie averted her eyes quickly from the royal presence. Franz Ferdinand was just as stuffy and pompous as she had anticipated he would be and at the thought of all he represented she felt quite ill. Not as ill, though, as she would have felt if

Gavrilo had realized she was a member, however reluctant, of the Archducal party.

She wondered again what he was doing in Sarajevo. He had said he was coming to Bosnia on a training exercise and she had thought a training exercise meant practising guerilla tactics in the Bosnian mountains. Then she remembered that he had once attended high school in Sarajevo and that he probably still had lots of friends in the city. Was that why he didn't want her to speak of their meeting to anyone? Because he was absent without leave from the training exercise, visiting friends?

A majordomo-like figure announced that dinner was served and the Archduke and Duchess led the way into the opulent dining-room. Natalie sighed. It was going to be a long tedious evening with nothing to look forward to but the visit next day to a school and a hospital.

The school was an Augustinian convent school and after acknowledging what Natalie thought were the far too long speeches of welcome, the Duchess handed out small presents to the pupils, pictures of the Archducal family for the older children, candy for the little ones.

In the afternoon, with the visit to Sarajevo's hospital behind them, the Duchess's party returned to Ilidze and Natalie accompanied her mother for a stroll in the nearby park.

'I wish I'd been able to bring Bella with me,' she said wistfully as a small girl ran past them, a puppy at her heels. 'She'll be missing me and pining.'

'She'll be doing no such thing,' her mother said briskly. 'She'll be eating a proper diet for once instead of having her teeth ruined with chocolate biscuits and she'll be having to do as she's told for a change, which will be very good for her.'

★   ★   ★

That evening dinner had again to be endured in the Archduke's presence. All through the long meal Natalie wondered where Gavrilo was dining. No doubt he would be at a *kafana* similar to the *Golden Sturgeon*, making one cup of coffee last an entire evening and fiercely discussing the cause of Slav nationalism with old school-friends. Looking around the high-ceilinged room, catching scraps of boring conversation about manoeuvres and the rose gardens at the Archduke's favourite residence, the estate and castle of Konopisht and of how the German Emperor intended visiting there in the very near future, Natalie wished fervently that she was in a smoke-filled *kafana* with Gavrilo.

Seeing the glum expression on her face Katerina leaned towards her. 'Cheer up,' she whispered encouragingly. 'There are only another two days to endure and it isn't as difficult a situation for us as it is for Papa.'

The next morning the Archduke and his aides again left early in the morning for the army manoeuvres which were taking place in remote and mountainous countryside. The only gentleman not to accompany the Archduke was Alexis Vassilovich. Despite both the Archduke's and Count von Hötzendorf's satisfaction at being able to talk unofficially with a representative of that thorn in their flesh, the Serbian government, they had no intention of allowing him to view Austrian army manoeuvres.

As Alexis had too much sense ever to have expected to be invited to the manoeuvres, he was indifferent to his exclusion from them. The visit was going far better than he had privately hoped. Despite von Hötzendorf's war-mongering belligerence, Franz Ferdinand's conversation was full of sound common sense. If any man was going to be able to solve the nightmarish problem of Slav dissatisfaction within the empire it was the Archduke and as far as

Alexis was concerned, the sooner he became Emperor, the better.

All the next day Natalie was perturbed by the genuine warmth with which the Duchess was greeted in Sarajevo wherever she went. Her own liking for the Duchess had not diminished in the slightest but it was worrying that Sarajevans, chafing under the Habsburg yoke, should also apparently like her unreservedly.

'Perhaps it is because they know that even when the Archduke is Emperor, she will not have the title Empress,' Katerina said when she broached the subject to her. 'I know that the Archduke isn't fooled by all the flags and bunting. After all, the civic authorities are in Austrian pay and they are the ones who have arranged it all. Papa told me both the Archduke and the Count are horrified by the lack of security precautions, especially as it is so well known that Sarajevo is a hotbed of Slav nationalism. Apparently when Emperor Franz Josef visited four years ago an entire Austrian garrison lined the streets and hundreds of suspected subversives were taken into custody. Nothing like that has been done for this visit. Papa says the only police on duty are the local police and they are Slav, not Austrian.'

Natalie was glad to hear it. It meant that when the day came when Bosnia rose in force against her Austrian masters and when Russia and Serbia came gloriously to her aid, Sarajevo's police force would not be a problem, but an asset.

Her rare attack of despondency came to an end the next night when dinner was a far more glamorous affair, with civic dignitaries from far and wide in attendance. The Sarajevo garrison band were colourfully arrayed on the hotel lawn and the dining-room windows were thrown open so that the melodies they played could be clearly heard. There were tunes by Schumann and Franz Lehar and Strauss and when 'The Blue Danube' was played she was reminded of her mother's Summer Ball and of Julian Fielding so romantically proposing to her.

She looked across at Katerina, wishing that she could share her secrets about Gavrilo and Julian with her and saw that Katerina was listening to the gentleman seated next to her with a dreamy, far-away expression in her eyes. The gentleman in question was a boring-looking dignitary, bald and fat and at least fifty and Natalie dismissed any idea of his being the object of Katerina's reverie.

'. . . and so your warnings about our being in danger in Sarajevo were quite wrong after all,' the Duchess was saying to a stern-faced gentleman seated across the table from her. 'It just goes to show that things don't always turn out the way you think they will. Everywhere we have gone here we have been greeted with friendliness and cordiality and we are very happy about it!'

'Who is the gentleman the Duchess is speaking to?' Natalie asked her next-door-neighbour.

The Archduke's junior aide was more than happy to enlighten her. 'Dr Sunaric, Vice-President of the Bosnian parliament. He was very nervous about the Archducal visit. He thought the locals were in an ugly mood and . . .' He broke off in embarrassed confusion as he remembered Natalie's nationality.

'And what?' Natalie prompted impatiently, uncaring of his *faux pas*.

The aide, sensing that no offence was going to be caused and wanting to remain the object of her undivided attention, said, '. . . and he thought the Archduke and Duchess faced definite danger from Slav nationalist fanatics.'

Natalie regarded him pityingly. 'Slav nationalists are

not thugs,' she said as if speaking to a three-year-old child. 'When we choose to fight the Habsburgs it will be with an army and . . .'

The aide's eyebrows rose nearly into his hair. Natalie, realizing that her remark had been a severe breach of good manners, seated as she was at a Habsburg dinner table, had the grace to blush. 'It will happen one day,' she said defiantly, but choosing her words with more care. 'Serbians and Bosnians, whether Orthodox or Moslem, will be united.'

'And Catholic Croats and Slovenes and Montenegrins?' The junior aide was regarding her with a mixture of amusement and genuine curiosity. 'What about them?'

'They will be united with us as well. We will all be united, irrespective of religion, in a great kingdom to be known as Yugoslavia . . .'

'*Natalie!*' The agonized warning hiss was from Katerina.

Natalie looked around, saw that her mother was frowning fiercely at her and regretfully abandoned the subject so dear to her heart.

'Tell me what it's like to be one of the Archduke's aides,' she said to her new acquaintance who at least was not bald or fat or nearly fifty. 'Do you spend much time in Vienna? Is it as elegant as Paris?'

'Thank goodness today is our last day,' Katerina said next morning as they dressed. 'With a little luck we should be on the train home by mid afternoon.'

Natalie breathed in as Helga laced her into a corset that reduced her naturally slender waist to a minuscule eighteen inches.

'It isn't another hospital again, is it?' she asked ill-humouredly. 'Why do hospitals always smell so vile? Why can't antiseptic be rose-scented?'

Katerina smiled her slow, gentle smile. 'It isn't another

99

hospital,' she said to Natalie's relief. 'There's to be a brief reception at the City Hall, a visit to the National Museum and then lunch at the governor's residence.'

'And then the Archduke and his party return to Vienna?'

Katerina nodded. 'And we return to Belgrade.'

'Good.' Natalie had enjoyed the previous evening and the flattering attention she had received from the Archduke's personable young aide, but she was missing Bella and the novelty of being part of the Archducal party, in however unofficial and minor a capacity, was fast fading.

'There are to be six official cars in the procession,' Paul Nikitsch-Boulles said to Alexis, 'plus a car for yourself and your family. The mayor and the commissioner of police will ride in the lead car. The Archduke and the Duchess will be in the second car with General Potiorek and Count Harrach. In the third car will be Count Boos-Waldeck, Countess Lanjus and the General's adjutant, Lieutenant Colonel von Merizzi. The remaining three cars will bear various members of His Highness's and General Potiorek's suites and your own car will bring up the rear. It has been arranged that the Archduke and his entourage will travel from Ilidze to Sarajevo by train in order that an official reception can take place at the station. The procession including the car that will take you and your family down to Sarajevo, will commence from the station and travel along a pre-arranged route to the City Hall.'

Alexis nodded. Like Natalie, he was looking forward to the moment when he would step aboard the train for Belgrade. It was a fiercely hot day and though there was a pleasant breeze in Ilidze, he knew there would be none in Sarajevo.

Grateful that the car hood was down Alexis shepherded his family into the waiting Daimler.

'. . . and he thought Belgrade not sophisticated because it doesn't have an opera-house as Vienna does,' Natalie said indignantly to her mother as she recounted some of her conversation with the Archduke's aide.

The chauffeur put the car into gear, pulling away from the hotel, picking up speed swiftly as the road began to wind steeply down to the valley floor.

'He isn't Austrian,' Natalie continued, not wanting her family to think she had been voluntarily consorting with the enemy. 'He's French. Don't you think it strange that the Archduke should have an aide who is French?'

Alexis made a non-committal noise, his thoughts on the report he would be making to Prime Minister Pasich when he returned. Zita made no reply at all. She was thinking of how much she liked the Duchess and of how unfair it was that her marriage was marred by her not being treated as the wife to the heir of a throne should be treated. Katerina was also silent, lost in private thoughts and Natalie lapsed into silence, gazing at the glorious scenery, wondering if Bella was missing her.

The city, in its mountain bowl, was as stiflingly hot as Alexis had anticipated as their car brought up the rear of the Archducal procession. Habsburg yellow and black flags drooped from windows, streamers decorated the streets, spectators stood in clusters staring curiously, some even cheering.

'Over there, across the bridge, is the new army barracks,' Alexis said to Zita, pointing the building out to her as their Daimler trundled leisurely down Sarejevo's broadest street on its way to the City Hall. On their left hand side were shops and cafés and the majority of onlookers were standing there, in the shade of awnings. On their right was a narrow pavement, an embankment, and the glittering olive waters of the Miljacka river.

The bomb, when it came, came from the left.

Alexis was aware that something was wrong a second or so before the explosion. There was a faint, detonating sound, as if a tyre had blown out and he half expected to see one of the cars in front swerve to a sudden halt. Instead he saw a small black object fly through the air, quite obviously aimed at the Archducal motor car. Seconds later there came an explosion that brought the four cars in front of him to chaotic, panic-stricken stops.

'*Alexis! For the love of God! What's happened?*' Zita demanded white-faced as their car skidded to a standstill.

'*Christ only knows! A bomb . . .*'

'*There are people hurt, Papa!*' Though many people had immediately begun to run from the scene, others were milling around prone and bleeding figures on the pavement. Katerina began to scramble from the car, intent on giving what help she could.

'*Stay where you are!*' Alexis shouted at Natalie as she began to follow.

'But, Papa . . .'

'DO AS I SAY!'

Natalie fell back in her seat, as shocked at having her father speak to her in such a way as she was at the outrage that had just taken place.

'Stay here!' Alexis said tersely to Zita and then, satisfied that his family were unhurt, he vaulted from the Daimler and sprinted up the smoke-filled street towards the Archducal car.

It had swerved to a halt several yards ahead of the car that had been following it. With vast relief Alexis saw that both the Archduke and the Duchess were still seated and that they were looking back over the folded-down hood of their car at the scene behind them, their expressions shocked and deeply anxious.

'*It's Merizzi who'd been hurt!*' General Potiorek was shouting. '*Where the hell is Fischer?*'

Dr Fischer, the Archduke's doctor, was running from his own car to the General's as fast as his stout physique would allow.

'Let's get everyone away from here!' Alexis shouted to the agitated Potiorek. 'There may be another attempt!'

In the car, Countess Lanjus was attempting to staunch the flow of blood from the back of Merizzi's head with a handkerchief.

'The car is damaged,' Potiorek said tersely as Fischer scrambled into the car. 'The engine is dead.'

'Then get everyone transferred to the other cars,' Alexis ordered, not caring that his speaking to a general in such a manner was a heinous breach of protocol. 'Can Merizzi be moved?'

Fischer nodded, his face grey. It could have been the Archduke who had been injured. If he had been, he might have died. And if he had died he, Fischer, would have gone down in history as the man who failed to save him.

Other people were racing to the scene. An Austrian general Alexis had never seen before was saying competently, 'Ambulances for the injured are on their way. I've telephoned the garrison hospital and all available army surgeons are also on their way.'

'Thank God,' Alexis said shakily, his heartbeat beginning to steady. 'Were any members of the public killed?'

'I don't think so. My name is Appel. I'm the commanding general of the local army camp. I was following you on my way to my office just off the Quay.'

'The Quay?' Willing hands were assisting Countess Lanjus into one of the other cars. Merizzi was in the professional care of Dr Fischer. The Archducal car had already left the scene.

'Appel Quay. The street we're in.'

Alexis looked around him dazedly seeing, as if for the first time, the many bridges and the wide, shimmering river.

'My name is Vassilovich,' he said, 'Alexis Vassilovich.'

'Tell your driver to continue straight to City Hall,' Appel said as with a scream of tyres ambulances began to arrive. 'God knows what sort of a greeting the Archduke is going to receive when he arrives. No-one will have been able to tell officials there what's happened. They're going to learn the news of the attempt on the life of the heir to the throne, from the heir to the throne himself!'

Unsteadily Alexis made his way back to the Daimler. Katerina had already returned to it, the hem of her pink silk dress thick with dust from kneeling beside the injured, scattered bloodstains on the skirt.

'Were any members of the public killed?' Alexis asked for a second time as he climbed back into the car.

Katerina shook her head, her eyes dark with distress and shock. 'No, but there were over a dozen people hurt, some badly.'

The Daimler began to move, easing its way around the ambulance that had arrived for Lieutenant-Colonel Merizzi and then picking up speed as it followed in the wake of the other undamaged cars.

'Alexis . . .' Zita's voice was thick with dread. 'Alexis . . . what will happen if . . .'

His eyes met hers. 'If the would-be assassin is a Serb?' he finished for her. 'God only knows, my dear. God only knows.'

Natalie said nothing. She still felt that, if she wasn't very careful, she would faint. The sight of the injured had shocked her inexpressibly. She had never seen so much blood before. And now her parents were suggesting that it had been shed by a Serb.

'Did they catch him?' Alexis was asking.

Zita nodded. 'He was young. We couldn't see clearly because of the crowd that surrounded him when he was caught, but he looked to be little more than a boy.'

'God damn him,' Alexis said viciously, sure the would-be assassin was a Serb nationalist fanatic. 'Thank God his attempt didn't succeed. If it had done . . .'

He left the sentence unfinished. If the Archduke had been killed there would be no hopeful future for Slavs living within the empire and no peaceful future for Slavs living outside it. 'Thank God,' he said again, suddenly feeling far older than his forty-eight years. 'The sooner Franz Ferdinand is aboard his train for Vienna, the better.'

When the Vassilovich Daimler sped up to City Hall Franz Ferdinand was on the steps, giving his scheduled speech thanking the city for its welcome.

'It gives me special pleasure to accept the assurances of your unshaken loyalty,' he said to the agonized-looking Moslem mayor standing by his side, 'and affection for His Majesty, our Most Gracious Emperor and King . . .'

As Natalie saw the Duchess by his side, smiling bravely, her heart went out to her. She didn't look like a woman who had just narrowly missed being blown apart by an assassin's bomb. She was as matronly and as dignified as ever, only her lack of colour, accentuated by her white lace dress and large white hat, betraying her shock.

'. . . I thank you cordially, Mr Mayor, for the resounding ovations with which the population received me and my wife, the more so since I see in them an expression of pleasure over the failure of the assassination attempt.'

Despite his being a Habsburg, Natalie was aware of grudging admiration for him. In his light blue, tightly-buttoned field-marshal's uniform, a fountain of green peacock feathers sprouting from his peaked hat, he looked dramatically magnificent.

His speech over, a little girl approached the Duchess, handing her a bunch of roses. The Duchess bent forward a little to take the bouquet from her and with fresh horror Natalie saw a long, fine scratch on her neck. Had it been caused by a bomb splinter? Was that how near the motherly Sophie had been to a hideous death?

'The Duchess is going to go upstairs to receive a delegation of the town's Moslem ladies,' Zita whispered to her. 'We're to remain in the City Hall's vestibule. With luck we might even be given a cup of tea. I've never been more in need of one in my life.'

As the Duchess was escorted upstairs the Archduke and his entourage, Alexis included, disappeared into one of the downstairs rooms.

'I wonder if Lieutenant-Colonel Merizzi has had to be operated on?' Katerina said unhappily as chairs and refreshment were brought for them. 'I wonder if all the other people who were injured are going to be all right?'

They were questions it was impossible to answer. Zita remained silent, aware of how grim the political situation would be if the Archduke's attacker proved to be Serbian. Natalie remained silent also, trying to blot out all thoughts of the motivation behind the attack. The very prospect of it having been committed in the name of Slav nationalism filled her with nameless horror. Was the terrible scene she had just witnessed the ugly reality behind all her exciting meetings in the *Golden Sturgeon*? If so, what did it make Gavrilo and Nedjelko and Trifko? What did it make herself?

'It won't have been a Serb,' she whispered fiercely to herself. 'It must have been a madman. It *has* to have been a madman.'

'There's been a telephone call from the hospital,' her father said an hour later when he rejoined them. 'Merizzi's injury isn't serious. The Archduke intends visiting him at the hospital before continuing on to the museum.'

'Dear God!' Zita stared at him appalled. 'He's not still continuing with his programme, is he?'

Alexis nodded wearily. 'Yes. The only change is to be the route. Instead of driving through the narrow streets of the old city as had been planned, we're to drive back down Appel Quay to the hospital and then go from there to the museum.'

Zita breathed in deeply. The Duchess was making her way down the stairs, the Archduke and his entourage were emerging from their meeting and there was no opportunity for her to put the very grave doubts she felt, into words. Tight-lipped she waited until the official party had made their exit and then followed Alexis out to the waiting Daimler.

The cars, with the exception of the bomb-damaged car, left the City Hall in the same order they had arrived, with the Mayor's car in the lead and the Vassilovich Daimler bringing up the rear.

Incredibly, Appel Quay was still full of people and this time when the royal procession appeared, the cheers were full of enthusiastic and sympathetic warmth.

'General Appel tells me the would-be assassin tried to jump in the river before being captured,' Alexis said grimly, as their car sped down towards the spot where the bomb had been thrown. 'It would have been better for him if he had succeeded.'

Natalie, her butterfly-brain rescuing her from thoughts she couldn't yet bear to contemplate, said musingly, 'Isn't it strange that the General's surname is the same as the name of the street?'

Alexis's mouth softened slightly. It was typical of Natalie to light on such an inconsequential fact at such a traumatic time. 'Perhaps it's because . . .' he began.

He got no further. The Mayor's car had turned off the

107

Quay and was following the original route, speeding down Franz Josef Street, the city's main shopping thoroughfare.

The Archduke's driver had begun to follow him and then, as General Potiorek shouted at him to continue on down the Quay, he braked hard, beginning to back out of Franz Josef Street and once again into the Quay.

It was then, as the Archduke's car was nearly at a standstill and as the following cars had slowed down in order that when it re-emerged on the Quay they would still be behind it, that the shots rang out.

It was a moment no-one present would ever forget; a moment that was to live in their memory, as bloodily fresh as the day it happened, for ever.

As Alexis and the Archduke's aides sprang from their cars, General Potiorek could be heard shouting at the Archduke's chauffeur to drive with all speed towards the Governor's Residence.

Amid all the shouts and the struggle taking place only yards away as attempts were made to arrest the attacker, Katerina sat numbly in the rear of the Daimler, staring after the Archduke's car, watching as the Duchess's head slipped towards her husband; as her lavish white hat fell from her head, rolling in the dirt and the dust of the grimy street.

'*We've got the bastard!*' Natalie heard someone cry.

'*No we haven't! He's got a gun!*'

There were other shouts, a whole cacophony of them as the violent fight continued.

The Archduke's attacker, incongruously and immaculately dressed, fought like a devil. From where she was seated Natalie could see his dark suit, his white shirt with a stiff round collar, his high button shoes. And she could see the gun in his hand. She saw him lift it to his temple, saw a spectator hurl himself on him, seizing hold of his arm. She saw someone else grab him by his collar; saw him twist free only to be caught hold of again. Two of the Archduke's aides had their sabres drawn and were striking out at him. Dozens of hands were trying to seize him. She saw an official-looking man race to the scene and pitch into the mêlée. She saw him seize hold of the struggling figure; saw the figure in question hit out with a clenched fist and then, as his victim sank to his knees, saw him again lift the gun, bringing it down on the man's head.

It was his last act of violence. There were too many hands on him for him to be able to struggle further. The gun was wrested from him and he was dragged away, still kicking, still struggling.

Natalie remained immobile, not hearing anything that her mother was saying to her; that Katerina was saying to her. She had seen everything that had taken place with nightmarish clarity. She had seen the gunman step from the crowded pavement when the Archduke's car had been reversing back into the Quay. She had seen him take aim and then, as he pulled the trigger once and then twice, she had seen him turn his head away as if he couldn't bear to watch the deed he was committing. And before he had done so, she had seen his face and she had recognized it. She couldn't, in a million years, have failed to do so. It was a face she knew very well. A face she had last seen only a few short days ago. It was the face of her friend, Gavrilo.

Chapter Six

'Take my wife and daughters immediately back to Ilidze,' Alexis was saying to their chauffeur, the skin so taut across his cheekbones it looked like parchment. He turned to Zita. 'I'm going to the governor's palace. I have to find out the extent of the Archduke's injuries.'

'And the Duchess's,' Katerina said, ashen-faced. 'I saw her fall against the Archduke. Her hat fell into the street.'

'Jesus God.' It was the first time in his life that he had blasphemed in front of his wife and children. None of them noticed.

'As long as the attacker wasn't a Serb,' Zita said again as she had after the bomb attack. 'Please God, don't let him be a Serb.'

Alexis wasn't listening. He had already turned on his heel and was striding towards the nearest available official car.

Neither Zita nor Katerina were aware of Natalie's catatonic-like state as their car sped them out of the city and into the hills. In deep shock themselves, only a display of normality from her would have seemed odd.

Natalie felt as if she were dying. Her safe, secure, orderly world had shifted on its axis and toppled into mayhem. Never again would she be innocently naïve, thinking of Slav nationalism in terms of gallant glory in which no-one really got hurt; no-one really died. Now she knew differently. Now she knew how childishly immature she had been; how foolishly gullible.

She wondered what would happen to Gavrilo and immediately shut the thought from her mind. She couldn't think about consequences; about Gavrilo or the Archduke or the Duchess, or she would lose all control. She would break down; go mad.

She sat staring sightlessly at the wooded hillsides she had thought so pretty only a few short hours ago. Perhaps Gavrilo's shots had missed the Archduke; perhaps the bullets had been blanks and Gavrilo had meant only to frighten, not to kill; perhaps, like the bomb attack, things weren't as bad as they appeared to be.

'Tea,' Zita instructed the minute they entered the hotel, 'and a brandy.' She looked at her daughters' white, exhausted faces. 'Three brandies,' she amended, judging them to be medicinal.

'I need to lie down,' Natalie said, speaking for the first time. It wasn't strictly true. What she needed was to be alone. Somehow she had to live through the time until her father either telephoned or returned with news of the Archduke's and the Duchess's injuries. Somehow she had to stop herself from thinking; somehow she had to stay sane.

To her vast relief Katerina said, 'I'll stay with Mama. She'll need someone with her if Papa telephones with news.'

Natalie walked alone to their bedroom, shutting the door behind her. 'It's going to be all right,' she said fiercely to herself as she sat down unsteadily on the edge of the bed, her fists clenched so tightly her knuckles were white. 'The Archduke hasn't been hurt. He's going to return to Vienna this afternoon, just as we are going to return to Belgrade. What I thought happened, didn't happen. It was a prank; a scare. *It's going to be all right!*'

Lunch-time came and went and still there was no tele-phone call. In her private sitting-room Zita stared at a French ormolu clock, ceaselessly twisting the rings on her long slim fingers. It had been nearly eleven when the gunman had opened fire and now it was nearly two.

It was ten past two when Natalie heard the car approach. She leapt from the bed and ran to the window, watching as it sped up the tree-lined drive and skidded to a halt on the gravel fronting the hotel. A rear door opened so precipitately it rocked on its hinges and her father emerged, his face strained, his shoulders hunched. She didn't wait to watch him enter the hotel, she spun on her heel, running to join her mother and Katerina.

'He's dead!' Alexis said the instant he strode in on them. 'He's dead and so is the Duchess!'

'No! It isn't possible!' Zita stumbled to her feet. 'There must be a mistake, Alexis! They can't *both* be dead!'

Alexis covered his eyes for a moment with his hand, struggling for composure. 'They died within minutes of each other,' he said when he could trust himself to speak. 'There was no hope for either of them. Not the remotest of chances.'

He walked unsteadily across the room to the sideboard and poured himself a glass of water. He was going to have to recount what had happened to the king and the prime minister and a score of government officials when he returned to Belgrade and it was important that, right from the beginning, he did so with absolute accuracy.

'The Archduke was hit in the neck,' he said, wishing that neither Katerina nor Natalie were present. 'He remained seated upright for several seconds and at first General Potiorek thought he hadn't been seriously injured and then Potiorek saw there was blood coming from his mouth and minutes later he lost consciousness.'

'And he never regained it?' Zita's eyes were wide with horror, her pupils so dilated no iris could be seen.

Alexis shook his head. 'No. Potiorek says that when the Duchess fell against him he said, "Sophie dear! Sophie dear! Don't die! Stay alive for our children," and then when Count Harrach tried to support him and asked him if he was suffering badly, he said faintly, "It is nothing. It is nothing."'

No-one spoke. No-one was capable of speaking. At last Zita said thickly, 'And the Duchess? What happened to the Duchess?'

Alexis blanched. Recounting the way in which the Archduke had died had been bad enough. Detailing the way in which the Duchess had died was going to be even more of an ordeal. Keeping his voice as tightly controlled as possible he said, 'She must have turned towards the Archduke, trying to protect him, and a bullet passed through the car door and the upholstery of the seat and into her groin. She died from internal bleeding. The doctors haven't said so, but she must have been dead before she was carried into the palace.'

Zita sank down on to the nearest chair. 'Her poor children,' she whispered, ashen-faced. 'Who will tell them? Who will break the news?'

'A telegram has been sent to their tutor.'

He braced himself for what was to come and seeing the movement Zita said with fresh fear, 'What is it? What haven't you told us? Have there been other deaths? Has . . .'

'The assassin was a Serb. A Bosnian Serb as was the would-be attacker who threw the bomb. I've already telegraphed Belgrade with the news. God only knows what is going to happen when it's made public. There won't be a Serb in Sarajevo safe from Austrian retaliation, and that includes ourselves.'

'Then we're going back to Belgrade today, as planned?'

'We're leaving immediately. The sooner I can speak to Pasich about Princip the better. He may not be one of Apis's dupes but . . .'

'*Princip?*' Katerina grasped hold of the back of a chair for support. '*Did you say the assassin's name was Princip?*'

Alexis nodded, his nostrils pinched and white. 'The police got his name out of him immediately, though nothing else. His name is Gavrilo Princip and the would-be assassin's name is Nedjelko Cabrinovich . . .'

There was an anguished cry and as all eyes turned towards her, Natalie slid unconscious to the floor.

'*Water! Quickly!*' Zita cried, rushing to her side. Alexis hurriedly refilled his glass, spilling droplets on the sideboard's polished surface in his haste. Katerina remained where she was, still holding on to the chair, her thoughts in chaos.

'She's coming round.' There was a sob of relief in Zita's voice as Natalie's eyes began to flutter open. Alexis went down on one knee beside her, sliding an arm beneath her shoulders and lifting her so that she was resting against him.

'Take a sip of water, darling,' Zita urged her anxiously as Alexis held the glass to her lips. 'You'll soon feel better.'

Natalie, doubting it, obeyed.

'Lift her on to the sofa, Alexis.' Zita's initial panic was ebbing. 'She'll be all right in a few minutes. It was the shock of hearing all those ghastly details . . .'

'No.' At Katerina's interruption both Zita and Alexis turned to look at her in astonishment.

'No,' she said again as Natalie's eyes flew wide in a vain plea for her to say no more. 'It wasn't the shock of hearing about the Archduke's and Duchess's death. It was something else.' Her eyes held Natalie's. 'You have to tell Papa,' she said, knowing there was no alternative, knowing that even if Natalie never spoke to her again she had to force her to admit to her friendship with Princip. 'You have to tell Papa,' she said again. 'He has to know.'

Alexis swung Natalie up in his arms and crossed the room, laying her down on a sofa.

'What is it I have to know?' he demanded curtly. 'If you are wasting precious time recounting trivialities I shall be extremely displeased. It is essential that I make my report to the king and the prime minister at the earliest possible moment . . .'

'It isn't a triviality, Papa.' Her eyes still held Natalie's, pleading for forgiveness and support. 'Natalie knows a young man named Gavrilo Princip. He's a Bosnian Serb and . . .'

Alexis swung his head back to Natalie and at her terrified, corroborating expression the blood drained from his face. 'Holy God,' he whispered, suddenly looking prematurely old. 'Holy, holy God.'

It was Zita who took command of the situation. 'How?' she demanded fiercely. 'How can Natalie possibly know a Sarajevan?'

There was silence. Katerina's eyes held Natalie's. At last, realizing the terrible situation in which she had inadvertently put her father, Natalie said falteringly, 'He's been studying in Belgrade, Mama. I met him at the Conservatoire and . . .'

'You saw him shoot the Archduke?' Alexis interrupted harshly. 'You recognized him?'

She nodded. 'Yes, I . . .'

'No more!' Alexis, immediately aware of implications that had not yet occurred to either his wife or daughters, was again in control. 'Not another word while there's the remotest chance of our being overheard. I'm ordering our bags to be taken down to the car and this subject has not to be discussed again until we're safely in Serbia, is that understood?'

They left the hotel virtually unnoticed. The Duchess's maids were in a state of near hysteria, the hotel maids, who had been as charmed by the Duchess as Natalie and Katerina had been, were openly crying.

The Vassilovich train, which had been ready to leave for over an hour, steamed out of the station at Ilidze, the window-blinds down.

Not until the border formalities had been completed and they had crossed into Serbia did Alexis reopen the subject. Sitting in a leather winged-back chair in the parlour-car he said to Natalie, 'Now tell me everything you know about Gavrilo Princip and tell me every single detail of your acquaintance with him.'

Natalie clasped her hands together tightly on her knees. 'I met Gavrilo and Nedjelko at the Conservatoire,' she began unhappily.

'Nedjelko?' Alexis had thought he had suffered every shock he could possibly suffer. Now, incredibly, there were even further horrors. 'Nedjelko Cabrinovich?'

Natalie nodded and Zita gave a low moan and covered her face with her hands.

'I liked them,' Natalie continued with frank artlessness. 'They were full of enthusiasm for Slav unity and . . .'

'They were terrorists!' Alexis's voice was a whiplash. 'Subversives! The scum of the earth!'

Natalie's face became very still. Despite everything that had happened she could not think of the friends she had so liked in those terms. She struggled to think how best she could portray a true portrait of them and said, 'Gavrilo and Nedjelko are idealists, Papa. And they are educated.' She remembered that Nedjelko had not been a student, like Gavrilo and Trifko, but worked in a print shop. 'At least Gavrilo and Trifko are educated. They are students and . . .'

'Trifko?'

Natalie's stomach lurched sickeningly. Was she saying far more than was necessary? Was talking to her father going to help her friends or harm them further? And after the bloody crime they had perpetrated did she want to help them? She didn't know. Her head ached and she felt sick.

'Gavrilo and Trifko have been friends since they were children. They are the same age and . . .'

'And they're Bosnians? They're citizens of Austria-Hungary?'

Natalie remembered how they had always described themselves and said with a flash of her old fire, 'Legally they are citizens of Austria-Hungary but they are Slavs and their loyalty is to a united South Slav state.'

Knowing only too well now where Natalie's fervour for Slav unity had come from he said grimly, 'Did you only ever meet at the Conservatoire? Were you ever seen with them anywhere else?'

'The *Golden Sturgeon*,' Natalie said reluctantly. 'It's a café in the old part of the city.' She leaned forward in her seat. 'They never talked of assassinating anyone, Papa. I'm sure Gavrilo didn't know his gun was loaded. He's a gentle person. He's quiet and well-mannered and though he has very little money he's always lending what he has to friends . . .'

'*Don't dare eulogize him!*' Alexis's face was so contorted with fury it was barely recognizable. 'He's an assassin whose act will very likely plunge our country into war!'

Natalie shrank back in her seat, appalled at the anger she had unleashed. 'I didn't know what he planned to do. I didn't even know he was still in Bosnia . . .'

There was a long, terrible pause and then Alexis said in a voice dangerously flat and unexpressive. 'You knew he had left Serbia for Bosnia? He told you his plans?'

Natalie's hands were now clasped so tightly her nails were scoring her flesh. 'He said it was to be a training exercise . . .'

The word Alexis uttered was one not even his wife was familiar with. 'Thank God,' he said, when he had himself under control again. 'Thank God you didn't know he was in Sarajevo. Thank God no-one saw you with him.'

Natalie remembered the Oriental bazaar; remembered the Austrian officer forcing his way through the crush to reach her side; remembered the expression of relief and then annoyance in his eyes; remembered the way Gavrilo had been holding her arm, how urgently he had been speaking to her.

'I was seen with him, Papa,' she said, her lips almost bloodless. 'I met him by accident in the Oriental bazaar. One of the Archduke's officers came in search of me, to help me through the crush, and he saw me with him.'

Alexis's ability to speak abandoned him. The situation was far, far worse than he had first assumed it to be. The instant the Austrian officer recognized Princip as being the youth Natalie had been talking to, the Austrian government would issue a warrant for her arrest. As he thought of what would follow, not only for Natalie but for Serbia, he felt physically ill.

On her mother's side of the family Natalie was a Karageorgevich. The Austrians would have no further to look for proof that the plot to kill the heir to the Habsburg throne had been hatched in Serbia and at the highest possible level. They would have all the excuse they needed to launch an attack against Serbia and to crush her, and Serbia, perceived by the rest of Europe as being the villain of the piece, would be friendless. Not even Russia would come to her aid if it was believed the ruling House had connived at the Archduke's and Duchess's deaths.

Alexis released the window-blind, staring out at mountains and valleys, at a village clustered around its onion-domed church, at a group of distant figures working in the fields and at gaily dressed women laundering clothes by the banks of a river. It was a scene of peaceful peasant life that could be seen all over Serbia and war would ravage and end it within days. All because his lovable, unthinking, foolish daughter had become acquainted with two nationalist fanatics and been seen with one of them shortly before he had committed his monstrous crime.

'What are we to do?' Zita asked, putting all her trust in him, certain that he would never allow Natalie to be arrested.

Alexis dragged his gaze from the window. He had been considering and rejecting decision after decision and he was left with only one. He had not the slightest desire to put it into words and when he finally spoke it was with the very greatest reluctance. 'Natalie must leave Serbia before Princip is questioned about his friendship with her. You must accompany her . . .'

'Leave Serbia?' Natalie's voice was dazed with incredulity.

'. . . and travel immediately to Switzerland,' Alexis continued, disregarding her interruption. 'You must travel on the night train to Budapest and then on the Orient Express as far as Munich and then . . .'

'*Leave Serbia?*' Natalie was staring at him as if he had taken leave of his senses. '*I can't leave Serbia, Papa! I shall never leave Serbia!*'

Until now Alexis had been looking directly at Zita. Now he turned his full attention towards Natalie. 'You have no choice,' he said grimly. 'You were seen with Princip by an Austrian officer. It will be assumed by the Austrians that you were well aware as to why Princip was in Sarajevo. The charges they will bring against you will be that of an accomplice to his crime and in Bosnian law an accomplice is as guilty of the crime committed as the perpetrator.'

'You mean that Natalie will be charged with murdering the Archduke and the Duchess?' Katerina asked disbelievingly. 'But that's not possible, Papa! It can't be!'

'It's very possible,' Alexis said, looking ten years older than he had when he had first left the hotel that morning.

'Uncle Peter would never allow it!' Natalie's eyes were black pits in a chalk-white face. 'He would never agree to my being returned to Bosnia to stand trial in an Austrian court!'

Outside the carriage window the scenery had changed. There were no longer wooded hillsides and turbulent, rushing streams. Instead there were orange-tiled, verandahed houses and dusty, mud-baked streets.

'He might have to,' Zita said, deep circles carved beneath her eyes. 'If the Austrians once believe the plot to kill the Archduke was hatched in Serbia they may very well declare themselves at war with us. In order to prevent that happening Peter will have to do everything in his power to convince them that neither he nor his government knew anything about it and part of that convincing will be having to co-operate with Austrian demands regarding the arrest of suspects.'

'Even if the suspect is a member of his family?' Katerina asked, hardly able to believe her ears.

'*Especially* if it's a member of his family,' Alexis said with stark brutality. 'For him to shield a Karageorgevich would be tantamount to admitting the assassination was hatched with royal connivance. War would then be inevitable. It's a choice Peter would never make. Not even for Natalie.'

'For how long will I have to go away?' Natalie asked,

barely able to force the words past her lips.

'If the officer in question doesn't recognize Princip as being the youth with whom you were in conversation at the bazaar, if no other witness steps forward to say that Princip was talking to a young female member of the Archducal party and if Princip volunteers no information about you when questioned, then it may only be for a few months.'

Their train was easing into Belgrade station.

'And if not?'

'If not? Then it might be for years.' His voice was so distorted by pain it was almost unrecognizable. 'It might be for ever.'

That evening Katerina knocked on her father's study door and when he opened it to her she said unhappily, 'I have to speak with you, Papa. There's something else you must know.'

Without a word he waited for her to enter the room and then closed the door. 'About Natalie?' he asked tautly.

She nodded. 'Cousin Max also knows Gavrilo Princip. He saw Natalie with Gavrilo in the *Golden Sturgeon* and told Vitza about it. Vitza told me.'

'Dear God in heaven! Does Vitza know him as well?'

'No. She only knew his name because Max had told her it.'

Alexis's mind raced. If Max Karageorgevich knew Princip it might mean that Max was also one of Apis's dupes. Though he had no way of proving it, he was certain Princip and Cabrinovich were Black Hand members who had acted on Apis's instructions. Was Max Karageorgevich a member of the Black Hand also? Was it perhaps Max who had suggested to Princip that he strike up a friendship with Natalie? A friendship that might lead to contact with Prince Alexander?

Another thought struck him and his blood ran cold. What if Vitza began to talk of Natalie's friendship with Princip? What if she told her grandmother? If Eudocia once knew, the whole world would know.

'Don't talk of this with anyone else,' he said, striding for the door. 'I'm going to talk to both Max and Vitza now.'

The door rocked on its hinges after him. She heard him shout for a carriage to be brought round to the door. Weakly she sat down on the nearest chair hoping fervently that neither Max nor Vitza yet knew it was Princip who had shot the Archduke and Duchess; hoping that when they did know they would never breathe a word about Natalie's friendship with him.

'You've been recalled,' the British minister said to Julian bluntly. 'I'd be grateful if I were you. The Austrians aren't going to take the assassination of Franz Ferdinand lying down. God alone knows what the repercussions are going to be. Reports are already coming in of Croat and Moslem anti-Serb demonstrations in Sarajevo. That will give the nationalists something to think about.'

Julian didn't give a damn about the nationalists. He was reeling beneath the news that he was to leave Belgrade.

'When am I to leave, sir? Was any reason for the decision given?'

'Leave? What? Oh yes.' The minister dragged his thoughts away from the disturbing reports coming in from Sarajevo and said, 'By the end of the week. No sense in wasting time. And don't worry as to reasons. You've performed brilliantly during your time here. London knows that and it's probably the reason you're being recalled early. No doubt you'll be speedily *en route* to a far more coveted post. Paris perhaps, or Petersburg.'

Six months ago, before he had fallen head over heels in love with Natalie, Julian would have been delirious with joy at the prospect of being given a post in either city. Now he said, 'If there's any chance of the decision being overturned I'd be very grateful, sir. The only place I want to be at the moment is Belgrade and . . .'

'Decisions from London are always final.' The minister rose to his feet, signalling that the interview was at an end. 'Even if they weren't, it would be senseless questioning this one. The Balkans are Europe's powder keg and this damn fool assassination could be the spark that ignites it. If it does, and if there's war again in Europe, every member of the Legation staff will be hard on your heels, haring back to London. Your advantage is that you will at least have a seat on the train.'

Julian didn't return to his office. He walked straight out of the Legation and into the Kalemegdan Gardens. If he left Belgrade without there being any kind of understanding between himself and Natalie, he might never see her again. The thought was unimaginable. Obscene. He walked without seeing anything around him. He had only days left in which to propose to her again. And if she still refused him?

He came to a halt in a corner of the garden that dropped steeply towards the point where the Sava river merged with the Danube. If she refused him it would only be because the proposal had come too soon after his first proposal to her. She needed time to get used to the idea that she was old enough to fall in love and marry. She needed to grow up a little. If he had remained in Belgrade he would have known when the time was right to propose to her again and to be accepted. But he wasn't going to be in Belgrade.

He stared down a bank awash with tamarisk trees towards the fast moving Sava and the majestic, glittering Danube. He had to keep in contact with her. He had to be able to write to her. And to do so he had to have Alexis Vassilovich's permission.

With his mind made up as to the course of action he was going to take he turned away from the magnificent view, striding purposefully through the Gardens towards Prince Milan Street and the Vassilovich *konak*.

'I'm sorry, sir,' the footman said to him distractedly. 'Madame Vassilovich and Mademoiselle Natalie are leaving for Switzerland tomorrow and no-one is being received.'

For the second time that day Julian felt as if he had been pole-axed. '*Switzerland?*'

For a dazed moment he wondered if, in the wake of the Archduke's assassination, Alexis Vassilovich was so apprehensive of Austrian reprisals against Serbia he was sending his family as quickly as possible to a safe haven. He dismissed the idea as ridiculous. If that had been the case Katerina would also have been leaving for Switzerland and besides, Alexis Vassilovich was not a man to panic in such a manner.

'I'm sorry, sir,' the footman said again apologetically.

In the circular, marble-floored entrance-hall Julian could see travelling trunks with labels clearly marked *Geneva*. It was then, as the footman began to close the door on him, that he heard the harrowing sound of sobbing.

He didn't hesitate. It was against all rules of good manners and etiquette but he strode past the protesting footman certain that something was dreadfully wrong, utterly determined to find out what it was.

As the footman called for assistance in order to eject him, Katerina came running into the entrance hall.

'Laza . . . what on earth . . .' She came to an abrupt halt, her cheeks flushing scarlet.

'It's not the footman's fault I've gained entrance,' Julian said, striding quickly towards her. 'He told me no-one was being received.'

Above their heads, from the direction of the bedrooms, the sound of heart-broken sobbing continued.

'What the devil is happening?' he asked urgently. 'Why isn't your father receiving anyone? Why are your mother and Natalie leaving for Switzerland in such a hurry? Is it Natalie who is crying?'

'I can't tell you.' Her voice cracked slightly and he realized that she, too, was near to tears.

'Then I'm going to speak to your father,' he said, turning away from her and walking determinedly across the entrance hall in the direction of Alexis Vassilovich's study.

'No! Please don't!' She ran after him, catching hold of his arm. 'Papa is so worried and . . .'

He halted, staring down at her, 'Worried about what?' he demanded. 'About the assassination in Sarajevo?'

'Yes . . . No . . .'

Her distress was so deep she looked as if she were about to faint.

'Katerina, for heaven's sake . . .' He slipped an arm comfortingly around her shoulders as he would have done if she were a cousin or a close family friend. 'What's happened? Please tell me. Does it concern Natalie?'

The temptation to lean against the comfort of his broad shoulder and to tell him everything nearly overcame her. If they had been engaged then surely she could have told him? And surely they were on the brink of being engaged? Why else would he be so deeply concerned about her distress or attempting to comfort her with such exquisite tenderness?

'I can't,' she whispered, wishing with all her heart that she could.

All the time they had been talking the sound of distant weeping had continued.

'It's Natalie who is crying, isn't it?' he asked, an odd edge to his voice.

She nodded and he gently released his hold of her.

'I'm going to talk to your father,' he said, and before she could protest again he turned away from her, walking swiftly down the corridor that led to Alexis's study.

When he reached the door he hesitated only for the very briefest of seconds and then, Natalie's sobs still ringing in his ears, he knocked sharply.

'What the devil . . .' he heard Alexis exclaim tautly and then the door was yanked open.

'I'm sorry, sir,' he said quickly, before Alexis could give vent to his wrath. 'I need to speak to you and it's extremely urgent that I do so today.'

Alexis hesitated and Julian said, 'It's about Natalie, sir.'

Alexis hesitated no longer. Certain that the British must have received information linking Natalie with Princip and that Julian had been sent by his minister he said tersely, 'Come in. What is it you have to say to me?'

Julian wiped a bead of sweat from his brow. He was accustomed to ticklish situations but this was one for which he had no precedent. Deciding that the best way of dealing with it was to come straight to the point he took a deep breath and said, 'I want to marry Natalie, sir.'

Alexis gaped at him. He had been expecting to hear that the British knew of Natalie's meeting with Princip in Sarajevo and that probably, thanks to their superbly efficient Secret Service, they even knew about her meetings with him at the *Golden Sturgeon*.

'*Marry?*' he said incredulously when he had recovered his powers of speech. 'Marry *Natalie*? Surely you mean Katerina?'

Julian shook his head, unsurprised by Alexis's assumption. Katerina was, after all, of marriageable age. At seventeen, Natalie was still precociously young. 'No, sir,' he said firmly. 'I want to marry Natalie.'

'And you've come to ask my permission to propose to her?' Alexis struggled to gather his scattered wits. 'It's out of the question. She's far too young . . .'

'I know that, sir. What I would like from you is permission to write to her . . .'

'How the devil did you know she was leaving the country?' Alexis demanded in fresh alarm. If a British diplomat knew, Austrian diplomats might also know. 'We only arrived back from Bosnia yesterday!'

'I didn't know, sir. I was told this morning that I'm being recalled to London and so my first thought was to propose to Natalie again . . .'

'Again?'

'. . . and if she refuses me again, to have your permission to write to her until she is older and does accept my proposal.'

'*Again?*' Alexis had thought nothing could take his mind from the fear that the Austrians would demand Natalie's arrest before she was safely aboard the Orient Express. He had been wrong. '*Again?*' he repeated, stupefied. '*You've already proposed marriage to my seventeen-year-old daughter without asking my permission?*'

Julian flushed scarlet. 'Yes, sir. I'm sorry, sir. If I could have your permission now, to propose to her again . . .'

Alexis drew in a deep breath, about to tell Julian Fielding exactly what he thought of his English impertinence. Then he remembered the hell he was in. He remembered that Zita was at that very moment lying down in a darkened room, overcome with grief at the prospect of being parted from him. He remembered the long, lonely months, possibly even years, that lay ahead of them.

He said sharply, 'You're leaving for London this week?'

'Yes, sir.'

'And you're in love with Natalie and want to marry her?'

'Yes, sir.' Julian's discomfiture was beginning to turn to bewilderment.

'And you come from a good family? You have excellent career prospects? A private income?'

'Yes to all three questions, sir,' Julian said, wondering what on earth had happened to change the tenor of the conversation so drastically.

The tips of Alexis's waxed moustaches quivered. 'Wait here,' he said peremptorily, striding towards the door. 'I must speak to my wife.'

The door slammed and Julian stared after him, more bewildered than ever. Why did Alexis need to speak to Zita? What on earth was going on? Slowly, sensing that his wait was going to be a long one, he sat down. He still hadn't asked why Zita and Natalie were leaving so suddenly for Switzerland. He still didn't know why Natalie was sobbing so broken-heartedly.

He looked around the room. There were several hunting trophies on the walls and a half dozen water-colours, all landscapes. A large group photograph hung nearby and even from where he was sitting he could recognize the exotically garbed figure of King Nikita of Montenegro, his daughters standing and sitting around him.

He stood up and crossed the room, looking at the photograph more closely. It had obviously been taken some years ago. Princess Elena, now Queen of Italy, looked scarcely old enough to be out of the schoolroom. With difficulty he differentiated between the Princesses Vera and Xenia and recognized Princess Militza.

The other faces he was unsure of. There was a willowy, ravishing looking creature on the far end of the back row, a dark-haired laughing-eyed young woman standing next to her, and there were another two elegant figures sitting on the ground on either side of the king's booted feet, large flower-bedecked hats almost obscuring their faces. He tried to remember the names of Nikita's other daughters and failed, all he could remember was that one of them was married to a Russian grand-duke and another had married Prince Franz Joseph of Battenberg.

His attention went back to the two girls at the far end of the back row. He had the most curious feeling of having met one of them, and quite recently. He frowned, pondering. Princess Militza had been at the Vassilovich Summer Ball but he couldn't remember any other female members of the Montenegrin royal family being there. When recognition came it almost took his breath away. It was Zita. And if it was Zita, then the vibrant-eyed young woman next to her could only be Princess Zorka.

He continued to gaze at the photograph, intrigued. He had known that Zita had acted as Zorka's lady-in-waiting during the years of Zorka's marriage to King Peter but he hadn't realized how far back the relationship extended, nor had he realized that Zita was regarded as being almost a member of the Montenegrin royal family. He was just beginning to muse on the political advantages of such a relationship when the door opened and Zita walked into the room, Alexis behind her.

'We need to talk to you,' Alexis said abruptly to him. 'We need to talk to you in the utmost confidence.'

Zita sat down, her hands clasped tightly in her lap.

Alexis remained standing, his eyes holding Julian's with burning intensity. 'Do you still wish to marry my daughter?' he asked bluntly.

Despite his certainty that something was very seriously wrong, Julian answered without hesitation. 'Yes,' he said and was aware of Zita's small gasp of relief.

Alexis crossed to his desk and sat down behind it. 'Then I want you to do so.' A pulse throbbed at the corner of his jaw. 'I want you to do so tonight.'

Julian wasn't at all surprised that Alexis had had to sit down before making his request. He, too, wished to sit down but there was no chair within reach. 'You have to tell me why,' he said, retaining a composure Alexis was always to remember with respect. 'You have to tell me why it's so important Natalie leaves Serbia.'

Alexis nodded. He had known, from the moment he had come to his decision regarding Julian and Natalie that he would have to tell Julian everything. 'There is very little to tell,' he said heavily, 'but what there is, is disastrous.'

Julian had guessed as much long ago. He waited.

'Unbeknown to us Natalie made friends, some time ago, with students who meet in the *Golden Sturgeon* café. One of them, Gavrilo Princip, she met again by accident while we were in Sarajevo. They were seen together by an Austrian army officer well aware of her identity.' He paused and then said tautly, 'It was Princip who assassinated the Archduke and Duchess.'

It was Julian's turn to gasp.

'You have my word for it that though the assassination plot was hatched in Belgrade, King Peter and those closest to him had no knowledge of it. Austria, however, will prefer not to believe that. Princip is a Serb and Austria will use the assassination as an excuse to mount an attack against Serbia and annihilate her. In order to prevent their doing so King Peter is going to have to comply with any demands they might make regarding the arrest of Serbian suspects within Serbia.'

At the thought of Natalie standing in an Austrian courtroom charged with complicity in murdering the heir to the Habsburg throne, Julian felt so giddy he thought he was going to black out.

'With circumstances as they are, you can see why I am so desperate that Natalie leaves the country at the earliest possible moment. My wife is prepared to accompany her but if she does so, it will mean our being separated for what could be a cruelly long length of time.' Alexis shielded his eyes with his hand for a moment and then said with heart-stopping frankness: 'I love my wife very much, Mr Fielding. I don't want to live months, and perhaps years, separate from her. By marrying Natalie and taking her with you to London, you can save me from such a fate.'

The blood was drumming so hard in Julian's ears that when he spoke he could hardly hear his voice. 'What if Natalie still doesn't want to marry me?'

'She'll marry you,' Alexis said, rising to his feet, 'if you'll have her.'

Julian tried to think coherently and couldn't. He wanted to marry Natalie more than anything else in the world, but he certainly didn't want her to be forced into marrying him.

Zita, seeing his difficulty, said quietly, 'I think it quite possible that Natalie only refused you because, at seventeen, the idea of marriage took her totally by surprise.'

'She is still only seventeen,' Julian said, stalling for time as he struggled to come to a decision, knowing that when he did so it would be the most important decision of his life.

'She may still be only seventeen,' Zita said bleakly, 'but she has aged years in the last twenty-four hours. We all have.'

It was true. He could see lines around her eyes that had never been there before and Alexis looked far older than when he had last seen him.

'Let me speak with her,' Alexis said, moving away from his desk and crossing once more to the door, 'and then the two of you must speak together.'

'May we speak together in private, sir?'

Alexis nodded. 'Of course.'

He left the room and Zita said awkwardly, 'Would you like some tea, Mr Fielding?'

Julian nodded, suppressing the fierce desire to ask instead for a large whisky or a large brandy. He said instead, striving to bring normality into a situation so far from normal it beggared belief: 'I was looking at the photograph of King Nikita and his daughters. Was it taken in Cetinje?'

'Yes, have you been there? I know visiting diplomats often regard Belgrade as being unsophisticated, but Montenegro's capital really *is* unsophisticated. In 1889, when that photograph was taken, Cetinje was little more than an overgrown village and the royal palace was simply a two-storeyed villa situated on the main street.'

Julian breathed a sigh of relief. He had been wondering what he and Zita could possibly talk about as they waited for Alexis's return and now the problem was solved. In the bizarre situation in which both of them were they could at least talk about Cetinje without embarrassment, and perhaps about Princess Zorka as well.

'He's a handsome young man, of excellent family, with a brilliant future in front of him,' Alexis said, knowing that he wasn't exaggerating, certain that one day Julian Fielding would be an ambassador.

'I can't marry him, Papa!' Natalie felt as if she were in the seventh circle of hell. 'I'm not in love with him!'

'But you like him?' Alexis persisted.

'Yes, I like him . . .'

'And you think him handsome?'

'Yes, but I don't want to marry him! I don't want to marry anyone!'

Alexis frowned, wondering how best to continue. Whatever happened Natalie had to leave Serbia and knowing her temperament as he did, he was convinced she would be far happier as the wife of a rising young diplomat in a glamorous European city than she would be living quietly in Geneva with her mother.

'I want you to listen to me very carefully,' he said, knowing that she was on the brink of hysteria. 'Love doesn't always come before marriage. In the right circumstances, between the right people, it often comes after. I wasn't in love with your mother, nor was she in love with me, when we married. It was a marriage arranged by our parents and we agreed to it because we trusted their judgement. If you marry Julian Fielding you will have an advantage we didn't have, for he is already in love with you. And you must bear in mind that if you don't marry him you will still have to leave Serbia, and instead of living in London or Paris or Petersburg you will be living in Geneva with your mother.'

She remained silent, her forehead pressed against the window-pane as she looked down into the garden with eyes swollen with crying.

'Having a daughter marry and leave home and live far away is in the natural order of things,' Alexis continued with devastating frankness. 'Having a wife living a thousand miles away is not, and it will break my heart.'

The agony in his voice was more than she could bear. He had come to her asking her to make a choice and she knew now that she had no choice. From the moment Julian Fielding had offered to marry her and take her with him out of the country there had been only one course of action she could possibly take.

She turned her tear-ravaged face towards him. 'If it means you and Mama being able to stay together, then of course I will marry him,' she said, knowing that somehow, for her parents' sake, she had to find the strength to be able to do so with dignity.

'Thank you, my dear,' he said unsteadily, folding his arms around her and holding her close.

She hugged him tight, fresh tears springing to her eyes, wishing with all her heart that she had never met Gavrilo and Nedjelko at the Conservatoire; that she had never accepted their invitation to meet again in the *Golden Sturgeon*; that she had never gone to the Oriental bazaar.

'I've told Julian he can have a few words with you in private,' Alexis said when he could trust himself to speak. 'I think the Italian drawing-room will be as good a room as any, don't you?'

With a heavy heart she followed him from her bedroom and down the grand staircase. The door of the main salon was open and she could see Katerina sitting strategically near to it, making a poor pretence of reading *Madame Bovary*. There was no opportunity for them to speak to each other, the most she could do was flash her a look of despair before following her father into the Italian room.

'Julian Fielding is in my study,' Alexis said, remaining near the door. 'I'm going back there now to tell him you are ready to speak with him and I shall see to it that you are not disturbed while you do so. The wedding is going to have to be within hours.'

'When will we leave Serbia?' Her voice was barely audible.

'He told me he was due to leave at the end of the week but that isn't going to be soon enough. Even before we left Bosnia the police were rounding up all Princip's and Cabrinovich's known friends and relatives. A demand that you are returned to Sarajevo for questioning could come at any minute. I'm going to ask Pasich to speak to the British minister and to ask if, as a special favour, Julian can be allowed to leave tomorrow. I'll tell him we have relatives in London and that a family crisis has necessitated your sudden marriage and made it obligatory for you to leave for London with the utmost urgency.'

She didn't speak, there was nothing further she could possibly say.

Fully aware of how deep her homesickness was going to be, Alexis felt as if his own heart was breaking. 'I'm sorry, my dear, so very, very sorry,' he said inadequately and then, his eyes suspiciously bright, he left the room, walking towards his study, leaving her alone.

When Julian entered minutes later she was still standing where Alexis had left her. She met his eyes with dread, certain he was about to launch into a flowery, romantic declaration of his feelings for her. If he did, she knew she would not be able to cope. She would have to tell him that she wasn't in love with him; that in all probability she would never be in love with him.

He gave her a wry smile. 'You really have landed yourself in an unholy mess, haven't you?' he said sympathetically. 'What on earth possessed you to begin frequenting *kafanas*? Don't you know the coffee at the British Legation is far superior?'

She gave a strangled cry, half a sob and half an hysterical laugh of relief and as he crossed the room towards her she ran to meet him.

His arms closed round her. 'God, what a silly goose you've been,' he said thickly, hardly daring to breathe in case he destroyed the sudden rapport he had created between them.

'I'd no idea anyone was going to be killed! Especially not the Duchess!' It was as if a dam had broken, the words came rushing in an anguished torrent. 'I *liked* the Duchess! I still can't believe Gavrilo killed her! Even though I saw him do it I still can't believe it! And then Papa said that I would have to leave Serbia and that it might be for years and years and oh, I can't bear it! I *love* Serbia! I'm every inch a Karageorgevich! Katerina isn't. Katerina wouldn't mind living in London or Paris or Petersburg but I'm going to hate it! I'm going to die!'

'You're not going to die, my little one,' he said tenderly, an edge of amusement in his voice. 'Everything is going to be very strange for you at first but wherever we find ourselves, London, Paris, Petersburg, or maybe even Brussels or Rome, life will be exciting and fun.' He hooked a finger under her chin, tilting her face to his. 'Far more fun than Geneva,' he added with the crooked smile that was quickly becoming comfortingly familiar.

'I didn't want to go to Geneva,' she said, shuddering at the very thought. 'I lived there when I was a little girl and every day I was there I cried and cried because I wanted to be in Serbia instead.'

He stared down at her thoughtfully. 'Is that why you have agreed to marry me? Because you couldn't bear the prospect of returning to Geneva?'

She shook her head and said with earth-shattering honesty, 'No, I told Papa I would marry you because I couldn't bear the thought of him and Mama being separated. They love each other very much, you see.'

He saw. He had known, of course, that she hadn't agreed to marry him because she had suddenly discovered she couldn't live another second without being his wife, but he had hoped she had realized that she was in love with him, if only a little. He said slowly, already knowing the answer, 'You're not in love with me?'

Gold-green eyes held his. 'I like you,' she said truthfully, 'and if I have to leave Serbia then I would rather live with you anywhere, than in Geneva with Mama.'

He took a deep, steadying breath. Liking was the most he was going to get from her for the time being and he had to decide if it was going to be enough. She stirred against him, sensing his indecision, slipping her hands up against his chest so that she could see into his face more clearly.

The movement unleashed all the desire that he felt for her. He wanted her more than he had wanted any woman before in his life; more than he would ever again want any woman.

'And I would rather live with you, under any circumstance, than without you,' he said thickly.

For the first time in days a hint of a smile touched the corners of her mouth. Julian Fielding had a talent for making her feel safe and secure and he was criminally handsome. A criminally handsome husband would at least be diverting company through the long agony of her temporary exile.

Katerina watched the comings and goings between the Italian drawing-room and her father's study in ever increasing bewilderment. What on earth was going on? Why had her father left Natalie alone and then very obviously sent Julian in to speak to her? Had her father told Julian about Natalie's friendship with Gavrilo Princip and the disastrous meeting in the Oriental bazaar? Was Julian offering Natalie advice of some kind and if he was, why was he doing so in such extraordinary privacy?

When Natalie and Julian finally emerged, hand-in-hand, her bewilderment deepened. Natalie was still pale and drawn but there was a new calmness about her and for the first time since she had been told she would have to leave Serbia she was not crying. They began to walk towards Alexis's study door and she sprang from her chair, hurrying to intercept them.

'What is happening?' she asked urgently.

It was Natalie who answered her. 'Julian is being recalled to London,' she said, her voice husky with fatigue. 'I'm going to go with him. It means Mama won't have to leave Papa and . . .'

'Recalled to London?' Katerina felt as if the ground were shelving away at her feet. Her eyes flew to his. 'You can't be recalled!' she protested, sick with horror. 'Not so suddenly! And what does Natalie mean by saying she is going with you? How can she go with you? Who will chaperone her?'

Julian shot her his easy smile. 'Don't worry, Katerina,' he said, intending to be reassuring. 'Natalie won't need a chaperone. We're to be married this evening.'

Chapter Seven

Katerina swayed and as she did so the study door opened and Alexis said peremptorily, 'I'd prefer it if all discussions took place behind closed doors, Natalie.'

'Yes, Papa,' Natalie said contritely, her hand still comfortably in Julian's.

'Papa . . . I don't understand . . .' Katerina's shock was so deep she thought she was going to lose consciousness. 'Julian says he and Natalie are to marry . . .'

'Behind closed doors, please,' Alexis repeated, wondering why neither of his daughters seemed able to understand the need for absolute discretion.

He opened the door wide so that they could all file past him. Only when it was safely closed behind them did he say to Natalie, 'From what I overheard I take it you have agreed to marry Mr Fielding?'

'Yes, Papa.'

Alexis gave a deep, shuddering sigh of relief. No matter how fraught and difficult the next few months were going to be, they were going to be bearable. Although he would be parted from his daughter, he wouldn't be parted from his wife. Under such circumstances he could survive.

'Then the next step is for the King to be informed. The situation is going to have to be fully explained to him. Once it is, I think we can rely on him to see to it that Mr Fielding is released immediately from his duties. There is an Orient Express departure from Budapest tomorrow morning. The wedding will take place in time for you both to be aboard it.'

'But Papa . . . please . . . surely Natalie and Mama would only be in Switzerland for a few months,' Katerina protested, the blood drumming in her ears. 'Surely it isn't necessary for Mr Fielding to . . . to . . .' she tried to say the word 'marry' and couldn't do so. '. . . to go to such lengths,' she continued, not daring to look in Julian's direction, knowing that she would break down completely if she did so.

'We have no way of knowing how long Natalie might be obliged to remain abroad,' Alexis said gravely. 'The officer who saw her with Princip may have paid no attention to Princip and not recognize him as being the Archduke's murderer. There may be no demand for Natalie's arrest. If there isn't, and once the assassins have been tried and sentenced and the affair is over, then she will be able to return to Belgrade. If, however, a warrant *is* issued for her arrest there is no telling how long she will have to remain abroad. Certainly she will have to do so until the Austrians can be persuaded to drop all charges against her. Even if they do, she will still be unable to return if political embarrassment will be caused by her doing so. That being the case it is far better that she travels to Britain as Mrs Fielding, than that she travels to Switzerland with your mother.'

For a sick, giddy moment, Katerina wondered if she were mad or if everyone else were mad. How could her father possibly think the situation warranted Julian sacrificing himself in such a manner? And how could Julian do so? It didn't make any kind of sense. Even if Natalie accompanying him to London was a more practical alternative than their mother having to accompany her to Switzerland, why was it necessary for him to marry her? A chaperone could be found to travel with them and surely in London Julian had female relatives with whom Natalie could stay?

'Papa . . .' she began hesitantly, about to put her thoughts into words and to bring sanity into an insane situation. 'Papa, don't you think that perhaps . . .' She got no further. She had been so terrified of establishing eye contact with Julian that she had scrupulously avoided looking in his direction. Now both he and Natalie moved slightly, entering the periphery of her vision and for the first time since she had entered the room with them she became aware that he was still holding Natalie's hand.

'Yes, Katerina?' Alexis prompted, looking at his pocket-watch, trying to estimate how long it would take him to reach the *Konak* and explain things satisfactorily to Peter, how long it would then be before the British minister was contacted and the wedding arranged.

Katerina stared at the two clasped hands. Natalie's nails were short and buffed to a pearly sheen. Julian's hand was sunbronzed and capable. She remembered how he had held her hand as they had waltzed at the Summer Ball. She remembered how close he had held her just a very short while ago, before he had spoken privately with her father, before he had then entered the Italian drawing-room and spoken to Natalie. When he and Natalie had walked from the room together she had assumed he was holding Natalie's hand in platonic comfort. She did so no longer. Slowly, with a sense of inescapable doom, she lifted her eyes to his.

He was looking at her with affectionate concern. In a moment of barbarous reality she realized that affection was the most she had ever seen in his eyes.

'Katerina?' Alexis prompted again, putting his watch back in his waistcoat pocket, anxious to be on his way. 'You were saying?'

'Nothing, Papa. It doesn't matter.' The pain in her

chest was so crushing she didn't know how she was continuing to breathe, let alone to speak. He didn't love her. He had never loved her. She remembered her shy confidence to her father, indicating otherwise, and burned with shame. How could she have been so foolish? How could she have read so much into so little?

'Will you excuse me, Papa?' she said stiffly, knowing she had to leave the room before even the remnants of composure abandoned her. 'I have a headache. I'm going to lie down for a while.'

He nodded. She certainly looked as if she needed to lie down. He hadn't realized just how greatly shocked she would be at the prospect of being parted from Natalie. It was understandable, of course. There were only two years between them and they had never spent so much as a night apart. As the door closed behind her he knew with a heavy heart that his family's unity was being destroyed and that there wasn't a thing he could do about it.

'I'm going to the *Konak*,' he said abruptly. 'Julian, you need to pack and you need to be available for an interview with your minister. Zita, will you see to it that Natalie has a suitable dress to wear for the ceremony?'

Without any more ado he followed Katerina from the room and it was only as he was stepping into his landau that he remembered their conversation on the night of the Summer Ball. Surely she had intimated to him that *she* was the one in which Julian Fielding was romantically interested? Wasn't that the reason he had been so disorientated when Julian had asked his permission to propose to Natalie, and to do so for a second time?

'The *Konak*,' he said tersely to his coachman. Obviously he had made a mistake. He remembered the stunned disbelief in Katerina's eyes when she had first learned Julian and Natalie were to marry and wasn't so sure. 'Damn and blast,' he said beneath his breath, wondering if life was ever going to be uncomplicated again. '*Damn and blast!*'

Katerina leaned against the bedroom door, her hands splayed against the wood, tears streaming down her face. When had it happened? How long had Julian been in love with Natalie? Why, oh why, hadn't she been aware of it? If she had been aware of it she wouldn't have allowed herself to have fallen in love with him. Now it was too late. She loved him and she didn't know how to stop loving him.

Dimly she heard voices in the hall and a carriage being called. It would be for Julian. He would be returning to his legation. In another few moments Natalie would be coming to confide in her. She pushed herself away from the door, crossing to the wash-stand. She couldn't throw herself down on the bed and sob her heart out as Natalie had so recently done. It would cause comment. Someone, her mother or her father or even Natalie, might guess the reason for her anguish and then she would never be able to face Natalie and Julian again.

She poured water into the bowl with an unsteady hand. Had Julian perhaps already guessed her feelings for him? Did he know she was in love with him? She thought back over all their conversations together, conversations she had treasured, mistaking entirely their tone and intent. She had said nothing shamingly revealing. She had simply assumed that his interest in her, and in her family, was because he was falling as much in love with her as she was with him. And she had assumed wrongly. It had been Natalie in whom he had been interested, Natalie with whom he had been falling in love.

Tears, hot and scalding, coursed down her cheeks. She bent her head over the bowl, splashing cold water on her face. She had, at least, an excuse for tears. Until Natalie was safely aboard the Orient Express her freedom was in jeopardy, and even when she was safely aboard, no-one knew when she would be returning home. In those circumstances, distress on her part was natural. What wouldn't be natural was if she broke down completely.

She lifted her head, pressing a towel to her face, struggling for control. Somehow she had to survive the wedding. She had to survive seeing Natalie and Julian leave aboard the night train for a new life together and she had to survive a future bereft of the hope that one day Julian would love her as she loved him.

The door burst open and Natalie said, her voice breaking, 'I don't know how I'm going to bear it, Katerina!' She threw herself face down on the bed. 'All Papa keeps saying is that I might be away for years and years! Why should I be? Gavrilo won't admit to knowing me. I doubt if he'll even admit to knowing Nedjelko! And now in order that Mama and Papa are not to be separated I have to marry an Englishman!'

Her voice broke completely. 'What if the Austrians don't ask for me to be extradited? What if I'm able to come back in a few months time, when Gavrilo's trial is over? Will Julian divorce me or will I have to stay married to him even though I will be living in Belgrade and he will be in London or Paris or Timbuktu?'

Slowly Katerina put her face towel down. 'Is that what you intend to do? Return to Belgrade and leave him?'

Natalie pushed herself up on one elbow and stared at her. 'Of course! What other choice is there?'

Katerina clasped her hands tightly together. 'You could stay with him. Surely that's what he is expecting you to do?'

'Stay with him? Even when it is safe for me to return to home?' Natalie's voice was incredulous. 'You can't mean it, Katerina. No-one can expect that of me, not even Papa.'

It was Katerina's turn to stare. All through the nightmare of hearing the plans for Natalie and Julian's marriage it had never occurred to her that Natalie was oblivious of what was expected of her. Or was she oblivious? Perhaps the marriage was merely an act of British eccentric gallantry. Perhaps Julian had made it quite clear to Natalie that it was to be a marriage in name only.

Hope entered her heart, so slender and tenuous she hardly dare put the question that had to be asked into words. 'Julian is in love with you, isn't he?'

'Of course he's in love with me.' Natalie was affronted. 'Why else would he have offered to marry me? But I'm not in love with him. I told him I wasn't in love with him when he proposed to me at the Summer Ball and I told him so again, today.'

Katerina remembered her happiness that evening, her certainty that Julian was about to ask her to marry him, the ecstasy of being held in his arms as they had waltzed to 'The Blue Danube'. And yet some time that evening he had proposed to Natalie.

'I didn't know he had proposed to you before,' she said stiltedly, wondering if there was a limit to pain, wondering if she had finally reached it. 'And if he is marrying you because he loves you, then he will most certainly expect you to stay with him and to travel with him wherever he is posted.'

Natalie sat up on the bed, hugging her knees. 'I won't do so,' she said vehemently, dark curls tumbling around her face. 'I'm marrying him only so that Mama and Papa won't be separated. I can't be expected to be unhappy for the rest of my life, just because I was seen with Gavrilo hours before he killed the Archduke, and I'm not going to be. I'm going to return home just as soon as all the fuss dies down.'

The fuss was a long way from dying down. In King Peter's study in the *Konak* both the King and Prime Minister Pasich heard Alexis's story in grave silence. He had given them his eye-witness account of the assassinations immediately on his return from Sarejevo. Now he told them of Natalie's meetings with Princip and Cabrinovich in the *Golden Sturgeon*, of her accidental meeting with Princip in the Oriental bazaar and of how Max Karageorgevich had also admitted to knowing Gavrilo, though not personally.

'Apparently a well-wisher pointed Princip out to him, telling him that he was a troublemaker. He says that's all he knows of him and that he's never had a conversation with him. He said he was perturbed to see Natalie in such company and that he asked Vitza to let Katerina know of it. Apparently he was sure Katerina would be able to deal with the situation and put an end to any further such meetings. He has also, of course, sworn on his life not to mention Natalie's acquaintanceship with Princip to anyone. As to Natalie, I have arranged for her to leave the country this evening. All that is necessary is for arrangements to be made enabling Mr Fielding to leave with her.'

Pasich, older even than the King, stroked his long white beard. 'I'll see to it immediately,' he said as Alexis had known he would. 'You're quite right in thinking it the safest course of action. The Austrians have already demanded a Moslem suspect be extradited from Montenegro. Quite what King Nikita is going to do isn't yet clear. The attitude of the Montenegrins is that Princip is a hero.'

'Our attitude has to be that he is not,' King Peter said in a voice sepulchral with fatigue. 'Alexander, as Regent, has ordered an eight-day period of mourning. His shoulders are broad enough and young enough to bear this burden. Mine, I'm afraid, are not. When I handed over my responsibilities to him, I did so not a day too soon.'

There was no way Alexis could disagree with him. Peter's shoulders were stooped, the rheumatism in his hands and legs more noticeable than usual.

'The news from Vienna is not good,' Pasich continued, taking Alexis into his confidence as always. 'The militarists are clamouring for war. They've been itching for years to draw the sword against Belgrade and now, thanks to Colonel Dimitrievich, they have an excuse to do so.'

Alexis felt as if cold water were being trickled down his spine. 'Apis? He's admitted involvement?'

A tremor passed over Pasich's aged face. Ever since Dragutin Dimitrievich had murdered King Alexander, thereby enabling Serbia to return to Karageorgevich rule, he had been a thorn in his flesh he could have well done without.

'Colonel Dimitrievich is saying nothing. However, I have it on good authority that he put the plan to assassinate the Archduke before the Black Hand Central Committee on 14 June and that the committee, realizing what the consequences might be for Serbia, opposed it.'

'But if they opposed it, why did it then take place?' Alexis asked, wondering who on earth was doing Pasich's spying for him.

'Because Colonel Dimitrievich doesn't give a hang for any judgement other than his own,' Pasich said bitterly. 'He told the committee he would rescind his instructions to the assassins, but as we know to our cost he did not do so. The result is that Austria suspects Serbian involvement in the assassination and her suspicions, God help us, are correct. Our task now is to deny such involvement vociferously in order to avoid finding ourselves in a war for which we are not yet prepared.'

'And we would not be able to do so if a Karageorgevich were implicated in the crime,' King Peter said quietly. 'There is no time to be lost. Mr Pasich, you must speak immediately with the British minister. Alexis, you must speak to my personal priest. As Mr Fielding is not a member of the Orthodox Church and as there is no time for him to be received into the Church, the wedding ceremony will, of necessity, be both curtailed and private. It will, however, take place. On that you have my word.'

It took place at seven o'clock that evening in the *Konak*'s private chapel. There was no incense, no massed choirs chanting gloriously, no awe-inspiring nuptial mass.

Natalie wore a close-fitting, whale-boned cream-silk dress, the slightly open neckline and the long tight sleeves flounced with matching lace. She carried no bouquet and wore no jewellery. Her only adornment was a myrtle wreath in her hair, signifying her virginity.

King Peter, Alexis, Zita and Katerina sat on spindly-legged gilt chairs in an arc behind her.

'Isn't Sandro going to be there?' she had asked Zita disbelievingly when arrangements for the ceremony had been explained to her. 'How can I be married if Sandro isn't there? And what about Great-Aunt Elena and Great-Aunt Eudocia and Vitza and Max? Isn't *anyone* going to be there?'

'As Regent, the full responsibility of this crisis with Austria has fallen on Sandro's shoulders,' Zita said, her own pain at the necessarily mean arrangements for the wedding, extreme. 'He's trying to ensure that if the worst comes to the worst and Austria does declare war, Russia will come to our aid. With negotiations like those going on he can't possibly be expected to attend a wedding.'

She didn't add that even if he could have attended the wedding it would have been most unwise for him to do so when at any moment there might come a demand from Vienna that he authorize the bride's arrest.

'The officer who saw Natalie with Princip has had time

in which to make a report,' she had said to Alexis when he had returned from the *Konak*. 'As no request has been received from the Austrians for Natalie's extradition does that mean he hasn't made one? That he didn't recognize Princip? That Natalie is leaving the country needlessly? Marrying needlessly?'

Alexis's still handsome face was grooved with lines of anxiety. 'I don't know, my dear,' he had said truthfully. 'The Austrians have apparently requested a Moslem be extradited from Montenegro. What his connection with the crime is, and how they got his name, I have no idea. Natalie could be next. It is a risk that can't possibly be taken.'

And so it hadn't been taken. Zita sat calm and outwardly composed as Natalie was married, not to a scion of a European royal house as had always been envisaged, but to a minor member of the British Diplomatic Service.

She wasn't the only person present concealing a burden of grief. Katerina was dying by inches unable to understand why, when she loved Julian with all her heart and would have done everything in her power to make him happy, he had chosen instead to marry Natalie, who did not love him at all and had no intention of even staying with him.

Alexis sat through the short ceremony ram-rod straight, racked by doubt and guilt. What if his judgement had been wrong all along? What if there was no real danger to Natalie at all? No possibility of grave political consequences if she remained in Serbia? What if he had emotionally blackmailed her into marriage with a man she did not love, all for no good reason? The thought seared him like a red-hot brand. Why, oh why had he taken her with him to Sarajevo? She hadn't wanted to go. He was the one who had insisted she accompany him and this nightmare was the result.

King Peter was also anguished. Pasich had told him only minutes earlier that a telegram had been received from Vienna. The Austrian authorities in Bosnia wished to question Natalie regarding her meeting with Gavrilo Princip in Sarajevo on 26 June. He sighed heavily. No-one but themselves and the British minister knew of the wedding now taking place and, God willing, only the same number of people would know about her departure for Britain as Mrs Julian Fielding. As far as the Austrians were concerned it would be as if Natalie had disappeared into thin air.

He had no intention of telling Alexis about the telegram until Natalie's train pulled out of Belgrade station. There was no sense in causing further distress before what would be an extremely painful leave-taking. Remembering how it had once been proposed that Natalie marry Alexander he sighed again and tried to concentrate on the vows his troublesome young relation was making in a remarkably steady voice.

'I can't go through with it!' she said in a far from steady voice an hour later as she was being helped out of her wedding-gown by her mother and Helga. 'I can't leave home!'

She looked across the room at Katerina, overcome by panic. 'I can't do it!' she said again, looking to Katerina for help as she had done when she was a small girl and Katerina had seemed always wiser, always more capable. 'I won't know anyone in London! I didn't want to be married! I don't want not to see you for ages and ages and ages!'

Katerina quickly crossed the room towards her, putting her arms around her, hugging her tight. 'And I don't want not to see you for ages and ages,' she said, fighting back an onrush of tears.

They clung together, overcome by the enormity of what was about to happen to them. All their lives, despite their differences in temperament, they had been each other's best friend. Now they were to be separated and neither of them knew how they were going to bear it.

'I'll go downstairs and make sure the trunks have been loaded into the carriage,' Zita said thickly, knowing that this was the last opportunity Natalie and Katerina would have to be alone together. 'Will you help me please, Helga?'

With eyes red from weeping Helga left the room with her.

Natalie said plaintively, 'I never imagined what my friendship with Gavrilo and Nedjelko would lead to, Katerina. I had no idea. It all seemed so exciting, dreaming and planning of a united South Slav state. It was all such fun, slipping away from the Conservatoire and meeting with them in the *Golden Sturgeon*. I felt as if I were a student and a revolutionary and it was so very romantic. I thought how proud great-grandfather would have been of me. I never thought of what being a revolutionary really meant. I never ever thought it through.'

'It's a Karageorgevich family failing,' Katerina said wryly. 'Great-grandfather never thought things through either. If he had done, he would never have lost his throne.'

For the first time in her life Natalie allowed a criticism of her great-grandfather to pass unchallenged. 'I wish I were you, Katerina!' she said with passion. 'I wish I was calm and sensible! I wish I were the one who was remaining in Belgrade!'

Katerina bit back the words that rose to her lips. Instead of saying she also wished they could change places, she said lightly, 'Don't be an idiot, Natalie. If you were me, I would be you and then where would I be?'

Natalie's resilient buoyancy came to her aid. 'In an almighty mess,' she said with a near hysterical giggle.

Despite all her inner agony Katerina smiled. 'I love you, little sister,' she said huskily. 'Come back home safely.'

Beneath the dark mass of her hair, the pale triangle of Natalie's face was almost mystically determined. 'I will,' she said, investing the words with all the solemnity of a vow. 'I'm never going to do anything stupid ever again.'

Katerina's smile deepened. It was possible to imagine many things but Natalie never again being rash or unthinking was not one of them.

'It's time you got dressed,' she said gently. 'What are you going to wear?'

Reluctantly Natalie walked across to her armoire and opened the doors. 'My Serbian-blue costume,' she said with quiet certainty. 'And I shall wear it again, when I return.'

The jacket was nip-waisted, a peplum flaring provocatively over the hips, the collar and cuffs trimmed with sable, the long skirt so narrow she could take only the shortest of steps in it. With it she wore pearl-grey Louis-heeled shoes and a small, round nonsense of a hat, a brilliant yellow feather sticking provocatively straight up in the air.

There was a lump in Katerina's throat as Natalie unobtrusively secured the hat with a hat-pin. Yellow braid edged the light-blue uniforms of the country's most élite regiment and by wearing yellow with blue, Natalie was as near to being in Royal Army uniform as it was possible for her to be.

There was a light knock on the door and Zita entered. 'It's time to go, sweetheart,' she said with a composure she was far from feeling.

Natalie turned away from the mirror. 'I'm ready.' Her

voice was steady, her eyes dry. She had long ago made up her mind not to cause her mother further distress by giving way to her grief. 'Has Julian already left?'

'Yes. He's gone to the British Legation and he's leaving for the station from there. Another attaché at the Legation is going to accompany him. When he boards the train he will do so separately from yourself. Prime Minister Pasich advised Papa that no-one should know the identity under which you have left the country. If the Austrians remain unaware of your marriage to Julian they won't be able to ask the British government to hand you over to them. With luck they won't even know when, or how, you left the country.'

'But she'll be seen at the station,' Katerina protested, wondering how Natalie's brave yellow feather could fail to be seen, or Natalie recognized.

Zita led the way out of the room. 'Natalie will board the train quickly and quietly. She is to travel in a private compartment and we will say goodbye to her there. We will not stand on the platform to wave her off or be conspicuous in any way.'

'I feel like a fugitive,' Natalie said bitterly as they reached the head of the grand staircase.

A spasm crossed Zita's fine-boned face. 'You are a fugitive,' she said quietly, 'and you must behave as one, both on the Budapest train and the Orient Express. When the Orient Express stops in Vienna, don't alight for a walk. Don't even do so when it reaches Munich. Germany is Austria's closest ally and the Germans would most certainly detain you if Austria asked them to do so.'

Natalie stumbled. Despite all the explanations her father had made to her, it still seemed incredible to her that so much fuss could be caused over so minor an incident. She hadn't sought Gavrilo out in Sarajevo. She hadn't even spoken to him for long. As a consequence, and because she was a Karageorgevich, she was being bundled across Europe like a hunted criminal.

It was customary, if a member of the family were leaving Belgrade for any length of time, for the household staff to line up ceremonially at the door in order to say goodbye. Only her father was in the marble-floored entrance hall. Apart from Helga, no-one knew she was leaving. No-one even knew she was a bride.

The door was open, the carriage waiting. Dusk was thickening into night. With a stab of shock she realized that by the time she boarded the train and it set off on its journey through Serbia to Hungary, it would be dark and she would not be able to look out and see the Serbian countryside.

Bella was whining at her feet and picking her up, hugging her close, she stepped out of the house and walked a few short steps across the courtyard to the carriage. Her trunks had already been taken down to the station in order that they could be taken aboard as unobtrusively as possible. Because of the importance of the train arriving in Budapest in time to make the connection with the Orient Express, the Belgrade to Budapest night train always left exactly on schedule and so careful timing for the boarding of both herself and her luggage was essential.

The journey to the station was a short one and Natalie tried to imprint every sight and every sound in her memory. In Prince Milan Street a young boy was carrying a lamb in his arms. She wondered if young men would carry lambs in their arms in London and doubted it. Trams were still running and in one, a woman wearing a loose Zouave jacket of maroon velvet embroidered in gold sat next to a moustached man in a western suit. A group of gypsies sat on the curb, one of them nursing a violin. An old man in baggy trousers and knee-high boots, an astrakhan cap on his head, sat outside a café drinking a glass of *sliovovitz*. Ochre-walled houses boasted rickety verandahs. Acacia trees sprouted in the tiniest of gardens.

'The train is in,' Alexis said with relief as their landau trundled over the cobbles of the square fronting the station. 'Now remember. There are to be no goodbyes on the platform. We are to draw no attention to ourselves whatsoever.'

'Will Julian be joining us to say goodbye?' Katerina asked, forcing herself to sound indifferent.

'No. There is to be no contact between Julian and Natalie until the train crosses from Germany into France.' He stepped down from the landau. 'The next few minutes are not going to be easy for any of us. I want no public tears. No acknowledgements of anyone who may recognize us.'

As he led the way into the cavernous station he was bitterly regretting his decision that they all see Natalie on to the train. It had been Zita who had pleaded with him that they do so. 'It's terrible enough her being forced to leave in this way, without her having to go to the station and board the train alone. If Julian were going to be with her I wouldn't ask it, but he isn't going to be with her. Please, Alexis. Please don't let's say goodbye to her in the house. Let us all be together until the last possible moment.'

Because of the guilt he felt, he had given in to her. As he strode quickly to Natalie's specially reserved compartment at the rear of the train he hoped fervently he wasn't going to regret doing so.

The minute they were in the compartment he pulled down the window-blinds. 'The train leaves in ten minutes,' he said, wondering how on earth he was going to live with himself if her departure, and the marriage that was enabling her to depart without inconvenience to himself, proved to be unnecessary. 'We haven't long.'

No-one needed reminding. No-one knew what to say. Words of any sort seemed inadequate.

At last Alexis said gruffly, 'I wouldn't have allowed you to marry Julian Fielding if I wasn't utterly sure of the depth of his love for you, or of my conviction that you will find happiness with him.'

'Yes, Papa,' Natalie said, knowing she could never find happiness with anyone who wasn't a Slav; knowing her father would not have encouraged her to marry if it were not that it saved his being separated from her mother.

The final whistle blew. Alexis kissed her on the cheek and then turned away and opened the carriage door, too overcome to speak.

'Be happy, darling,' Zita said, her long-held composure threatening to abandon her. 'Goodbye, God bless.'

Katerina was the last to leave the compartment. 'I love you and I'm going to miss you,' she said fiercely. 'Look after yourself! Write to me!'

As the carriage door swung closed behind her, Natalie stood for a moment, alone in the centre of the carriage, unable to comprehend the enormity of what had just happened.

The train began to pull out of the station and as it did so she ran to the window, releasing the blind, slamming the window down, leaning as far out as possible.

Katerina was following Alexis and Zita out of the station. Natalie gave a choked sob, knowing that she could not call out, knowing that if she did so her father would also turn round and that the last parting expression she would then see on his face would be one of anger.

Futilely she began to wave and then, miraculously, Katerina turned around, waving in response.

With tears pouring down her face Natalie waved and waved, the yellow feather in her hat streaming in the wind as the train picked up speed. Even when Katerina was no longer discernible she continued to wave. She waved until her arm ached; until the station was nothing but an indistinct blur; until not even the lights of Belgrade were visible in the enveloping darkness.

Chapter Eight

For hour after hour she sat by the window, Bella in her arms, too heartsick to walk along the train and into the dining-carriage. An attendant brought water and biscuits for Bella and a glass of milk for herself and she sipped at it, staring out into the blackness, wondering what would have happened if she had succeeded in the mission she had been given and had persuaded Sandro to meet with Gavrilo and Nedjelko and Trifko.

The mere thought made her blood run cold. That disaster, at least, had never taken place. Sandro was not involved. She had never, thank God, mentioned Gavrilo or Nedjelko or Trifko by name to him.

She hugged Bella closer, pressing her face against the comforting warmth of her silky fur, reliving again and again the ghastly seconds in Sarajevo when Gavrilo had stepped from the pavement and shot the Archduke and Duchess at point-blank range. She was certain he had never intended killing the Duchess. If he had intended a second victim, it would have been General Potiorek. The more she thought about those few vital seconds, the more certain she was that the Duchess had thrown herself across her husband in an effort to save him and, intercepting the bullet, had died. Then Gavrilo had turned the gun on himself.

She had seen him do so quite clearly. It had been an interfering spectator standing behind him who had seized hold of his arm and prevented him from committing suicide. The man had been wearing a fez and she hated him with all her heart. If he had not acted as he had, Gavrilo would have died quickly and cleanly in the street. Instead, in the mêlée that had followed, he had been nearly lynched and there was no telling what brutality he had suffered since, while being questioned.

Beads of sweat broke out on her forehead as she thought of the physically fragile Gravilo being tortured. Again and for the hundredth time she wondered why, at that particular street corner, at that particular time, it was Bosnian Moslems who were standing thickly on the pavement and not Bosnians who would have been more sympathetic with Gavrilo's aims. Non-Moslems would not have helped the police arrest Gavrilo, they may even have prevented Gavrilo's arrest and enabled him to escape. Moslems had, however, always been favoured by the Austrian authorities as part of their policy of encouraging divisions within the country's mixed racial and religious community and it was Moslems loyal to Austria whom Gavrilo had found himself among when he had fired his fatal shots.

No-one had asked her how she now felt about Gavrilo. Not her father or mother or Katerina. Not even Julian. For a while she had been uncertain as to what her feelings were. The Duchess's death had distressed her profoundly and in the immediate aftermath of the killings it had seemed inconceivable to her that she should still regard herself as being Gavrilo's friend. Yet as the shock of what had happened faded she found to her incredulity that she still did so. She understood his fierce Slav nationalism and his virulent hatred of all things Austrian. As a Bosnian, he had lived daily under the oppression of Austro-Hungarian misrule and she knew that he had seen the act he had committed as being not a crime, but a patriotic act of liberation.

Wearily she rose to her feet, pulling her sleeping berth down from the wall, wondering if Trifko had also been in Sarajevo and if he, too, had been arrested. As she undressed she wondered which of them had first thought of striking at Austria by murdering the heir to the Austrian throne; from where Nedjelko and Gavrilo had got their weapons; what would happen to them when they were tried. She climbed into the narrow sleeping berth, making a space for Bella next to her, wondering about something so terrible she had not yet been able to put it into words. Wondering if her friends would hang. When she woke in the morning, she felt as if she had not slept at all. She wished that Julian were with her, so that she had someone to talk to. She wasn't sure, but she thought that Julian would understand her feelings about Gavrilo. She hadn't, as yet, been able to talk about them with anyone. She wondered if she would see him if she went into the dining-carriage for breakfast. They were both under strict instructions not to speak to each other and her father had told her to stay in her compartment and not run the risk of being recognized by fellow-travellers in the parlour and dining-carriages.

She kissed the top of Bella's head and released the window-blind. They were no longer in Serbia and the scenery that met her eyes, though beautiful, did not warm her heart. The rivers were not Serbian rivers, the lakes not Serbian lakes. She wondered how long it would be before they reached Budapest. The attendant had promised her he would take Bella for a walk when the change-over to the Orient Express was made and she was hoping she would also catch a glimpse of Julian.

By the time she had finished dressing they were drawing into the station. Porters came for her luggage, an attendant came for Bella. Her father had given her strict instructions on how she was now to behave. She was to leave the

Belgrade train quickly and quietly and board the Orient Express in the same manner. A private compartment had been booked for her. She wasn't to speak to anyone on the platform, not even Julian.

Knowing she couldn't speak to him didn't stop her looking for him as she walked across the platform to the waiting train. She saw him almost immediately. Tall and broad-shouldered, his hair gleaming gold in the morning sunlight, he was talking to an elderly gentleman who also looked to be British.

At the sight of him her spirits rose buoyantly. She wished she could run down the platform and join him. In their short time together in the Italian drawing-room she had discovered that in his company things no longer seemed to be as bad as they appeared. He was able to put things into perspective for her. She wanted to be able to talk to him about her nightmare that Gavrilo and Nedjelko would be hanged. She wanted him to comfort her and she knew that he would do so.

When she was safely on the train and in her compartment, she lowered her window, leaning out to see if he was still there. He was still with his companion, still deep in conversation. Mindful of her father's stern instructions she didn't call his name but she waved furiously. The movement caught his attention, he looked directly towards her and grinned. Incredibly, despite all her nightmares and all her grief at no longer being in Serbia, she grinned back complicitly. He was her friend and he understood her and for the short time she was going to be away from home, he would make her exile bearable.

As a guard exhorted all passengers to board the train and as Julian turned reluctantly away from her in order to do so, she reflected on how much worse things could have been. It could have been the ornately dressed French attaché, Monsieur Quesnai, who had fallen in love with her and who had asked her father if he could make her a proposal of marriage. What on earth would she have done if her father had suggested she marry Monsieur Quesnai? A chuckle rose in her throat and wishing that Katerina were with her so that she could share the joke, she closed the window and waited for the attendant to return Bella to her.

The tedium of the journey, alone in her private compartment, was crushing. She couldn't enjoy the scenery because with every change in the landscape she was forcibly reminded of how far from home she was travelling. Every time a border was crossed and her documents examined she expected a contingent of soldiers or police to arrive and place her under arrest and her nerves were stretched to breaking point. She was travelling under her married name. Prime Minister Pasich had handed her travel documents to her himself, the ink on them still wet.

That night, as she lay in her wagon-lit cuddling Bella, it occurred to her that Julian was probably very nearby. Whatever the reason given for Mrs Julian Fielding travelling in seclusion, it would surely look very odd if their sleeping compartments were not adjoining. She suddenly felt less lonely. Tomorrow morning they would reach Vienna and by the afternoon the city would be safely behind them and the worst would be over. In another twenty-four hours they would be in France and she would be able to come out of seclusion, knowing it would not matter if she were recognized.

She slept restlessly, waking up to the brief, tormenting belief that everything that had happened on and since 28 June, was nothing but a hideous dream. The realization that it was reality came with the force of a fist being punched into her stomach.

As they drew into Vienna her anxiety mounted. Surely,

if the Austrian authorities were now seeking her and if they knew she was aboard the train, this was where they would arrest her. She allowed Bella to be exercised only with the greatest reluctance and immediately the attendant had left the compartment with Bella at his heels she crossed to the window in order to pull the blind down.

The station was draped with black crêpe and black flags hung everywhere. Julian was on the platform twelve yards or so away, his back towards her. She didn't wait for him to turn so that she could wave to him. She tugged the blind down against the lavish display of national mourning and sat in the muted light wondering what Katerina was doing in Belgrade, if Vitza and Max had been told of her departure to Britain and if Sandro had minded not being at her wedding and not saying goodbye to her.

When finally the whistle blew and the train began to steam once again on its way she let out a deep, shuddering sigh of relief. There was still a long way to go before they would be out of Austria, but the worst was over. She was sure now that she would not be arrested. The officer at the Oriental bazaar had not recognized Gavrilo. Gavrilo hadn't spoken about her when questioned, and would not. She was as safe as she had been a week ago, before she had left Belgrade for Ilidze.

She released the window-blind. Was it only a week ago? It seemed a lifetime. She remembered laughing with Katerina on the car ride from Ilidze down into Sarajevo, happily untroubled by any premonition of disaster. Perhaps, where she was concerned, there had been no disaster at all. If the Austrians did not wish to question her she could return at any time to Belgrade and her journey to Britain could be seen as being a holiday.

And Julian? A small smile touched the corners of her mouth. Being married might prove to be very interesting. In her mind's eye she again saw his broad shoulders and narrow hips, his thick tumble of blond hair and his finely chiselled mouth. Her smile deepened. Marriage to Julian was going to be more than interesting. It was going to be the most fun she'd ever had.

All day the train steamed through Austria towards Germany. When she woke in the morning they were in Munich. By evening they were in France. Sunnily she showed her documents to the official who knocked on her compartment door. Buoyantly she dressed for dinner, knowing that Julian would be waiting for her in the dining-carriage. Hoping that a dress that had been the height of fashion in Belgrade would not be shamingly *passé* in France, she tucked a wriggling Bella under her arm and for the first time since she had boarded at Budapest, walked down the corridor to the public carriages.

He was seated facing her as she entered. There was a bottle of champagne on the table and flowers. He flashed her his heart-stopping smile and rose to meet her.

'Have you been all right?' he asked, concern in his eyes and something else. Something that sent a shiver of anticipation down her spine.

She sat down, settling Bella beside her, feeling suddenly ridiculously shy. 'I've been bored,' she said frankly. 'I thought we were never going to get out of Austria. It went on and on and on.'

'We're out of it now,' he said comfortingly, sitting down again. 'And Germany. You won't have to see either country ever again.'

She was about to say that it wasn't true, that she would have to travel through them when she returned home, but she thought better of it. It would be tactless to bring up the subject of her return before they had even arrived in Britain, especially if it wasn't an event he was anticipating.

'I'm starving,' she said as the appetizing aroma of hot

soup reached her from a nearby table. 'All I've done for three days is eat off trays.'

He laughed, wanting to feast his eyes on her and trap her hands between his, knowing he must do nothing that would disconcert her and spoil their easy camaraderie. Common sense had told him right at the outset that he had to take things slowly. He felt a rising in his crotch and wondered for how much longer he could do so. They had been married for three days and he still had not kissed her on the mouth.

'What would you like?' he asked, turning his thoughts away from bed with superhuman effort. 'Quail or chaud-froid?'

She chose the quail and when they came they were deliciously fat and stuffed with chestnuts.

'Have you heard any more news from home?' she asked, knowing that he would have bought newspapers both in Vienna and Munich. 'Is Sandro managing to convince Emperor Franz Josef that Uncle Peter and his government had absolutely nothing to do with Archduke Franz Ferdinand's death?'

'Not according to Austrian newspapers.' Julian's thoughts were suddenly very far from bed. 'The *Reichspot* had a headline on its front page announcing that although the assassin was a Bosnian, the guilt for the crime lay with Serbia. It said Serbia's foreign policy had encouraged the crime and that Serbia's existence was a constant threat to Austrian security.'

She put down her knife and fork, suddenly not hungry any more. 'Does that mean there is going to be a war?'

His frown deepened. 'I'm not sure. If there is a war I can't see Russia remaining on the sidelines. She's always regarded herself as Serbia's big brother and I'm sure she would come to her aid.'

'Of course she would!' Natalie's innate optimism swiftly

165

re-asserted itself. 'And so it won't matter that Serbia isn't yet ready to go to war.' She picked up her spoon again. 'Austria will be defeated, Bosnia and Herzegovina will be freed from Austrian rule and Gavrilo will have succeeded in what he set out to do, which was to liberate his country.'

It occurred to Julian that as the wife of a diplomat, Natalie was going to be far from ideal. He would have to explain to her the need for caution and reticence whenever they were in public and politics were under discussion. He wondered what would happen if he had the ill-luck to be re-assigned to Berlin or Vienna and shuddered. The prospect of Natalie at Potsdam or Schönbrunn Palace garden parties was too horrendous to contemplate.

He said divertingly, 'The Archduke's and Duchess's funeral is to be held tomorrow in Vienna. No heads of state are to be in attendance. The official explanation is that the Emperor is too old and infirm to be able to cope with the exertion of a long funeral.'

A waiter removed their plates, another refilled their champagne glasses.

'I don't believe that for a minute,' Natalie said with beguiling forthrightness. 'It's been done so that Uncle Peter won't have to be invited to the ceremony.'

Julian grinned. Beneath Natalie's riotous mass of thick dark curls, now anchored in a becoming chignon, there was an amazingly quick brain. 'I think you're right,' he said as they were served with lobster. 'If one monarch was invited, they would all have to be invited, including King Peter. Can you imagine the embarrassment that would have caused, with Austrian newspapers declaring him to be the villain of the piece?'

Natalie giggled. She had never drunk more than a glass of champagne at a time before and it was an extremely pleasant sensation. She was feeling wonderfully relaxed and she was also, whenever she looked straight into

166

Julian's amber-brown eyes, beginning to feel something else as well. Something she had never felt before and which both excited and disturbed her.

He stretched his hand across the table, taking hold of hers. 'Let me tell you about England,' he said, an unmistakable throb of patriotism in his voice. 'Let me tell you about my family.'

She didn't particularly want to know about Britain and until now it had never occurred to her even to wonder about his family. It was nice, though, to have her hand once again in his as he told her about the family house overlooking Regent's Park and the ancestral home in Northumberland.

'You'll like Northumberland,' he had said enthusiastically. 'There's a wild, untamed feel to it . . .'

Her eyes had lit with genuine interest. 'Like Serbia? Are there mighty rivers like the Danube and the Sava?'

He laughed, thinking of the North Tyne and the Tweed. 'There are some big rivers, though none as mighty as the Danube, and there are scores of burns, the Usway, the Fallowlees, the College, the Chirdon, the Blacka . . .'

'Burns? What are burns? I don't understand.'

'Northumberland is near to Scotland and burn is Scots for a small stream.'

The waiter came to remove their plates of barely touched lobster and reluctantly he released her hand.

'There are wonderful stretches of coastline as well,' he added. 'We can sail and swim.'

It didn't sound at all like Serbia and she wasn't sure that she wanted either to sail or swim.

Strawberries were placed on their table. Neither of them made a move towards eating them.

'The last twenty-four hours must have been very stressful for you,' he said, and this time both her hands were trapped in his.

167

She thought of Vienna and the station draped with black crêpe and shivered, then she thought of what Gavrilo and Nedjelko must be undergoing and said in a low voice, 'The only terrible thing that has happened to me is my having to leave home. I can't stop thinking about what must be happening to Gavrilo and Nedjelko. I can't stop thinking about what will happen to them after they are tried and sentenced.'

Julian looked around swiftly to make sure no-one was within hearing distance. The tables nearest them had been vacated and the waiters were at the far end of the carriage. He said very quietly, 'Don't give yourself nightmares about it, my love.'

It was the first time he had ever called her his love and she liked it. It made her feel very sophisticated and secure. What was more, she knew that he was now going to vanquish her demons for her.

'From what you have said about them they were both highly intelligent,' he continued. 'They would have known what the consequences for their deed were. They weren't frightened of risking them and I doubt if they are frightened now.'

'But when they are tried . . . if they are hanged . . .'

'They won't be hanged.'

At the certainty in his voice, her heart almost ceased to beat. 'What do you mean? How do you know?'

Julian looked around the carriage again. The vacated tables had not been taken. The waiters were nowhere in sight.

'Knowing that you might be arrested as well and be charged as an accessory, and knowing that in Bosnian law an accessory to murder is considered to be guilty of the deed itself, I made it my business to know. The maximum charge for either murder or treason is death, but not if the accused is under twenty at the time the crime was ommitted. You told me Gavrilo was studying for his high-school graduating examination. He can't be twenty yet. The most he can be is nineteen.'

'He is nineteen, and so is Nedjelko!' Natalie's relief was absolute. He had done what she had known he would do. He had put an end to the dreadful images that had tormented her every time she had closed her eyes and tried to sleep.

He said now, the heat at the back of his eyes deepening, 'I think it's time for bed, don't you?'

She sighed, sad that their lovely evening together had come to an end but happy in the knowledge that she would finally sleep restfully. Bella was already asleep and had been for a long time. She picked her up lovingly. 'Good night,' she said as Bella stirred and made a little snuffling sound and fell asleep again. 'Thank you for finding out about Gavrilo and Nedjelko and the law about their ages.'

He stood up and said carefully, 'Now that we are no longer in Austria or Germany we don't have to travel apart, Natalie.'

She looked at him uncomprehendingly. 'No. I know. And I'm glad. I'm looking forward to our being together tomorrow as we travel to Britain.'

He said gently, 'We're married, Natalie. In the normal way of things we would have been sharing a wagon-lit ever since leaving Belgrade.'

Her cheeks flushed with colour. Surely he couldn't be suggesting they consummate their marriage now? On a train?

He could read her mind as clearly as reading a book. A small smile crooked the corner of his mouth. For a seduction as important as this one was going to be, a narrow bunk in a swaying wagon-lit was hardly the ideal setting. Especially when it would also have to be shared with a frolicsome puppy.

'My wagon-lit is next door to yours on the left-hand side,' he said, accepting that he would have to be patient for a little longer. 'If you have a nightmare and want someone to talk to, give me a knock.'

'Thank you.' Her first reaction was relief. Hard on its heels came disappointment.

He walked out of the dining-car and down the corridor with her and then, as she paused outside her wagon-lit, he put his hands gently on her shoulders and turned her towards him.

'Good night,' he said, and lowering his head to hers he kissed her full on the mouth.

It was an intensely pleasant experience and one she wanted him to continue. He didn't do so. He raised his head from hers, looking down at her, an expression she couldn't quite understand in his eyes.

'Good night, my love,' he said huskily.

It was only when she was tucked up in bed, Bella at her feet, that she realized what the expression in his dark brown eyes had been. It had been amusement.

Britain was nothing like she had imagined. With what she now realized was colossal ignorance, she had expected it to be similar to Switzerland. Crisp and neat and sanitized. Sanitized it certainly wasn't. The docks and railway station were dismally grubby and coated heavily with bird droppings.

'Isn't it wonderful?' Julian was saying ecstatically. 'Didn't you love the white cliffs? Every time I see them, when I'm returning from a long spell abroad, I get a lump in my throat.'

Natalie remained tactfully silent. To her jaundiced eyes the cliffs of Dover had also looked grubby and she couldn't imagine why the British made such a fuss about them. The Kentish countryside, however, was pretty and her spirits began to rise. She liked the untidiness of the fields and the many small woods and occasionally there were streams that reminded her, just a little, of home.

Her pleasure died as they drew into London. The suburbs seemed to stretch into infinity. She had never imagined a city could be so large or, despite the hot July sun, so grey. She understood, now, why so many Englishmen referred rudely to Belgrade as being a glorified Balkan village. Compared to London, Belgrade *was* a village, a colourful village with an exotic hotch-potch of building styles and nationalities. London wasn't colourful. There were no yellow-walled houses with verandahs creaking with flowers. There was no-one in peasant dress of any description. No plum trees or acacia trees. No violin-playing gypsies.

'What do you think, my love?' Julian was saying elatedly. 'Isn't it magnificent?'

'It's very big,' she said truthfully, not wanting to be impolite.

The first thing she saw as they walked from the station was a news-stand. She looked eagerly at the headline of the paper prominently displayed and was mystified to see no mention of Sarajevo or of the terrible Austrian threat Serbia was now under.

Crowds milled around them. Crowds totally un-interested in Serbia. Her hand tightened in Julian's as homesickness swamped her. She had naïvely thought Belgrade the centre of the world. Now, with a slam of shock, she realized that it was very far from being so.

Julian was greeting a chauffeur by name. The motor car waiting for them was a blue-green Mercedes with pale cream leather upholstery. Deeply impressed she momen-tarily forgot about Britain's incredible lack of interest in Austro-Serbian relations.

The streets were even wider and the buildings even

grander than they had appeared from the train. With relief she saw that her costume and yellow-feathered hat were not embarrassingly *passé*. All skirts were narrow and nearly all hats small and head-hugging. She saw several skirts, very long and tight at the ankle, worn with a kind of tunic reaching to just below the knee. They looked very dashing and surprisingly Russian and she determined on a shopping expedition at the soonest possible moment.

'I sent a telegram from Belgrade,' Julian said as the Mercedes weaved through a bewildering maelstrom of private motor cars, horse-drawn carriages and bicycles. 'Mother and Father will be expecting us, though I doubt whether Diana will be at home, not in July.'

'What about your older brother?' she asked, suddenly aware that her attention had wandered when he had been telling her about his family and not wanting to make any *faux pas* when she was introduced to them.

'Edward will be in Northumberland. He's a country man by nature and looks after the family estate. He loathes London.'

A short while ago Natalie would have been in agreement with Edward. Now she wasn't so sure. She had become aware of an agreeable feeling of excitement in the London streets and though the buildings were grey, they were even grander than she had first supposed. They would have magnificent ballrooms. As she thought of the balls to which they would be invited it occurred to her that London was perhaps not as appalling as she had first thought.

The Mercedes purred to a halt in front of a grandiose house set back from the road a little. There was no small park surrounding it, no ornate courtyard. She reflected that none of the other large houses she had seen had been set in private parks and that very few had been fronted by anything that could be described as a courtyard and that it was obviously the custom in London not to have either.

'Here we go,' Julian said as the chauffeur opened the door for them. 'Mother and Father are going to love you. I know they are.'

'You have told them about me, haven't you?' she asked in sudden apprehension.

He grinned, his hair falling low across his brow, suddenly looking more English and foreign to her than he had ever done. 'My telegram was terse and to the point. RECALLED STOP MARRIED STOP NO PROBLEMS STOP.'

'Will you tell them *why* we married?' His arm was lovingly under hers and he was leading her towards the front door. 'Will you tell them about Sarajevo?'

He didn't answer her. The heavy front door had swung open and a butler could be seen, waiting to greet them. She picked Bella up, tucking her under her arm, frantically wondering why she hadn't asked all these questions when they had been on the train.

'Welcome home, sir,' the butler, an elderly man, was saying genially. 'Welcome to London, ma'am.' If he found it odd to be addressing a miss scarcely out of the schoolroom as ma'am he gave no sign of it. His manner was genuinely welcoming and her sudden rush of panic began to die.

If a Serb married and brought a husband or wife home to the *zadruga*, they were immediately incorporated into the family. Her own parents would most certainly have regarded any husband she or Katerina brought home to Belgrade as being part of their family.

The butler, moving ahead of them, opened a pair of double doors and with her hand securely in Julian's she walked with him into a drawing-room densely packed with furniture and *objets d'art*.

There were two people in the room. A grizzled-haired,

bearded man, far older than she had expected him to be, and a woman possibly in her mid-fifties, beautiful with the kind of beauty that is bone-deep and that never completely fades.

As Julian strode forward, shaking his father's hand, kissing his mother on the cheek, Lady Fielding's eyes met Natalie's. They were very cool and very clear and there was not a hint of welcoming warmth in them. Instead there was a chill that would have frozen the Sava.

Deeply disconcerted Natalie set Bella down, certain she must have made a mistake.

'My wife, Natalie,' Julian was saying with pride. 'Natalie, my mother. My father.'

'Welcome to England,' Lady Fielding said with a slight, polite smile. There wasn't the least intonation of sincerity in her words and with deep shock Natalie realized she had made no mistake. Julian had been wrong in thinking his mother would love her. Lady Fielding was never going to love her. She was never even going to like her.

'Natalie's maiden name is Karageorgevich,' Julian was saying, wanting his parents to know right from the outset that their new daughter-in-law wasn't an obscure Balkan peasant. 'She is a member of the Royal House of Karageorgevich.'

His father's eyebrows rose in genuine interest. 'Are you indeed? I met King Peter once, years ago, in Switzerland. He wasn't king then, of course. He was in exile and passing his time by translating John Stuart Mill's *Essay on Liberty* into Serb. Curious choice of book I thought. Are you familiar with Mr Mill's works, Miss . . . Miss . . .' he broke off in confusion.

Julian said with a hint of amusement in his voice, 'As Natalie is your daughter-in-law I think it's quite in order for you to call her by her first name.'

'Yes, of course, stupid of me.' His father shot her a

sheepish smile. 'Apologies for being such a bumbler, my dear. The truth of it is, it's rather difficult for me to believe that you *are* my daughter-in-law. Julian's telegram only came three days ago and we had no prior warning. He never mentioned in his letters that he was contemplating becoming engaged and . . .'

'Natalie must be tired,' Lady Fielding interrupted, clearly impatient with her husband's attempts to put Natalie at her ease. 'I'm sure she would find a cup of tea welcoming. I'll have one of the maids show her to her room and a tray sent up.' Without waiting for Natalie to express an opinion she pressed a button by the side of the elaborate marble mantelpiece.

'*Our* room, I hope?' Julian said and though his voice was pleasant there was an underlying note of steel in it.

'Of course, dear,' his mother said, unfazed. 'I've had the double room on the second floor made ready for you.'

A maid entered, little older than Natalie. 'You rang milady?' she queried respectfully.

'Yes, Ellen. Would you show Miss . . . Mrs Fielding into the bedroom that has been prepared for her and arrange that tea is sent up to her.'

Natalie looked towards Julian.

'I think that would be a good idea, my love,' he said, an expression in his eyes she couldn't quite read. 'I need to explain to my parents that there is nothing untoward about my being recalled to London so suddenly and that my being so was the reason for our rather hasty marriage.'

She nodded, knowing now that he would never in a million years confide the Oriental bazaar episode to his mother.

She followed the maid out of the room and before the door closed behind her she heard his mother say in deep pain, 'My dear Julian. Whatever were you thinking of? A *Balkan* and a child at that. As for the dog . . .'

'It's a nice looking little dog,' his father interrupted inconsequentially. 'It will make a good gun dog one day . . .'

The door closed. Seething with fury she followed the maid up two flights of stairs and into an opulently furnished room. From the window there was a magnificent view of rolling grassland and trees and she realized that it must be the public park of which Julian had spoken.

'I'll have tea sent up immediately, Miss,' the maid said, adding uncertainly, 'Would you like me to take the little dog down to the kitchens? I'm sure Cook will be able to find something nice for her. A beef bone perhaps, or some chicken left-overs.'

It was a kind offer and Natalie handed Bella to her saying, 'You'll take good care of her, won't you? Everything will be very strange to her.'

'Yes, Miss. Don't worry, Miss. I have a dog of my own at home.'

As the maid took Bella out of the room, Natalie wondered where her home was. Kent, perhaps. Wherever it was, it wasn't as far away from London as Belgrade.

Slowly she took her hat off and dropped it on a chair, then she crossed to the windows and stood, looking out over the park. *Balkan*. She hugged her arms in an effort to stop herself shaking with rage. It had been uttered as the worst possible kind of insult. Never would a Serb have greeted a guest in such a way. Especially a guest who was also a daughter-in-law.

The maid returned with a tea-tray and informed her that Cook was making a great fuss of Bella and that she was not to worry about her. Later still, when the tea was cold, Julian entered the room.

'I thought you would be resting,' he said as she turned away from the window, her close-fitting costume jacket still buttoned.

176

'I can't live here,' she said starkly, her eyes big and grave. 'Your mother doesn't want me here, nor does she want Bella.'

He crossed the room towards her and put his hands gently on her shoulders. 'My mother's behaviour was appalling,' he said, making no attempt to excuse or explain it. 'It won't be in the future. You have my word.' He slid his arms around her, holding her close. 'You *can* live here, Natalie. It will only be for a short while. I'll soon be given a fresh posting. In the meantime we can enjoy London together,' a hint of laughter entered his voice, 'and Father liked Bella. He thinks she will make an excellent gun dog.'

It was nice being held so close. She could hear his heart beating and smell the faint tang of his cologne. His lips brushed her temple and then he moved a hand to her hair, removing the pins from her chignon and letting them drop to the floor. She remained perfectly still, her heart beginning to pound in short, slamming little strokes. Was he about to make love to her? Now? In the middle of the afternoon?

As the last pins fell to the floor her hair tumbled around her shoulders in a riot of waves and curls.

'I think you should take your jacket off,' he said huskily, hooking a finger under her chin and raising her face to his. 'I think we should go to bed.'

Natalie thought they should go to bed too. A most delightful sensation was spreading through her body and she wanted to be even closer to him. Slowly, her eyes never leaving his, she raised a hand to her jacket and began to undo the tiny covered buttons.

Heat flushed the backs of his eyes. Without a word he turned from her, drawing the curtains, plunging the room into muted light.

She pushed the jacket back off her shoulders and it slid down her arms and then on to the floor.

He came back to her, lifting her lightly in his arms, carrying her towards the bed. 'There's nothing to be afraid of,' he said thickly as he laid her down. 'I'm not going to hurt you. I'm going to be very, very gentle.'

She lay watching him as he pulled off his shoes and socks, his jacket and tie, excitement spiralling through her. She had never seen a man naked and it seemed incredibly strange that now she was about to do so, the man in question was one she regarded merely as a friend.

Deftly he undid his collar-button, removing his high starched collar.

She wondered if she should tell him she had only the haziest idea of what married lovemaking entailed. In the normal way of things her mother would have told her everything she needed to know, but her wedding had been so sudden, and there had been so many things to arrange, that the vital mother and daughter conversation had never taken place.

He took off his shirt, his chest muscles rippling, his shoulders looking even broader than they did when he was clothed.

'My mother didn't . . .' she began hesitantly, 'I don't know . . .'

'It doesn't matter.' His trousers were snug on his hips and she felt her cheeks flush as he unbuttoned them. They dropped to the floor and her flush deepened. Without the least trace of embarrassment he lay beside her on the bed, propping himself up on one arm, looking down at her with an expression that sent the blood fizzing along her veins.

'We're going to take this very slowly,' he said, unbuttoning the first pearl button on her high-necked blouse. 'We have all the time in the world . . .'

He undid another button and another. When they were all undone he slid his strong, well-shaped hand up beneath her camisole, cupping her breast, his thumb brushing her nipple, his mouth coming down warm and demanding on hers.

She didn't hesitate. At the touch of his hand on her flesh desire had roared through her. Not knowing quite what was to come next, not caring as long as the magnificent, wonderful sensation continued, she slid her hands up into the coarseness of his hair, her mouth opening willingly beneath his.

'I love you,' he said hoarsely afterwards as they lay nakedly together, limbs still abandoningly entwined, bodies glistening with perspiration. 'I love you with all my heart and I'm going to love you for the rest of my life.'

She gave a contented, satisfied murmur, her face nuzzled against the side of his neck.

His arms tightened around her as he waited for the words he so desperately wanted to hear. They didn't come. He fought disappointment. They would come. She couldn't have responded sexually to him as she just had done if she didn't love him. It simply wasn't possible.

The next day, a week to the day that the Archduke and Duchess had died in Sarajevo, he showed her London. They strolled hand-in-hand through Regent's Park, ate mouthwatering strawberry ice-creams in Gunter's, visited Westminster Abbey and fed the pigeons in Trafalgar Square.

She was far from home, still in a state of intense anxiety about Gavrilo and Nedjelko, still waiting tensely to hear what Austria's ultimatum to Serbia was going to be, and yet she was incredibly, extraordinarily, happy.

It was a state of bliss that didn't last long. The headlines in the morning papers were that two more assassins, Trifko Grabez and Danilo Ilich, had been arrested.

'Do you know them?' Julian asked her, wondering

how many more people were involved and were going to be arrested.

'I know Trifko.' She thought of their meetings in the *Golden Sturgeon* and a tremor ran through her. She had never liked Trifko as much as Gavrilo and Nedjelko, but the thought of him standing trial on charges of treason and murder was horrific.

'And Ilich?' Julian persisted.

She shook her head. If Nedjelko had thrown the bomb at the Archducal motor car, and Gavrilo had fired the shots that had killed the Archduke and Duchess, what were Trifko's and Ilich's crimes?

From that moment on they bought every edition of every newspaper. In mid-week there came reports that scores of people had been arrested in Bosnia and charged with complicity in the crime and at the end of the week Julian received a letter from Alexis telling him the Austrian government had requested Natalie's extradition from Serbia. He decided not to tell her. Events in Sarajevo and Belgrade were causing her enough anxiety without his adding to it needlessly. There was nothing the Austrians could do about Natalie. She was in London and she was safe.

On 23 July Austria delivered its long threatened ultimatum to the Serbian government. All publications directed against Austria-Hungary were to be suppressed. All anti-Austrian propaganda was to be eliminated from schools. All illicit traffic in arms was to stop and all officials who had helped the conspirators to cross the border were to be punished. All army officers and civic functionaries guilty of propaganda against the Habsburg monarchy were to be removed from their positions. Two Serbians, an army officer and a student, were to be arrested, suspected of complicity in the assassinations. All nationalist societies were to be dissolved.

Natalie could no longer complain that Britain was not

interested in events taking place in Sarajevo and Belgrade. Newspaper headlines screamed the details of the ultimatum and declared that war was imminent. Germany declared it would support Austria-Hungary if Austria-Hungary declared war on Serbia. Russia and France declared they would support Serbia.

The Serbian reply to the ultimatum was delivered within the deadline stipulated and met virtually all the points in the ultimatum. It was rejected.

On 28 July a telegram was sent from Vienna to the Serbian government, informing them that war had been declared and that evening the Austro-Hungarian armies attacked Belgrade.

Natalie was distraught. Julian spent nearly every waking moment at the Foreign Office, giving his superiors the benefit of his first-hand knowledge of the government in Belgrade.

On 1 August, as Russia ordered a general mobilization, Germany declared war on her. Two days later she declared war on France.

'Britain will be next,' Julian said, red-eyed from lack of sleep. 'If she is, I shall enlist immediately.'

Panic bubbled up into her throat. 'But if you do, I'll be alone here with your parents! I couldn't bear it! I couldn't survive it!'

'You'll have to,' he said gently, taking her into his arms and rocking her as if she were a child. 'Everyone is going to have to bear colossal burdens.' He didn't add that not all would survive them.

All next day, a Monday and a Bank Holiday, he was at the Foreign Office. Hourly the tension mounted. Germany had declared her intention of attacking France through Belgium. If she did so, Britain would honour a long-standing commitment to defend Belgium from any such invasion. The invasion came.

As crowds gathered in Whitehall and outside Buckingham Palace, news spread that Britain had presented Germany with an ultimatum. Belgium's neutrality was to be honoured by Germany. She had until midnight, Berlin time, to make a satisfactory reply. If none were received, then Great Britain and Germany would be at war.

Midnight in Berlin was eleven o'clock in London and at ten o'clock Julian left his nerve-wracked colleagues in the Foreign Office and hurried home to Cambridge Gate.

'Is it going to be war?' his mother asked tensely, hurrying into the hall as he entered the house.

'We won't know for nearly an hour,' he said, knowing in his heart already; having known for days. 'I'm going to take Natalie down to Whitehall. I want her with me when Big Ben strikes eleven.'

She was in their bedroom, sitting on the edge of the bed in her nightdress, listening to the wireless, hoping to hear news of Serbia.

'Get dressed,' he said peremptorily, yanking open her wardrobe door and snatching at random at a blouse and skirt. 'We're going down to Whitehall.'

She didn't ask any questions and she didn't argue. She scrambled into the clothes he tossed towards her and then, her hair tumbling hoydenishly around her shoulders, she ran with him from the house.

The chauffeured Mercedes took them as far as the edge of Trafalgar Square and could go no further owing to the crowds that had gathered there. It was ten to eleven.

Julian flung the car door open. 'Come on,' he said, ignoring the horrified expression on his chauffeur's face. 'Let's join the crush.'

There was a sea of straw boaters, a forest of fiercely waving hand-held Union Jacks. Every now and then, for no reason that Natalie could see or think of, a whole section of the crowd burst out in loud cheering. Many men had beer bottles in their hands. There were children holding on to balloons and she remembered that the day had been an English holiday.

'Let's try and reach the War Office!' Julian shouted over the din, hauling her after him through the bizarrely festive throng.

All along Whitehall the windows blazed with lights. Policemen massed the fronts of many buildings. Official cars were parked two deep.

Suddenly the mood of the crowd changed. Silence fell. Solemnly Big Ben began to strike the hour.

A woman standing near to Natalie began to cry. Another began to pray, very softly, beneath her breath.

Slowly, irrevocably, the chimes continued.

Julian slid his arm around Natalie's shoulders.

The last stroke sounded and faded away on the hot night air. For a long moment the silence continued and then someone shouted, *'Down with the bloody Kaiser'* and pandemonium broke out.

'Is Britain now at war with Germany?' Natalie asked uncertainly. 'Will you be enlisting? Will you be going away?'

He nodded, damning Princip, damning the Austrians and their high-handed ultimatum, damning the insane German army scything its way through Belgium, damning everyone and everything responsible for the ending of their too-short time together.

All around them the mood had returned to one of frenzied carnival, a rowdy rendering of the 'Marseillaise' vying with a bawdy music hall song. He said sombrely, 'I report for officer training immediately. I leave in the morning.'

Chapter Nine

Katerina returned home from saying goodbye to Natalie lonelier and more bereft than she had ever been before in her life. She had no close friend to turn to; no-one who could take Natalie's place. Certainly Vitza would not be able to do so. Natalie was catastrophically impetuous, infuriatingly self-centred, but her innate gaiety and buoyant vivacity ensured that life with her was never dull.

As the Vassilovich carriage-horses trotted through the now dark streets, Katerina was sure that not only was it going to be exceedingly dull in the future, it was also going to be aridly bleak. Her heart hurt, as if it were physically bruised. To think of Natalie was also to think of Julian. She had hoped to catch a glimpse of him at the station, to see him for one last time, but he had followed her father's advice to the letter and had not so much as looked out of his carriage window.

As the landau turned off the street and into the courtyard she reflected that if he and Natalie had not married, and if he had not proposed marriage to herself, she would not only be feeling devastated by his return to Britain, she would have the added misery of knowing it was extremely unlikely she would ever see him again. Now, ironically, that was not so. She was his sister-in-law. She would be aunt to his children. They would undoubtedly continue to see each other, however intermittently, for the rest of their lives.

Alexis's secretary was in the entrance hall as they entered the house.

'A Major Zlarin wishes to speak with you, sir,' he said respectfully. 'It's official business.'

Alexis nodded. There was going to be lots of official business in the next few days. He only hoped none of it would centre around Natalie.

'I'm going to bed, Alexis.' There were deep dark rings shadowing Zita's eyes. She turned to Katerina, kissing her lovingly on the cheek. 'I think you should too, my dear,' she said, aware that Katerina was as emotionally exhausted as herself. 'Today has been traumatic and we both of us need a good night's sleep.'

Katerina nodded in agreement. She had no intention of staying up any longer. There was no point. There was no-one to talk to over cups of cocoa; no-one in whom to confide.

As she began to walk up the grand staircase towards the room she would never again share with Natalie, she saw a tall, uniformed figure emerge from the Italian drawing-room behind her father's secretary. As they walked towards her father's study he looked upwards, towards her. He was in his early thirties with typically high Slavic cheekbones and olive skin. His hair was black and sleek and he exuded an air of indisputable authority. She looked away, thinking about Julian again, wondering how long it would be before her father received a telegram from him announcing that he and Natalie had arrived safely in England.

At breakfast the next morning Katerina said curiously, 'What did the major want with you last night, Papa? Was it anything to do with Sarajevo?'

Alexis hesitated, he had still not decided whether to keep the news of Austria's request for Natalie's extradition from her, in order to spare her further anxiety.

Zita, who believed that as a family they should all share everything, the bad news as well as the good, saved him from having to make a decision.

'Uncle Peter sent Major Zlarin with the news that the Austrians have asked for Natalie's extradition,' she said, her voice carefully controlled and calm. 'Apparently the terms of the request were most cordial and even a little hesitant.' She sliced an apricot with a pearl-handled fruit-knife. 'It would seem they are not at all sure of their ground. Sandro has replied to them, saying that Natalie returned from Sarajevo incubating scarlet fever and that she is at present too unwell to be questioned. Eventually he is going to inform them that a young man accosted Natalie and made a temporary nuisance of himself when she became detached from the Archducal party at the bazaar, but that she certainly didn't later recognize him as being Gavrilo Princip, that she is quite sure he was not and that her presence in Bosnia for questioning is unnecessary.'

'Apparently Sandro is hopeful that the matter will be pursued no further,' Alexis finished for her. 'Whether he is right or not only time will tell.'

As the week progressed and the Bosnian authorities announced the arrest of Danilo Ilich and Trifko Grabez, Alexis spent longer and longer hours at the *Konak*. On Sunday, a week after the assassinations, Katerina and Zita were taking afternoon tea in the garden when Alexis strode across the lawn towards them, grim-faced.

'What is it, darling?' Zita said apprehensively, rising to her feet as he approached. 'Is it more bad news?'

He shook his head. 'No, thank God. But both Sandro and Pasich think the Austrians are eventually going to declare themselves at war with us. I think they are right and I've decided it's about time we talked about what will happen to us, as a family, when they do so.'

Katerina put down her cake-fork and pushed her plate and slice of almond cake away from her, her appetite gone. 'What do you mean, Papa?' she said, her tummy tightening into unpleasant knots. 'Isn't it bad enough that we are separated from Natalie? Why should anything else awful happen to us?'

He sat down on an insubstantial looking garden chair. At forty-eight he was still handsome, still superbly physically fit. 'I fought the Turks, and if Austria declares war against us, then I shall fight the Austrians,' he said starkly. 'Sandro has already made it quite clear that as Crown Prince Regent and Commander-in-Chief of the Army, he doesn't intend issuing orders from the rear. He's going to call on every Serb to defend his country and he's going to lead the fighting from the front. The least I can do is to follow his example.'

'It may not come to it.' Zita's hands were clasped tightly in her lap, the knuckles bone-white. 'We must pray it doesn't do so.'

'Major Ivan Zlarin has been given instructions to defend Belgrade from attack across the Sava,' Alexis continued grimly, as if she hadn't spoken. 'He has promised me that as he will be in Belgrade and as I, most likely, will not be, he will afford you as much of his protection as he possibly can. That being the case, I think you should both become acquainted with him. He will be joining us for tea in five minutes or so.'

Katerina looked towards her mother. A week ago they had been a happy, united family with no cares other than Bella's infuriating habit of chewing every slipper, shoe and boot that she could find. Now Natalie and Bella were in Britain and soon, if Sandro's and Prime Minister Pasich's premonitions were correct, her father would be leading volunteer irregulars into battle.

A uniformed figure emerged from the rear of the house

and began to cross the terrace, striding towards the flight of stone steps leading down to the lawn.

Zita looked towards him meditatively, narrowing her eyes against the sun's glare. 'Is Major Zlarin married?' she asked with interest.

Alexis shook his head. 'No, he's a career soldier. Men like that don't have time for marriage.'

It had been over a week since Zita had smiled but a smile touched the corners of her mouth now as she said fondly, 'Don't be silly, darling. He simply hasn't met the right girl yet.'

As Major Zlarin approached, Katerina was aware her first impression of him had been correct. There was something very forceful about him, something almost threatening.

When he took hold of her hand, bowing slightly over it, his touch was cool and firm. It was with something of a shock that she met his eyes. They were very dark, very intense, and the admiration in them was blatant.

'I'm so glad you were able to join us for tea, Major,' Zita was saying, the loose sleeve of her turquoise chiffon dress fluttering in the air as she poured tea into a wafer-thin cup. 'It means my husband is also with us and for that I am grateful. I've seen very little of him since we returned from Sarejevo.'

Major Zlarin looked even more incongruous than Alexis, sitting on one of the fragile-looking garden chairs. He was a big man and there didn't look to be a spare inch of flesh on him. Everything was hard muscle.

'You were the witness of an historic event, Ma'am,' he said as he took the cup and saucer from her.

He had a clipped way of speaking and once again the faint touch of a smile brushed Zita's mouth. Unless she was very much mistaken, Major Ivan Zlarin was far more at ease issuing and receiving orders than he was in feminine company.

'So my husband tells me. It is his opinion that Princip's action will precipitate us into war.'

Major Zlarin's eyebrows rose slightly and Alexis said, 'My wife and daughter are fully aware of the situation in which Serbia finds herself. I have been telling them of the provisional arrangements that have been made in case of enemy attack and that you have very kindly promised to do all you can in the matter of affording them protection.'

'To do so will be an honour,' the major said, looking with uncomfortable directness towards Katerina.

Katerina dropped her eyes. If Major Zlarin was hoping to conduct a discreet flirtation he was going to be disappointed. Her heart and mind were full of Julian and she had no desire to flirt with anyone, least of all a stern-looking man more than ten years her senior.

The major circumspectly returned his attention to Alexis. 'I think, however, that perhaps it might be best if your family were to leave Belgrade now, before any attack is made.'

Alexis frowned as if he were considering the suggestion and Katerina said with a suddenness and vehemence that took them all by surprise: 'No, Papa! If Belgrade comes under attack there will be scores of injured, perhaps even hundreds. The medical sevices will need every possible willing volunteer. I may not have nursing experience but I have lots of common sense and I shall offer my services immediately.'

'No, my dear. That would be most unsuitable . . .'

'Surely not,' Zita interrupted composedly. 'After all, I shall be with her. I think we shall both make extremely able volunteer nurses.'

It was a blatant statement of her own intention to remain in Belgrade should it come under attack. Their eyes met and held and as he saw her determination he knew it would be futile to attempt to change her mind.

'Then if that is the decision you have both taken, I had better tell you exactly what the position is,' he said, conceding defeat and not altogether unhappy at the choice his wife and daughter had made. 'Belgrade cannot be easily defended and the Prince Regent has decided that only a small division be spared in the attempt to do so. The main bulk of the army will be elsewhere, trying to prevent Austro-Hungarian forces from sweeping over the borders to the north and west and I shall be with them. Major Zlarin and his men will prevent any crossing of the Sava from Hungary.'

It sounded strange to hear her father referring to Sandro so formally and Katerina wondered when she would see him again. The weekly family tea parties at the *Konak* had come to a very abrupt halt and she hadn't even had the opportunity to speak to him about Natalie.

Though she was scrupulously avoiding all eye contact with him, she was aware that Major Zlarin was again looking in her direction. She continued to think about Sandro and the heavy burden that was now on his shoulders. She knew that by nature he was a pacifist, but she also knew he would fight like a tiger to save his country from Austrian domination.

'And of course that is what they want to do,' her Great-Aunt Eudocia said a week later, seconds after she had swept into the Vassilovichs' drawing-room, Vitza and Max in her wake. 'Austria wants to incorporate Serbia into her monstrous empire, just as she has Bosnia and Herzegovina. Well, she's not going to do so.'

Max looked towards Katerina. 'Care for a walk?' he asked, clearly unwilling to sit through another of his grandmother's tirades.

Katerina nodded. She hadn't spoken to Max since Natalie had left for Britain. Her father had told her that

Max did not know Gavrilo Princip personally, that Princip had simply been pointed out to Max as being an undesirable and that when Max had seen Princip with Natalie and when he had told Vitza of Natalie's *sorties* into the *Golden Sturgeon* he had, quite naturally, referred to him by name.

'There is absolutely no link at all between Max and Princip,' he had said to her with relief when he had returned from his interview with Max, 'and the subject is not to be spoken of again. Is that understood, Katerina?'

She had nodded and asked one last, final question. 'And Sarajevo? Does Max know about Natalie's meeting with Princip in Sarajevo?'

'Good God, no! Nor is he to! We have enough problems at the moment without compounding them by trumpeting them to your Karageorgevich cousins!'

She had found it interesting that her father hadn't chosen to confide in Max and was about to ask him his reasons when she realized that it would be tactless to do so. Her father quite clearly didn't want to say another word on the subject, and had no doubt told Max and Vitza not to either.

Now, as she and Max left the room together, she wondered if he had accompanied his grandmother to the house with the express intention of flouting her father's wishes. As a small boy he had always been determinedly single-minded and it was a trait he hadn't grown out of.

Her assumptions were correct. Almost the instant they set foot on the terrace he said abruptly, 'What's the truth about Natalie's meeting with Princip, Trina? Had she met him before? Did she know what he was planning to do in Sarajevo? Is that why she's been bundled off to Britain? Because she's implicated in the assassinations?'

'Don't be an ass, Max!' She tried to give a derisive laugh

but it only sounded artificial and brittle. Wondering why on earth she had been foolish enough to have accepted his invitation to go for a walk she said with as much sincerity as she could muster, 'Natalie barely knew Princip. The day you saw them together it just happened that he sat at her table. That's all there was to it. Sorry to disappoint you, Max. If you're looking for a great drama you'll have to look elsewhere.'

'To a scandalously hasty and highly unsuitable marriage for instance?' he asked dryly. 'If Uncle Alexis wasn't panic-stricken over Natalie's friendship with Princip why did he marry her so precipitately to an Englishman? And why did the happy couple hare out of the country minutes after the ceremony as if the hounds of hell were at their heels?'

'You talk the most utter rot,' she said crossly. 'What sort of books do you read? English Bram Stokers? There were no hounds of hell at Julian and Natalie's heels. Only a shoal of good wishes.'

He grinned suddenly. 'Have you read Bram Stoker? Only an Englishman could have conjured up *Dracula*.'

For a vastly relieved moment she thought he had abandoned the subject of Natalie and then he said, 'And there was no shoal of good wishes, Trina. There was no-one at the wedding to proffer them. Grandmama said it couldn't have been a more hasty or shabby affair if Natalie had been eight months pregnant.'

'It's time Great-Aunt Eudocia kept her opinions to herself,' Katerina said with a blaze of rare anger. 'How dare she insinuate such a thing?'

'Well, when was the last time you remember any member of the family marrying in such undignified haste and without there being a huge family gathering and celebration? And why were no explanations or apologies given?'

'Why should there have been? Surely at the present moment people have more important things to worry about?'

'You mean Austria's reaction to Franz Ferdinand's death?'

She nodded, hoping the conversation would now veer on to a more general topic.

He shrugged, beginning to walk in the direction of the rose garden. 'Austria is old hat,' he said dismissively. 'Anyone in their right mind knows she'll attack us sooner or later. I'm more interested in the subject you're so keen to get away from. Namely, why Natalie was coerced into marrying an Englishman.'

'She wasn't coerced. She's very much in love with him.'

Max snorted derisively. 'Don't give me that, Trina. Natalie in love with an Englishman? Natalie is Slav through and through. Can you imagine Natalie wanting a son who is half-English? I can't. Where will he be educated? Eton? And can you imagine Natalie choosing to live anywhere but Serbia? The idea is ridiculous.'

'You're talking rubbish as usual, Max,' she said, wishing her throat wasn't so painfully tight, wishing she had remained in the drawing-room and endured Eudocia's opinions on Austria-Hungary. 'Natalie will be happy living wherever her husband lives.'

Max halted, his hands gracelessly in his trouser-pockets. 'Glad it wasn't you,' he said unexpectedly. 'I thought it was when I surprised the pair of you strolling around here the night of the Summer Ball. What was he doing? Trying to drum up family support? I should think he needed all he could get.'

They were standing beneath a huge truss of roses. Katerina remembered her happiness that night; her certainty that Julian was about to propose to her. Instead he had waylaid Natalie in the Italian room and he had asked her to be his wife. And Natalie had refused him. She wasn't remotely in love with him and if it hadn't been in order to spare their parents from being separated, she would never have married him.

'What will you do if it comes to war, Max?' she asked, changing the subject, hating the lies she was being forced to tell about Natalie's feelings for Julian, knowing that if she continued Max would most certainly see through them.

For once he looked at her as he spoke to her. 'Don't you know the slightest thing about me?' he asked bitterly. 'I'm an army officer and a Karageorgevich and Karageorgevich men have always fought.'

She had the grace to blush. Four years ago, when he was only twenty-one, he had covered himself with military glory while fighting the Turks. She had forgotten only because it was so difficult to imagine Max as a hero.

'I'm sorry, Max. I wasn't thinking . . .'

A bird landed in the roses and a shower of carmine petals fluttered down on to his shoulders. 'Do you ever think?' he asked abruptly. 'About me, I mean?'

'In what way?' The question was so odd she didn't know how to answer it. 'As an army officer? I so rarely see you in uniform that . . .'

'No,' he said tersely. 'Not as an army officer.'

For a moment she thought he was going to explain what he had meant but instead he merely shrugged his shoulders and turned away from her, beginning to walk back towards the house.

She stared after him in exasperation, relieved that his questions about Natalie had come to an end and hoping that she wouldn't have to suffer a similar barrage from Vitza.

Reluctantly she began to follow him back to the house, taking care not to catch him up, wondering if he gained pleasure from being so insufferably rude; wondering if the day would ever come when she would have a pleasant, civil conversation with him.

Eighteen days later, the tension under which they were all living, came to a climax.

'It's arrived,' Alexis said tautly as he hurried into the house on returning from the *Konak*. 'The Austrian Minister delivered it by hand to Pasich a little over an hour ago.'

Katerina put down the book she had been reading. Zita said sharply, 'Delivered what? An ultimatum?' She had been arranging white roses in a shallow bowl. Now she dropped them, hurrying across to him.

He nodded, sinking down into a chair, covering his eyes with his hand. 'It's a quite ridiculous document. Utterly insolent.'

She knelt down by the side of his chair, taking hold of his other hand, saying sombrely: 'What is going to happen? What kind of reply is going to be made?'

He dropped the hand that had been covering his eyes. 'We'll acquiesce to their demands. One of them was the arrest of two Serbians. Bizarrely enough there was no mention of the Black Hand or Apis and there was no mention of Natalie, thank God.'

'If we acquiesce to their demands will it be the end of the affair?' she asked uncertainly.

He shook his head, squeezing tight hold of her hand. 'No, my love. I doubt that Austria has the remotest intention of accepting any reply made to her. Sandro has decided to mobilize in order to be in readiness for every eventuality. I'm to go to Shabatz to take command of the irregulars who are already volunteering in droves.'

'You're going now? Today?' Her face was almost as pale as the roses she had been arranging.

'Yes, my love. With God's good grace the precautions Sandro is taking will prove to be unnecessary, but if they aren't . . .' He left the remainder of his sentence unsaid. If they weren't they all knew the hell that would follow.

'I think you're being ridiculously close-mouthed,' Vitza said to her pettishly two days later as she sat beside her on the large garden swing. 'I'm not asking you to talk to me about Natalie, though goodness knows I think you should. I'm simply asking you to tell me why an army major has walked into the house as if he owns it. It's quite obvious something is going on and it's utterly selfish of you not to tell me what it is.'

'There is nothing going on that you don't already know about,' Katerina said placatingly. 'Prime Minister Pasich is delivering his answer to Austria's ultimatum this evening. No-one believes the Austrian government is going to accept it. Major Zlarin is here because two of his men are being detailed here over the next few days.'

'I still think you know more about the situation than we do,' Vitza persisted mulishly. 'Max does as well. He thinks Natalie's marriage is definitely connected with the Princip affair. He thinks it is all very odd and it *is* very odd . . .'

Major Zlarin emerged from the house, two young soldiers in his wake, and began to walk round the side of the house towards the stables.

'What did you say the major's name was?' Vitza asked, changing the subject suddenly.

'Zlarin. Ivan Zlarin.'

'He's very attractive, isn't he? Very Slav and very male.' The major and the men with him disappeared from view and she said meditatively, 'I could have understood if Natalie had married a man like Major Zlarin, but why has she married a whey-faced Englishman?'

Katerina seldom lost her temper but she came close to doing so now. 'Julian Fielding is *not* whey-faced! And why should Natalie marry a man like Major Zlarin? He's nearly old enough to be her father!'

'I think older men far more attractive than young men,' Vitza said, trying to sound as if she had many mature admirers and failing badly. 'If there is a war, Max has arranged that I go with Grandmama to Nish. He says it's where Mr Pasich intends to move the government if Belgrade should ever be taken. It will be funny living so far south.' Her eyes were still on the corner Major Zlarin had so recently disappeared around. 'Do you think the major will be coming back?' she asked, clearly longing for him to do so. 'Do you think we could ask him what the latest news is?'

'No,' Katerina said firmly. Though she knew very little about Major Zlarin's character and personality she was quite sure he was a man who would have very little patience with the kind of fatuous questions Vitza would ask, or with the embarrassing simpering to which she would undoubtedly subject him.

The wait for Austria's reaction to the reply they had been given was nerve-wracking. Unable to bear the tension of waiting passively at home for news, Zita took Katerina with her to the *Konak*. Many other family members were also there, though not Eudocia or Vitza.

'Max has bundled them off to a friend's estate at Nish,' Zita said when Katerina wondered aloud where they were. 'He doesn't look remotely efficient, but there's far more to Max than meets the eye.'

It was Sandro who broke the news to his aunts and

cousins that Austria-Hungary had declared itself to be at war with Serbia.

'It is what we have expected,' he said gravely. 'But we are not friendless and the bullies of Vienna and Budapest are going to get an ugly shock. Russia is coming to our aid. The Tsar has already mobilized his armies. We are not going to be overrun by Austria-Hungary nor are we going to be forcibly annexed as Bosnia and Herzegovina were annexed. Every able-bodied man in the kingdom is being called to arms and is answering the call. My great-grandfather freed Serbia from Turkish domination and his spirit is far from dead. Austria-Hungary will come to regret bitterly the decision she has taken today. It will result not in victory for her, but in the destruction of her empire.'

He looked years older than he had done two short months ago when his unofficial engagement to the Grand-Duchess Olga had been announced in the same room. There was no sign at all now of endearing boyishness. The young man who had teased Natalie and played with Bella was now a sombre, grave-faced war leader.

'I think we should go home now,' Zita said quietly. 'That is where the hospital authorities will contact us should we be needed.'

Late that night there came the rare sound of a motor car roaring into the courtyard.

Abruptly Zita laid her embroidery down and walked swiftly out into the entrance hall, Katerina at her heels.

The visitor was Max. He was in army uniform and looked surprisingly authoritative.

'Yes, Max?' Zita asked anxiously. 'Have you brought a message from Sandro? From Alexis?'

He shook his head, looking beyond her to Katerina. 'No. I've just come to say goodbye.'

'Then would you like some tea, some *slivovitz*?' Zita asked, trying not to betray the surprise she felt.

'No,' he said gracelessly, still looking at Katerina. 'I haven't time.'

A startling suspicion occurred to Zita and she looked swiftly towards Katerina for confirmation of it. The suspicion died. Katerina was looking at Max with the same bewildered incomprehension she herself had done.

'Shall we go into the drawing-room and sit down for a few moments?' she suggested, wondering how any young Karageorgevich could be quite so charmless.

He shook his head. 'No. I must be going.'

The front door behind him was still open and Katerina could hear the engine of his staff-car still running. She wondered where he was going; if he were going to join her father at Shabatz on the Bosnian frontier. Most of all she wondered why he had gone to the trouble of visiting them in order to say goodbye, only to do so in such an offhand manner.

'Are you going to Shabatz?' she asked, as he continued to stand in the centre of the entrance hall, his officer's cap in his large, powerful hands.

'No. Tser.' He looked as if he were struggling to come to a decision. Finally he said abruptly: 'Look after yourselves, both of you. If you'd been my mother and sister I would have sent you to Nish whether or not you wanted to go,' and before either of them could make any reply he turned on his heel, leaving as precipitately as he had arrived.

'What a peculiar young man,' her mother said with a slight frown as they returned to the drawing-room. 'There are times when I find it hard to believe he's a Karageorgevich. Do you think perhaps his awkwardness stems from shyness?'

Despite all her tension Katerina giggled. 'Max isn't shy, Mama. He's just very, very odd.'

There came a distant booming sound and her amusement faded. It came again, this time nearer.

'It's begun,' Zita said tautly. 'It's artillery fire. The Austrians are trying to cross the Sava.'

Chapter Ten

Natalie stared up into Julian's sombre face in disbelief. '*Tomorrow?*'

He nodded, his arm tightening around her shoulders. All arrangements had been made days ago but he hadn't been able to bring himself to tell her. Right up to the last moment he had been praying that Germany and Austria-Hungary would pull back from the brink. It could have been done. Sir Edward Grey, Britain's foreign secretary, had been all for mediation and had put forward the suggestion that Austria should be summoned before a European court of justice and the matter settled there. Berlin had turned the suggestion down saying Germany couldn't possibly be party to summoning Austria before a court of justice when she was so clearly in the right. As a consequence the pace of mobilization had hotted up, each country determined that its armies would be in the best possible position by the time war was declared, each preparatory military measure taken occasioning a counter-measure by the opposing side until war was no longer merely possible but inevitable.

'But you can't go tomorrow!' Natalie protested as they were buffeted on all sides by a crowd running riot with patriotic zeal. 'I'll be all alone!'

'*Don't worry, love!*' a woman squeezed next to them shouted. '*You won't be on your own for long! It'll all be over by Christmas!*'

'Will it?' Natalie's eyes were fixed on Julian's face. He,

alone of everyone around them, was not in a celebratory mood. And he was a diplomat. He knew far more about the realities of the situation than the jingoistically singing and shouting Bank Holiday revellers did.

'They say so,' he said comfortingly, keeping the doubts he felt to himself. 'Let's get out of here. We've only a few hours left together and I don't want to share them with half of London.'

Extricating themselves from Whitehall was nearly as difficult as entering it had been. Newsboys were everywhere, shouting at the tops of their voices, *'Foreign Office official – ultimatum rejected!'* No-one seemed to want to go home. A group of Salvationists were lustily singing 'Onward Christian Soldiers' and nearby people were dancing to the rhythmic chant of 'Down with the bloody *Kaiser!* Down with the bloody *Kaiser!'*

Natalie clung to Julian as he forged a way through the crush and back to the point where they had left the chauffeured Mercedes. For the last week she had found international events hard to follow. If Britain had come to Serbia's aid by declaring war on Austria-Hungary she would have been shouting *'Zivio!'*, the Serb equivalent for 'Hurrah', as loudly as everyone else around her, but as far as she could understand this was not what had happened. Britain was at war with Austria-Hungary's ally, Germany, because Germany had marched her armies through neutral Belgium. And she didn't want to be alone in London just for the sake of Belgium.

'It isn't just for Belgium,' Julian had said to her patiently. 'It means Britain is Serbia's ally, just as France and Russia are. It means the Kaiser is going to get a bloody nose and the Habsburg empire is finally going to disintegrate.'

She held fast to that thought now as Julian pushed and shoved a way through the throng. If Julian's going away brought the day of South Slav freedom nearer, then she would conquer her horror at the thought of being alone in London. She would think of it as a sacrifice for a future Yugoslavia.

The Mercedes was still waiting for them, the chauffeur sitting with his window open, his cap pushed to the back of his head as he joined in the chant that had been taken up around him. '*Down – with – Germany! Down – with – Germany!*'

He stopped immediately he saw Julian, pulling his hat forward, springing out to open the rear door for them, his face scarlet.

Julian merely grinned. 'Get us home as quickly as possible,' he said, wondering how many days it would be before the young man enlisted and his parents had to find an older and less physically fit man to replace him.

Natalie scrambled into the car with relief. Trafalgar Square was now a sea of flag-waving, shouting humanity and the Mercedes's interior was a blissful oasis of comfort and calm.

'Why did I always think the British were reserved and undemonstrative?' she asked as the car began to inch its way out of the square and a group of young dare-devils began climbing Nelson's column, their shoulders draped in Union Jacks. 'They're just as crazily passionate as Slavs.'

'I thought you had already found that out,' he said in amusement, drawing her close.

She giggled and uncaring of the crowds pressing dangerously close to the sides of the slowly moving car, slid her arms around his waist. The heady, intoxicating pleasure of their lovemaking had come as a delicious surprise to her, so much so that there had been times when she had almost forgotten the circumstances under which they had married. Now, mindful of their coming separation she said huskily, 'I shall miss you, *chéri.*'

His arm tightened around her. He loved the way she often used French for endearments, Serb when she was angry. 'If the pundits are right and the war is over by Christmas, we won't be parted for too long.'

'What shall I do while you are away?' The car was now free of the worst of the crowds and picking up speed. 'Will I be able to do something to help with the war?'

'What on earth could you possibly do?' he asked, the amusement she always roused in him back in his voice.

'I don't know.' Her dark, delicately winged eyebrows pulled together in a deep frown. 'There must be something.'

She wondered what her mother and Katerina were doing in Belgrade. They would most certainly be doing something. She remembered the way in which Katerina had run from their Daimler in Sarajevo in order to help the injured after Nedjelko had thrown his bomb. Katerina wouldn't be sitting with her hands in her lap.

'I could be a nurse,' she said musingly, 'there's going to be a need for lots of nurses.'

'There's going to be a need for lots of *qualified* nurses,' Julian amended. 'There's also going to be a need for bandages. Rolling bandages is the sort of thing you and Mother could do at home.'

Her head had been resting comfortably against his shoulder. Now, hardly able to believe her ears, she pushed herself away from him, saying incredulously, 'You can't mean that? Rolling *bandages*? With your *mother*?'

She didn't know which idea most appalled her. Rolling bandages sounded to be the most boring occupation on earth and was certainly far too mundane a task for a Karageorgevich. As for embarking on such a task with his mother . . . She shuddered.

If Lady Fielding had exploded with wrath over their marriage Natalie would have understood and may even had some sympathy with her. What she didn't understand, because it was so totally foreign to her own volatile nature, was Lady Fielding's chill, contained, antipathy. The prospect of living with her without Julian's mediating presence was so appalling she felt physically ill. How he could envisage the two of them rolling bandages together was beyond all understanding.

'Well, what else can you do?' he was asking reasonably, impatient to reach home. Impatient to make love to her. 'There'll be lots of charities you can support and . . .'

With difficulty Natalie dragged her thoughts away from the domestic horror laying in wait.

'Serb charities? Charities that will send money to Serbia?'

'I was thinking of more general charities,' he said, mindful of her forays into Belgrade's *kafanas* and not wanting her to become involved with any Serb-dominated organization in his absence, however seemingly innocuous. 'The Red Cross, for instance.'

Natalie's interest waned. Raising money for charity sounded no more interesting than rolling bandages. She wanted to be doing something important; something exciting. She was sure that Katerina would be doing something exciting. Belgrade was under attack from Austro-Hungarian forces across the Danube and Sava and she longed to be there with Katerina; to know what was happening; to be involved.

As the Mercedes glided through the gas-lit streets she wondered what her father was doing, if he was fighting and if so, where. Sandro would be fighting. As Commander-in-Chief of all the army he would be leading his men from the front. Max would be fighting, too. He had covered himself with honour when fighting the Turks and would no doubt be doing so again now he was fighting the hated Austrians.

'Mother and Father will be waiting up,' he said to her as the car slid to a halt outside the house. 'I shall be leaving early in the morning and they'll want to say goodbye to me tonight. You go straight up to bed. I'll be with you as soon as possible.'

Natalie pushed her tumbled hair away from her face. It was now after midnight. How many hours were left to them? Five? Six? Begrudging his parents every minute of the time Julian was going to spend with them she stepped into the chandelier-lit entrance hall.

Almost immediately the drawing-room doors opened and Lady Fielding walked swiftly towards them, her long taffeta skirt crackling around her ankles. 'We heard the announcement on the wireless,' she said tautly to Julian, ignoring Natalie as if she didn't exist. 'We're now at war with Germany.' Her voice shook slightly and Natalie was intrigued. It was the first time she had heard a throb of emotion in that cool, flute-clear voice. 'I can still scarcely believe it. Can we *really* be at war with Germany? All because of a foolish incident in the Balkans?'

Natalie sucked in her breath and Julian said quickly, 'Go to bed, sweetheart. I shan't be long.'

For the first time Lady Fielding's eyes flicked towards Natalie. As her eyes took in her daughter-in-law's riotously unpinned hair a spasm of distaste crossed her face. Natalie read the look perfectly. In Lady Fielding's eyes she was an east European gypsy. A *Balkan*. Her eyes flashed fire. Only for Julian's sake did she keep silent. With a surge of self-control that neither her mother nor her father would have believed her capable of she crossed the hall and mounted the stairs, her head high, every line of her body declaring that far from being a gypsy she was a member of the Royal House of Karageorgevich.

Later, in bed, she said passionately, 'I hate your mother!'

'Don't. It's a useless exercise.' He lay on one elbow, looking down at her, his hard-muscled chest sheened with perspiration after their rapturous lovemaking. 'She didn't mean to be rude when she described the war as being triggered off by a damn fool thing in the Balkans. It's the way many English people view what has happened and you can hardly blame them.' With his free hand he began to stroke the inside of her thigh. 'Serbia and Bosnia are as remote to most of them as the stars.'

'She doesn't like me,' Natalie persisted, finding it hard to hold on to her indignation and fury when he was once again arousing in her the deep, delicious ache that only his lovemaking satisfied.

'True.' It was a truth so obvious he had long ago been forced to accept it. 'What you have to bear in mind, sweetheart, is that we cheated her of all the pleasures of a formal engagement announcement and of a splendid wedding at St Margaret's, Westminster. Even if our wedding had taken place in Belgrade, in the cathedral, she would have been happy. European royalty would have been among the wedding guests, King Peter would have been there, Prince Alexander, his sister and her husband, the son of Grand-Duke Constantine, Princess Xenia and Prince Danilo of Montenegro and perhaps even King Nikita. My parents would have been guests at the *Konak*, your father would have impressed my father with his political statesmanship, your mother would have charmed mine immediately and everything in the garden would have been lovely.'

His hand had moved over the tightly curling tangle of her pubic hair, his thumb gently brushing her clitoris.

'As it is, my mother hasn't met any of your family and finds it hard to believe in their existence. She's not a foolish woman but she's an unimaginative one. Our wedding was rushed and consequently, in her eyes, not respectable and so she thinks of you as being not respectable either.'

Natalie slid the palms of her hands up against his chest, succumbing lasciviously to the fierce, chaotic tumble of urges he was arousing in her. It no longer seemed important that his mother disliked her and she could no longer concentrate on the reasons he was giving for her not doing so. All she wanted was to be once more united with him, to be a part of him.

'Love me,' she whispered hoarsely. 'Now, *chéri*. Again.'

His eyes darkened with answering heat and as she parted her legs further, pulling him down on top of her, he abandoned his attempt to explain his mother's hostile reaction to her, entering her velvet-soft flesh with ardent urgency.

It was five in the morning when he left her. 'I'll write,' he said, dressing in civilian clothes for what he knew was going to be the last time for weeks, perhaps months. 'Diana will be home by the end of the week, so you will have company. You'll like her. She's enormous fun.'

Natalie sat on the bed in her lace-trimmed nightdress, hugging her knees, unconvinced. If Diana was anything like her mother she would most certainly not like her and anyway, she didn't want his sister's companionship. She wanted his.

'I'm going to miss you,' she said truthfully.

His fingers trembled slightly as he finished fastening his collar on to his shirt. He knew she would miss him and he was profoundly grateful, but he wanted her to say more. He wanted her to say she loved him.

'How will I hear news of Serbia now you are no longer at the Foreign Office?' she asked anxiously, the words he so yearned for remaining unsaid.

'You'll have to rely on the newspapers.' He kept his disappointment from his voice with difficulty. 'News from all the war fronts is going to be sparse, though. You mustn't expect too much.'

He put on his suit jacket and straightened his tie. His bags were already packed and waiting in the hall. He didn't feel like a warrior going off to battle. He felt like a man being cheated out of time with his wife by rabble-rousing, warmongering politicians, generals and emperors.

'Goodbye, sweetheart,' he said thickly.

She sprang from the bed, running towards him, flinging her arms around him. 'Come home safe!' she begged, wondering how she would survive in Britain if he did not do so. 'Come home before Christmas!'

He kissed her one last time, hard and deeply, and then he strode out of the room knowing if he stayed for even a second longer his self-composure would desert him.

She stood very still as his footsteps receded, as she heard him run lightly down the stairs, as he crossed the hall to the front door. The door opened and then closed. Very faintly she could hear the sound of the Mercedes's engine revving and then its distant throb as it faded into the distance. Then nothing.

Slowly she turned back to the bed and sat down on its edge. For the first time she was truly alone. Alone and among foreigners. Tears glittered on her eyelashes. How was she going to endure living beneath the same roof as her hostile mother-in-law? Who was she going to talk to? She had no friends in London. No blood relatives. She thought of her old friends and brushed her tears away, burning with shame. Gavrilo, Nedjelko and Trifko were enduring the horrors of Austrian imprisonment. Compared to them she had no burden to bear. Patriotic zeal pulsed through her. Somehow she had to be able to do something for Serbia.

Bella was cavorting at her feet and she picked her up, hugging her close. London was one of the biggest cities in the world and she couldn't be the only Serbian exile in it. She remembered the way exiled Bosnians and Croatians had gathered in the *Golden Sturgeon* and the *Acorn Garland* and the *Green Garland*. Wherever there were exiles there were meeting places for them. All she had to do was to find the meeting place for Serbian exiles in London.

Fizzing with purpose she scrambled back beneath the rumpled sheets to wait until the day had properly begun. Bella struggled to join her and she obligingly allowed her to do so. Life had purpose again. She wasn't going to be either bored or lonely. She would have her breakfast in bed as usual and then she would dress and take Bella for a walk, and in the course of it she would track down some fellow Serbs.

It wasn't as easy to do as she had supposed. London wasn't only vast, its streets and squares were a hideously complicated maze. She could find no heart to it, no easily obvious Bohemian Quarter. Tired and exhausted, having to resort to a taxi to get her home, she trailed into the Fielding home late in the afternoon.

'Milady has been most anxious about you,' the butler said in kindly warning as he opened the door to her. 'Miss Diana and Mr Edward have arrived.'

Natalie was uncaring. She didn't want to meet either of them. She wanted a hot bath, a substantial English afternoon tea and peace and quiet in order to work out a future strategy for the finding of fellow Serbs.

She had barely set foot in the entrance hall when all her hopes were dashed. The drawing-room doors opened and Lady Fielding swept out, resplendent in a gown of cream silk and a heavy rope of pearls.

'Natalie! Where *have* you been? London isn't Belgrade! You can't stroll the streets unaccompanied!'

It was the first time emotion of any sort had entered Lady Fielding's voice when talking to her and the first time she had condescended to address her by her Christian name. Natalie's puzzlement was momentary. Emerging hard on her heels from the drawing-room was a lively-faced, blonde-haired girl wearing a dress with a daringly *avant-garde* V-neck and a tall, lean young man who, apart from his narrow shoulders, bore a startling resemblance to Julian.

'I took Bella for a walk,' she said truthfully, adding even more truthfully, 'and I got lost. Even following the river didn't help.'

The blonde-haired girl didn't wait to be introduced. She darted past her mother, kissing Natalie effusively on either cheek, saying with husky, unchained laughter in her voice, 'I'm not surprised! If you follow the river you'll end up either in Gravesend or Henley! I'm Diana. Julian has told me all about you in his letters. A member of the Royal House of Karageorgevich! Lord, I'm so impressed! Do you know Crown Prince Alexander? Is he as dashingly attractive as his photographs? Does he really have to wear pince-nez or does he wear them in order to try and look older and even more distinguished?'

'You are being extremely vulgar, Diana,' her mother interposed crushingly. 'I'm sure Natalie doesn't have a close acquaintanceship with the Crown Prince and . . .'

'He's my cousin,' Natalie said to Diana, knowing she had met with a kindred soul, 'and my dearest friend.'

'There! I knew he would be!' Diana said triumphantly, tucking her arm companionably through Natalie's. 'Mama's being rather lax. She hasn't introduced you to Edward yet. Poor Edward is *en route* to the North Somersets. At least the North Soms are cavalry so he'll still be among his precious horses. Do say hello to Natalie, Edward. She'll be thinking you're deaf and dumb!'

The tall, leaner version of Julian stepped forward and shook her hand. 'I'm very pleased to meet you,' he said a trifle shyly. 'It must be difficult for you, being abandoned by Julian before you've had chance to make any friends in England.'

He didn't have Julian's strong personality but she sensed the same compassionate, generous nature and forgot that she had wanted to take her tea alone.

'I was looking for friends today,' she said engagingly, much to Diana's delight and Lady Fielding's horror. 'There must be other exiled Serbs in London and I want to meet with them.'

'You mean you've been out on your own . . . walking the streets . . . looking for *Serbs*?' Lady Fielding had turned the sickly cream-colour of her tea-gown. 'Dear Lord! What if you had been seen? Recognized? Edward, please explain to her that she *cannot* walk around London looking for . . . looking for *Serbs*!'

A suspicion of a smile tugged at the corner of Edward's mouth. 'You'll never find anyone just walking around London looking for them,' he said kindly. 'If you want to make contact with fellow Serbs, and I can understand your wanting to do so, there are easier ways of going about it.'

'There may well be,' his mother interrupted tartly. 'But it would be most improper for Natalie to take advantage of them.'

'I do not think my mother or father or Julian would think it improper,' Natalie said swiftly. 'I always made my own friends in Belgrade and my parents and King Peter never objected to my doing so.' She thought of Gavrilo and Nedjelko and the *Golden Sturgeon* and crossed her fingers so that the lie wouldn't matter.

'London is not Belgrade.' Lady Fielding's thin-bridged,

faintly aquiline nose took on a white, pinched look as she kept her fury at being spoken to in such a manner in check with difficulty. 'You are now married to an Englishman and you must adopt English manners and customs.'

'I don't think you're being very understanding about this, Mama,' Edward said gently. 'Natalie may be married to an Englishman but thanks to this wretched war she's not going to have the benefit of his companionship for quite some time. If she had been living in London for a little longer it wouldn't matter so much. Julian would have introduced her to his friends and they would now be her friends. As it is, she has no friends of her own and I think Julian would want her to make some.'

'He wouldn't wish her to do so unescorted and unintroduced!'

'I'll escort her,' Edward said easily, bending down and scooping up an exhausted Bella from where she had been lying at Natalie's feet. 'I've another three days in town before leaving for my regiment. Three days should be long enough to find out where Serbs meet in London.' He tickled Bella under her chin. 'This dog needs a drink. Do you think she would be happy with Lapsang Souchong or should I ring down to the kitchens for a bowl of water?'

Natalie flashed him a sunny, grateful smile and as he led the way back into the drawing-room for afternoon tea she said chattily, her arm still linked in Diana's, 'I'm sure Bella will adore Lapsang Souchong. She is a very well-bred dog and was originally a present from the Tsaravich to Crown Prince Alexander. Sandro had gone to St Petersburg to attend his nephew's christening. His sister, Hélène, is married to the son of Grand-Duke Constantine. While he was there he became unofficially engaged to one of the grand-duchesses and it was then that the Tsarevich gave him Bella.'

She and Diana had sat down by now and Diana was

staring at her wide-eyed. 'Crown Prince Alexander is to marry one of the grand-duchesses? Oh, which one? Do tell! And have *you* been to St Petersburg? Have you met the Tsar and Tsarina?'

Lady Fielding cleared her throat. 'I think this conversation is far too frivolous to be in good taste under the circumstances, Diana.'

'What circumstances?' Diana turned away from Natalie and looked towards her mother. She had very blue eyes and they were now very wide. 'Because of the war? But Russia and Serbia are our allies! We should be learning all we can about them! And don't you think it romantic that this little dog was originally the Tsaravich's? I do. I think it absolutely spendid.'

Her mother didn't deign to reply. She didn't believe one word of Natalie's prattle about the Tsar and Tsarina and Crown Prince Alexander. The girl was a charlatan as no doubt Julian would eventually discover. He had been taken in by far too obvious physical charms, charms that Lady Fielding found far too exotic to be merely Balkan. Far from believing her daughter-in-law to be a member of the Royal House of Karageorgevich, Lady Fielding was of the opinion that Natalie's raven hair and sweeping black-lashed eyes were indications she was not even Serbian but Armenian, and most likely Jewish-Armenian.

Natalie was uncaring of Lady Fielding's frigid antipathy. Diana was her friend, Edward had become her temporary knight in shining armour and tomorrow he was going to help her make contact with London's Serbian community. Life was fun and interesting again. She took another cream cake, wondering how she could possibly have allowed herself to become so despondent, wondering if London's exiled Serbs would regard her as Sandro's representative and if they would treat her accordingly.

* * *

They treated her with extreme respect, which was profoundly gratifying. Though there was no-one there of her own age group or social class the language spoken was her own. Talk was of nothing but Serbia, of how the Serbian army was rumoured to be holding thousands of Austrian troops at bay across the Danube and the Sava and of how even the arthritically-afflicted King Peter had taken up arms in his country's defence. By the time Natalie left the church hall in which they met she was more homesick than ever. She didn't want to be in London, not truly knowing what was happening in her country's fight for survival, her only news wild rumours. She wanted to be in the heart of Belgrade, as she was sure Katerina still was.

Over the next few weeks Diana's friendship was her salvation. Despite her angelic blonde hair and baby-blue eyes she was not classically beautiful as her mother was beautiful. It was her liveliness that gave her the illusion of beauty and it was her liveliness to which Natalie wholeheartedly responded.

All Diana's friends were fun and all too many of them were leaving London before Natalie could become properly acquainted with them.

'Cousin John has joined the Derbyshire Territorials, Rupert is with the Gloucester Yeomanry, Charles is training with the Grenadiers at Richmond,' Diana said despairingly, ticking them all off on her elegantly manicured fingers. 'There's going to be no-one left in London soon. Even the girls are dispersing as fast as flies in a thunderstorm. Every mother in the city seems bent on taking a Red Cross hospital or dressing-station to France. The list is endless, the Duchess of Sutherland, the Duchess of Westminster, Lady Dudley, Lady Forbes. All the daughters are going too, to nurse. Do you think that's what we should do, Natalie? Nurse in France?'

'I'd rather nurse in Serbia,' Natalie said fiercely. 'It said in *The Times* that a Dr Elsie Inglis is taking a Scottish Women's Hospital unit out to Serbia.'

Diana looked doubtful. Serbia seemed a mite too far away and, lacking the Duchess of Sutherland and the Duchess of Westminster's throng, not very appealing.

'I think I'd rather nurse in a hospital converted from a chateau or a casino,' she said with stark honesty. 'The Duchess of Westminster has set up her hospital in the casino at Le Touquet, among the pine woods. I can imagine myself there. I can't quite imagine myself in Serbia.'

Natalie could. She had wept when she had read of how Scottish girls were leaving for her homeland from Southampton. It seemed so unfair that they could go and she, a Karageorgevich, could not.

All through September her depression increased. September was a wonderful month in Serbia. As she took Bella for desultory walks around Regent's Park she thought of how plums would be being harvested for *slivovitz*, how the cattle would be returning from summer pasture, how the peasants in the villages would be celebrating the harvest with feasting, dancing the *kolo* with wild abandon to the heady music of flutes and violins. Then reality would assert itself and she would look around her at staid English nannies wheeling perambulators and at neat and tidy flower-beds where nothing turbulent or lavish was ever allowed to grow.

October was worse. In October *The Times* tersely announced that the trial of those accused of assassinating Archduke Franz Ferdinand and his wife had begun in Sarajevo.

She scoured every newspaper for days after for further news reports but though there were glaring headlines about Belgian cities falling to German troops and of how a decisive, victorious battle had been fought on the banks of the Marne, there was not a whisper of information about the trial of those who had triggered off the conflagration.

'I don't understand it,' she had wailed to Diana. 'How can there not be anything in the newspapers?'

'Well I don't understand it either. Ask Father. He'll know.'

Natalie's relationship with Julian's father had become, when Lady Fielding was not present, affectionately friendly.

'There won't be any information to speak of in British newspapers,' he said to her with gruff gentleness. 'It's an Austrian trial and Britain is an enemy belligerent. There won't be any British reporters present in the courtroom, nor will there be any reporters from Serbia, France or Russia. I imagine that the item in *The Times* was culled from an American newspaper, though I doubt if even the Americans have a correspondent attending the trial. They probably picked it up from an Austrian or German newspaper report.'

'Then how am I to find out what is happening?' she asked, appalled. 'How will I know when sentence is passed?'

He frowned slightly. 'Does it matter that you know, my dear? I'm rather perplexed as to why you are so concerned. Whatever happens to the young men who sparked off Europe's present carriage-ride to hell, it can have no bearing on current events. The victory on the Marne is good news of course but poor Belgium is suffering dreadfully. Ghent, Bruges and Ostend have all fallen.'

Sobs of frustration rose in her throat. Julian had stressed to her long ago the importance of no-one knowing about her friendship with Gavrilo. As a consequence his father had no inkling of it and so there was no way he could understand her passionate need for information. She wondered what he would say if she were to tell him of how very near she had come to being a defendant in the trial now taking place in Sarajevo. Instead she said, 'How can I get hold of American newspapers?'

'I'm not sure, my dear. I'll make enquiries of course. What you have to bear in mind is that any newspaper coming from America will be several weeks old by the time it reaches Britain and as the trial has already started it will very likely be over and done with long before you are able to read even an interim report of it.'

There was nothing she could do but wait in an agony of suspense for *The Times* to receive more information on the trial from *The New York Times*. She wondered how long she would have to wait; how long the trial would last.

It was the first week in November when the bald announcement that Gavrilo Princip, Nedjelko Cabrinovich, Trifko Grabez, Civijetko Popovich and Vaso Cubrilovich had all been found guilty of treason and murder. Gavrilo, Nedjelko and Trifko had been sentenced to twenty years in prison, Vaso Cubrilovich to sixteen years and Civijetko Popovich to thirteen years. Danilo Ilich, also listed as an assassin, and four of the plotters' principal helpers were found guilty of treason and being accessory to murder and, being over twenty years of age, had been sentenced to death by hanging.

By the time she had finished reading her hands were trembling so much that the newspaper fell from her fingers. Who were the 'principal helpers' who had helped her friends and who were now going to hang? Who were Civijetko Popovich and Vaso Cubrilovich? She had never heard of either of them, nor had she ever heard Gavrilo mention Danilo Ilich by name.

She hugged her arms wishing Julian was with her.

Julian knew how nearly her name had come to being listed with those of the 'principal helpers', how very nearly she had come to standing trial on charges of being an accessory. He would understand the mental and emotional trauma she was now undergoing and he would, as always, be able to comfort her. But wishing that Julian was with her was a futile exercise. He wasn't with her and he wouldn't be until his officer training was completed and he had leave before being posted to France.

At night, alone in the brass-headed bed they had shared so joyously, she cuddled Bella and tried to ward off nightmares by remembering that Gavrilo and Nedjelko and Trifko were not among those who were going to be hanged.

It was at night, also, that she most missed Katerina. All their lives they had shared a bedroom, giggling and gossiping together in the darkness before going to sleep. Now she had only Katerina's letters for company and they were often so delayed in arriving that she could never be sure if her mother and Katerina were still nursing or even if they were still in Belgrade.

For hour after hour she would lie in the darkness, comforted by the sound of Bella's gentle breathing, trying to imagine what was taking place at home, wishing she were there, wishing the war was over and that she could return.

By December she had even more to think about. Julian had written to her, telling he was leaving for France in a month's time and would be home for five days prior to sailing. Not only was she fervently looking forward to seeing him again, she had something quite momentous to tell him. Something about which she didn't truly know whether to be pleased or appalled. She was going to have a baby.

Chapter Eleven

As the sound of shelling intensified Katerina and Zita ran out into the courtyard. They weren't the only ones anxious to know from which direction the bombardment was coming. Windows in the maids' quarters were being thrown open and the butler and two footmen ran outside hard on Katerina and Zita's heels.

'The Austrians are trying to cross the Sava, ma'am,' the butler said tautly, echoing Zita's own immediate assessment of the situation. 'If they succeed the city will be overrun within an hour. Perhaps if we evacuated now, ma'am . . .'

'No.' Zita had made her mind up long ago about what action she would take if the city were overrun and evacuation did not feature in her plans.

One of the maids clustering at the windows began to cry and another sobbed hysterically, '*We're going to be killed! We're all going to be raped and killed!*'

A barrage of shellfire rained down on what Zita judged to be the Kalemegdan Gardens and she turned and looked towards the terrified faces crowding the open windows. Girls frightened half out of their wits were going to be a hindrance to her in the hours and days ahead, not a help, and she said to the still anxiously hovering butler, 'If any of the household staff wish to leave tell them they may do so.'

'Yes, ma'am. And yourself and Miss Katerina, ma'am? For Miss Katerina's sake perhaps it would be better if . . .'

'No,' Zita said again firmly and as she did so she was aware of a new, ominous sound merging with the thunder of exploding shells. It was the sound of hoof-beats and iron-rimmed wheels hurtling over cobbles. For a brief moment she wondered if she was behaving irresponsibly in choosing to remain in a city that was bound to be eventually overrun. She looked across at Katerina about to suggest, for her sake, that perhaps they should leave for Nish.

Katerina's eyes met hers. 'Should we make our way to the hospital now, Mama?' she asked, her eyes resolute, her voice perfectly steady.

Another flurry of shells came screaming over the city from the Hungarian banks of the Danube. This time they landed fearfully near, somewhere in the vicinity of Terazije Square.

Despite the horror they were caught up in a small smile touched the corners of Zita's mouth. In a terrifying situation she and her daughter were in fundamental agreement with each other and it was a gratifying sensation.

'Yes,' she said, turning and beginning to walk back into the house. 'We'd better go on foot. I don't want to put the horses at risk.' She turned to her unhappy butler. 'Make sure all the grooms are down at the stables. The horses must be terrified by the noise and they'll need reassuring and soothing. Tell the maids they can leave at any time but that while there is a bombardment they are safer in the house than out on the streets. And tell them to shut their windows and to draw their curtains so that if the windows are blown in they won't be injured by flying glass.'

'Yes, ma'am.'

'And have the cellars opened up. There are going to be hundreds of people fleeing the east of the city looking for whatever shelter they can find.'

'But the wine, ma'am!' the butler protested in horror.

'If city riff-raff shelter in the cellars not a bottle will be safe!'

'And not a bottle will be safe if the Austrians overrun us,' Zita retorted tartly. 'I'd rather the wine was drunk by fellow citizens than by Austrian troops!'

As they stepped into the chandelier-lit entrance hall Katerina said, 'We could turn the ballroom into a public shelter as well, it wouldn't be as safe as the cellars but it would hold a vast number and be far safer than the streets or the wood houses down by the Sava.'

'And if enough kitchen staff volunteer to stay we can provide soup,' Zita said, determining that if the kitchen staff fled she would make it herself. She turned again towards her dazed butler. 'Get Laza to supervise the preparing of the ballroom. Tell him that everything flammable should be removed and heavy material pinned over the mirrors and windows.'

'Yes, ma'am. At once, ma'am.'

As he hurried off to do her bidding two stolidly calm figures stepped forward. 'If you're going down to the hospital tonight, I will come with you,' Helga said flatly, a white, capacious apron tied over her serviceable gown as an indication that she was ready to undertake any task asked of her, no matter how bloody.

'And I shall come too, of course,' a less phlegmatic voice said with equal firmness.

Both Zita and Katerina stared at Miss Benson as if she were an apparition. As Natalie's governess she had had no tasks to perform since the day Natalie had accompanied them to Sarajevo. Zita never liked dismissing anyone and she had had too much on her mind to think of dismissing the quiet young Englishwoman who had striven diligently and in vain to further Natalie's classical education. She had simply assumed that Miss Benson would be looking around for alternative employment and that when such employment was found, she would then say her goodbyes.

Now she said doubtfully, feeling guilty for not having encouraged Miss Benson to return to Britain while it was safe for her to do so, 'Conditions are going to be extremely unpleasant in the hospital and the streets are very unsafe . . .'

'Just as they no doubt are in Bruges and Ostend and other cities the Huns and their allies are reducing to rubble,' Miss Benson said with asperity, her mousy hair pulled neatly off her face and secured in a bun, her hazel eyes resolute. 'I'm an Englishwoman and if I were not here, but home in Lincolnshire, I would be volunteering for a nursing unit in Flanders. As I'm *not* home, and not likely to be for some time, I shall nurse Serbian soldiers and civilians instead of Belgian and French soldiers and civilians. We're all allies together, aren't we?'

Helga cleared her throat and Zita and Katerina stared at her, appalled. Miss Benson said swiftly, 'I'm sorry, Helga. I didn't mean to insinuate . . . I wasn't referring to *you!*'

'I've never been ashamed of being German,' Helga said, unperturbed, 'and I'm not ashamed of being German now. I'm just going to forget about it for a little while. Injured men won't mind what accent I have if I'm tending them. They might even think I'm a Montenegrin.'

In all the years that Helga had been in Karageorgevich service it was the nearest she had ever come to a joke.

'Of course they won't mind,' Zita said, laying a hand reassuringly on Helga's arm, her eyes suspiciously bright. 'Now let's go. It's no use waiting for a lull in the shelling. There quite obviously isn't going to be one.'

It was the first time in her life that Katerina had ever known her mother to set off, on foot, down Prince Milan Street. Her amusement at the novelty soon vanished. Fires were raging in the east of the city and the night air was thick with the acrid smell of smoke and ash. Despite the obvious danger of being out in the open when shells were being fired so indiscriminately, the streets were thronged.

'*Don't go towards the rivers!*' a woman shouted out to them, a shawl pulled close around her head, half a dozen terrified children at her heels. '*The Austrians are trying to cross both the Danube and Sava! Head west, not east!*'

Carriage horses galloped wildly down the street, half demented by the roar and scream of mortars.

'The side-streets will be safer!' Katerina shouted to her mother. 'The fewer horses there are, the less chance there is of our being run down!'

Agreeing with her Zita plunged down the first alleyway she came to, hoping to God that her sense of direction wasn't playing her false and that they would emerge in the vicinity of the hospital.

'It never occurred to me the Austrians would be able to fire on us from across the river,' Miss Benson gasped as they hurried as fast as they dared over the treacherous cobbles. 'I always thought the river so pretty and even though I knew Hungary was on the opposite bank I never thought of it as being *near!*'

'It's near all right,' Helga panted as they turned into another, even narrower alleyway. 'The Austrians can shell Belgrade twenty-four hours a day if they choose to!'

Katerina was just about to say robustly that Serbian cannon could also fire on Austrian positions from the advantageous heights of the Kalemegdan Bluff when she saw the sign over the café they were hurrying past. It was the *Golden Sturgeon*.

It was crowded with students seeking shelter from the firing; students who were possibly homeless as Natalie had said so many of them were. She saw the little marble-topped tables and wondered if any of those taking shelter were friends of Gavrilo Princip's; if they realized that it was in that café that the holocaust now taking place had been initially so idealistically and recklessly triggered.

'I can hear our guns firing back!' her mother shouted to her over the crashing sound of artillery fire. 'Whatever their range they'll be able to hit whatever is in the water! The Austrians won't land! Major Zlarin won't allow them to!'

Katerina could only hope fervently that her mother was right. As they emerged from the alleyway she could see the lights of the hospital and lots of people, some of them injured, converging on it.

'Scores of houses by the river have been demolished!' a complete stranger shouted across to her. 'Even the *Konak* has been shelled!'

Katerina wondered how many female members of her family were taking shelter there and if any of them had been hurt. At least she didn't have Natalie to worry about. Natalie was safe in London and the English Channel was far broader than the Sava and Danube. London wouldn't be under shellfire nor, unless there was a catastrophe of mammoth proportions, was it ever likely to be.

As they hurtled into the hospital a nursing sister ran to greet them, saying with heartfelt relief, 'Thank God for extra pairs of hands! We have no wounded soldiery yet but the slums near the river have come under terrible shelling and we have lots of injured children. Do any of you have nursing experience?'

'I have,' Helga said, looking as efficient and capable as a hospital sister in her starched white apron.

'Then go up to Ward Three. The rest of you make your way to what was the staff dining-room. Porters and a handful of nurses are busy filling it with emergency beds. Tell the nurses you are taking over from them and they can go back to their wards.'

Katerina wondered if her mother had ever in her life been spoken to so peremptorily before and doubted it. She looked across at her, wondering if she was going to politely say that she had come to the hospital in order to nurse, not to make beds, but her mother's aristocratically beautiful face was unperturbed.

'When you have finished in the dining-room, come up to Ward Three,' the nursing officer said as a groaning woman was led past them, blood seeping through the makeshift bandage around her head. 'You're going to be thrown in at the deep end I'm afraid. Shell splinters don't make tidy wounds.'

Katerina had never made a bed in her life, especially a bed made up of a coarse linen sheet and a rough blanket. Miss Benson, seeing her dilemma, said: 'If we work as a pair we'll make up twice as many beds twice as quickly.'

Katerina agreed gratefully, noting with amazement that her mother had already set briskly to work, bed-making as if it were a task to which she had been born.

As they made up bed after bed the deafening noise of the bombardment continued, the hospital's walls shuddering with the vibration.

'Wounded soldiers are being brought in now,' a porter said to her as he brought her yet another armful of blankets from the store room. 'Word is that we've trounced the troop ships which were trying to land. It won't stop them from trying again, though. The sooner the allies send aid, the better.'

Katerina pressed a hand against her aching back, wondering by what route aid would arrive. It wasn't only men and ammunition that were needed. It was doctors and nurses and hospital supplies.

'Let's hope the Austrians haven't managed to cross the Sava anywhere else,' Miss Benson said to her quietly as they moved on to yet another bed. 'Parts of the river can be crossed from Bosnia, can't they? And what about the Drina?'

Katerina didn't want to think about the Drina. Her father was at Shabatz and if the Austrians made any attempt to invade from Bosnia he would be in the forefront of the fighting.

The night seemed endless. Occasionally there were respites. Suddenly the noise of gun and artillery fire would stop but it never stopped for long.

'We don't have enough shells and cartridges to keep this pace up for long,' the informative porter said to her as he squeezed the last makeshift bed into place. 'Where the hell are the Russians, that's what I'd like to know. And a few Frenchies wouldn't go amiss neither.'

Her mother interrupted the conversation by saying: 'There's no more to do here. Every possible bed is made up. Let's go along to Ward Three and be useful there.'

With a tightening of her tummy muscles Katerina followed her mother and Miss Benson from the bed-filled dining-room. She was by nature cool and calm and she knew that she possessed more than a fair share of common sense, but were those qualities going to be enough to enable her to cope with what lay ahead? She had never changed a dressing, never even seen a serious burn.

'Don't worry,' Miss Benson said, coming again to her rescue. 'We won't be asked to do anything beyond our capabilities. Our work will be to carry out all the mundane tasks in order that the nurses will have more time for emergency nursing.'

Katerina flashed her a grateful smile aware that in the last hour or so their relationship had subtly altered into one of friendship. She wondered what Miss Benson's Christian name was and said tentatively: 'I think we should be on first name terms, don't you?'

Miss Benson shot her an answering smile that made her plain face suddenly pretty. 'My Christian name is Celestria, but I much prefer to be called Cissie.'

In happy, new-found camaraderie they followed Zita up a flight of stone stairs and into the bloody mayhem of Ward Three.

Major Ivan Zlarin stood wearily on the heights of the Kalemegdan Bluff and looked across the now empty river towards the distant banks. It was dawn and respite from enemy shelling had come at last. He took a cigarette from a pocket of his jacket and lit it, inhaling deeply, wondering if the Austrians were going to hold fire long enough for his men to get some much needed rest. For one night they had held an Austrian invasion of Belgrade at bay. For how many more nights would they be able to do so?

He stared broodingly down at serpentine-green water littered with empty shell-cases. The river needed mining. If it were mined Austrian monitors would no longer be able to sail so close to the city and fire upon it with such impunity. He wiped beads of perspiration from his forehead. He had no mines, God damnit, nor had he any torpedoes and torpedo tubes. The only way he could continue to deter monitors and troop ships was by keeping them under constant artillery fire.

He blew a wreath of smoke into the acrid air. Geographically, he had the advantage. There were a whole series of heights looking down over the river and he had seen to it that all were equipped with cannon. If it weren't for the two islands in the Sava, he could have been said to be holding the upper hand.

The islands; his heavy black brows met as he frowned even more deeply. Gyspy Island and Little Gypsy Island were Habsburg possessions lying mid-way between the Austro-Hungarian banks of the Sava and the Serbian banks, providing a screen behind which Austrian monitors could take refuge from his shellfire.

He needed to capture the islands, but how? Without

228

monitors and mines and torpedoes how could he conduct any fight on either the Sava or the Danube? His deep thought was disturbed by the sound of running footsteps.

'I did as you asked, Major Zlarin!' a young corporal gasped, floundering to a halt. 'I went to the Vassilovich *konak* but neither Madame Vassilovich nor her daughter were there. A butler seems to have taken over and has opened the house to scores of people seeking shelter from the shelling. He said he was under Madame Vassilovich's instructions to do so and that she and her daugher are at the hospital and have been all night.'

'Injured?' Ivan snapped, forgetting temporarily all about the problem of the islands. 'Which of them was injured?'

'Neither, sir.' The corporal pressed a hand to his side and struggled to regulate his breathing. 'They're there as nurses, sir.'

A spasm of relief passed over Ivan's hard-boned face. 'And the city?' he asked, mindful that it was the city he was striving to protect.

'Not good, sir. Austrian howitzers got the *Konak* in their sights and part of the roof has gone. The British Legation has been shelled and a hole you could drive a tank through has been blasted in the eastern gable of the Russian Legation. The wood houses near to the river suffered the worst. Fires are still raging and people are taking advantage of the lull in the fighting and leaving the city in droves.'

'Go to the hospital. Tell Madame Vassilovich that my advice is for her and her daughter to leave immediately for Nish. Tell her you are under instructions to accompany them there and afford them protection. Do you understand?'

'Yes, sir. I'll go at once, sir.'

Jubilant at the thought of such an easy assignment the

corporal drew in a ragged breath, saluted, and set off at a trot down the hill towards the smoking, ravaged streets.

Ivan turned and looked once more out across the river. The sun was beginning to rise now, streaking the sky with long piercing fingers of gold and red. Katerina Vassilovich. Even at a moment like this, when the defence of the city rested on his shoulders, it was impossible for him to keep from thinking of her. She possessed an air of calm and tranquillity that had at first intrigued him and then had become vitally necessary to him. It was soothing to be in her company. She didn't chatter and giggle as so many girls her age did. There was emotional and intellectual substance to her and for the first time in his life he had found himself thinking more and more about marriage.

Zara would not be pleased at his decision. His widowed cousin, only a year or so his junior, had been his mistress for the last ten years. Until recently it had been an exceedingly satisfactory arrangement, then he had met Katerina and begun to be aware of how frumpily plump and middle-aged Zara had begun to look. He doubted if Katerina would ever look middle-aged. Certainly Zita Vassilovich didn't do so, though she was easily in her mid-forties, and Katerina possessed the same kind of Raphaelite beauty as her mother.

His eyes sharpened, all thoughts of love fleeing. From the eastern end of Gypsy Island Austrian monitors were again easing into view.

'*Get back to your positions!*' he shouted to his tired troops. '*Prepare to fire!*'

It was mid-morning before Katerina and Zita made their way home in order to check on the arrangements made in their absence for providing shelter for the city's poor. Both of them were more physically exhausted than they had ever been before in their lives. The sights that met their eyes as they hurried through wood-paved Terazije Square and down Prince Milan Street, did nothing to cheer them. Though there had been a lull in the bombardment much earlier in the morning, it had continued almost without a break ever since and house after house had sustained damage.

All around them people were fleeing. Ox-drawn carts laboured westwards piled high with domestic possessions and with the elderly and infirm. Children scampered alongside, some bright-eyed at the drama and excitement, others bewildered and frightened. Belgraders too stubborn to leave, or too poor to make the attempt, were valiantly shopping for bread and collecting water from public pumps as if shrapnel and incendiary bombs were an everyday part of their lives.

'As I think they are going to be,' Zita said as an electric-tram car rattled past them for all the world as if it were an ordinary morning. 'There's no real military purpose to this constant firing on the city. All the military targets are on the heights overlooking the river. This constant lobbing of shells and incendiaries is purely to cause panic and destroy property and it's my guess the Austrians are going to continue with it until the city is either completely deserted or flattened.'

'Or both,' Katerina said tautly as they passed a ramshackle little cottage with its upper storey completely blasted away. A black-garbed Moslem woman was standing in the doorway, silent tears rolling down her face.

Zita went across to her, saying gently, 'Your house is far too unsafe to stay in. Bring your family and belongings to the Vassilovich *konak* on Prince Milan Street.'

The woman knuckled her tears away, staring at her first in suspicious disbelief and then, when she realized that Zita was serious, in profound gratitude.

'If you know of anyone else needing shelter, tell them

they can find it there,' Zita added, saying as she returned to Katerina, 'Let's pray I'm right about the strength of the walls and the safety of the cellars. I'll never forgive myself if I'm not.'

Katerina didn't answer her. The great iron gates leading to the courtyard had come into view and she was fearful of what might meet their eyes when they reached them. The soundly-built *Konak* had been hit by shellfire and so it wasn't beyond the realms of possibility that their own home was damaged. Steeling herself for the worst she took a deep steadying breath as they approached the gates.

The roof, walls and windows were all intact and she let out a shuddering sigh of relief. Their own house was further west of the rivers than the *Konak* and the Legations. Perhaps it was out of reach of Austrian cannon and howitzers. Perhaps it would never be hit and the strength of its walls and cellars never put to the test.

'I'm going to check that the ballroom and cellars have been turned into suitable public shelters,' her mother said, a slight unsteadiness in her voice betraying her own vast relief, 'and that Cook is running a soup-kitchen. Then we must sleep before returning to the hospital, even if it's only for a couple of hours.'

Katerina nodded, so tired she wondered how she was still managing to walk. There were handcarts and ox-carts littered all over the courtyard, testament to how quickly word had spread that shelter was to be found within. Hoping fervently that her own bedroom hadn't been transformed into a sanctuary for strangers she accompanied her mother up the steps and into a house scarcely recognizable as being the one they had left only twenty-four hours earlier.

Children could be heard shouting and babies crying and there was a stale indefinable smell in the air.

There was no sign of the butler, instead it was Laza who greeted them.

'We're doing our best, Ma'am,' he said to Zita. 'Trouble is, word that you were offering shelter spread like wildfire and there's been far too many people coming, saying they were burned out, for us to cope with them properly. It's the sanitary arrangements that are the most difficult problem . . .'

Zita raised a hand slightly, motioning him to silence. In her eagerness to help the injured she had been blind as to where she could best, at the moment, be of use. Until Laza could cope in her absence her place was in her home, organizing it as a refuge for the public in a way no-one else would be able to.

She said quietly to Katerina, 'You get what rest you can. I'm going to stay here for a while.'

Katerina nodded, realizing the sense of her mother's decision. Wearily she began to climb the stairs to her room wondering how much longer the city could hold out without Allied help; wondering if the ballroom would ever again ring to the glorious notes of 'The Blue Danube'; if they would ever again enjoy leisurely afternoon tea on an immaculately kept lawn.

All through August and September the onslaught continued and all through August and September Major Zlarin and his men held the Austrian forces at bay. News of what was happening elsewhere in Serbia was sketchy and infrequent. Only at the beginning of October did word arrive from Alexis.

Katerina had opened the mud-marked envelope with trembling fingers. It was dated 17 September and at having confirmation that at least until then, he was alive, Zita felt almost ill with relief.

My dearest love,
I hope by now that you are safely in Nish. One of my men is

being seconded to Major Zlarin's forces and I am asking him to deliver this to Zlarin in the hope Zlarin will be able to get it to you, wherever you now are, by a military courier.

The first days here were the worst. The Austrians stormed across the Drina and succeeded in capturing Shabatz. Fighting was hard and hideous. Everyone realizes now we're up against a far tougher enemy than the Turk. Austrian artillery has to be the most powerful in the world and our field-guns are petty and ineffectual in comparison. We fought back, however, and by the end of August we had thrown the enemy into complete disorder, shelled them, charged them, and driven them back across the Drina in panic-stricken flight. We shall soon have Allied help and when that arrives the Austrians will be finished.

And now I come to something of a more personal nature; something which will, I think, surprise you. Max Karageorgevich led the fighting to free Shabatz of its invaders and did so with great astuteness and courage. As a fighter he possesses all the flair and élan that is so unfortunately lacking in his peacetime demeanour. We joined forces in clearing the last of the invader from Serbian soil and it was then he spoke to me of the matter which will, I think, be as much a surprise to you as it was to me. He wishes to marry Katerina.

Zita had been reading the letter aloud and at this point Katerina gave such a loud cry of disbelief that Zita faltered, looking across at her in dismay.

'He can't possibly wish to marry me! It's Max's sick idea of a joke! What did Papa say to him? He surely didn't believe Max was *serious*?'

Zita looked down again at the hastily pencil-written letter.

Max says it is a matter to which he has given a lot of thought. Apparently he called on Katerina immediately before

234

leaving for the front with the intention of making his feelings clear to her. He says he realized, however, that he should ask my permission before doing so and this, of course, he has now done. They are second cousins, of course, and you know what my feelings were on the subject when it was suggested Natalie might marry Alexander. However, as you can well imagine, I now bitterly regret the stance I took and have no intention of repeating my mistake. Max may be a Karageorgevich but he doesn't possess the notorious Karageorgevich qualities of hot-headed thoughtless temper, quite the reverse. In the rapidly changing world in which we are now living, I think I would rest easy knowing that Katerina was married within the family, especially to a man of whose lion-hearted courage there cannot be the faintest shadow of doubt. With Natalie now as far away from us as if she were on the moon, a zadruga-style marriage would be a great consolation to me, as I am sure it would be to you. Their children would be Slav, not half English, and would be brought up in what I hope, when this war ends, will be a United Kingdom of all South Slavs. There is no chance of any children Natalie may have, doing so. That being the case, a marriage between Max and Katerina would give me great happiness and would, I am sure, be in Katerina's best interest.

To return to the hideous present. It may be there will be no more fighting for a while in the north-west. Rumour has it the remains of the battalions we chased back across the Drina are now on their way to Galicia to take their place in the line against Russia. They'll have no better luck there. Perhaps by Christmas the war will be over and we will be reunited again. I pray so. All my love, my darling, to both yourself and Katerina. Alexis.

She lowered the letter to her lap, meeting Katerina's eyes with reluctance.

Katerina gave a choked cry of anguish. 'Not you as well,

Mama! You don't think I should marry Max, do you? Surely you realize it's an insane idea! Papa was not thinking clearly when he wrote to you. He had just spent weeks fighting the Austrians and naturally he was proud of the way Max conducted himself in battle. Any member of his family would be. *I'm* proud, but it doesn't mean I want to marry him, nor does it mean Papa is right in thinking that I should marry him!'

Zita said slowly, 'I don't think it would be wise to come to a hasty decision on this subject, Katerina. Max obviously cares about you a great deal . . .'

'Max has never given the slightest indication that he cares about me!' At the prospect of her mother agreeing with her father that Max would make her a suitable husband, panic welled up inside her. 'I've never yet had a pleasant, civil conversation with him! I don't even feel *comfortable* with him! How could I possibly marry a man with whom I don't even feel comfortable?'

'You couldn't,' Zita said with regretful practicality. 'But it is a pity you feel as you do. In many respects a marriage between yourself and Max would be ideal. It would please his grandmother enormously . . .'

'I'm not marrying in order to please Great-Aunt Eudocia.' Katerina said, so vastly relieved at her mother agreeing she couldn't marry a man she didn't even like that there was a glimmer of amusement in her voice.

Zita heard it and responded to it. The corners of her mouth quirked in a smile. 'Not even Papa would want that. We'll regard the subject as closed for the moment. You haven't told me yet how the American Red Cross is managing. Is it making life easier for you at the hospital? Is it true that English and Scottish nurses are also in the country, setting up medical units and field hospitals?'

Katerina nodded, glad to steer the conversation away from the subject of a possible marriage between herself and Max. 'The Serbian Relief Fund in Britain is funding them. I wonder if Natalie is involved in raising money for them?'

For a few brief, precious moments they talked of Natalie, both relieved that she was in a place of comparative safety; both wondering if she was homesick; both wondering when they would see her again.

Such moments, when they were together and when they could talk, were rare. During the last two months the city had been under fire for thirty-six days and thirty-six nights and leisure for gossip was a thing of the past. Because the streets were under almost constant shellfire Katerina rarely came home. Instead she slept at the hospital, as did Helga and Cissie. Major Zlarin was assiduous in offering protection, almost embarrassingly so. No matter how intense the fighting, a soldier was always spared to stand guard at the Vassilovich *konak* and to offer Zita whatever help she might need in the running of her public shelters and soup kitchen.

Every few days or so a soldier would also arrive at the hospital in order to speak to Katerina and check on her welfare. Always it was reiterated that Major Zlarin thought it would be wisest if they left the city and that when they decided to do so a military car and driver would be at their disposal to take them to Nish. Always the offer was politely refused.

On one occasion, Major Zlarin visited Katerina at the hospital. On being told a member of the military was asking for her, Katerina had hurried from her ward, her hair scraped back under her white gauze headdress, her white bibbed apron scattered with bloodstains. She had expected to find a corporal checking on her safety on Major Zlarin's behalf and was stunned to find herself face to face with the major himself.

'You look tired,' he said to her abruptly.

'I am tired.' She had been on duty for sixteen hours and had just assisted at an amputation. Not wanting him to use the fact of her tiredness as an excuse again to suggest it was time she and her mother evacuated to Nish, she said with a dismissive shrug of her shoulders, 'Everyone is tired. It doesn't matter. At least we're being of use.'

He had taken off his peaked cap in order to talk to her and despite his height she could see that his once gleaming coal-black hair was now thick with shrapnel dust. He, too, looked utterly exhausted.

She wondered when he had last slept; when he had last enjoyed a warm meal and was mortifyingly aware that he should have been doing so now. Since early morning there had been no bombardment, yet instead of snatching a precious few hours rest he had honoured his promise to her father and had come personally to check up on her safety.

Aware that she had sounded churlish instead of grateful for this sacrifice of his time, she said amelioratingly, 'Mama and I are both very appreciative for the protection you have given us. Having a military presence at the house has been a great help to Mama. Without it she thinks things would have got out of hand on a number of occasions.'

He gave a grunt that could have meant anything and then said, 'Your mother has been amazingly stubborn in insisting on remaining in the city, however, the time has regrettably come when both she and you are going to have to take my advice and leave for Nish.'

'No, I'm sorry, Major Zlarin. We couldn't possibly . . .'

'Austrian forces have re-taken Shabatz,' he said grimly. 'Our army is in retreat due to lack of ammunition. They are falling back and it's my belief that it's only a matter of time before the order is given to evacuate all military personnel from Belgrade.'

She felt her face drain of blood. 'You mean Belgrade will be handed over to the enemy? We will be occupied?'

'If the retreat isn't halted, those are the orders I think will be given. In such a situation it is unthinkable that you and your mother should remain in the city.'

She said a little less forcefully, 'Mama made up her mind long ago that she would stay in Belgrade no matter what happened . . .'

He said caustically, 'With all due respect, your mother can have very little idea of what will happen if enemy troops occupy Belgrade. Women and children will very likely be taken hostage and as members of the ruling house of Karageorgevich both you and your mother will be high on the list of any hostages sought out.'

The blood had begun to return to her cheeks again and she felt an uncomfortable stirring of embarrassment as the major's dark eyes relentlessly held hers. Was he intimating that she and her mother would face rape if they stubbornly remained in Belgrade? Not wanting to pursue the subject she said, 'What is the situation now, on the Sava and Danube?'

His heavy brows met in a deep frown. 'All the foundries, bakeries, and all the factories along the riverbanks have been razed to the ground but thanks to the help we've been given by the British, the Austrians are no nearer to invading than they were two months ago.'

'The British?' Katerina's eyes widened. She had seen no evidence of British troops in the city. 'They've sent men? A battalion?'

'They've sent one man and he's proving to be of more value than any battalion,' he said with grudging admiration. 'Thanks to Commander Cardale we have mines and torpedoes and a successful crossing of either the Sava or Danube by Austrian troops is now extremely unlikely.'

'Then that's good news!' Her usually gentle smile was devastatingly sunny.

Their eyes held and in that moment Ivan Zlarin made up his mind that he was going to marry her. The realization put an end to the ease of manner which had been growing between them. She was both a Vassilovich and a Karageorgevich and Alexis Vassilovich no doubt anticipated a much grander match for his eldest daughter than marriage to an army man. He wondered what Alexis's reaction would be when he asked permission to court her. It didn't occur to him to wonder what Katerina's would be. As a mature sophisticated military man of thirty-two, he was accustomed to securing all his objectives. Now he had made up his mind to secure Katerina he anticipated no difficulty he couldn't overcome.

'Speak to your mother about the likely occupation of the city,' he said with a return of his usually stiff manner. 'The sooner you are both in Nish, the better.'

She nodded, certain she would be wasting her time, anxious to return to the ward where by now she would be being acutely missed.

'I will. Goodbye, Major Zlarin. Good luck.'

He remained standing, his army hat in the crook of his arm, his brows still pulled together in a frown as he watched her hurry away from him and up the stone stairs towards her ward. Only when the last swish of her skirt was no longer visible did he turn and leave the building.

At the beginning of November Zita received another letter from Alexis. Its tone was far more pessimistic than his first letter had been.

Dearest Love, I hope this scrawl reaches you. As I write we're under fire and so it's going to be regrettably short, however, as a messenger is about to leave en route to Major

Zlarin I am seizing any chance, however remote, of making contact with you. Things are looking bleak at the moment. Still no reinforcements and now no shells for artillery and no cartridges for rifles. My irregulars have now joined ranks with the First Ban (of Shumadia, Max's division). When this ghastly war is over I haven't the slightest doubt that Katerina and he should marry. Try and bring her round to my way of thinking. If she were to agree it would be an enormous worry removed from my mind. My only other worry is you, you and you. The messenger is about to leave and so I must end. Keep safe, keep strong. All my love, my darling. Alexis.

This time Zita made no comforting comments to Katerina about the marriage being out of the question. Her marriage to Alexis had been arranged by their mutual families and it was one she daily thanked God for. If it was Alexis's judgement that Katerina would be happy with Max, then it was judgement she trusted.

Katerina was appalled. It was bad enough that her father was risking his life at the battlefront, without having to live with the knowledge she was going wilfully to disappoint him over something on which he had apparently set his heart.

At night at the hospital, worn out and weary on her canvas camp bed, she tried to imagine pleasing her father and marrying Max. It was impossible. He was as big as a bear and about as communicative. Why on earth had he taken into his head that he wanted to marry her? Why hadn't it been Julian who had wanted to marry her?

At the thought of Julian pain would engulf her, crippling in its intensity. Over the past few months she had tried to school herself not to think of him, but it was impossible. She would stare into the darkness of the dormitory she shared with Cissie and Helga and a dozen other volunteers, tears burning her eyes as she thought of what might have been. Together they would have been happy. Even after all that had happened she hadn't the slightest doubt of it, it was a certainty that wouldn't leave her, a certainty that was a constant torment. As Austrian cannon thundered across the Sava and Danube she would wonder where he was; if he was in France or Belgium; if he was in an infantry or cavalry regiment. Worse, she would wonder if he was wounded. If he was even still alive.

Ever since the day he had married Natalie she had kept her grief to herself, confiding in no-one. She had become quieter, more introspective, and because of the dreadful circumstances under which they were living the change that had taken place in her had gone unnoticed. Sometimes, as she faced the fact that she would never now have the love she craved, she wondered if it mattered who she married. With unwitting hurt her mother had pointed out to her that as she wasn't in love elsewhere she could at least *consider* Max as a suitor.

'Would it matter if I were in love elsewhere?' she had asked with a flash of rare bitterness.

Her mother's eyes had widened in surprise. 'But of course it would! If you were going to marry suitably elsewhere then Papa wouldn't be advocating you marry Max. He's doing so because it is quite obvious that whatever our future after the war, it is going to be far different from anything we have been accustomed to. There are going to be no grand balls thick with eligible young men. If the carnage goes on for much longer there aren't going to be *any* young men, eligible or otherwise. Papa wants to secure your future and in every practical way marriage to Max would do so.'

All through the remainder of November the war news grew worse. The retreat Major Zlarin had spoken of at the beginning of the month had not turned into a rout, but it had insidiously continued. In the face of tremendous odds the army had fallen back and fallen back again, digging new trenches, fighting hand to hand, praying for the promised reinforcements that still didn't arrive. The weather was now freezingly cold and heavy rain had turned the battlegrounds into a quagmire. Katerina could hardly bear to think of the conditions under which her father was living, never warm, never completely dry, never satisfyingly fed.

As the month came to an end the sense of panic grew. There were rumours that the troops were about to evacuate the city, that the railway bridge was about to be blown, that occupation by Austrian forces was imminent.

When Katerina saw a staff-car scream up to the hospital and Major Zlarin vault from it and sprint inside, she knew the rumours were true.

Quickly she turned away from the window, running from the ward, running down the stone steps, running towards the terrible news she knew she was going to be given.

He met her at a turn in the stairs. 'It's happened,' he said abruptly, his face sweat-streaked and exhausted. 'The army is in full scale retreat from Shabatz. All troops are falling back to Rudnik and the order has been given to abandon Belgrade. In another hour there won't be a Serbian soldier left in the city. You and your mother are to take my staff-car and go to Nish. I've already given the driver his instructions . . .'

'No.'

Disbelief flared through his eyes and then such frustrated fury that Katerina flinched as if she had been struck.

'For Christ's sake!' he bellowed, abandoning all civility and restraint. 'Do you want to be raped? Murdered? Dragged off across the Danube as a hostage? You have no *choice* but to leave for Nish! The miracle will be if you ever reach it!'

She shook her head, sick with a terror she was determined not to show, knowing that her mother would never leave, knowing that they were going to have to take their chances with the Austrians just as all the other nurses were going to have to.

'No,' she said again, 'I'll never forget your concern, Major Zlarin, and if you asked anything else of me I would comply without hesitation, but . . .'

'Marry me.'

The floor felt as if it were shelving away at her feet. She put a hand out to the wall, certain she was about to faint.

'Marry me,' he said again fiercely. 'Say yes and I'll honour your mother's insane conviction the two of you should stay. Say no and I'll put both of you under arrest and have you driven out of here in chains.'

'I . . .' She tried to speak and couldn't. Her throat was so constricted no sound would come. She stared at him in wide-eyed incredulity, the blood fizzing in her ears.

The noise from the streets had become deafening. There was the sound of truck engines revving, women sobbing, men shouting.

'I have an evacuation to oversee,' he said savagely. 'Quickly, yes or no?'

'Yes,' she said, having to lean her whole weight against the wall to save herself from slithering weak-kneed to the floor. 'Yes, I'll marry you.'

For a second his disbelief at her answer was almost as great as hers had been at his demand.

He took his pistol from his holster and pressed it into her unwilling hands, then he swiftly undid his ammunition-belt.

'Here. Take it. For Christ's sake don't be afraid to use it.'

244

As she clutched the hideous cargo to her breast he pulled her against him, his mouth coming down on hers in hard, unfumbled contact. For a brief second as he raised his head from hers their eyes held and then he turned on his heel, taking the steps two at a time, sprinting back to his waiting car.

Chapter Twelve

Waterloo station was crammed with returning and departing soldiers. Natalie felt as if she was drowning in a sea of khaki as she stood at the barrier, jostled on all sides by bulging kitbags, waiting for Julian's train to arrive. He wasn't expecting her to be there and there was no real reason for her to be there. He wasn't returning injured from the front as so many others were, nor was he returning from a vast distance. It made no difference. She had missed him mightily and she didn't want his mother to be present when they were reunited.

'It's not quite the done thing, you know, for people of our class to wait at railway-station barriers,' Diana had said, wondering if Natalie was unaware of the fact and would appreciate it being pointed out.

'Then it ought to be,' Natalie had responded, knowing that Diana was only trying to be helpful and not taking offence. 'All reunions should take place at the first possible moment and all separations at the last possible moment. Despite all the risks, when I left Belgrade my family came with me to the station and I would have been devastated if they hadn't done so.'

She tried to imagine returning and not finding her parents and Katerina waiting in a fever of impatience at the barrier, but it was impossible.

'What risks?' Diana had asked curiously. 'Serbia wasn't at war when you and Julian left for Britain. Why was there any risk involved in your family coming to see the two of you off?'

Not for the first time Natalie silently cursed the promise she had made to Julian not to talk to anyone about Gavrilo and the circumstances in which they had left Belgrade.

'It just was, that's all,' she said frustratedly. 'And no matter what your mother might think, Julian will be pleased to see me at the station. I know he will.'

Her mother-in-law thought public reunions on railway station platforms vulgar and had told her so. Natalie was uncaring. Despite the giddiness and gaiety of Diana's companionship, it hadn't been the same as being with Julian. She had missed his humour and his common sense and his ability to comfort. She had also missed his urgent, physical need of her.

As she stood at the barrier she felt hot and damp with longing. In an hour or so they would again be in bed together. She remembered the baby and with a flash of panic wondered if lovemaking would be dangerous for it. Surely it wouldn't be, so early on in pregnancy? She wished there was someone she could ask; someone she could talk to. Diana would be as ignorant as herself and she certainly couldn't broach the subject with Lady Fielding.

As the train began to steam into the station she pressed closer to the barrier. The longer her separation from her mother, the more she missed her. Her mother would have been able to tell her everything she needed to know about having a baby. At the thought of her mother her throat tightened. She wanted her mother to be near at hand when the baby was born. What if she wasn't? What if the war was still not over?

Belching steam the train slid to a halt and as it did so carriage doors were flung open and what seemed to Natalie to be an entire army was disgorged upon the platform. The fierce homesickness that had been about to engulf her vanished. Somewhere in the mass of humanity now streaming towards the barriers, was Julian. What if she missed him? What if he didn't see her in the crush?

'*Over here, Jimmy! Over here!*' the girl squeezed next to her shouted, waving so furiously she almost dislodged Natalie's yellow feathered nonsense of a hat.

Natalie adjusted it, standing on tip-toe in order to see more clearly the sea of approaching faces. She had worn the hat, which was totally unsuitable on a freezing December day, in the hope that Julian would see it and recognize it. Where was he? What if he had changed his plans? What if he wasn't on the train at all?'

'Natalie! *Natalie!*'

He was striding down the platform towards her, tall and broad-shouldered and incredibly handsome in his officer's uniform.

Pride and delight surged through her. He looked wonderful. He *was* wonderful.

The second he was through the barrier his arms were around her, lifting her off her feet, hugging her tight. Incredibly she found that she was crying. Tears were streaming down her cheeks as she clung to him in a fever of happiness, saying joyously, 'Oh, Julian! I'm so glad you're home! I've missed you so much!'

When he kissed her she was uncaring of the crowds around them. Her arms went round his neck and her mouth opened, her tongue sliding eagerly and urgently past his.

When at last he raised his head from hers he said thickly, 'God, Natalie! I can't begin to tell you how I've longed for this moment! I think I would have borne it better if I'd been in France or Belgium, but only being an hour's train ride away and not able to have leave, was utter torture.'

248

'For me too,' Natalie said fervently as he tucked her arm in his and then began to forge a way through the throng and towards the street. 'Have you heard from Edward? Has he written to you since he went to Flanders? His postcards to me are so cheerful that I don't believe a word in them. Have you heard anything about the war in Serbia? There's so little news. All the news is about the fighting in Belgium. What does it mean in the papers when it says things are at a stalemate? How can they be? I don't understand and no-one will explain.'

He grinned down at her. 'I'll do all the explaining I can while I'm home. I'm glad you've made such good friends with Diana. I knew you would.'

'Serbia,' she said again, refusing to be sidetracked into talking about Diana. 'Can't you find out what is happening from some of your Foreign Office friends? The newspapers were full of Bulgaria's declaration of neutrality and it made me so *cross* because Bulgaria's hand in glove with the Austrians and is just waiting for the right moment before attacking Serbia from the south. Why can't people *see* that?'

The Fielding Mercedes was waiting for them. Only the chauffeur had changed. Far too elderly for active service he opened the door for them and then eased himself arthritically behind the wheel, driving towards Piccadilly at a frustratingly decorous speed.

Sitting close together in the back seat their fingers interlocked.

'I missed you,' she said again, remembering the misery of countless afternoon teas taken with his mother present. She wondered when she should tell him about the baby and decided to wait until after they had made love. She didn't want to run the risk of him saying he couldn't make love to her if she was pregnant.

His fingers tightened on hers. Though in his time at

249

Cadet School there had been no special weekend leave passes for London there had been opportunities to visit the nearest town. Most of his companions had found professional sexual relief there, but he hadn't even been tempted to try. He loved Natalie and he missed her and he had kept his body clean for her. She had obviously missed him, too, for which he was profoundly grateful. Why, then, couldn't she say that she loved him? It was a mystery he couldn't fathom, one which endlessly tormented him.

With his free hand he tilted her face towards his. 'I love you,' he said, a raw edge to his voice.

It was a grey, chill day and in the shadowed interior of the car her eyes looked suspiciously bright. 'I know,' she said huskily, a leg pressed close against his. 'I've been looking forward so much to your coming home.'

For a moment he was tempted to put himself out of his misery and to ask her straight out if she loved him. Only the prospect that he might not receive the answer he craved kept him silent. Better not to know and to live in hope, than to risk having all hope dashed. They had five precious, glorious days to look forward to and he didn't want to spoil them. After this leave it might be months before he saw her again. If the present stalemate in the trenches didn't come to an end, it might be years.

He said, knowing it would make her happier than anything else he could say, 'I'll have a word with a few people and see if I can get hold of some up-to-date information about what's happening in the Balkans.'

'Thank you.' She snuggled closer to him. He was making everything all right, as he always did. She tried not to think about their next separation. His being in Flanders would be very different from his being at Cadet School in rural Surrey. What if he were injured? What if he were killed? She shut the thoughts from her mind. He wouldn't be killed. The war would end soon. He would return to the Foreign Office and somehow or other he would ensure he was again posted to Belgrade.

At the prospect of once again being home her heart soared. Her mother would no doubt hold a magnificent ball to celebrate her return. There would be parties at the *Konak* and afternoon strolls with Bella and the new baby in the Kalemegdan Gardens. The baby would be christened in the cathedral and would have to have a suitable complement of royal godfathers and godmothers. Alexander would be a godfather, of course, and perhaps Prince Danilo of Montenegro would be another. She wondered if, as Alexander's future wife, the Tsar's eldest daughter would agree to being a godmother. That might mean the Tsar and Tsarina being in attendance as well.

At the thought of such grandeur and glory she gave a deep sigh of satisfaction, beginning to be slightly more pleased at the prospect of the baby than she was apprehensive.

Mistaking the sigh Julian raised her hand to his mouth and kissed it. 'Not long now, my love. A dutiful hour or so with my parents and then we're off into Oxfordshire or Cambridgeshire in search of a quiet country inn.'

'And will we stay there for all of your leave?' she asked, her eyes widening.

He grinned. 'Every last little minute of it.'

At the thought of being so completely free of Lady Fielding, Natalie's cup was full and running over. 'Oh, *wonderful!*' she said blissfully. 'Bella will love to be in the countryside. We can take her for long walks and . . .'

He had forgotten about Bella. 'It might be difficult to find accommodation that takes dogs,' he began doubtfully, remembering how hopelessly trained she was.

Natalie's joy vanished. 'But she'll pine if we leave her behind! She'll be lonely at night without me!'

His eyes held hers, a horrid suspicion beginning to

251

form. 'What do you mean, she'll be lonely at night?'

Natalie looked a trifle sheepish. 'She sleeps with me. I was so lonely when you went away and the bed was so big and Bella was so small . . .'

It was his turn to sigh. He should have guessed. And though Bella may have been small four months ago, she wouldn't be small any longer. Knowing that the next five nights were going to be spent *à trois* with an atrociously spoilt spaniel he said with stoic resignation, 'All right. Bella comes with us but she sleeps on the floor. Is that understood?'

'Yes,' Natalie said, knowing very well that Bella would do no such thing. 'She will. I promise.'

It was heaven driving out of London. Julian had tossed a coin and headed north-west, towards Oxfordshire. Although his soft-topped Morgan was far less luxurious than the Fielding Mercedes, Natalie much preferred it. She sat cocooned in the fur Julian had bought her as an early Christmas present, cosy beneath a thick mohair blanket, Bella on her lap. The English countryside intrigued her. Compared to the Serbian countryside it was so neat and tidy, the fields and farmhouses arranged as if they were children's toys. Nothing was boring. High-hedged lanes gave way to woods and the woods in turn opened on to high ridges looking out over furrowed fields or on to small groupings of houses around a village green. Always the groupings were the same. At a distance would be the manor house, set in parkland, then there would be a farm or two, a church and parsonage, an inn, a cluster of small houses and in the centre of the village, an oak tree or a yew tree that looked as if it had been growing there for a thousand years.

The inn at which Julian stopped was thatched, had overhanging eaves and exquisite, diamond-paned windows.

As they stepped beneath a hooded doorway, Natalie felt as if she were stepping back into the Middle Ages. For the first time it occurred to her that she could tolerate a month or two in England every year, providing their time was spent in the countryside and not in the house at Cambridge Gate.

Immediately they signed the guest register they were offered afternoon tea. Impatient to hurl themselves into bed, but not wanting to make their intention obvious, they said they would take it in their room. They walked up the tortuously uneven staircase hand-in-hand, Bella scampering at their heels, praying that the unwanted tea would arrive quickly and that they could then lock their bedroom door and forget about the outside world.

'A baby?' He had been lying naked beside her in exquisite exhaustion. Now he sat upright so suddenly that a pillow fell off the bed. 'A *baby*?' he said again, looking down at her incredulously.

She giggled. She was lying on her back, her smoke-dark hair tumbling riotously over the pillow, her bare breasts bigger than he remembered them, the nipples silky and japonica-red. 'Yes. A baby. Our baby.'

'Are you sure?' His face was so fiercely elated it was transfigured. 'When did you find out? When is it due? Great God in heaven! I'd never thought . . . Never expected . . .'

His reaction was so intense she felt a strange, almost powerful feeling stealing through her. 'You're pleased?' she asked unnecessarily, pushing herself up against the pillows.

'Pleased? Of course I'm pleased! I'm over the moon!' Unable to contain himself he swung his strong, muscular legs from the bed and strode over to the window, opening it wide, uncaring of the light drift of snow that was beginning to fall. Somewhere in the distance a church bell was ringing for evening service. Cows in a nearby barn, waiting to be milked, mooed plaintively.

She shivered as the crisp, winter air rushed into the low-ceilinged room. 'I want the baby to be born at home, in Belgrade,' she said, reaching for the sheet and blankets that had been kicked to the bottom of the four-poster bed and pulling them against her breasts.

He spun around and she thought, as she so often did, how magnificent he looked naked. 'Belgrade? We won't be back in Belgrade for years,' he said, concern in his eyes. 'The war is at an impasse and talk of it being over by Easter is as pie in the sky as the earlier talk of it being over by Christmas.' He turned, closing the window. 'Even when it is over, travel will be difficult.'

He began to walk back towards the four-poster, saying comfortingly, 'That isn't to say we won't return at the first possible moment, because of course we will.' He slid into the bed, drawing her close. 'But it certainly isn't going to be before the baby is born, sweetheart. And it may not be for quite a long time afterwards.'

He couldn't see her face and the expression in her eyes. His arms were around her and her head was resting against his chest.

'Don't you intend applying for another posting in Belgrade immediately the war is over?' she asked, her voice sounding a little odd.

Presuming it was because she was speaking against his naked chest, he said, 'It would be wonderful if I were able to, but return postings are frowned on. With luck we'll find ourselves in another Slav capital, such as Petersburg.'

She lay against him, very still. She didn't want to find herself in St Petersburg. She didn't want to find herself anywhere but in Belgrade. All her apprehensions about the baby returned. How could she leave him and return home if she had a baby? He wouldn't allow her to take it with her. His ecstatic reaction at knowing he was going to be a father had been an indication of how devotedly paternal he was going to be. Which left the option of her leaving the baby with him and returning home alone.

She thought of Bella and of how fiercely attached to Bella she was. She couldn't imagine leaving Bella behind anywhere, under any circumstances, and if she was incapable of abandoning Bella, how could she possibly abandon her baby?

'I think we should celebrate by making love again,' he said, his lips brushing her hair, his arms tightening around her.

As always, he awoke a response in her, but it wasn't the same as before. Somewhere inside her something cold and hard had settled. She was his wife and separated from her family and her home because he had taken advantage of her father's panic over her friendship with Gavrilo. It had been a panic that had been unnecessary. The Austrians hadn't issued a warrant for her arrest. The trial was now over. If she hadn't been coerced into marrying him, she would be with her mother in Switzerland, secure in the knowledge that they would be returning to Belgrade the very second it was possible to do so. As passion flared within her and she drew her legs high, crossing them behind his back, so did resentment and steely determination. Somehow, despite all the difficulties, she would return to Belgrade. And when she did so, she would never again leave.

Christmas in the Fielding home was the most miserable Christmas she had ever experienced. The New Year was no better. Turkey had entered the war and her troops had attempted to cut Britain's Suez Canal artery with the East. Though they had failed, the attempt had meant large

255

numbers of Russian and British troops being pinned down in the Sinai desert when they might have been elsewhere.

Elsewhere, to Natalie, meant Serbia. In February came news that typhoid was raging throughout the country. More British Red Cross units and Scottish Women's Ambulance units were sent and Natalie lay sleepless night after night wondering if her family were among the dead and dying.

At the end of the month Julian wrote to her telling her he had been injured in the thigh and was being sent to the Duchess of Westminster's Hospital at Le Touquet. Diana had heartily regretted not having volunteered to nurse there and decided that the time had now come for her to volunteer her services to the Red Cross. When she did so, Natalie accompanied her.

Diana was told that as she had no previous experience she would be wise to apply to Guy's Hospital as a VAD probationer and Natalie, conspicuously seven months pregnant, was advised to join one of the many sewing guilds. She had duly gone along to the sewing guild that met at Claridges Hotel in Mayfair, taken one look at the cluster of upper-class, middle-aged ladies neatly and diligently stitching clothes for servicemen and the poor and had decided they would be far better off without her.

'Soldiers are having a tough enough time without having to fight their way into any odd-shaped garment I might make,' she said glumly to Diana who, home after her first week at Guy's, was sitting in a state of exhaustion, her feet in a bowl of hot water.

At the beginning of March there was more bad news from France. The list of wounded was horrendous and there seemed to be no end in sight.

Natalie had been relieved to think of Julian safe in his hospital bed and was torn between hoping he was hurt so badly he wouldn't be able to return to the front and praying his injury wasn't so severe it would leave him with a permanent limp.

At the end of March she met Nikita.

She had persisted in visiting the church hall in Camden in which her fellow Serbs met, even though the atmosphere was disappointingly staid. Her mother-in-law thought it outrageous she was continuing to do so now that she was so heavily *enceinte*, but Natalie was uncaring. Now that Diana was nursing at Guy's life had become extremely boring. Her advanced pregnancy precluded her from seeking relief from it by riding in the park or even from walking very far and a few hours of being lapped in her native tongue was welcome diversion.

Immediately she set eyes on Nikita she knew she had found a soul-mate. He was only a few years older than herself and tall and slenderly built. There was a whippy look to him that indicated he would be an ugly customer in a fight – and there was something else about him that made it obvious he would not need much excuse to join any fight that was going. With a mop of thickly curling black hair and lashes as long as a girl's fringing dark fiery eyes, he could easily have been mistaken for her twin. He was also quite obviously feeling as bored and as out of place in the decorous church hall as she was herself.

As a heavily pregnant lady her place was with the other married women, embroidering and talking and keeping an eye on the many small children running about. The men stood or sat in groups at the other side of the church hall as divided from their womenfolk as if they were in church. Their wives rarely approached them, women unknown to them never.

Natalie had no time for such conformity. She looked across at the newcomer, realized he would have been far more at home in the *Golden Sturgeon* and knew she had found a kindred spirit. Oblivious of her condition she walked across the hall towards him.

Her prey, aware that she was heading unmistakably in his direction, looked extremely disconcerted.

'Hello,' she said disarmingly, as if they had just met at a *Konak* tea party or the Vassilovich Summer Ball. 'My name is Natalie Fielding. I haven't seen you here before. Have you any news of what is happening in Serbia? How long is it since you were there?'

'I'm not Serbian, I'm Croatian,' he said suspiciously, wondering if her husband was perhaps one of the men standing nearby him. He looked around, but there was no-one English-looking in the hall and with a name like Fielding her husband couldn't possibly be a Slav.

'Croatian, Bosnian, Serbian, it doesn't make any difference, does it?' Natalie said, aware of his discomfiture and blithely ignoring it. 'When this war is over and the Habsburg empire is no more, we'll all be one country. You do believe in a future Kingdom of all South Slavs, don't you?'

His eyes returned to her, the alarm fading, interest growing. 'With Croatians, Bosnians, Serbians, Slovenes all equal? Yes. That's why I'm in London. I'm a member of the Yugoslav Committee.'

'The Yugoslav Committee?' Natalie had never heard of such a thing. Excitement began to spiral through her. 'What is the Yugoslav Committee?'

He looked around to see if the men he had been standing with were still listening to their conversation. They weren't. Disconcerted by Natalie's advanced state of pregnancy they had edged away, not wanting to be singled out by her as he had been.

'Do you know Ante Trumbich who used to be Mayor of Split?'

She shook her head.

'Trumbich and Franjo Supilo, editor of *Novi List* . . .'

'I haven't heard of *Novi List* either,' Natalie said, unabashed by her ignorance.

'Then you should have done,' he said rudely. 'It's a leading journal of the Serb-Croat movement. Trumbich and Supilo and Ivan Mestrovich met with a group of Serbian exiles from Bosnia in Florence last November and . . .'

'Who is Ivan Mestrovich?' Natalie asked with interest, her excitement mounting. She felt as if she were in the *Golden Sturgeon* again; as if she were once again at the centre of events, plotting and planning for the day when a Karageorgevich would rule a Kingdom of all South Slavs.

'Mestrovich is Dalmatian and a sculptor,' he said impatiently. 'He's also one of the acknowledged leaders of the movement calling for the union of Dalmatia with Croatia and as he's now joined forces with Trumbich and Supilo . . .'

'My father is Alexis Vassilovich, a personal adviser to King Peter,' Natalie said, determined not to be left out of the name dropping. 'King Peter is my uncle. My mother is a Karageorgevich.'

She had expected him to be impressed. He wasn't.

'Do you always interrupt people when they are telling you something? When Mestrovich, Trumbich and Supilo met in Florence they formed the Yugoslav Committee, the aim being to promote the idea of a Yugoslav federation. I'm a member of it and I'm in London to set up the headquarters here.'

Natalie was entranced. He was a nationalist in the same mould of Gavrilo and Trifko and Nedjelko. He was setting up a nationalist organization in London and she would be a member of it. There would be no more long hours of tedious boredom. From now on she would be able to work

259

actively for the day when all south Slavs would be united, no matter what their religion. Life would be just as interesting as it had been in Belgrade when she had had her weekly meetings at the *Golden Sturgeon* to look forward to.

Somewhere in her brain a warning bell rang.

It was her meetings at the *Golden Sturgeon* that were responsible for her present predicament. Hadn't she told Katerina that she bitterly regretted them? Hadn't she said she would never be so foolish again?

'We don't meet here of course,' her new-found friend said, his eyes sweeping contemptuously around the church hall. 'The people who come here are not politically educated.'

'I am,' Natalie said serenely, ignoring the warning bell, hungry to be involved in exciting events again.

'You?' For the first time he abandoned sullen rudeness and grinned. His teeth were very even, very white. 'You're a woman. You should be sitting with the other women, minding babies and embroidering.'

Natalie's patience was fast running out. 'What's your name?' she demanded, determined to take him down a peg or two.

'Kechko. Nikita Kechko.'

'It might interest you to know, Nikita Kechko, that I used to meet with Gavrilo Princip, Trifko Grabez and Nedjelko Cabrinovich in the *Golden Sturgeon* in Belgrade,' she said, forgetting entirely her vow to Julian that she would never speak of her friendship with Gavrilo to a living soul. '*And* I met Gavrilo in Sarajevo the day before he shot the Archduke. Now do you think I should be minding babies and embroidering?'

His eyes held hers and suddenly she was aware of a physical reaction she hadn't felt for months, a reaction she hadn't thought possible now she was so heavily pregnant.

'Prove it,' he said abruptly.

His shirt was open at the throat, revealing a strong, olive-toned neck. She wanted to lick his flesh, to slide her hands inside his shirt, running them over his shoulders and chest. His trousers fitted snugly, a buckled leather belt low on his narrow hips. She wondered what he would look like naked; what he would be like in bed.

For the first time in her life she was shocked with herself. How could she be so sexually aroused by a stranger when she was within weeks, perhaps days, of giving birth? Surely it wasn't natural. And it most certainly wasn't loyal.

She thought of Julian lying injured in his hospital bed in France and for the first time wondered what sort of loyalty it was she owed to him. Their marriage wasn't, after all, a conventional one. She hadn't married him because she was in love with him. She had married him in order that her parents wouldn't be parted. That being the case, she surely didn't owe sexual loyalty in the way she would have if they had married for love. It was an interesting thought and one that would, no doubt, be of importance in the future. At the moment, however, she was eight months pregnant and indulging in lascivious thoughts was not only undignified, it was probably abnormal. Checking them with difficulty, she said, answering his question, 'Gavrilo is shy with women. Trikfo has no time for them, Nedjelko has.'

'Mother of God,' he said softly. 'You do know them.'

The expression in his eyes had changed and she knew that from now on he would take her seriously. She wondered from where he knew Gavrilo and Nedjelko and Trifko; if he had met them in Sarajevo before they had left Bosnia for Serbia, or if he had met them in Belgrade.

Before she could ask he said, 'Is that why you're in London?' Respect had replaced patronizing amusement. 'You came to avoid being extradited?'

For the first time it occurred to Natalie that her flight could be seen as being the stuff of which legends are made.

'Yes,' she said, enjoying her feeling of importance. 'But I'm going to return at the first possible moment.'

His eyes flicked to her swollen stomach. 'And your husband? He's English?'

As he moved his head slightly she saw a thin white scar slicing through his left eyebrow. She wondered if it had been caused by a knife blade. She could imagine him in a knife fight. There was something very feral about him. Something very dangerous.

'Yes. He was a diplomat in Belgrade and . . .'

'NICKY!'

Natalie broke off in mid-sentence as a burly, bearded figure descended on them, resplendent in boots and breeches and traditional embroidered waistcoat.

'I'm going to have to go,' Nikita said to her swiftly. 'We'll meet again. Here. I'll introduce you to the Yugoslav Committee.'

'Greetings, my friend!' a deep bass voice boomed. 'How are you? I'm sorry I'm late.'

Looking as if he had just stepped off a Balkan hillside and not a London street the newcomer engulfed Nikita in an affectionate bear hug.

Natalie wondered if he was a member of the Yugoslav Committee, if he might even be Ante Trumbich or Franjo Supilo or Ivan Mestovich. She didn't wait to be introduced and to find out. Slav male dignity was easily affronted and aware that her advanced pregnancy would be an embarrassment to Nikita she turned on her heel and walked away as quickly as her bulk would allow.

She wasn't the least despondent at their conversation coming to such an abrupt end. They had said all that was necessary. At the thought of being introduced to active nationalists elation sizzled through her. She was going to be at the centre of events again; actively involved in shaping the destiny of her country.

As she stepped out into the busy street she wondered what Julian's reaction would be when she wrote him with the news. The chauffeured Mercedes was waiting for her and as she crossed the pavement towards it, she frowned. Julian would not be pleased. In fact, he would be quite seriously displeased. As the chauffeur arthritically clambered out from behind the wheel and opened the nearside rear door for her, she decided that it would be best not to write to France with news of Nikita and her impending involvement with the Yugoslav Committee.

For a second, as the chauffeur closed the door behind her and she sank back with relief against the leather upholstery, she was overcome by a sensation of *déjà-vu*. She dismissed it, resting her hands on her swollen stomach. This moment hadn't happened before. It wasn't identical with the one when she had determined not to tell Katerina about her visits to the *Golden Sturgeon*. This was different. Nothing bad was going to come out of her friendship with Nikita. This time she was going to be sensible about things. This time she was going to be careful.

Chapter Thirteen

As Major Zlarin sprinted down the stone hospital stairs and out into the chaos of the street Katerina stared after him, the pistol he had thrust into her hands clutched close to her chest, scarcely able to believe the enormity of what had happened. From out of nowhere, without the least encouragement, he had asked her to marry him. It was incredible. Unbelievable. And what was even more incredible, what was absolutely beyond all belief, was that she had accepted him.

A posse of soldiers surged past her carrying an injured comrade and she pressed herself back against the wall to enable them to pass. What on earth had she been thinking of? How could she possibly have agreed to marry a man she scarcely knew? A man she had never yet addressed by his Christian name? It was the kind of thing Natalie might have done. As she thought of how little Natalie had known Julian before marrying him, she realized that it was, in fact, *exactly* what Natalie had done. Natalie, however, had had good reason to marry Julian. Dazedly she wondered as to the reasons behind her own untypical heedless, reckless behaviour.

There was only one, but it was sufficient. If she married Major Zlarin, she could not be emotionally blackmailed into marrying Max. Her fingers tightened on the pistol. She may have behaved recklessly but she hadn't behaved senselessly. Whatever the circumstances she couldn't possibly marry Max and her father's letters had left not a shadow of doubt that that was now the match intended for her. Traditionally even Serbian peasant marriages were arranged affairs with young men, as well as young women, marrying in accordance with their parents' wishes. Such arrangements were considered to be the natural order of things and it was very rare that the parents' say in the choice of a son-in-law or a daughter-in-law was defied. Now that her own parents were in agreement that she should marry Max, so logically suitable in so many ways, refusing to do so would be near impossible.

The noise of panic in the street was growing louder, the rumble of distant cannon-fire intensifying. Unregretful of the momentous decision she had just taken she turned and began to run back up the stairs towards her ward. She had to tell her mother and Cissie and Helga that the army was retreating to the south and that Belgrade was going to be totally exposed to Austrian occupation. And she had to tell her mother that Major Zlarin had asked her to marry him and that she had accepted him.

'Dear God,' Cissie whispered, when Katerina gasped out her news about the retreat. 'What will happen to us? What are we going to do?'

'We're going to do what nurses have always done in these situations,' Zita said, her fine-etched face exhausted and resolute. 'We are going to carry on caring for the injured. If that also means caring for the enemy then so be it.'

Katerina had been holding the pistol low, half hidden in the folds of her skirt and neither her mother nor Cissie had noticed it. It was Helga who saw it first.

'*Mein Gott!* Did the major give you that?' she asked, her eyes widening.

Katerina moved her hand slightly, bringing the pistol into full view. All three of them stared at it, appalled.

'Yes. It's for use in an emergency.'

'You shouldn't have taken it from him.' The lines of strain around Zita's mouth had deepened. 'What if you use it in panic? What if you kill someone?'

For the first time Katerina wondered if her mother had any real understanding of what might happen to them when the Austrians arrived. She said patiently, 'If I hadn't taken it from him, and if he hadn't known we had at least one weapon with which to protect ourselves, he would never have allowed us to stay in the city. He would have had us arrested and put us aboard one of the trains taking the troops south.'

'Did Major Zlarin say from where the army was retreating?' Zita asked, deciding not to pursue a subject that could have no satisfactory outcome. 'Will Papa and Max be retreating through Belgrade? Is there any chance of our seeing them?'

All the time they had been talking they had been jostled and pushed as relatives of the sick rushed in to say last goodbyes before joining in the general evacuation.

Katerina regained her balance after a kerchiefed woman, all her worldly goods in clumsy bundles, half fell against her. 'He said it was a full-scale retreat from Shabatz.'

'Then that will include your father and Max . . .'

'They won't be coming through Belgrade, Mama,' Katerina said before Zita could raise her hopes. 'All forces in the north-west will be falling directly back on Rudnik.'

'And then what will they do?' Cissie asked, not understanding.

'They'll hold out until reinforcements come,' Zita said, praying to God that Serbia's allies would not let her down, 'and when they do, they'll hurl the Austrian forces back across the Sava and the Danube and not one Austrian or Hungarian will ever set foot on Serbian soil again.'

'We'd better get back to the wards,' Helga said as a patient stumbled past them with the aid of a makeshift crutch. 'The patients are panicking.'

'Let's hope they are not doing so with good reason,' Cissie said quietly. 'It may not be comfortable but I think you should wear that pistol on a belt beneath your skirt, Trina. Then it won't be taken off you.'

Katerina nodded, more grateful every minute that Major Zlarin had given her some form of protection.

On the wards chaos reigned. News of the army retreat and of the evacuation of all troops from the city had spread like wildfire. Patients not fit enough to sit up were struggling to get to their feet, intent on fleeing. The nursing staff, as fearful of what treatment might be meted out by the occupying Austrians as their patients, pleaded with them to be calm. Some patients, unable to walk even on crutches, had hauled themselves to the windows and thrown them open. As the troops streamed past in the street below, *en route* for the train station, there were encouraging shouts of, '*Come back soon and chase the bastards into the Danube!*'

No-one hurled abuse. Everyone knew the men were reluctantly obeying orders, orders that were necessary if a line further south was to be held until reinforcements arrived.

'They'll be back,' a blind old man, both legs amputated, said confidently. 'And when they are, the King himself will lead them back into the city. Old as he is, he's fighting with his troops. Come on everyone, three cheers for King Peter! Three cheers for Crown Prince Alexander! They're Karageorgevichs and no-one ever kept a Karageorgevich down!'

The hurrahs were deafening and for once Katerina didn't feel as if she was all Vassilovich. Half of her was Karageorgevich and at the moment she was so proud

267

of the fact that it was a physical pain.

The silence, when the hurrahs died down, was monumental. The last train south had gone and there were no more hurrying soldiers in the streets. The nurses went about their tasks, exchanging apprehensive glances with each other. Suddenly, very faintly, there came the sound of triumphant martial music. Katerina went to a window and leaned out. The music grew louder. It was a band and behind the blaring of the band there was the tramp, tramp, tramp of hundreds of marching feet.

'They're coming,' Cissie said unnecessarily.

Katerina felt her stomach muscles tighten. The pistol was uncomfortably secured beneath her skirts. With clammy hands she continued with her task, changing the dressing of a young girl badly injured by shrapnel splinters.

A patient at the end of the ward, propped against the wall and looking out of the window, said tersely, 'They're coming in with flags waving, God damn them, and they're heading for the *Konak*.'

Katerina finished her task, her hands trembling. In another few minutes the yellow and black flag of the Habsburgs would be flying from the *Konak*'s flag-pole.

There was no silence now. As the Austro-Hungarian forces marched into the centre of the city they whistled and shouted exultantly. There was the sound of doors being rocked back on their hinges, of shouted protests and abuse.

Feet thundered up the stone hospital stairs. The door at the end of the ward was flung open and three Austrians, rifles at the ready, burst into the ward.

No-one moved.

'This hospital is now under the control of Austro-Hungarian forces,' one of the men, an officer, barked. 'All occupants are henceforth prisoners of war. Long live the

Austro-Hungarian Empire! Long live Emperor Franz Josef!'

'*May he rot in hell!*' a young boy, who had fought under Major Zlarin and who had half a leg blown away, shouted rebelliously.

Reaction was instant. The two soldiers accompanying the officer sprinted towards his bed, took up positions at the foot of it and raised their rifles. As pandemonium broke out and as the boy tried to hurl himself protectively from the bed to the floor, they took aim and fired, shooting him through the heart.

Zita didn't hesitate. For the first time in her life her cool, dignified self-control abandoned her. Before Katerina could stop her she rushed towards the officer, slapping him across the face with all the force of which she was capable.

'*Murderer!*' she spat, her eyes blazing, her voice fearless. '*Butcher!* Is this to what the mighty Austro-Hungarian army has sunk? Shooting wounded and defenceless boys in cold blood? Have you no honour any more? No pride?'

The first instant she had moved the two soldiers had swung towards her, rifles raised. Katerina's hand closed over the pistol beneath her skirt. Was she going to have to use it now? So soon? Even if she did, it wouldn't save her mother's life. She couldn't shoot all three Austrians before at least one of them retaliated.

Her hideous dilemma was solved as the officer, not taking his eyes from Zita's, motioned for his men to lower their weapons. 'The Austro-Hungarian army will not be abused by Balkan scum,' he said tersely, aware from her speech that Zita was no ordinary nurse. She had the bearing and arrogant confidence of a member of the aristocracy and his eyes narrowed speculatively. If the order was given for hostages to be taken, he would select her first and quite possibly score a coup. For the moment what he wanted was her co-operation. Hundreds of Austrian soldiers had been injured in earlier, opposed attempts to take the city and nursing care for them was desperately needed.

'If you are in charge of this ward it is your duty to see that no insults are offered,' he continued, wondering how quickly he could evict the present patients on to the street. 'If they are, the perpetrators, whether male or female, will be executed.'

He looked around the ward, saw Cissie and said abruptly, 'She comes with us. If there is not complete co-operation she will not return.'

'No! Never!' Zita said forcefully, moving swiftly in order to stand protectively between Cissie and the soldiers who had begun to walk towards her.

'It will be better for the patients if I go without a fuss,' Cissie said to her quietly, her voice perfectly steady.

Torn by indecision Zita looked across to Helga. Deeply unhappy Helga nodded her head. '*Ja*,' she said reluctantly, her advice as practical as always. 'That is so.'

The officer spun round towards her. 'You! You are German?'

Helga squared her shoulders. '*Ja*,' she said again.

She was standing by the bed of a man with appalling head and facial injuries, one hand comfortingly on his shoulder. A Serbian army jacket lay conspicuously across the foot of the bed.

'You are a traitor,' the officer said icily and then, to his men, 'Shoot her.'

This time Katerina unhesitatingly lifted her ankle-length skirt and feverishly reached for the pistol. She was far too late. As her fingers closed around it two shots rang out simultaneously and Helga pitched forward, blood spurting from her mouth and chest.

'*No!*' Zita screamed, dashing towards her. As she did

so, she saw Katerina's intention and shouted again, this time with far different emphasis, '*No!*'

At the same moment, a squad of Austro-Hungarian soldiers raced into the ward, rifles at the ready. With sobs choking her throat Katerina released hold of the pistol and let her skirt fall. Her mother's protest had not been squeamishness. To shoot now would achieve nothing. It was too late to save Helga's life. Revenging her would cost their own lives and perhaps the patients' lives as well.

No-one had seen her action. The wounded and dying were being evicted at bayonet point from their beds, Cissie was being marched from the room, Zita was cradling Helga's head in her lap, weeping.

It was a scene of nightmare and it was taking place within the first half hour of Austrian occupation. As Katerina knelt at her mother's side, by Helga's body, she wondered what further horrors lay in store and thanked God that Natalie was not with them and would not have to endure them.

As the hours of occupation turned into days and the days turned into first one week and then two, Katerina mentally apologized time and time again to Major Zlarin. He had been utterly right when he had said that neither she nor her mother had any conception of what life under the heel of the enemy would be like. The yellow and black flag of the Habsburgs flew from the *Konak*'s flag-pole. Drunken soldiers looted both bomb-damaged houses and undamaged houses at will. The slaughter of civilians became an everyday incident. Old women were stood on chairs in the street to be hanged. Rape was commonplace. Retaliation impossible.

The Austrian high command moved into the Vassilovich *konak*, and Zita and Katerina rarely left the hospital. For ten horrendously long days they had no news of Cissie and then, unescorted and barely able to walk, she returned to the hospital.

It was Katerina who saw her first. She dropped the dressing tray she was carrying on to the first available surface and rushed towards her.

'Cissie!' she gasped, throwing her arms around her. 'Oh my God! We thought we were never going to see you again!' Tears of relief streamed down her face. 'Where did they take you? What happened to you? Are you all right?'

Even as she asked her last question Katerina knew that it was an utterly foolish one. Cissie was quite obviously far from all right. Her skin had lost its rain-fresh English bloom and there were deep, haggard shadows carved beneath her eyes.

As she drew her friend gently towards the nearest chair she said fearfully, 'Did they hurt you, Cissie? Did they beat you?'

'They raped me,' Cissie said, her voice barely audible, terrible in its lack of emotion. 'I don't want your mother to know. I don't want anyone to know apart from yourself.'

'But Cissie, she *has* to know!'

Cissie shook her head. 'No. I can't speak about it, Katerina. I don't want to be questioned about it. I don't want people to look at me and to remember . . .' Her voice cracked slightly, emotion showing for the first time. 'I want soap and hot water. Is there any? Can I have a bath? Can I have lots of baths?'

There was nowhere else for Cissie to stay but the hospital and the hospital was full of wounded Austrian and Hungarian soldiers. Katerina wondered how Cissie could possibly bear being in such close contact with them. She had begun to help out on the wards again and as Katerina watched her tend the Austrians and Hungarians as

272

diligently as she had the Serbian wounded, her admiration for her British friend soared sky-high.

At the end of the second week of occupation rumours began to fly that the Allies had finally managed to re-provision the army.

'If it's true, they'll fight their way back north again,' Zita said, her eyes ferociously bright. 'They'll chase these animals out of Belgrade and I hope every last murdering one of them drowns in the Sava!'

Katerina, remembering the terrified, bewildered old women who had been chivvied at bayonet point from their homes and executed in the streets, heartily concurred.

The atmosphere among the Austrians changed. Anxiety clearly began to replace triumph. News came of battles being waged along the Rudnik–Souvabor line, battles the Serbian army was winning. With the same speed with which it had been realized the city was to be abandoned to the enemy, came the realization it was about to be liberated. Wounded Austrians and Hungarians struggled from their beds as wounded Serbians had done before them, intent on fleeing from the city and back across the Sava to safety.

As the mayhem in the streets increased and as gunfire could be heard, drawing nearer and nearer to the city, Zita said to Katerina, 'The Austrian high command will have abandoned the house. I want to know what damage has been done to it. It's the first place your father will make for if he's with the returning troops and I want to leave a message there for him. I want to make sure he knows where to find us.'

Katerina didn't argue with her. After all the horrors they had endured, a walk through streets filled with panicking Austrians, when their own troops were within hearing distance, seemed almost as risk-free as a peacetime walk in the Kalemegdan Gardens.

It was Cissie who put the first doubt into her mind. 'The Austrians won't retreat empty-handed,' she said when Katerina told her where Zita had gone. 'They're going to take hostages. When your mother walks into the Vassilovich *konak*, so obviously its mistress, she's going to be arrested and hauled off across the Sava.'

'Mama thinks the high command will have already left the city,' Katerina said, anxiety beginning to stir. 'She thinks the *konak* will be empty.'

'For her sake, I hope she's right. But even if the high command have left, there may be lesser ranks still there. And if it's been deserted entirely, there will be looters.'

Katerina's anxiety was now fully fledged. Of course there would be looters. What on earth had she been thinking of, allowing her mother to walk unprotected into a situation bound to be highly volatile?

'I'm going after her,' she said, swiftly taking off her white apron with its prominent red cross on the bib. 'If neither of us comes back don't come after us. Wait until there are friendly troops in the city first.'

She didn't wait for Cissie to make a response. Pushing her way out into a corridor crammed with walking wounded all intent on fleeing the hospital and the city, she shoved and jostled her way out on to the street. It was quite obvious that the battle for Belgrade was taking place on its outskirts and that the one intention of all Austrian and Hungarian soldiers within the city was to leave it as fast as possible.

As she headed towards Prince Milan Street she was appalled at the scale of damage. Every other house was wrecked; the university, once the city's pride and joy, was entirely demolished; the streets had been cratered by bombs; everywhere cellars were exposed, great shells having broken down their walls and gouged their way deep into the earth.

The *Konak*, though damaged, still stood; as did their own house. At first it seemed blessedly deserted and then, as she hurried across the marble-floored hall and into the first of the downstairs salons, she heard her mother scream.

She raced back into the hall, the loaded pistol in her hand. Where had the scream come from? Upstairs or downstairs? The Italian room? Her father's study? The ballroom?

'*Mama!*' she shouted, panic bubbling up in her throat. '*Mama! Where are you?*'

There came an animal-like cry of pain from the direction of her father's study, the crash of falling furniture and then her mother shouted frantically: '*Get out, Katerina! Run. Run!*'

Katerina had no intention of getting out. She raced towards the study, the pistol heavy and slippery in her sweating hand. This time she was going to use it. This time nothing was going to stop her.

Her mother had been flung to the floor, blood streaming from a blow to her mouth. The bodice of her gown was ripped, exposing her breasts, her skirts pushed high. The Austrian was straddling her, his belt undone, his engorged penis in his hand.

He didn't even bother to lift his head and look towards Katerina as she ran into the room. 'If you're the daughter,' he said with contemptuous disdain, about to ram himself into Zita's exposed flesh, 'you must wait your turn.'

Katerina didn't hesitate. She lifted the pistol with both hands and squeezed the trigger hard. There was a brief second when, sensing danger too late, the Austrian turned his head towards her, the expression in his eyes changing from lascivious anticipation to one of stupefied disbelief.

The bullet hit him between the eyes, as perfect a shot as

if she had spent her entire life handling firearms. As blood and shattered bone spurted and he fell backwards, Zita screamed dementedly, *'Get him off me! For the love of God! Get him off me!'*

Katerina dropped the pistol, running towards her. 'Are there any other soldiers in the house?' she demanded frantically, seizing hold of the Austrian's shoulders. 'If there are we've got only minutes, perhaps seconds!'

Zita shook her head, struggling from beneath the Austrian's weight, racked by hysterical sobs. 'No! I don't think so! Oh my God, Katerina! What are we going to do?'

Katerina pantingly let go of the Austrian's carcass. 'We probably don't need to do anything,' she said, fighting to keep hysteria at bay, struggling to think clearly. 'The Austrians are leaving the city as fast as their legs will carry them. In another hour or so there's going to be no-one left to find the body and exact retribution.'

'But until then?' With shaking hands Zita was attempting to cover her breasts with the torn remnants of her blouse.

'We hide it,' Katerina said, terrified that at any moment someone would walk in on them. 'I'm going to drag him to the head of the cellar steps and push him down. While I do, go upstairs and see if any of your clothes are still in the closets. You can't walk back through the streets like that and we have to go back to the hospital. We can't stay here.'

Zita pressed the back of a violently trembling hand to her mouth, tears streaming down her face. 'Please God let your father and Max be among the troops who enter the city. Max and Major Zlarin were right. We shouldn't have stayed. For the last two weeks we haven't even been nursing our own wounded, we've been nursing Austrians and Hungarians. We should have gone to Nish with Vitza and Eudocia.'

'No, we shouldn't,' Katerina said briskly, knowing that her mother was on the verge of breaking down completely. 'We're Belgraders and our place is here. In years to come you'll be glad that we stayed. Now go and find another blouse.'

As her mother dazedly obeyed her, Katerina again seized hold of the Austrian's shoulders. She still hadn't told her mother about Major Zlarin's proposal of marriage and of her answer to him. As she tugged the body out of the study and towards the door leading to the cellar head, it occurred to her that she should do so before the army flooded victoriously back into the city. If her father and Max were among the victors and reunion with them was only hours away, it would help if her mother was no longer viewing Max as a prospective son-in-law.

The Austrian's body was horrendously heavy. Time and again she had to halt, panting for breath. Blood smeared the carpet and she wondered if she was wasting her time. Anyone entering the *konak* would be aware that an act of violence had recently taken place. She remembered that the house had served as Austro-Hungarian headquarters and that prisoners had no doubt been questioned in it. Blood on the carpet would arouse no undue curiosity.

Reaching the cellar door she yanked it open with relief. Hiding the body was perhaps totally unnecessary, but it was better to be safe than sorry. If Austrian officers returned and found their murdered comrade she didn't want an innocent person being shot in retribution.

Summoning the last remains of her strength she dragged the cumbersome body to the head of the stone steps and pushed. It buckled over, slithering and sliding down into the darkness. Panting harshly she turned her back on it, shutting the cellar head door firmly behind her. With luck it wouldn't be found until after it had ceased to matter.

Her mother was waiting for her in the hall, dressed in an

incongruously resplendent matching afternoon dress and winter coat.

'If we're going to be liberated I want to be dressed for the event,' she said defensively.

She no longer looked like a woman who had suffered near rape. Though her face was still ashen, her eyes were no longer in shock. They were those of a woman who had herself in control again. A woman who wasn't going to let the action of a now-dead stranger upset her equilibrium.

Sensing the change that had come over her mother in the short while they had been apart, Katerina felt relief flood through her. Her mother had changed into the most elegant outfit she could find not just in order to celebrate the city's liberation, but as an act of defiance towards the outrage she had suffered. The colour of the dress and coat was royal purple and she wondered if the colour, too, had been chosen on purpose. The coat was narrow and twelve inches or so shorter than the equally narrow ankle-length dress. The lapels and cuffs were edged in black braid and if her mother had also been wearing a hat she would have looked as if she were about to attend a *Konak* tea party.

Reading her thoughts a ghost of a smile touched the corners of Zita's mouth. 'I have every intention of stepping inside the *Konak* before today is over. I wonder if Peter has thought to give orders that no-one is to remove the Habsburg flag until he is able to do so himself? I hope he has. I want to be there when he hauls it down and tramples it underfoot.'

They began to walk out into the courtyard and she said, her smile fading, 'I wonder how his arthritis is after all these months of fighting? A lesser man would have simply stayed with his government in Nish, not shared the hardships of the trenches with men anything up to forty years his junior.'

Katerina's eyes darkened apprehensively. She was

wondering how her father had fared. Though only in his forties, not his sixties, he was still no longer young and the last few weeks of winter damp and cold would have taken their toll.

As they stepped out into Prince Milan Street it became obvious that the fighting was now in the city itself. As sniper-fire whistled over their heads, they ducked into the first gateway they came to, pressing their backs against a high stone wall.

'Should we go back to the house?' Zita asked, still deferring to Katerina's new-found authority.

Katerina shook her head. 'No. We're going to be needed at the hospital. If we take it slowly and carefully we'll be all right.'

A fleet of Austrian staff cars roared down the street, heading towards the river.

'They're going!' Zita said exultantly. 'Every last Austrian officer is running away! Oh God, *please* let your father be among the troops about to enter in triumph. And Alexander. And Max.'

Katerina put her head cautiously around the corner of the six-foot high gateway. What looked to be an entire division of Austro-Hungarian troops was surging down the street, racing after their fleeing officers. She ducked back again, wondering how long it was going to be before they could continue on their way.

'I need to talk to you about Max,' she said as the troops began to thunder past, only feet away from them.

Zita had to raise her voice to a shout in order for it to be audible. 'Your father will tell you everything you need to know! When the wedding will take place! Where you will live!'

A fresh outburst of gunfire added to the din. Katerina took a deep breath. She should never have started the conversation under such grotesque circumstances but now she had done so, she was determined to finish it.

'I'm not going to marry Max!' she shouted as a fresh barrage of shots flew over their heads. 'If Papa consents, and I think he will, I'm going to marry Major Zlarin!'

Zita's jaw dropped. '*Zlarin?*' she asked increduously. 'But when did the two of you become acquainted? Where? I don't understand.'

Despite the danger of the position in which they were, with enemy forces fleeing through the streets and bullets flying, Katerina felt a spasm of amusement. Never in her life had she seen her mother so stunned.

'Nothing has been going on behind your back,' she said as the number of running soldiers began to thin. 'I haven't seen him on any occasions you don't know about. He asked me to marry him when he came to the hospital and gave me the pistol. I accepted.' She gave another cautious look around the corner of the gate. The road was now clear of enemy soldiers and she said decisively, 'Come on. Let's make a run for it.'

'*Wait!*' Her mother clutched hold of her arm. 'What do you mean, he asked to marry you when he gave you the pistol and you accepted? Hadn't he given you any indication previously of his feelings? How long had you been secretly in love with him? Why hadn't you told me?'

'Not now, Mama. We've got to get back to the hospital. Can you hear distant cheering? Do you think the army is at the city gates?'

Together, hand-in-hand, they broke into a run, taking the shortest route. In every street and every alleyway Belgraders were pouring out of their homes eager for their first glimpse of their returning, victorious army.

'*They're here!*' came the cry. '*They're here!*' And long before Katerina and Zita reached the hospital Serbian cavalry was pouring into the city to be greeted by a deliriously grateful population.

'*Shall we stay here and join in the fun?*' Katerina shouted to her mother as they were deafened on all sides by Slavic hurrahs of '*Zivio! Zivio!*'

Zita nodded vigorously, her hideous ordeal nearly forgotten in the dizzying exhilaration of welcoming back an army so obviously, unequivocally triumphant.

From open windows winter flowers began to fall as women and girls raided vases and gardens. Chrysanthemum after chrysanthemum, white and yellow and flaming orange, were hurled over the heads of the exultant heroes until the ground beneath their feet was a literal carpet of petals.

A joyous-faced girl next to Katerina held the ceremonial sash she had embroidered for her bridegroom to wear on their wedding day. Squeezing a way to the front of the crowd she ran out into the street, hurling it around the neck of a delighted soldier. Other girls began to do the same until the marching men began to look like an army of festive bridegrooms.

When shots again began to ring out from the direction of the Sava no-one was perturbed. Everyone knew it was only their own troops helping the last of the Austrians and Hungarians back across the river into Hungary.

When Alexander rode down the street the cheering was at fever pitch. Tears poured down Katerina's face. For the first time in weeks she wished desperately that Natalie was in Belgrade; that she, too, was sharing this wonderful moment.

Shouts of '*The King! The King!*' went up in a tornado-like roar as a ramshackle open-topped car trundled into view. Katerina's throat hurt with the intensity of her cheers. Elderly and arthritic her uncle had fought alongside his troops like a common soldier. Never again would she feel less proud of her Karageorgevich heredity than her Vassilovich one. Not since the elderly Frederick the

Great had ridden into battle with his troops had a king of his age acted in such a way.

In her vibrant purple Parisian coat and dress Zita stood out from the crush around her as if she were wearing a tiara. Peter saw her and in disbelief and concern instructed the officer driving the car to halt.

Zita seized hold of Katerina's hand. 'Come on,' she said abandoning a lifetime of cool dignified reticence. 'We're Karageorgevichs and this is our moment just as much as it's Peter's and Sandro's and Max's and Papa's,' and before Katerina could protest she dragged her after her through the crowd, out into the street and across to the car.

Peter's grizzled eyebrows were high in disbelief. 'Zita! My dear girl! I had no idea you were still in the city! And Katerina, too!' He motioned them to join him. 'You should both have been at Nish . . .'

'We've been nursing at the hospital, Sir,' Zita said as she sat in the rear seat, overwhelmingly grateful that she had changed into an elegant outfit and looked as if she were a member of the royal family and not a scullery-maid.

Katerina sat beside her, well aware that she looked every inch a scullery-maid. Her serviceable blackberry-blue dress was splattered with bloodstains and tendrils of sweat-soaked hair had escaped from her neat chignon and were clinging damply to her temples and the nape of her neck.

The crowd didn't care. It was obvious from King Peter's action that they were members of his family; members who had quite voluntarily stayed in the city to suffer under enemy occupation.

As the battered staff car once more revved into life the deafening roars of 'Zivio! Zivio!' were as much for them as they were for the King and his troops.

'Alexis is leading his men in somewhere behind the

282

cavalry,' Peter said, acknowledging the cheers as they neared the *Konak*. 'And young Max is also leading troops into the city. He and his men fought their way north like devils. I'm going to have him promoted to brigadier. He'll be the youngest brigadier in the army and one day he'll be our youngest general.'

At the prospect of being flung so soon into Max's company Katerina shot her mother an anguished glance. Max's conversations with her father would have convinced him that he was on the point of becoming engaged to her. Who was going to tell him differently?

Zita, interpreting the glance correctly, laid a comforting hand on hers. 'Don't worry, my love. Immediately I see Papa I will tell him of Major Zlarin's proposal to you and of your desire to accept it.'

Katerina didn't correct her mother by saying that she had already accepted the proposal. If her mother wanted to believe that circumstances were normal and that she was waiting for her father's consent before accepting Major Zlarin's offer of marriage then she was quite happy to allow her to do so. All that mattered was that her father abandoned all thought of Max as a son-in-law. He had always been a loving and tolerant father and she was certain that now she had made her own choice as to a husband he would respect that choice and give her his blessing.

She wondered where Major Zlarin was, if he were among the troops who had fought their way north and re-taken the city.

As the staff car rumbled into the *Konak* courtyard euphoric, near hysterical Belgraders thronged after it. The Habsburg flag had already been hauled to the ground by a triumphant student. Too much a gentleman to show his intense disappointment at not being able to haul it down himself, Peter courteously allowed the proud young man to present it to him. For a brief second he held it aloft so that there might be no mistaking the object he held and then, as the crowd roared themselves into a near frenzy, he threw the yellow and black flag to the ground, spat on it and trampled it underfoot.

Katerina found entering the *Konak* after its occupation by the Austrians an even worse experience than entering her own home. Though her own home had suffered vile desecration it had not been stripped of its contents. In the *Konak*, room after room was totally bare.

'They brought furniture vans from Hungary, your Majesty,' a distraught official told the king. 'Nothing remains, not even your Majesty's personal photograph albums.'

Haggard-faced, his rheumatically afflicted hands clasped behind his back, King Peter walked through the rooms of his plundered palace.

Katerina and Zita, sensing it was a tour of inspection he wished to conduct alone, remained in the now echoingly empty Grand Salon.

They were still there when a weary but triumphant Alexis strode in on them.

Zita entered his arms like an arrow entering the gold, tears of thankfulness streaming down her face.

'Oh my love! Oh my darling!' she gasped between kisses. 'Are you all right? Have you been hurt? Are you going to be staying in Belgrade? Is the worst over now? Is the war drawing to a close?'

He hugged her close, hair that had previously only been grey at the temples now grey all over. 'I'm not staying,' he said thickly, knowing the worst news must be broken at once. 'The enemy may have been chased across the Sava but they still have to be chased across the Drina.'

Reluctantly he released her and turned towards Katerina, his eyes suspiciously bright. 'Has it been very terrible, my darling?' he asked, taking her in his arms and rocking her against his chest as he had used to do when she was a little girl. 'Was I grossly neglectful in allowing the two of you to stay?'

Katerina thought of the nightmare that had taken place only an hour or so ago. She wondered if her mother would ever tell him all the details of what had happened and doubted it.

'No,' she said, not wanting him to feel the slightest measure of guilt for a decision that had been taken in defiance of his wishes.

Zita said, her eyes carefully avoiding Katerina's, 'There was an incident at home. An Austrian officer was shot and killed. His body is down the cellar steps.'

Slowly he released hold of Katerina, his eyes holding his wife's. 'An incident?' he asked, his voice raw with dread. 'What kind of incident? And which cellar steps? Our house has a score of cellars.'

'The ones nearest the downstairs public rooms,' Katerina said, coming to her mother's rescue. 'It's nothing for you to worry about, Papa. We'll tell you all about it later. But if you could have the body removed . . .'

Despite her elation at the expulsion of the Austrians and her joy at their family reunion, her face was pale with strain. That she and Zita had witnessed unspeakable horrors was obvious, as was their reluctance to put those horrors into words. It was a reluctance he understood. He, too, had no desire to talk of what he had seen and done since they had last been together.

He said: 'I'll send men to remove it immediately. Meanwhile, what is all this about Major Zlarin wishing to marry you? He told me when his troops and mine joined forces at Rudnik. He was exceedingly apologetic at speaking to you without having spoken to me beforehand but I assured him that, under the circumstances, I quite understood.' A slight smile touched his mouth, the first time it had done so in months. 'I was tempted to tell him that it wasn't the first time a young man had omitted such a politeness when courting one of my daughters.'

Katerina tried to smile in return and failed. He was referring to Julian's initial proposal to Natalie on the night when she had been so certain he was going to propose to herself. For weeks she had successfully kept all thoughts of Julian at bay. Panic welled up in her throat. If she succumbed to them now she would never be able to marry Major Zlarin. And if she didn't marry Major Zlarin she would have to live with the knowledge she was causing her father great distress by not agreeing to marry Max.

'Is Major Zlarin with the troops who have entered the city?' she asked, struggling to drive Julian's image from her mind.

Alexis nodded and then, sliding his arm around Zita's waist, taking Katerina's hand in his, he said gravely, 'I want you both to listen to me very carefully. Belgrade may be back in Serbian hands but Serbia itself is far from being so. Austro-Hungarian forces still have to be routed from the north-west. Shabatz and all the towns and villages around it still have to be re-taken. That being the case, very few of the troops who have just entered the city will be remaining. We will be leaving almost immediately to consolidate the victories of the last few days and to ensure that no enemy troops remain anywhere in the country.'

Zita leaned against him, knowing there was going to be no closer physical reunion than the kisses they had just exchanged. Reading her thoughts, sharing her feelings, his arm tightened around her.

'What I am going to ask of you now is going to be difficult for both of you. We have already had one hasty wedding in the family, without ritual and any kind of celebration. Now I am going to ask that we have another.'

286

Zita pulled away from him, horrified. 'What are you talking about? You're surely not suggesting that Katerina should marry Major Zlarin in the same . . . the same unsatisfactory manner in which Natalie married?'

'I'm suggesting that the wedding takes place without prior preparation,' he said gently. 'That doesn't mean it has to take place privately, in the palace, as was the case with Natalie. This time the wedding will take place in the cathedral, but I want it to take place within the next few hours, before I leave the city.'

'But why?' Zita asked despairingly, all hope of seeing at least one of her daughters married with pomp and ceremony fast disappearing. 'I don't understand!'

'The war we are now in is not a war purely between Serbia and Austria. It is a world war, and it is not going to be over by Easter or even by next Christmas. When I leave the two of you this time there is no telling when we will be reunited and I would like to see Katerina married before I leave. Now do you understand?'

Looking down into her bewildered face he saw that she did not. Gently he drew her once again into the circle of his arms. He had not wanted to put his reason for wanting a hasty marriage between Katerina and Major Zlarin into brutally blunt words but knew now that he had no option.

'I'm not a young man any more,' he said sombrely. 'The fighting at the front is going to be long and hard and I think it very likely, my darling, that I might not survive it.'

She gave an anguished cry of protest.

He ignored it, saying steadfastly, 'Now do you understand why I want to see Katerina married before I leave again for the front?'

She nodded, tears glistening on her eyelashes. 'And Major Zlarin?' she said tremulously, 'Will he be agreeable?'

'I've already spoken with him and the answer is yes. Both his parents are dead. No feelings will be hurt at his marrying in such a manner, or at least no feelings that he cares about.'

Katerina felt as if a bottomless pit had opened at her feet and if she were about to fall headlong into it.

'But, Papa . . .' she said, appalled at his premonition that he would die on the battlefield; appalled at the prospect of marrying a near stranger in such haste. 'We are not yet even officially engaged! And you won't die! I know you won't! When the war is over and when you return to Belgrade, then we can celebrate with a wedding!'

'I doubt if this war is going to be over for years,' Alexis said heavily. 'And though I hope you are right and that I do return, I can't help feeling the chances are very heavily against it. To see you married now, before I go away, will give me great peace of mind, Katerina.'

She was at the edge of the pit, beginning to slip. There was nothing she could say without revealing that she was not hopelessly in love with her bridegroom-to-be.

'And Max?' Zita was saying. 'He will have to be told – and quickly.'

'I'll undertake that task,' Alexis said, thankful the worst was over and that arrangements could now be made. 'In ordinary circumstances he could have served as Zlarin's best man, as it is he will probably not want to be in attendance at all.'

'Then there will be a best man?' Zita asked intensely relieved that the wedding wasn't going to be quite as makeshift as Natalie's had been. 'And will Katerina have a bridesmaid to escort her to the cathedral?'

'The wedding will be as traditional as we can make it in the time available,' Alexis promised. 'The problem is going to be bridesmaids. Everyone will no doubt flock back from Nish now that the city is free of Austrians, but there's no telling just when Vitza and other family members will arrive.'

'That doesn't matter,' Katerina said, grateful that there was at least one problem it was within her grasp to solve. 'I would like Cissie to be my bridesmaid. I don't need anyone else.'

'Then the sooner you and Cissie get together with Helga and plan what you will wear, the better.'

Katerina and Zita stared at him, appalled.

As the expression on their faces registered on him he said sharply, 'What is it? Has Helga been hurt?'

'She's dead,' Zita said in a cracked voice. 'She was shot in front of us. Executed as a traitor because she nursed Serbians.'

'Dear God,' Alexis whispered, his face taking on an ashen pallor as he drew them both close, realizing that he hadn't come near to imagining what both of them had suffered.

During the next hectic few hours, as arrangements for her wedding went ahead at breakneck pace, Katerina wondered if Natalie had felt the same mounting panic she was now feeling. She must have done, for she had had even less warning that she was to be married and her bridegroom hadn't even been of her own choosing.

When Zita had suggested that under the circumstances she might like to break with tradition and speak with her bridegroom before the ceremony, Katerina had shaken her head emphatically. If she saw him she might panic totally. She was being coerced into nothing that wasn't of her own choice. The pity was, that it wasn't as she had imagined it would be.

She had anticipated that by the time they married they would have come to know each other well; that the war would be over; that Natalie would be in

Belgrade and would be her chief bridesmaid.

As it was she was marrying with no more preparation than Natalie had done. Her mother had been unable to beg, borrow or steal a wedding gown and so she had said that she would wear one of her summer dresses. The dress she decided on was of white chiffon. It swirled floatingly around her ankles and she made it festive by pinning a small posy of white winter bud-roses to the bodice.

She left for the cathedral from the *Konak*. The streets were still thronged and word quickly spread that the bride was King Peter's niece; that she had voluntarily stayed in the city throughout its occupation and was marrying the officer who had commanded the troops responsible for keeping Austro-Hungarian forces at bay all through September and October.

Accompanied all the way by cheers and shouted good wishes her carriage trundled through the bomb-cratered streets, the horses picking their way with infinite care.

As she stepped out of her carriage at the cathedral what looked to Katerina to be an entire division of soldiers were waiting to greet her. For the first time in months rifles and pistols were let off without deadly intention as they shot off volley after volley into the air, announcing her arrival in age-old fashion.

None of her family had yet arrived back in the city from Nish and she entered the cathedral knowing the only wedding guests would be her parents and a handful of Major Zlarin's fellow officers. It was the near-emptiness of the imposing incense-filled interior that made the presence of the unexpected guest so instantly obvious.

He was stood facing the front of the cathedral, his back towards her.

Katerina's hand tightened on her father's arm. He had told her Max would not be at the ceremony. He had told her that he had told Max of her engagement and imminent marriage to Major Zlarin and that Max had taken the news with commendable stoicism.

She looked from the back of his head to where Major Zlarin was waiting for her. He, too, had his back firmly towards her. Suddenly the panic she had been fighting ever since she had known they were to be married so soon, convulsed her. She gasped and stumbled, only her father's swift support preventing her from falling.

Max turned his head and looked towards her. As their eyes met she suddenly saw beyond his mask of infuriating brusqueness and rudeness. He was brusque and rude because beneath that bear-like façade he was cripplingly shy. She wondered why she hadn't realized it before. Her mother had. Her mother had guessed the night he had come to say goodbye to them. Suddenly he no longer seemed repellent and odd; suddenly he seemed blessedly familiar and reassuring.

She looked away from him and towards her husband-to-be. His back was still firmly towards her, ramrod straight, far from familiar and light years away from being reassuring.

As she kept on walking, drawing nearer and nearer to him, it occurred to her for the first time that she was quite possibly making the biggest and most far-reaching mistake of her life.

Chapter Fourteen

Natalie had never missed or wanted her mother as much as she did when she was having the baby. She couldn't believe how horrendous labour was. No-one had prepared her for it. When she had asked the family doctor what she might expect, he had said merely that he would take care of everything and that all she had to do was be 'a good girl'. It was advice she had found singularly unhelpful. In theory she supposed that she could have asked her mother-in-law but in practice she would rather have gone kicking and screaming into hell. Diana, for all her nursing experience at Guy's, had been utterly useless.

'Wounded soldiers don't have babies,' she had said pragmatically. 'All I know is that lashings of hot water and towels are necessary.'

'What on earth for?' Natalie had asked, her perplexity deepening. 'I shan't want a bath when I'm giving birth and the baby isn't going to need vast quantities of bath water. It will probably be able to fit into a decent sized kitchen bowl.'

Diana, who knew less about kitchen bowls than she did midwifery, said reassuringly, 'I shouldn't worry about it. No-one else seems to. When the baby is ready to arrive it simply arrives and that's all there is to it.'

As she lay in a specially prepared bedroom in her in-laws' house, Natalie knew from three hours painful experience that Diana had been exceedingly over optimistic.

Other babies might very well arrive simply and uncompli-
catedly. Hers wasn't doing so.

'How much longer is this going to go on?' she demanded
of the midwife. 'I've been in labour for three hours now.
Surely three hours is long enough for a baby to be
born?'

'Three hours is no time at all, Mrs Fielding,' the
midwife said in amusement. 'The doctor has looked at you
and he's gone on his way. He wouldn't have done so if he'd
thought the birth was imminent.'

'Gone on his way?' Natalie forgot about the intermittent
pain cramping her stomach and the intolerable ache in her
lower back. She pushed herself up against the pillows.
'What do you mean, "gone on his way"? He's in the house,
isn't he?'

The midwife's amusement deepened. Society mothers
always had an inflated idea of their own importance and
this one seemed to think she had been highly incon-
venienced merely at having had to take to a bed.

'Doctors are busy men, Mrs Fielding,' she said
patiently, busying herself laying out scissors and string
and soap in readiness for the doctor's eventual return.
'And they are busier than ever now there are so many war-
wounded. You need to rest and conserve your strength.'

Natalie stared at her in deepening horror. Conserve her
strength? For what, for the Lord's sake? If this wasn't
labour, what was?

During the next two hours she blamed her increasing
misery on everyone she could think of. Julian, for having
made her pregnant in the first place; his mother, for not
having ensured she had a doctor who would have speeded
events up a little; her father, for having insisted she leave
Belgrade and persuading her that marriage to Julian was
the best way of doing so; Gavrilo, for being responsible for
her having to leave Belgrade; and Katerina, for not having

293

physically prevented her from meeting him in the *Golden Sturgeon*.

'We're nearly there, Mrs Fielding,' the doctor said encouragingly as she pushed and pushed, panting for air.

Natalie was glad to hear it. She was never going to have a baby again. The pain was vile, the indignity beyond all bearing.

'And again, Mrs Fielding!' the doctor exhorted cheerfully. 'I can see the baby's head! Easy now, try and relax.'

Through eyelashes beaded with perspiration Natalie shot him a look of pure venom. He was a certifiable madman. In Serbia it was customary for midwives to bring babies into the world unassisted by doctors and Natalie now understood why. No woman would have made such a ridiculous request at such a time. He might just as well have asked her to fly to the moon. Her body was out of her control and all she could do was to let it get on with whatever was happening to it.

The pain reached a crescendo she didn't know how she was going to survive; she felt as if she were being split in two; as if she were enduring death by medieval torture.

There was a gush of warm liquid, a lusty yelling, and it was over. She gave fervent thanks to God and turned her attention to the mucus-covered, squalling infant on the bed.

He was beautiful. Just as nothing had prepared her for the rigours of labour, so she was totally unprepared for the overwhelming love she instantly felt for the kicking scrap of humanity that was her son. In one swift second she forgot her vows never again to become pregnant. If this was the result then she wanted a baby every year. He was wonderful; incredible; magical beyond anything she had ever imagined.

It seemed an eternity before his umbilical cord was cut

and he was bathed and powdered and dressed in a little tie-string vest, a frilled and beribboned nightdress and a muslin napkin. Finally, when she knew she would die if she had to wait a moment longer, he was wrapped in a shawl and placed in her arms.

His hair was still damp and plastered slickly to his head and it was impossible to tell its true colour. It was dark though, far darker than Julian's Anglo-Saxon fairness. The colour of his eyes, too, was nearly impossible to distinguish. Diana had told her that all babies were born with blue eyes, but her son's eyes didn't look a true blue. They were grey, the colour of English bluebells before they opened. She wondered if he was going to look more English than Slav and, if he did, if she would mind.

He made a little mewling sound, his tiny fingers struggling to be free of the shawl. She loosened it gently, knowing the answer immediately. No matter how English his colouring might prove to be, it wouldn't matter in the slightest. All that mattered was that he was hers and that he was healthy. She wondered how soon it would be before she could return to Belgrade with him. She wondered if it would matter having the christening when he was several months old.

'What are you going to call him?' Diana demanded when she was allowed in the bedroom to see them both.

'Stephen.'

Diana's carefully plucked eyebrows rose in startled surprise. 'Stephen? Is that your father's name?'

Natalie looked towards the crib, loath to take her eyes off its contents for even a second. 'No. Papa's name is Alexis and Stephen will be Stephen Alexis.'

'You can't just name him after your father,' Diana said reasonably. 'If you do, Pa will be most dreadfully hurt.

295

And what abut Julian? Won't he be expecting his son to be named after him?'

Natalie frowned slightly. She had never seriously discussed names with Julian. 'Stephen Alexis Julian,' she amended, wishing that Julian was a little more Slavic.

Diana decided to forgo the subject of her father's name being included as well. New mothers were notoriously touchy and she didn't want Natalie bursting into postnatal tears.

'Why Stephen?' she asked again. 'Is it a Karageorgevich family name?'

Natalie shook her head. 'No. George and Alexander are the most common Karageorgevich male names. I'm calling him Stephen after Stephen Dushan Nemanya who was crowned Tsar of all the Serbs in 1346 when Serbia was an empire.'

'Very nice too,' Diana said good-humouredly, grateful that the Tsar's first Christian name hadn't been as much of a tongue-twister as his other two names. Her mother was going to find it hard enough to come to terms with Stephen as a first name. Dushan would have pole-axed her.

'The baby will be christened at St James's when Julian is next on leave,' her mother-in-law said frostily when the subject came under discussion and Natalie told her of her plans to have Stephen baptized in Belgrade Cathedral. 'It could be years before it's safe to travel to the Balkans and a young child most certainly couldn't make such an arduous journey. It's out of the question.'

Natalie thought of the luxury of the Orient Express and did what she always did when in conflict with Lady Fielding. She ignored her. It was the only way she could survive the situation. If she once gave rein to her volatile temper she doubted if her mother-in-law would live to tell the tale.

A month after Stephen's birth she again met Nikita at the church hall. This time he greeted her like an old friend, vastly relieved that the bulk that had been the baby had now disappeared.

'We're not staying here, among these old women,' he said, his disparaging glance taking in the men as well as their wives and daughters. 'I have people I want you to meet.'

'Good,' Natalie said in happy anticipation. 'Are they the friends you spoke about before? The ex-mayor of Split and the journalist and the sculptor?'

'Maybe, though maybe not. They're important people. They're in meetings all the time with men such as the editor of the British *Times* and Mr Seton-Watson.'

Natalie had no idea who Mr Seton-Watson was but as he was obviously important, and as she knew from the attention her father-in-law gave to every announcement in *The Times* that its editor was important also, she was impressed.

The ex-mayor of Split and the journalist and the sculptor were not at the café to which Nikita took her, but there were lots of other Slavs there, all young and all nationalistic.

Natalie was in heaven. It was just like being in the *Golden Sturgeon* again, only instead of talking endlessly over cups of coffee and small glasses of *slivovitz*, her new-found friends talked endlessly over cups of English tea.

Her relationship to King Peter gave her immediate status, just as it had done with Gavrilo and Trifko and Nedjelko. She was questioned endlessly as to what his policy was with regard to the creation of a new South Slav state and, even more importantly as Alexander was now Regent, what Alexander's policy was.

As before, Natalie had no real idea. She and Alexander

had gossiped, played tennis and romped with Bella together, they hadn't discussed politics. As before she took great care that no-one should suspect her ignorance as to her cousin's political views. As nearly all Nikita's friends were Croats, not Serbs, the subject most under discussion was not union between Serb and Serbian, as it had been in the *Golden Sturgeon*. Instead the preoccupation was with exactly how equal partnership between Serb and Croat in a new South Slav state would actually be achieved. Such semantics left Natalie cold. All that mattered to her was that the new state would be, by another name, the glorious medieval empire ruled over by Tsar Stephen and that this time Alexander would be its Tsar.

There had been a few slight frowns when she had happily referred to this idyllic vision of the future.

'We're working for constitutional, democratic and parliamentary union, not for an enlarged Serbia,' one of the older men said to her cautioningly.

Natalie had met with this hair-splitting before and had little patience with it. Union between the Slavic states, at present unwillingly part of the Habsburg empire, and Serbia, would obviously result in an enlarged Serbia and she had never been unable to understand why her non-Serbian friends could not see that.

'It would be a monarchy, of course,' the pedant allowed, 'headed by the Karageorgevich dynasty. If King Peter abdicates in favour of Alexander, then Alexander Karageorgevich will be Yugoslavia's first king.'

Natalie was glad to hear it.

'But not tsar,' the pedant continued stuffily. 'Yugoslavia will be a kingdom, not an empire.'

As far as Natalie was concerned he was again splitting hairs. If Croatia, Slovenia and Bosnia, and quite possibly Montenegro and parts of Macedonia as well, united in one state with Belgrade as its capital and Alexander as its king, then Serbia would be an empire again.

Seeing her irritation Nikita said, changing the subject, 'Have you read about the latest battle at Gallipoli? The British and French have occupied two strongly fortified lines of Turkish trenches.'

'Trenches, bah!' the elderly man who had taken Natalie to task said disgustedly. 'What is the good of trench warfare? It wears men out and kills them without achieving anything.'

This time Natalie found herself in agreement with him. Julian had been declared medically fit and released from hospital and was again in Flanders. His letters home were as inconsequential and cheerful as Edward's and Natalie wasn't fooled by them in the slightest. Once again he was enduring the stalemate of trench warfare, once again he was living without even basic sanitary comforts.

There were times, when she wasn't with Nikita and his friends and the conversation didn't centre entirely on the war and what might happen after the war, when it was hard to remember the conditions being suffered in Flanders and Gallipoli. In many respects life in London was exactly as she imagined it had been in peacetime. Stephen was regularly wheeled around St James's Park by the nanny employed by her mother-in-law. Though Diana was still a VAD at Guy's she had plenty of time off and her free time was spent as it had always been. She lunched in smart restaurants with friends, went to parties and danced until the early hours of the morning. Much to her mother-in-law's furious disapproval, Natalie often accompanied her.

'Julian wouldn't mind,' she said to Diana truthfully. 'He wouldn't want me to be bored.'

'With all your interesting new friends I don't see how you could possibly be bored,' Diana had said enviously,

'Will Nicky really be a member of the government when this new kingdom of the South Slavs is founded after the war?'

Natalie frowned slightly. Nikita had long since asked her to call him Nicky and it irked her that Diana had begun to do so also, giving the impression that she, too, was an intimate friend. As for Nicky one day being a member of the Yugoslav government, she couldn't remember having ever given Diana that impression but as the belief obviously made Nicky ultra-respectable in Diana's eyes she saw no harm in allowing her to cling to it.

'All the founding members of the Yugoslav Committee will hold government positions,' she said, trying to sound suitably authoritative.

That Diana knew of Nicky's existence was a source of irritation to her. It had been accidental. She and Diana had been enjoying ices at Gunther's. Deep in conversation they had stepped out into the street and walked headlong into Nicky. From that moment on Diana had been like a woman obsessed, wanting to talk about nothing else.

'Are you sure he isn't a Karageorgevich?' she had demanded the minute they were out of earshot. 'He looks like a Karageorgevich. All dark and damn-your-eyes, just like a Balkan bandit.'

'He's not a Karageorgevich,' Natalie had responded, crossly. 'He's not even Serbian. He's a Croat. And what do you mean by likening Karageorgevichs to Balkan bandits? Prince Alexander is nothing remotely like a bandit. He's very intellectual.'

'I'm sorry,' Diana said, appalled by the realization she had been unintentionally insulting. 'I meant it as a compliment. I meant bandit in the Byronic sense; mad, bad and dangerous to know.'

'Karageorgevichs are none of those things,' Natalie said archly, conveniently forgetting a family history thick with murder, kidnappings and skulduggery. 'We're *royalty*, not riff-raff.'

'Of course you are!' Diana agreed warmly, looking forward to a future in which she would be a guest at the Royal Palace in Belgrade, 'and I wasn't insinuating anything else for one moment. It's just that Nicky is so dashing and his hair is so dark and curly that he reminded me of Byron, dressed in Albanian costume and about to fight the Turk for Greek independence.'

Natalie's knowledge of Byron and his connection with Albania and Greece was distinctly sketchy and so rather than risk revealing her ignorance of English poets and British history she allowed herself to be mollified.

'He is *excessively* romantic looking,' Diana eulogized as she paused to buy a posy of gardenias from a flower-seller. 'How did you meet him? Was he a friend of Julian's in Belgrade?'

'I met him at the Serbian exiles club,' Natalie said truthfully, leaving the second part of Diana's question conveniently unanswered and adding quickly, 'He's a friend of Mr Wickham Steed, the editor of *The Times*.'

Diana was not at all fazed at Natalie having made friends with a young man to whom she had not been properly introduced, choosing to believe that Wickham Steed, a friend of her father's, had introduced her to Nicky.

'Julian is going to be awfully pleased with all the diplomatic contacts you are making,' she said guilelessly as they continued to stroll through the late summer crowds. 'It's going to be an enormous help to him after the war, when he returns to the Foreign Office.'

Natalie made an inarticulate sound that she hoped Diana would take for one of agreement. Privately she doubted very much that Julian was going to be pleased with her. It was far more likely that he was going to be far

301

from pleased. In fact it was quite possible that he was going to be exceedingly displeased.

Irritation at the chance meeting between Diana and Nicky swept over her afresh. If Diana had remained ignorant of Nicky's existence, Julian wouldn't have to be told about her friendship with him. Even despite Nicky's credentials as the friend of Mr Wickham Steed and Mr Seton-Watson, Julian was not going to be impressed. He was immediately going to class Nicky in the same category as Gavrilo and Trifko and Nedjelko and he was going to assume that her friendship with him would lead to disaster, just as her friendship with nationalists in Belgrade had led to disaster.

It was the end of November when he wrote her, telling her that he had leave and would be home for Christmas. Despite her misgivings as to what his reaction would be when he was told of her friendship with Nicky, Natalie was overjoyed. He would cheer and comfort her as he always did and the war news was such that she was in desperate need of cheer and comfort.

The attempt to storm the Gallipoli peninsula had ended in total retreat; Serbia was as cut off from her allies as she had ever been. Even worse was the news from Serbia itself. All through the autumn Austro-German troops had been attacking in force along the Danube front while four hundred thousand Bulgarian troops had hurled themselves across the western frontier. The result had been catastrophic. When news of what was taking place in Serbia had finally reached London it was disclosed that the Serbian army was in retreat and marching without food and adequate clothing across the snow-covered mountains into Albania.

Natalie had at first been disbelieving and then prostrate with grief. How had it happened? Why, why, why hadn't the Allies ensured that munitions reach Serbia? At the thought of Austrian and German chiefs of staff inhabiting the *Konak* and Austro-German and Bulgarian troops strutting Belgrade streets she had been physically sick. Not even Stephen's existence had eased her heartache. What had happened to her father? Was he, too, marching in rags across treacherous icy mountain passes into Albania? Were Max and Sandro with him? And what of her uncle? How could he, arthritic and elderly, survive the hell of such a journey?

'Napoleon and his army successfully crossed the Alps,' Diana said to her, trying to take a positive attitude to the news.

'Napoleon made his march after long and careful preparation,' Natalie said bleakly, remembering her childhood lessons in all things French. 'He didn't make the crossing with inadequate means of transport and no provisions.'

Diana was suitably chastened. She couldn't imagine how she would feel if her father or Julian or Edward were retreating over mountains in temperatures which Natalie had assured her would be well below zero. She said tentatively, changing the subject, 'Where will your mother and sister be now? Will they still be in Belgrade?'

Natalie's heart-shaped face became even paler. 'I don't know. They may have gone to Nish, but the Austrians and Germans and Bulgarians will be in Nish now as well.'

They both fell silent, not wanting to put into words their fears of what Serbia's civilian population might now be suffering.

She had no warning of his arrival, he simply walked into the house. A maid ran to the nursery where Natalie now spent nearly all her time, to tell her the news. Natalie promptly thrust her son into his nurse's arms and ran out into the corridor and towards the stairs, Bella at her heels.

He was still in the large hallway, his kitbag at his feet, being greeted by his mother. She called his name from the head of the stairs and as he raised his head, his eyes meeting hers, his mother might as well have not existed.

'Julian! Oh, *Julian!*'

As he strode to the foot of the stairs she hurtled down them and into his waiting arms.

Dimly she was aware of her mother-in-law's frigid disapproval, dimly she was aware that they were being watched round-eyed by half the household staff. She didn't care. He was home and he would somehow find out from his friends at the Foreign Office exactly what was happening in Serbia and where her family were.

'Oh, I've missed you so much!' she gasped truthfully when at last he released her.

Before he could reply Lady Fielding said freezingly, 'Shall we go into the drawing-room? The hall is not the most suitable place for a family reunion, and can you please stop that dog from racing around in circles and barking in such an annoying manner?'

'Julian hasn't seen Stephen yet,' Natalie protested, ignoring completely her mother-in-law's references to Bella. 'You must come upstairs *this minute*, Julian, and say hello to your son. He's absolutely wonderful. He hardly ever cries and he and Bella adore each other.'

Taking hold of his hand she began to lead him up the stairs, Bella still skittering excitedly around their ankles, and it was only then that she realized just how badly he had been injured.

'You're limping!' she said, her eyes widening in shock. 'You didn't tell me you had a limp. You said you had been declared fit for active service again!'

'So I have,' he said easily. 'A limp counts for nothing, these days. Ignore it. I do.' And with his hand tightening

304

on hers he continued to walk up the stairs and towards the nursery.

Her delight and pride, as he bent over Stephen's crib and very tenderly lifted him from it, was marred by concern. For the first time she was able to look at him clearly and she was shocked by the change in him. He was still incredibly handsome, still tall and wonderfully broad-shouldered, his combination of dark-gold hair and brown eyes still as striking as ever, but there were lines on his face that had never been there before and he had lost so much weight that he looked positively emaciated.

'Hello, old chap,' he was saying tenderly to his chortling son as he cradled him awkwardly in his arms. 'You don't know me yet, but you soon will do. I'm your Pa.'

Natalie dragged her thoughts away from the horrors he had so obviously endured since they were last together and said proudly, 'Isn't he absolutely gorgeous? His eyes were almost blue when he was born but they're hazel now. His hair isn't remotely like yours though. Even when he was newly born it was obvious it was going to be nearer my colour than yours. I still can't make up my mind whether he's going to look more English than Slav, or more Slav than English. He's going to be handsome though, isn't he?'

'Very handsome,' Julian said thickly, gazing down at the son he had feared he would never see. 'And I like the name. Is it for Stephen, last Tsar of Serbia?'

She nodded. 'I knew you wouldn't mind. I named him after you and Papa as well. Stephen Alexis Julian.'

Very gently Julian laid Stephen back down in his crib. 'We have to go back downstairs,' he said regretfully. 'I haven't seen Pa yet and if we lock ourselves in our room before I do so, we'll never hear the last of it.'

'Tell me what happened to you when you were injured,'

she said, her eyes holding his as his arms closed once more around her. 'Was it far worse than you made out in your letters? Will you always have a limp?'

'Will it matter to you if I have?'

She shook her head. 'No,' she said with patent truthfulness. 'All that matters to me is that you are alive.'

He felt weak with thankfulness, not because his limping would not offend her, but because her reply told him that she loved him.

As always, her uninhibited response to him in bed convinced him of her love more than any number of words. There were times when his happiness was so great, as opposed to the horrors he had left behind him, that he felt both mentally and physically disorientated. Instead of being a mere day and a half away, Flanders could have been as far away as the moon.

At a welcome home party that Diana and Natalie arranged for him there were two bands, one American and black, the other Hawaiian. The food was light years removed from the food of the trenches. Instead of bully-beef there were avocados and terrapin and soft-shell crabs and instead of enamel mugs of bitter tea there was champagne and plentiful supplies of claret and brandy.

Though the dancing had continued until dawn and everyone invited declared it a great success, he had not enjoyed it. It had seemed bizarre and excessive and he found it hard to credit that such shenanigins, amid rooms awash with hot-house orchids and roses, could be regarded as normal when across the Channel men were dying in their thousands in conditions of unimaginable vileness.

Natalie sensed his deep inner repugnance to the jollities Diana so assiduously arranged for him and sympathized totally. She, too, found it hard to party when her inner thoughts were on the sufferings being undergone by her country's retreating army.

'Can you find out for me if my uncle is still with his troops? If it is Sandro who is leading the army across the mountains and into Albania?' she had asked him as they lay in bed, wrapped in each other's arms, their bodies exhausted and satiated after lovemaking.

He had been able to find out very little. 'There's been no communication with the Serbian High Command for months,' he said when he returned from a visit in Whitehall. 'The rumours are that both King Peter and Prince Alexander are with the troops now struggling to make a crossing into Albania. As to what is happening in Belgrade and Nish, there are no reports whatsoever, not even rumours.'

The lack of information to even someone with Julian's diplomatic contacts was a crushing disappointment to her but it was one that had to be borne. Another burden was the weight of his annoyance when Diana's careless talk left her no option but to tell him about Nicky.

'A Croat nationalist?' he had asked, dumbfounded. 'After everything that happened after you made friends with Princip you've been foolish enough to make friends with a Croat nationalist? Can't you understand that these people are only interested in trying to use you? In trying to exploit your family links?'

'You're wrong,' she had said stubbornly, hating the fact that they were on the verge of an argument. 'All that matters to Nicky and his friends is that I am a South Slav, just as they are.'

'Being a South Slav has nothing whatsoever to do with it!' he exploded, running his hand through his hair. 'If you weren't a Karageorgevich members of the Yugoslav

Committee wouldn't even give you the time of day!'

'You don't understand,' she said tightly, wishing that she could have kept Nicky a secret from him, wishing that Nicky and Diana had never met. 'The Yugoslav Committee is respectable! The editor of *The Times* is in sympathy with the Committee's aims! It is the kind of organization Papa would have joined . . .'

'Your father would not have wanted you involving yourself with nationalists of any kind,' he retorted grimly. 'Have you forgotten what happened last time? You nearly found yourself in an Austrian court on a charge of complicity in the assassination of Archduke Franz Ferdinand!'

'You're wrong,' she said again, mutinously. 'No warrant was ever issued for my arrest. The Austrians never requested my extradition.'

He turned away from her sharply, thrusting his fists deep into his trouser pockets. When Alexis had written to him, telling him of the Austrian request for her extradition, he had determined never to tell her, seeing no point in causing her further distress by doing so. Now he was sorely tempted to tell her exactly how close she had been to standing trial alongside Gavrilo Princip and his cronies.

She stepped close up behind him, sliding her hand conciliatingly through his arm. 'Don't let's fall out,' she said huskily. 'There are only another four days before you return to the front. Don't let's spoil them.'

His anger had melted instantaneously. He knew far more about the Yugoslav Committee than she could possibly guess and, to be fair to her, what she had said about it was true. It *was* respectable. Through its dealings with the British government it had acquired the *de facto* stature of a kind of government-in-exile for the South Slavs still under the rule of the Habsburg monarchy. Thanks to Yugoslav emigrants in North and South America it had both funds and military recruits.

Whether Nikita Kechko was as respectable as Trumbich, Supilo, Mestrovich and other eminent members of the Committee was another matter entirely and one he intended finding out. For the moment, however, he and Natalie were on loving terms again and he didn't intend to waste another moment discussing a subject that could only cause tension between them.

Natalie was equally glad to drop the subject. She had known Julian wouldn't approve of her participation in nationalist activity. He was an Englishman, not a South Slav, and he couldn't possibly understand the age-old dream of South Slav unity.

It was Diana who exasperatedly brought the subject up again.

'I think we should invite Nicky to next Sunday's cocktail party,' she said to Natalie as she accompanied her to the nursery to say goodnight to Stephen. 'Some of Julian's Foreign Office colleagues have been invited, the ones not medically fit for active service and a scattering of others who are also home on leave. Nicky is just the sort of person they should be meeting. He'll be able to tell them everything they've ever wanted to know about the Balkans and . . .'

'No,' Natalie said firmly, unable even to imagine Nicky in her mother-in-law's drawing-room.

'But why ever not?' Diana's carefully pencilled eyebrows rose in surprise. 'It would be the perfect opportunity for Julian to meet him and . . .'

Natalie suppressed a shudder. She had done her best to give Julian the impression that Nicky was a mature, respected intellectual in the mould of Ante Trumbich and Franjo Supilo and Ivan Mestrovich. If he once met him he would be instantly disillusioned for though Nicky was, of course, respectable and intellectual, he didn't look it. As Diana had once so tactlessly pointed out, he looked like a Balkan brigand.

'Nicky isn't in London this weekend,' she lied as they reached the nursery door. 'He's attending a meeting in Bath . . .'

'*Bath?*'

'There are a lot of South Slav emigrants in Bath,' Natalie said quickly before Diana could think up any awkward questions. 'Oh look, doesn't Stephen look gorgeous when he's ready for bed?'

The last few days of Julian's leave flew by with terrifying rapidity. One minute they were on a hearth rug before a roaring log fire happily playing with Stephen and Bella, the next a maid was packing Julian's kitbag for him and he was dressing in hideous khaki again.

She sat on the bed, watching him, all the joy and comfort ebbing away. 'You haven't spoken about it,' she said quietly. 'You never speak about it.'

He turned away from his dressing-table mirror towards her. 'It?'

'The war. Flanders.'

A shutter came down over his eyes. Slowly he turned back to the mirror and finished fixing his collar. 'What is there to say?' he said at last. 'It's beyond description. Words can't capture it, they can only trivialize it.'

She remained silent and, his collar fastened, he walked towards her, sitting down beside her and taking hold of her hand. 'The fighting isn't the worst part,' he said gently. 'At least when we're actually fighting the adrenalin is running. The worst part is the day-to-day living in the trenches; the dreariness of being among rats; the permanent stench of death and decay, the dirt and the unceasing drain of casualties.'

'When it started, people who were supposed to know said it would be all over by Christmas,' she said, leaning against the comfort of his broad shoulder. 'This is the second Christmas and it still isn't over. Surely it must be over soon? Surely it can't go on for much longer?'

She didn't know it, but she was echoing his mother's words to him. 'How much longer will the war go on? When will it end?' It was a question every man, woman and child in all the countries involved, wanted answering and there was no answer. The war had become a murderous treadmill grinding round and round without any significant retreat or advance, with the beginning no longer distinguishable and the end nowhere in sight.

'I don't know,' he said heavily. 'I wish to Christ I did.'

Her hand tightened on his. 'How much longer before you have to leave?'

'The car is already waiting for me. Five minutes. Ten at the most.'

'Make love to me,' she said urgently. 'Make love to me one more time before you leave.'

He had no time in which to undress. Unbuttoning his trousers he made love to her as if she were a French whore, his khaki uniform scratching her skin, his jacket buttons scoring her flesh.

It was savage, primeval lovemaking in which tenderness was abandoned and naked need was all.

'Oh God, I love you!' he panted, as the climax of his life built up inside him. 'Only you! For ever!'

In hungry, hoarse tones she urged him on and as he exploded inside her, shouting out in triumph, her own cries sounded as if they had been torn from her heart.

Afterwards, when he had gone, she sat for a long time at the window, staring sightlessly out over the park, wondering how long it would be before they were reunited again; how long it would be before the war was over and they would be able to travel to Belgrade together, taking Stephen with them.

In January came news that King Nikita of Montenegro had capitulated to Austro-Hungary and fled to Italy, leaving his son behind to demobilize the army and await Austro-Hungarian occupation.

Natalie was heart-sick. She had never been overly fond of King Nikita, finding him tiresomely egotistical, but she remembered how devoted her mother had been to his daughter, Zorka. Tears glittered on her eyelashes. At least in dying young Zorka had been spared the anguish of seeing her beloved country occupied by a long-hated enemy.

In February came news that Albania had been invaded. Natalie was distraught. If Albania had been invaded, what would happen to the Serbian troops who had trekked over the mountains? Would they be killed? Captured? She had hurried to the café in Camden where she regularly met with Nicky and his friends, wanting to know their views on the situation.

'They'll have to take refuge somewhere else,' Nicky said to her starkly. 'Robert Seton-Watson thinks they'll make for North Africa or Corfu.'

She was just about to ask if Mr Seton-Watson knew where the necessary ships would come from when there came the sound of someone entering the café in a hurry.

Seconds later Natalie sensed someone approaching behind her. She turned around to see who it was, her eyes widening in disbelief.

'Mrs Fielding, I'm sorry to disturb you,' the most junior of her mother-in-law's maids said in obvious distress. 'But I had to find you and the chauffeur said you'd be here.'

'What's happened?' Natalie asked bewilderedly.

The maid tried to speak and couldn't. Instead she burst into tears.

Fear seized hold of Natalie, so monstrous that as she

tried to rise to her feet she stumbled. *'Is it Stephen?'* she demanded, white-lipped. *'Has something happened to Stephen?'*

The maid shook her head. 'No, Mrs Fielding. It's young Mr Fielding. There's been a telegram. He's dead. Killed in action.'

Natalie gasped and swayed. Her friends had all risen to their feet. Someone had hold of her arm, someone else was asking if the café proprietor had any brandy.

'Which one?' she demanded in a choked voice. 'Mr Edward or Mr Julian? *Which one?'*

The maid stared at her, in growing horror, comprehension slowly dawning. 'I . . . I don't kn . . kn . . know, Mrs Fielding,' she stammered.

'Oh God!' Natalie pressed the back of her hand to her mouth, struggling for composure. 'Did the chauffeur bring you here? Is he outside?'

'Yes, Mrs Fielding. He's waiting to take you back to the house . . .'

Natalie never remembered leaving the café. Nicky and his friends surged out on to the pavement after her and she remembered only the concern on their faces as she half fell into the rear seat of the Mercedes and the chauffeur closed the door for her.

'Quickly!' she said, dry-mouthed when he slid once more behind the wheel. 'For the love of God, *quickly!'*

With scant regard for the other traffic on the road he swept down Camden High Street and into Park Way. She could hear the blood drumming in her ears, her heart slamming against her rib cage. She didn't want Edward to be dead; Edward with his strong outdoor physique and his kind, gentle manner; Edward who loved Northumberland so and who had never wanted to leave it. The thought of Edward being dead was monstrous. Obscene. Yet if it wasn't Edward . . .

313

Panic rose up in her throat, threatening to choke her. What would she do if it was Julian who had been killed? What would happen to her and Stephen? How would she survive without the comfort he gave her? The laughter? The lovemaking?

In Albany Street the car slowed to a standstill, enmeshed in a midday traffic-jam.

'Can't you force a way through?' she asked the chauffeur frantically.

He shook his head. 'No, madam. It's hopeless. There's nothing for it but to sit it out.'

Natalie hadn't the remotest intention of sitting it out. She flung the door open and as the maid and chauffeur stared at her in disbelief she scrambled out of the car.

The pavement was almost as crowded as the road and as she began to run old and young pedestrians alike had to jump smartly out of her path. She was uncaring of the consternation she was causing. She had to reach home. She had to find out if it had been Edward or Julian who had been killed.

She ran the length of Albany Street and into Chester Court. Panting for breath, her hair beginning to fall from its pins, she dodged across the road and into Cambridge Gate, running, running, running.

Chapter Fifteen

When Katerina stepped out of Belgrade Cathedral on her husband's arm she had no idea where they would now go, the situation was such that a honeymoon was out of the question. The Austro-Hungarian army may have been put to flight but it would no doubt re-attack at the first opportunity. She wondered if her husband would remain in Belgrade to defend it and, if he did, if he would have private quarters into which she would be expected to move.

'Can you hear the gunfire?' he asked her with a slight frown as Belgrade's newly liberated population surged around them, shouting congratulations. 'The army must still be flushing out Austro-Hungarian stragglers.'

Even as he spoke his own men began again to shoot triumphantly into the air for all the world as if the wedding was taking place in a country *zadruga* and Katerina was unable to hear the gunfire to which he was referring, or to make her own voice heard.

The hastily arranged wedding-breakfast was to take place in the *Konak*, though as the Austrians had stripped the palace of its furnishings Katerina was uncertain if there would be a table for the food or even chairs for the few guests to sit on.

Reflecting that her wedding was proving to be just as bizarre and hotch-potch as Natalie's had been, she allowed her husband to hand her into the waiting carriage, a ripple of shock running through her as his hand touched hers.

Her cheeks burned as she thought of the intimacies to come. How on earth was she going to survive them? At least when Natalie had married Julian she had been on familiar enough terms with him to be able, without awkwardness, to address him by his Christian name. How could she possibly address Major Zlarin as Ivan? She couldn't even *think* of him as Ivan.

Panic welled up in her as their carriage began to trundle away from the cathedral. Why didn't he smile across at her and try and put her at her ease? Why wasn't he aware of her difficulty? It would be so easy for him to solve it for her. All he had to do was to say he hoped she would soon get used to the sound of his name on her lips. Given such an invitation she might have found herself speaking his name quite easily and with only a little shyness. If Julian had been in the same position, he would have solved all constraint by being lovingly teasing.

Her hands tightened in her lap. She mustn't think of Julian. To think of Julian would be to open the door on more pain than she could possibly bear. He was married to Natalie now and, as marriage to Natalie was what he had wanted he was, presumably, happy.

As their carriage continued through shell-blasted streets still chaotic with rejoicing citizens and triumphant soldiery, she wondered if Natalie, too, was happy. It was hard to think of any reason why she shouldn't be. Though Britain was at war, she hadn't been invaded as Serbia had been invaded. London citizens hadn't been dragged out on to the streets and raped and shot as had happened daily in Belgrade during the weeks of Austrian occupation. Natalie hadn't had to endure the harrowing sights she and Zita had witnessed.

Over and above all those considerations, Natalie had Julian to love and care for her. That being so, how could she be anything else but happy? True, she hadn't been in love with Julian when they had married but that was because she had been so young it had never occurred to her to think of him, or anyone else for that matter, as being a possible suitor. Now that they were married, Katerina didn't see how Natalie could be anything else but in love with him. For Natalie, everything had worked out for the best. Her ill-advised friendship with Gavrilo Princip and their catastrophic meeting in Sarajevo had resulted not in disaster for her, but in great good fortune.

As many of the troops who had greeted them at the cathedral with volleys of rifle-fire continued to ride riotously alongside their carriage, she looked across at the man she had married in growing apprehension. He was still frowning slightly, his thoughts obviously on the last pockets of fighting taking place down near the river. She wondered if even Max would have been so absorbed in military matters if riding with his bride to his wedding breakfast, especially a bride he had not previously courted and who it could be assumed was feeling shy and ill at ease.

'They'll be back of course,' he said suddenly, 'and as long as they don't have Bulgaria as an ally we might be able to rebuff them yet again.'

'And if Bulgaria joins with them?' she asked, grateful that the silence had been broken, however unromantically.

'Then they'll overrun us,' he said, his frown deepening.

He was in dress-uniform and with his assertive jawline and magnificent physique, looked splendidly imposing. As the officer-in-charge of the forces who had kept the enemy at bay across the Sava all through September and October, he was a hero in the eyes of all Belgraders and she knew she must be the envy of countless young women. Certainly Vitza, when she returned to the city and heard of the wedding, would be envious.

As she tried to gain comfort from the knowledge and as

317

she wondered vainly how to prolong the conversation and how to bring a more personal element into it, he said with obvious concern, 'You haven't yet told me how you and your mother fared during the occupation. Was it very bad? Did you have to use the pistol I gave you?'

She hesitated, wanting to be able to communicate with him, yet not wanting to mar her wedding day by dwelling on the hideousness of the last few weeks and especially the hideousness of her mother's near-rape and the nightmare that had followed it.

'You were right when you told me it would be grimmer than I could possibly imagine,' she said at last. 'It was. And I did use the pistol. I've already told Papa of the circumstances and I will tell you too, of course, but not now. I don't want to remember horror today. I just want to be happy that the Austrians are in full flight and . . .' she hesitated again, a slight blush rising to her cheeks, '. . . and that it is our wedding day.'

With vast relief she saw his habitually brooding expression soften. 'I'm sorry it isn't a more traditional wedding,' he said with such obvious sincerity that she felt her apprehension beginning to ebb. 'You know, of course, that it was your father who was anxious the wedding take place now and not later?'

She nodded, feeling her blush deepening. 'He thinks the war is going to continue for a long time, perhaps for years,' she said, anxious that he should understand why her father had suggested their wedding take place so quickly and that he should not think it had been at her own urging. 'He says that this time when he leaves for the front it could quite possibly be years before he is home again and I think . . .' her voice trembled slightly, '. . . I think he wanted to ensure that he saw me married. I think he was fearful that if he didn't do so now, he might not be alive to do so in the future.'

Ivan nodded, 'He didn't quite say as much to me, but I was aware of the fear that prompted his request and I was, of course, more than happy to comply with it.'

As if sensing how disconcertingly formal he sounded he stretched out a gloved hand to hers, saying in a slightly more relaxed manner, 'I appreciate how difficult our marrying so quickly must be for you.'

'It is difficult,' she said frankly, her hand shyly answering the pressure of his. 'But as long as we are both aware of the difficulties they won't last for long.'

Their carriage was turning into the *Konak*'s courtyard and he said with equal frankness, 'There's been no opportunity for me to say so before, but I'm deeply honoured that you accepted my proposal of marriage.'

It was her turn, now, to feel awkward. Though he hadn't said so specifically, she knew he was referring to the fact that she was a Karageorgevich. In normal times, a marriage between a daughter of the House of Karageorge and an army major would have been considered highly irregular. She would have been expected to marry within her own extended family circle or, if she married outside it, to marry a man of title and wealth, perhaps a member of the Russian nobility or a Polish princeling.

For the first time she wondered what Ivan thought her motivation had been in accepting his proposal. Did he think she had fallen in love with him at first sight, as he had apparently fallen in love with her? And if he did, should she disabuse him of the idea? Should she be honest with him and tell him that though she wasn't in love with him yet, she was certain she soon would be? Should she tell him about Max?

The carriage rocked to a halt in the courtyard and as scores of people wishing them well surged around it, she realized the difficult decision would have to be made later.

Behind them other carriages were turning in off the

street; her parents' carriage; the best man's and brides-maid's carriage; the carriages containing the sprinkling of guests, some of them family members, some of them Ivan's fellow officers.

As Ivan stepped down from the carriage and turned, offering her his hand, she was aware of a moment of pure happiness. The war was turning in her country's favour; her uncle and Sandro were back in Belgrade; all the Vassilovich and Karageorgevich family members possible were again gathered together; her parents were reunited and by marrying Ivan Zlarin she had given her father peace of mind.

Ivan's men had dismounted and were beginning to form a ceremonial pathway for them. As they did so a young woman carrying a baby pushed her way directly in front of Katerina, thrusting the baby in her arms. Knowing that by tradition the baby would be a boy Katerina kissed him while her well-wishers cheered themselves hoarse.

After, when she had handed the baby back to his mother, other age-old symbols of good luck and prosperity were pressed on her. With her arms full of wheat loaves and bottles of red wine she entered the palace as laughingly laden as a peasant girl returning from market.

All through the first part of her wedding breakfast, her optimism about her married future never faltered. It was a junior officer who ended it. Not a guest, he had entered the room as discreetly as possible and asked permission to speak to Ivan.

At first Katerina was barely aware of him. In looking happily around the long banqueting-table she had realized for the first time that Max had accompanied them back to the *Konak*. He was seated at the far end of the table and, flanked by two of Ivan's military friends, was drinking heavily and joylessly.

'They are five of them, sir,' she heard the young officer

say to Ivan. 'All Austrians and all mere boys. They were found hiding in the *Konak* stables.'

Ivan gave an irritated shrug of his shoulders. 'Have them shot,' he said peremptorily.

Katerina forgot her distress at Max's obvious misery. It was Ivan, now, who had all her attention. She turned towards him, deeply shocked. 'Surely they don't have to be shot if they are so young? Can't they be sent to a prison camp?'

'If the Austrian army hadn't behaved like animals at Shabatz, maybe they could have been,' he said dryly. 'As it is, they killed all prisoners and wounded and I gave orders yesterday that we would return the compliment and that no prisoners were to be taken in Belgrade.'

He turned again to his waiting officer. 'Have them shot,' he ordered again. 'At once.'

'Yes, sir.'

As the officer saluted Katerina felt panic bubble up in her throat. She, herself, had killed an Austrian but it had not been in cold blood and on her wedding day.

She said tautly, 'I understand how you feel about the men the Austrians slaughtered, I understand because of the crimes they committed here, in Belgrade. But even though I understand I don't want any Austrians executed on my wedding day. It would be something I could never forget.'

'I'm sorry if my decision is causing you distress,' he said with obvious sincerity. 'It's one with which you should never have been burdened and you can rest assured that the officer in question will be severely disciplined.'

All around the table their guests were keeping their eyes tactfully averted, pretending that nothing was amiss. Only Max was openly watching their exchange of words, the expression on his heavy-featured face unreadable.

'I don't *want* him disciplined,' Katerina said, her horror

increasing. 'I don't want *anyone* disciplined or executed or treated harshly in any way at all!'

Max had risen unsteadily to his feet. No-one took the slightest notice of him. All attention, however much the pretence was otherwise, was centred on the bride and groom.

'My decision is a military one and it is pointless our discussing it any further,' he said, an edge of impatience creeping into his voice. 'We should be enjoying our wedding breakfast, not discussing matters which have no place at such a time.'

As he was talking Max had begun inebriatedly to walk from the room. Ivan diplomatically ignored him.

'Have you seen the number of wedding gifts we have received?' he asked, changing the subject. 'Where on earth are we going to store them all?'

She had no idea, nor did she care.

She said in a choked voice, 'You don't seem to understand how important this is to me. Please, as a special favour . . .'

Distantly, from the courtyard, a rifle-shot rang out.

Ivan's best man sprang to his feet. 'It's time for some music and some dancing!' he announced boisterously. 'Where's the gypsy band? Tell them we're ready to begin dancing!'

Another shot rang out and Katerina knew it was too late for any further pleas. The gypsies bounded in and there were shouted demands from the guests for them to play a wedding *kolo*.

Katerina felt frozen inside. How could she lead the dancing in the *kolo* when two young boys had been executed and another three, within hearing distance of the music, were about to be so? Why had Ivan been so obdurate? Surely a gesture of mercy on their wedding day would not have been interpreted by anyone as a sign of weakness?

Ivan had taken her hand in his and was drawing her to her feet. 'We must lead the dancing,' he was saying reasonably, as if nothing untoward had happened.

Conscious that all eyes were now on her, she forced herself to comply with his request, listening all the time for further sounds of rifle-fire.

None came. In a sea of misery she wondered if it was because more than one man had been shot by the previous volleys of fire.

As the band began to play and a huge circle was formed, she looked across at her husband and saw the familiar small frown creasing his strongly marked brows. Was he, too, aware of the oddness of the two separate volleys of rifle-fire? She had no way of telling. The communication that had begun to burgeon between them was now at an end, not just temporarily but permanently. In a moment of stark reality she knew she had been wrong in thinking she could learn to love him. His personality was too stern and too unbending for her ever to be able to do so. All she was going to be able to do was to go through the motions of being a loving wife just as now, her heart totally untouched by the music, she was going through the motions of dancing.

As the *kolo* eventually came to an end she saw Max re-enter the room. Gracelessly he began to walk in their direction and in growing alarm she realized that he was intent on speaking with Ivan.

'Congratulations,' he said to him with rude off-handedness a few seconds later, ignoring her completely. 'Welcome into the Karageorgevich family, Major Zlarin.'

'Thank you, Major Karageorgevich. I deem myself highly honoured . . .'

'We are, of course, a family with a bloody history,' Max continued, cutting him short. 'To listen to our enemies you'd think each and every one of us was a barbarian,

323

including King Peter and Prince Alexander. It isn't true, of course. We are only barbarians on the battlefield. That being the case, and not wanting there to be any confusion in the public mind about Karageorgevich honour, I have just returned from attempting to rescind your recent order for the execution of five prisoners.'

Ivan drew in a savage intake of breath and Max continued unperturbed, 'Unfortunately I was too late to prevent the execution of two of the men, or should I say boys as they could have been no older than seventeen. The remaining three, however, are on their way to a prison camp.'

'You've over-reached yourself, Major!' Ivan's voice shook with the force of his anger. 'You'll be court-martialled for this insult! Ruined!'

'I don't think so,' Max said disinterestedly. 'There isn't a military tribunal in the country would sanction the court martial of a Karageorgevich. Especially one about to be promoted to brigadier. Your own court martial, however, would be a relatively easy matter to arrange. Good day, Major.'

Still avoiding all eye contact with Katerina he turned on his heel, walking away from them with the obvious intent of leaving the room for good.

'Let's dance,' Katerina said quickly, before Ivan's wrath exploded and he made his fury with Max public. 'They're playing a *Machvanka* and it's my favourite.'

He was rigid with fury, his nostrils pinched and white, his mouth a thin hard line. For a moment she thought he wasn't going to respond to her and then he nodded, saying tightly, 'Yes. Of course.'

The danger was over. As they again led the dancing she felt weak with relief, knowing that if he had embarked on a public feud with Max he would have been professionally destroyed by it. As it was, she knew that Max would not gossip about the incident, that as far as he was concerned it was over and closed.

Her heart hurt with the force of the gratitude she felt for him. He, alone of everyone who had overheard Ivan's tersely given order, had appreciated the monstrosity of it. As Ivan whirled her around in time to the music and the skirts of her white chiffon dress floated around her ankles, she wondered when she would be able to thank him; and if she would ever be able to do so adequately.

That night, and for the next three nights, it was arranged they stay at the *Konak*. It had been Sandro who had suggested the palace for their honeymoon and Katerina had been deeply appreciative. It meant she would be among familiar surroundings in what she feared were going to be the most stressful few days, and nights, of her life.

Her premonition didn't fail her. When, that night, Ivan entered their bedroom from his dressing-room, his sleek black hair shining with water droplets, a tie-belted silk dressing-gown hiding his nakedness, his first words did nothing to create a sense of ease between them.

'I have a confession to make,' he said succinctly.

She was sitting in bed, decorously attired in an exquisitely embroidered nightdress, her arms protectively clasped around her knees. Her heart, already racing as if it were about to explode, began to race even more swiftly and more erratically.

'Yes?' she said hoarsely, grateful at least that a confession would delay the inevitable moment when he joined her in bed, wondering if the time had come when she should tell him why she had accepted his proposal of marriage.

The candle-lit room, plundered of its sumptuous furniture and fittings, had been hastily refurnished with

325

basic necessities. These did not include sofas or chairs and he remained standing a yard or so from the bed, his hands pushed deep into the pockets of his dressing-gown.

'I'm fourteen years your senior and our marriage has been very . . . precipitate. It would have been unnatural if I had not had certain friendships in the past and I am not going to burden you with a confession of all of them. The majority were merely youthful escapades and of no moment then and certainly of no moment now.'

He paused, seeking for the right words with which to continue and she said hastily, 'But there's no need for you to make any confession of past relationships! I don't expect it. It never even occurred to me that . . .'

'One relationship you must know about,' he said, interrupting her with the same lack of empathy with which, at the wedding breakfast, he had refused her pleas that he show mercy to the Austrians. 'It concerns a family member, a woman you will no doubt meet some time in the future and so it would be most remiss of me not to speak to you about it.'

Katerina felt her cheeks beginning to burn. Whatever it was he was about to tell her, she didn't want to know about it. Instead of making their first night together easy he was, by the very formality of his manner, making it even more fraught than it need be.

'Please, Ivan,' she pleaded, 'it really isn't necessary . . . I'd rather know about your life when you were a little boy, where you lived, the things you liked doing . . .'

His frown intensified and she knew that he was not listening to her and that, no matter how much he might believe himself in love with her, he was never going truly to listen to her or understand her. His inflexible personality was, quite simply, incapable of it.

'Zara is my cousin,' he continued relentlessly. 'She was widowed ten years ago and it was then we began our . . .

relationship. It is now over and has been ever since I first met you.'

She knew that the moment had come for her to make her own confession and was totally unable to do so. He was a man whose pride would never enable him to cope with the knowledge that she had married him without being in love with him, nor could she tell him she would quickly learn to love him as she had initially intended doing, for she doubted now that she ever would.

The expression in his eyes and the tone of his voice changed as he said thickly, 'You're the most beautiful woman I have ever seen, Katerina.'

She knew that he was going to make love to her without there being any bridge of understanding between them and her arms tightened around her knees. Countless other women had endured the same fate and at least her husband loved her; at least he was in the prime of life, good-looking and a hero.

As she tried to think of all the ways in which she was fortunate he walked to the side of the bed and blew out the candles on the night-table. In the thick darkness she heard the slither of silk as he discarded his dressing-gown.

Unless she were to seem ridiculous, she knew she could no longer remain sitting, her arms around her legs. Exercising all the will power of which she was capable she slid her legs flat, her heart slamming against her rib cage as he slid into bed beside her.

His own breathing had become harsh and heavy and she wondered if he, too, were nervous. His hands reached out for her, assured and knowledgeable, and she knew that he was not.

'I love you,' he whispered fiercely, drawing her against the heat and hardness of his body.

It was the body of a stranger and as his mouth closed on hers and she struggled to respond to him, she became aware of the faint lemon tang of his cologne; a cologne heart-achingly familiar. Memories came rushing back; Julian speaking to her at *Konak* afternoon tea parties, dancing with her at the Summer Ball, walking with her in the moonlit rose garden.

Suddenly, as with ownership in his fingers he began intimately to caress her, she knew a life-line had been offered her. In the inky darkness she could imagine it was Julian who was making love to her; Julian to whom she was lovingly responding. She knew she would suffer guilt and shame afterwards, but afterwards could take care of it itself. It was now that mattered. Now, that had to be survived.

When, four days later, he left with his troops for the north-west border, her relief was crippling in its intensity. Conscious of her lack of radiant happiness and aware of both her mother's and Cissie's concerned curiosity, she avoided all opportunities for confidential feminine chats by spending all day, every day, nursing at the hospital.

Soon she was there day and night. During the Austrian occupation there had been an outbreak of typhus in the north of the country among Austrian troops. Now, though there were no longer any Austrian troops on Serbian soil, the epidemic spread. Within weeks the entire country was devastated by it.

One morning, exhausted to the point of collapse after yet another night without sleep, Katerina said fearfully to Cissie, 'I think I'm infected, Cissie. I feel terrible.'

Cissie paused in what she was doing, wiping perspiration from her forehead and looked at her critically.

'You look terrible,' she said bluntly. 'Let me take your temperature.'

'I can't! I'm going to be sick!'

She grabbed hold of the nearest bowl and as she vomited Cissie filled a glass with water.

'Here,' she said after a little while. 'Drink this.'

Katerina's hand shook slightly as she accepted the proferred drink. She had known, when she had begun nursing typhus patients, the risk she was running and had thought herself prepared for any consequences. Now she realized how wrong she had been. She wasn't prepared at all. She was horrifically frightened.

'Let me take your temperature,' Cissie said again, 'and let me check your pulse rate.'

When she had done so she said, 'Is this the first morning you've been sick?'

Katerina shook her head. 'No, I was sick yesterday morning. I thought then it was just over-tiredness. I still don't have any spots and to be truthful, I don't feel feverish, just vilely nauseous.'

'You'll probably feel like that for a while,' Cissie said without the least trace of concern. 'For three months or so at least.'

Katerina stared at her, her eyes widening.

For the first time since typhus had been diagnosed in Belgrade, Cissie grinned. 'You are a simpleton, Trina. You haven't typhus. You're pregnant.'

'*Pregnant?*' For a moment she was disbelieving and then she pressed the back of her hand to her forehead. She hadn't the slightest temperature. She felt her pulse. Despite her tiredness it was strong and steady. Relief and joy swamped her. She wasn't sick. She was having a baby. A baby she wanted more than she wanted anything else in the world.

All through the spring the typhus epidemic raged and all through the spring there were no further direct attacks by the Austro-Hungarian army.

In July, there came reports of Austro-Hungarian troops and German troops, massing in huge numbers in Hungary and the rumour was that they intended forcing their way through Serbia to Constantinople.

All through late summer and early autumn the country waited for the inevitable onslaught. Alexander appealed to the Allies for help and was told that aid would come from Bulgaria. Alexander, knowing that Bulgaria was only waiting for the most advantageous moment to enter the war alongside Germany and Austria, protested vainly. Even when Bulgaria began mobilizing her army, the Allies refused to believe her intention.

In October, when three hundred thousand Austrian and German troops began a tremendous attack upon the Danube front and Bulgaria threw off her mask of deceit and simultaneously hurled four hundred thousand troops across the western frontier, Serbia was without Allied aid.

By November it was obvious that defeat was inevitable. It was Zita who broke the news to Katerina.

'Sandro sent news this morning,' she said, walking in on Katerina in the nursery where she was breastfeeding Peter. 'Apparently there can be no question of the remnants of the army falling back. There is no longer anywhere for them to fall back to. There is going to have to be a complete retreat.'

Katerina's arms tightened around her son. 'But where to? And what will happen to us? The Austrians behaved barbarically in the few weeks they were in Belgrade. What will they do when they have the entire country at their mercy?'

Zita's cameo-like features were ivory-pale. 'Sandro intends leading all remaining troops over the mountains and into Albania, to Scutari. Even though he is ill, the King is going to accompany him.'

Gently Katerina lifted Peter from her breast, holding him in one arm as she fastened her blouse. 'And Papa and Ivan? Will they be going as well?'

'Sandro still has no word of Ivan. Your father, however, will be going. As we will be going.'

Katerina felt the blood drain from her face. 'Across the mountains? In winter? How can we? Peter is only eight weeks old!'

'And what will happen if we stay?' Zita asked tautly. 'I doubt if any of us will survive. This way at least we will all be together.'

As her eyes held her mother's, Katerina realized there was no choice. A year ago they had barely survived a few weeks of Austrian occupation. As Karageorgevichs they would certainly not survive a long-term occupation. She thought of the mountains and cold terror gripped her heart. The tracks they would have to follow would not be suitable for motorized transport or even ox-wagons. Their only means of conveyance would be pack-horses; their only food would be that which they were able to take with them.

They left on 24 November, part of an exodus over two hundred thousand strong. In a long endless line, the Austro-Hungarian and German armies hard at their heels, they headed south-west. The mountains proper began at Lioum-Koula and that evening, as Katerina tucked Peter in his thickly blanketed crib, she did so by the lights of a hundred scattered fires as all the transport and food wagons that could be taken no further, were burned.

Day after day they trudged through snow and ice, climbing to windswept plateaus several thousand feet above sea-level, descending into narrow gorges running between towering black walls of basalt and then climbing again to yet another plateau of breathtaking grandeur and desolation.

Many died of cold and disease and hunger. Every morning Katerina woke she expected to find Peter dead in his eiderdown-padded carrying-crib. Every morning she was greeted, instead, by healthy crying.

When the mountains were finally behind them a sea of mud lay ahead of them. Exhausted, malnourished pack-horses keeled over and died in their tracks; even Zita could no longer ride but had to toil through an ankle-deep and often knee-deep, quagmire.

When Scutari was reached a sick and exhausted Sandro made the decision to ship the remnants of his army to Corfu. There, still in close vicinity to possible fields of action in Albania and Salonica, his troops could be rested, reorganized and re-equipped. The Italians who were in control of the area refused to assist him or provide him with transport. There was nothing for it but to trek another hundred miles through malarial coastal lowlands to Valone where, hopefully, the French would come to their aid.

To Katerina, time no longer had any meaning. Alexis had obtained fresh pack-horses and an ox-wagon in Scutari and as she sat next to Zita, Peter in her arms, squashed by the many weak and infirm who had been squeezed into the wagon beside them, her mind drifted hallucinatedly to the blissfully carefree days of early 1914. She was again at afternoon tea parties at the *Konak*; walking in Kalemeg-dan Gardens with Natalie; dancing with Julian at her mother's Summer Ball.

When at last they were aboard a French ship bound for Corfu she said reflectively to Zita, 'Do you realize it's nearly Christmas again? If Gavrilo Princip had not shot the Arch-duke, and if Austria had not then declared war on us, Sandro would now be officially engaged to Grand-Duchess Olga.'

'And thousands upon thousands of people, probably millions, would not have died,' Zita said thickly. 'It doesn't bear thinking about, does it? Do you think Princip will ever realize the enormity of his action?'

'How could he?' Katerina looked around at the raggedly dressed, emaciated figures around them. 'He's locked away in a prison cell. How could he possibly imagine the depth of the suffering that has been caused? No-one who has not seen it could imagine it. It's beyond imagination.'

Only days later Sandro told her he had received confirmed reports of Ivan's death.

'I'm sorry, Trina,' he said gently.

They were on the balcony of the villa that was now the Vassilovich home. In the distance, beneath a diamond-bright winter sky, the Aegean glittered like glass.

'Thank you for taking the trouble to tell me yourself, Sandro,' she said stiltedly, not daring to analyse the emotions roaring through her.

'It was the least I could do.' His voice was bitter.

As she looked into his familiar, now haggard face, she felt a shaft of pain that was not for herself or for Ivan. On the terrible trek across the mountains Sandro had been very ill, so ill that he had had to undergo surgery under the most primitive of conditions. His illness and the crippling burdens, military and political, that he had shouldered over the last eighteen months, had taken a savage toll. He was no longer the handsome young man who had teased her and who had laughed and joked with Natalie and played with Bella. Careworn and still physically fragile he looked a man in his late thirties, not his mid-twenties.

She said with sudden passion, 'Oh God, Sandro! When will this war be over! When will things be as they used to be?'

'Things are never going to be as they used to be,' he said

333

bleakly, 'the entire world has changed and it's never going to be the same again.'

'But surely some things will be the same!' she protested, appalled. 'When the war is over we'll be together as a family again. Natalie will come home and . . .'

At the expression in his eyes the words died on her lips.

'What is it?' she asked fearfully. 'Why are you looking at me like that? What have I said?'

He blanched, saying tautly, 'I thought your father would have told you . . .'

'Told me what?' Never, during all the horrors she had experienced since the war had begun, had she been more terrified. 'Has something happened to Natalie? Something that's been kept from me?'

The pale February sunlight gleamed on his dark hair and his gold pince-nez as he said awkwardly, 'During the last days of peace the Austrians demanded Natalie's extradition. They suspect her involvement with Gavrilo Princip. They suspect she met him the day before the assassinations in Sarajevo.'

Behind her, in the villa, Peter began to cry. For the first time since he had been born Katerina did not rush to his side.

'But what the Austrians suspect doesn't matter now!' she protested bewilderedly. 'When the war is over and they are defeated they won't be in a position to do anything about their suspicions!'

'Maybe not, but whatever the situation after the war one thing is certain and that is that questions are going to be asked by the entire world about the true nature of Serbia's involvement in Archduke Franz Ferdinand's assassination. If Natalie's association with Gavrilo Princip comes to light it will be seen as evidence that the House of Karageorgevich, and therefore Serbia itself, instigated the assassination plot and are responsible for triggering off the bloodiest war the world has ever seen. If that happens my only defence on Serbia's behalf will be to show that ever since the assassination Natalie has been *persona non grata*. There mustn't be the faintest suspicion that, knowing of her involvement, I and my government condoned it.'

'I don't understand . . .' Katerina could feel the blood draining from her face. 'What do you mean, *persona non grata?*'

'Natalie can never again be received at court, Trina. She can never return to Belgrade.' His voice was unsteady. 'She can never, ever, come home.'

Chapter Sixteen

Natalie ran up the steps of the Fielding home, her heart hammering as if it were about to burst. She had never been given her own key to the house and she had to ring the bell and wait in frantic anxiety for the butler to open the door.

When he did so she hurtled past him into the hallway. From somewhere upstairs came the sound of weeping. She wondered if it was her mother-in-law or Diana; if it was for Edward or for Julian.

Now that the moment had come when she could ask and have her question answered, she couldn't force the words past her lips. Her throat was so tight she felt as if she were about to choke. Gasping for breath she came to a halt outside the drawing-room door and the butler said, his voice betraying his inner distress, 'Sir Archibald and Miss Diana are in the drawing-room, Mrs Fielding.'

She grasped hold of the door knob, her palm slippery with sweat. She could ask the butler whether it had been Julian or Edward who had died, but she didn't want to hear the news from a butler. If Julian was dead, she wanted to be told by someone who loved him.

With her chest still hurting from her long, agonized run, she opened the door and entered the room.

Her father-in-law was standing near the marble fireplace, the telegram still crushed in his hand. Diana was sitting on one of the sofas, silent tears streaming mascara down her face. The minute Natalie entered the room she sprang to her feet, running towards her.

'Oh, Natalie! I'm so glad you're here! Do you think there could possibly be a mistake? Do you think Edward could be alive after all?'

All through spring the house remained in deep mourning. Lady Fielding retreated to her bedroom, displaying a passion of grief of which Natalie had not thought her capable. Sir Archibald withdrew into long, sombre silences. Diana no longer partied when not on duty at Guy's but instead went for long lonely walks in the park.

Natalie, too, grieved for Edward, but she had not known him long or intimately and her grief was not as savage and as all-consuming.

As the weeks went by and Diana remained wretchedly solitary, Natalie's loneliness increased until she could hardly bare it. She had Stephen, of course, but Stephen was only nine months old and though she loved him with all her heart, he couldn't yet be a companion to her.

Inevitably she began to spend more and more time with Nicky. From the moment she had met him, heavily pregnant, she had been physically attracted to him. Within weeks of Stephen's birth she knew it was an attraction fully reciprocated. Her problem was what to do about it.

She knew what she wanted to do about it. Julian's love-making had made her more than aware of her capacity for sexual enjoyment and it had been six long months since he had been home on leave. Deeply sensual by nature she was finding her celibacy an increasing burden, and she wasn't at all sure that it was necessary.

As she took Stephen for a daily walk in his pram in the park, she pondered on the oddness of her marriage. She had not *chosen* to marry Julian. Surely, then, she wasn't as morally bound to be faithful to him as she would have been if she had fallen in love with him and married him in

337

a normal manner? She thought of her mother and Katerina and knew that far from being in agreement with her reasoning, they would be deeply horrified by it.

As Stephen sat in his pram, chewing happily on an ivory teething-ring, she looked out over the park lake, frowning deeply. Was there any real reason why they should be? If she hadn't agreed to marry Julian her mother would be embarking on her third year of living in Geneva. As it was, thanks to the sacrifice she, Natalie, had made, her mother had been able to remain in Belgrade. Under those circumstances, surely her mother was in no position to censure or criticize her?

As for Katerina . . . Natalie sighed. Katerina was so naturally honourable she couldn't imagine her ever doing anything of which she need feel guilty or ashamed. And how could Katerina understand the cataclysmic demands of instant, unreasoning, overwhelming sexual attraction? Katerina had never been in love and when the time came when she *did* fall in love, Natalie doubted that it would be a case of love at first sight. Katerina was too coolly sensible to let her heart rule her head. When Katerina married it would be to someone eminently suitable and she would do so only after a long, decorous courtship. Katerina would never have to wrestle with her conscience in the way that she, Natalie, was now having to do. Katerina's love-life was never going to be anything but serenely uncomplicated.

Satisfied that she need not trouble herself about the opinions her mother and Katerina might one day have of her if she were to have a love affair with Nicky, her frown cleared. Whatever her decision, it was one over which she need not torture herself. The bizarre circumstances of her marriage were such that behaviour that would normally be regarded as outrageous was, in fact, only to be expected.

She watched a duck as it skimmed low across the surface

of the lake, the sun glinting on its jewel coloured plumage. The main problem was, of course, that Julian would not be in agreement with her.

A child on roller-skates raced past her. She was so deep in thought she hardly noticed. Where Julian was concerned, surely the solution was simply never to confide in him? It wasn't, after all, as if he intended selflessly putting her happiness over and above his own. He had told her quite categorically that when the war was over he would not be applying to return to Belgrade; that instead he was hoping for a posting in Paris or St Petersburg. That being the case, surely she was entitled to embark on a relationship with a man she had begun to think of as her soulmate; a man who, if circumstances had been different, she would have *chosen* to marry?

The answer was so obviously in the affirmative that a delicious shiver of anticipation ran down her spine. She wouldn't, of course, *hurt* Julian. He was her best friend and she was very, very fond of him. She would take great care that he never became aware of her changed relationship with Nicky. There was, after all, no reason why he should ever do so. All she had to be was careful.

Nicky sensed the decision she had taken the instant they next met. His white teeth gleamed as he flashed her a dazzling smile of supreme satisfaction.

'We will not stay to the meeting,' he said with typical male Slavic high-handedness. 'We will go to bed.'

It was what Natalie had intended but she had not expected the matter to be put quite so bluntly. Reminding herself that there was a world of difference between the passionate, impatient temperament of a Slav and the restrained, refined temperament of the average Englishman she forgave him his unromantic directness.

Nicky was being true to himself as she was now going to

339

be true to herself. For the first time in her life she was head over heels in love. Her affair with Nicky was going to be a taste of what her life would have been like if she had never met Gavrilo; never gone to Sarajevo; never been obliged to marry an Englishman. It was going to be a union of minds as well as bodies for they shared the same political dreams and aspirations in a way she and Julian would never do. She remembered Julian's adamant intention never to apply for a return posting to Belgrade. How could there be the least mental affinity between them when he was so uncaring as to the central passion of her life?

There were no such barriers between herself and Nicky. Nicky understood utterly her fierce love of home and country; he understood why she had had no choice but to give Gavrilo and Trifko and Nedjelko all the moral support possible; he understood why she could never reconcile herself to self-imposed exile in London or Paris or St Petersburg. He was her soul-mate; her other self.

With adrenalin coursing through her veins she turned her back on the meeting and, accompanying him to the small bedsit he rented above a shop in Camden High Street, turned her back also on marital fidelity.

In July came horrific reports of the fighting on the Somme. Natalie waited in terror for a telegram informing her that Julian was among the dead. Instead, towards the end of August, she received a pencil written postcard from him telling her little else but that he was still alive. She had cried with sheer relief, at first mystifying Nicky and then annoying him.

'Why are you reacting like this?' he asked crossly when, tears glittering on her eyelashes, she told him the news. 'It's me you love, remember? Not him.'

'He's my best friend,' she said truthfully. 'How else should I react?'

340

'He's a man you were forced into marrying,' he said exasperatedly. 'An Englishman. How can anyone be best friends with an Englishman?'

Natalie had laughed at his idiocy and been pleased by his jealousy. 'If you knew him you would easily understand.'

'Well, I don't know him,' Nicky said dismissively, pulling her close against him, 'nor do I want to talk about him.'

Afterwards, back home at Cambridge Gate, Natalie sat on her bed with her legs curled up beneath her, Bella by her side. When she had embarked on her affair with Nicky she had not anticipated complications. Now, however, because of Nicky's attitude towards Julian, she could see complications looming. What would happen when Julian came home on his next leave? What if Nicky insisted on a confrontation with him? She shuddered at the very thought, putting her arm around Bella and hugging her closer, wishing that, just for once, life could be problem-free.

In September life became, if not problem-free, decidedly more optimistic. A new offensive was launched by the allies from Salonika and in the forefront were Serbian troops, well rested and well drilled after their months of recuperation in Corfu. Led by Alexander, the army's advance was rapid. Soon they were again on Serbian soil, fighting the Bulgarians, and Natalie was euphoric, certain that both her father and Max were with them.

In November came news that Emperor Franz Josef had died and that his successor was to be his great-nephew, the young Archduke Karl. Natalie wondered if Gavrilo would be told of the emperor's death and, if so, what his reaction to it would be. As always when she thought of Gavrilo she wondered where he was being imprisoned, whether it was in Bosnia or Austria; if he had contact with Trifko and Nedjelko; if his cough was still troubling him.

In December came news of another death.

'Rasputin's been murdered,' Diana said as she entered the nursery.

Natalie was impatiently waiting for Stephen's nurse to finish dressing him in his leggings and coat so that she could take him for a walk.

'Murdered?' Her exquisitely winged eyebrows rose nearly into her hair. 'Who on earth by? The *Bolsheviks*?'

'Nothing so boring!' Diana said, her eyes alive with their old sparkle. 'It says in *The Times* that he was murdered by two close relatives of the Tsar.'

Stephen had struggled free of his nanny and was tottering gleefully towards her on chubby legs.

'*Noblemen*?' Natalie was incredulous. 'But who? Who would *dare*?'

Diana bent down and scooped her nephew into her arms. 'The murder took place at the home of Prince Felix Youssoupov, so I assume he is one of them. I can't think of a more glamorous murderer, can you? He was in London some years ago and *everyone* fell in love with him. At fancy-dress balls he wore an eighteenth-century Russian dress of gold and pearls and sables, with embroidered boots and jewelled scimitar. Even Mama thought him eligible.' She gave an exaggerated shiver of horror. 'I wonder if he used the scimitar to murder Rasputin?'

At such unsuitable talk in front of a small child Stephen's nanny drew in an outraged hiss between her teeth. The ladies of the house ignored it.

'Does it say in *The Times* how he was killed?' Natalie asked with unashamedly prurient curiosity. 'Does it say what the empress's reaction has been?'

Diana eased Stephen a little more comfortably on her hip. 'It does indeed say how he was murdered. He was . . .'

Stephen's nanny interrupted her, her voice agonized. 'Mrs Fielding! I must protest! This is a most unsuitable conversation to be conducting in front of an eighteen-month-old child!'

Natalie regarded her balefully. Ever since Stephen had been born, nanny had been a thorn in her flesh. British mothers, apparently, did not take their children for walks in the park. That was nanny's province. Nor did they romp and play with their children at bedtime. That was no-one's province as, according to nanny, children made giddy and excited at bedtime would then be unable to sleep. Nor did they sing foreign, incomprehensible songs or tell stories about heroes with unpronounceable Slavic names.

Well aware of the deep disapproval in which she was held, Natalie said with remarkable patience, 'I think you're worrying unnecessarily, Nanny. At eighteen months old, Stephen is far too young to understand our conversation and . . .'

'Murdra! Murdra!' Stephen chanted merrily, pulling at the carefully arranged blonde kiss-curl lying against Diana's cheek.

Diana made a strangled sound as she tried, unsuccessfully, to turn a giggle into a cough. Bright spots of angry colour appeared on Nanny's cheeks.

Natalie said, keeping her own giggles under control only with the greatest difficulty, 'I shall take Stephen for his walk now, Nanny.'

Nanny knew when she was beaten but had no intention of accepting defeat without a last salvo of shots.

'Yes, Mrs Fielding. If you insist on doing so, Mrs Fielding. I would be negligent in my duty, however, if I didn't point out to you that it is a bitterly cold day; that there is an influenza epidemic; that . . .'

'I appreciate your concern,' Natalie said, walking towards the door, 'but Stephen is warmly dressed and though you think the day cold, it is nothing like as cold as a Serbian winter day.' She paused at the door as Diana carried Stephen out into the corridor, knowing very well that her next few words would very rapidly find their way back to her mother-in-law. 'And as Stephen will one day have to become accustomed to Serbian winters, he might as well start by becoming accustomed to London ones.'

Later, in the frost-bound park as Stephen clutched hold of the railings edging the lake in order to watch the ducks being fed and as Bella skittered around their ankles, Diana said curiously, 'When the war is over, you don't really intend Stephen spending long periods of time in Belgrade, do you?'

Natalie pressed her fox-fur collar a little closer to her chin. One of the disadvantages of her affair with Nicky was that she could no longer confide whole-heartedly in Diana for fear of revealing more than she intended.

She said obliquely, 'Belgrade is my home,' then, changing the subject, she said, 'You haven't finished telling me about Rasputin's murder. How did he die?'

'I think he must have died quite horribly,' Diana said with unladylike relish. 'The newspaper report said he was poisoned, shot and bludgeoned before being dumped in the River Neva.'

Natalie shuddered. 'Prince Youssoupov and his accomplice didn't leave anything to chance, did they?' Another thought struck her and she stopped walking, her green cat-eyes widening. 'Goodness! I wonder if Hélène's husband was involved in the murder?'

'Hélène?'

344

'Sandro's sister. She married one of Grand-Duke Constantine's sons and it was while Sandro was in St Petersburg attending the christening of their first child that the Tsarevich gave him Bella as a present.'

Diana began asking her if she knew the Grand-Duke personally but Natalie didn't hear her. She was lost in a reverie of a world that was no more: Sandro teasing her at an afternoon tea party; Bella tumbling over their feet; her mother and Katerina walking the length of the *Konak's* grand drawing-room arm-in-arm, deep in conversation; Vitza in an incredibly unflattering royal-blue dress; her uncle proudly announcing that Sandro was to marry the Grand-Duchess Olga.

Homesickness, so acute she didn't know how she was going to survive it, swept over her. She hurt with the longing to have her mother's arms around her again; to be in the bedroom she had shared with Katerina, drinking cocoa and sharing secrets and confidences; to smell the heady fragrance of plum blossom and to hear the familiar rattle of trams in Prince Milan Street.

'. . . I do think Russian men extremely handsome,' Diana was saying dreamily, 'don't you?'

Natalie made a non-committal reply and before Diana should see the unshed tears glittering on her eyelashes she walked across to Stephen, lifting him away from the railings, pressing his rosy, chubby cheek against her own.

Spring was even grimmer than it had been in 1915 and 1916. Julian's public-school classical education was finally put to use by the army and he was posted to Salonika in the belief that his knowledge of Greek would be more useful there than it was in Flanders.

Natalie's euphoria at the thought of him fighting within hailing distance of Alexander and her father was short-lived. All the gains Alexander and his army had made the previous autumn had been reversed. Winter had put an end to the drive into Serbia and now the Serbian army and its allies were marking time in Salonika, enduring a stalemate every bit as bitter as the one being suffered in Flanders.

The news from Russia was even worse. In Russia there was revolution. Natalie was distraught.

'The newspaper reports say nothing as to the whereabouts of the imperial family or what is to happen to them,' she said to Nicky, deeply distressed. 'How can Russia function without a monarchy?' She thought of Serbia without a Karageorgevich king and a cold shiver ran down her spine. 'How can *any* country function without a monarchy?'

Nicky merely grinned. They were in the café in Camden that had become a second home to them both. The friends they met with there had not yet arrived and apart from an elderly man with a shabby mongrel dog at his feet, they had the place to themselves.

'Russia will function a damn lot better without the Romanovs than it ever did with them,' he said, shocking her unutterably.

'You don't mean that!' It was the first time he had ever expressed an opinion with which she had not been in total agreement. 'You can't!'

He shrugged, amused by her dismay, knowing it was occasioned by the fear that if Russia could so easily dispense with its ruling dynasty, other countries might also seek to do so. 'How can you be so surprised by what has happened?' he asked reasonably. 'All winter the newspapers have been full of reports of Russians queuing for hours, days sometimes, for bread. There's been no coal either. Factories are standing idle and those who aren't starving to death are freezing to death. In those circumstances it's only natural there's been revolution. The miracle is, that it didn't happen months ago.'

'I don't agree,' she said mutinously, thinking of the glorious wedding that was to have taken place in the Cathedral of Our Lady of Kazan between Sandro and the Grand-Duchess Olga and that now would not happen. 'The Tsar could have abdicated, the throne could have passed to the Tsarevich . . .'

From beneath the table there came a whine as, perfectly on cue, Bella tugged at her lead in an effort to reach the mongrel and to socialize.

'I sometimes wonder if you read anything through to the end,' Nicky said, an edge of impatience in his voice. He dragged a crumpled copy of *The Times* from his pocket and laid it on the table, smoothing the creases. 'It says here, at the end of the article about the revolution, "the first abdication form prepared by the generals passed the throne to the Tsar's son, aged twelve. This was changed at Nicholas's request, in favour of his brother the Grand-Duke Michael. The grand-duke has since renounced the throne as there is so much hostility towards the Romanovs that the provisional government could not guarantee his life."'

Nicky was wrong in thinking she hadn't read the article through to the end. She had. Many times. And she still couldn't comprehend the enormity of it. How could a dynasty as mighty as the Romanovs be removed so speedily and totally from power? And what would now happen to them? She stroked Bella, wondering if they still had their dogs with them. She wondered, too, what would now happen between Sandro and Olga. Would they still marry? Would Sandro be kept informed of her whereabouts? Another thought struck her and she gasped, her eyes widening.

'Perhaps the imperial family will seek exile in Britain!' Her mind raced ahead to all kinds of possibilities. 'Perhaps

347

Hélène and her husband will come with them? Perhaps there will be a wedding between Sandro and Olga here, in London?'

Nicky snorted derisively. Natalie ignored him. If Sandro married Olga in London then she would un-doubtedly be asked to be a bridesmaid. A smile of deep relish touched the corners of her mouth. Vitza would be so jealous she would never, ever, forgive her.

The summer came and went and the imperial family remained immured in Russia. In September there came news that they had been moved from what had once been St Petersburg and was now Petrograd, to Tobolsk, a small town in Western Siberia. In November the Bolsheviks overthrew the provisional government and Nicky told Natalie that not only would Russia now negotiate a separate peace with Germany, but that in his opinion the imperial family were now doomed.

'And Hélène and her family too?' Natalie had asked, white-faced.

He had nodded, tight black curls tumbling low over his brow and she had turned away from him, knowing that he didn't care as she cared; knowing that he couldn't comfort her as Julian would have comforted her.

If the news from Russia was of unrelieved grimness, the news from Serbia's government-in-exile in Corfu was, to Yugoslav Committee supporters' ears, headily optimistic.

The leader of the Committee, Ante Trumbich, had met with Premier Pasich and a formal agreement had been reached concerning the future formation of a Kingdom of all South Slavs. It was agreed that it would be a constitutional, democratic and parliamentary monarchy headed by the Karageorgevich dynasty, that there was to be equality among the three national groups, Serbs, Croats and Slovenes and that the Orthodox, Roman Catholic and Islamic religions were to be exercised freely and publicly.

Though the dream couldn't come into existence until the war was over, and only then if the Allies were the victors, it was a hundred times nearer to becoming a possibility than it had been when Natalie had met Gavrilo and Trifko and Nedjelko in the *Golden Sturgeon* and schemed of somehow bringing such a day about.

Again and again, as 1917 merged into 1918, Natalie found herself thinking of Gavrilo. Never, in a million years, could he have imagined the devastation and slaughter that his murder of Franz Ferdinand had occasioned and was still occasioning. She wondered how he would endure the burden on his conscience and if, when all the Serbs, Croats and Slovenes who had lived in vassalage in the Austro-Hungarian empire were living freely and equally in a Kingdom for all South Slavs, he would find in their freedom a measure of solace.

Her own solace as the war dragged on into its fourth year were Julian's letters from Salonika and her mother's and Katerina's letters from Corfu. When the first letter from Corfu had arrived in the spring of 1916 she had sobbed with sheer relief.

'They're safe!' she had said to Diana, tears streaming down her face. 'My mother and sister are in Corfu and they're safe!'

Minutes later she had said incredulously, 'I don't believe it! It isn't possible! Katerina is married!'

She had raised her eyes from the letter and stared at Diana with such a dazed expression on her face that Diana had laughed.

'Why shouldn't she be? She's older than you, isn't she? Who has she married? Does he have a wonderfully exotic title?'

349

Feeling totally disorientated Natalie had lowered her eyes again to the letter. After a moment or two she had slowly shaken her head. 'No. His name is Zlarin. Major Zlarin.'

Diana had hoped for a minor royal princeling but had had the good manners to hide her disappointment.

'Mama says he is a hero,' Natalie had said, continuing to read. 'She says he and his men protected Belgrade for weeks, holding massive Austro-Hungarian forces at bay across the Sava.'

She had looked up again from the letter, her eyes huge in the delicate triangle of her face. 'There's a baby!'

Diana had giggled, 'There often is when people marry. Is it a boy or a girl?'

'It's a boy.' Her shocked eyes had held Diana's. 'Mama says he was born in September 1915, only two months after Stephen was born! How could he have been? It would mean Katerina married Major Zlarin in 1914 and she didn't even *know* a Major Zlarin when I left Belgrade in June 1914! Her having a baby in 1915 is an absolute impossibility! Mama has written the year wrongly. She must have intended to write 1916 or even 1917.'

Diana had taken the letter from her. It had been written in English, flamboyantly in purple ink and the hand-writing was not that of someone liable to make an error. It was large and flowing and self-confident.

'Your mother hasn't made a mistake,' she had said a few seconds later. 'She says the baby's name is Peter and that he was born shortly before they made the nightmare trek across the mountains to the Adriatic.'

She had lowered the letter to her lap and looked across at Natalie. 'The Serbian army retreated in the winter of 1915, so your nephew *must* have been born in September 1915.' She made a quick calculation on exquisitely red-lacquered nails. 'Katerina could have married him as late as December 1914, which means that if she met him immediately after you and Julian left for England she would have known him for six months.'

She had frowned slightly. 'Six months wouldn't be considered a respectable length of time for an English debutante to meet, become engaged and married to someone, but perhaps things are different in Serbia?'

'They are not,' Natalie had said, her voice still thick with shock. 'Engagements are very long and formal and the bridegroom is nearly always someone known to the family.'

'That wasn't the case with you and Julian,' Diana had pointed out as a waiter had assiduously refilled their coffee cups. 'Perhaps your sister's and Major Zlarin's love story is as unconventional as yours and Julian's. Perhaps they fell in love at first sight just as you and Julian so obviously did. Perhaps they married without ever being engaged. Perhaps they even eloped.'

She had poured a small amount of cream into her coffee cup and waited for Natalie's comments. Natalie had been unable to make any. For the first time in her life she had been rendered speechless.

Before she had recovered from the shock of her mother's letter another letter arrived with the same postmark. This time the handwriting was Katerina's and she had torn it open with trembling fingers, glad that Diana was not with her.

Dearest, dearest Natalie, I can't believe that I'm really able to write to you at last! So much has happened since you left for England that I don't know where to start. I know that Mama has already written you with news of my marriage and so I must begin this letter with the news Sandro broke to me himself only a few hours ago. Ivan is dead. He died in the fighting near Shabatz but Sandro only received confirmation of his death after we arrived here. Helga, also, is dead. Her death was terrible and I find it nearly impossible to write about. She was nursing with us at the hospital when Belgrade first fell to the Austrians . . .

As Natalie had read of Helga's death; the suffering Katerina and her mother had witnessed during the Austrian occupation; the horrors of the typhoid epidemic; the fall of the country to Austro-Hungarian forces; the hellish trek across the mountains of Montenegro and Albania, she had felt as disorientated as when she had first learned of Katerina's marriage. If she hadn't left Belgrade when she had, she too would have suffered and witnessed untold horrors. And she hadn't done so. She had suffered nothing worse than agony of mind over Julian's safety, first in Flanders and now in Salonika.

The knowledge of all she had been spared had filled her with irrational guilt. With all her heart she had wished she had been with her mother and Katerina during their dark, dreadful days in Belgrade and during their epic crossing of the snow-bound mountains. And she had wished that she was with them now, in Corfu.

In March, Nicky's prediction that the new Bolshevik government in Russia would seek a separate peace with Germany, was fulfilled. In May came newspaper reports that the Tsar and his family had been moved from Tobolsk to Ekaterinburg, a place of which Natalie had never heard. In July came reports that the entire family had been murdered.

Natalie had wept unashamedly, pressing her tear-streaked face against Bella's soft fur. There would be no marriage now between Sandro and Olga, no alliance between the once mighty Romanovs and the House of Karageorgevich.

From the war fronts the news had never been so optimistic. In August British forces broke through the German lines in France and the Kaiser began to talk in terms of ending the war. In September Allied forces, among them the Serbian army under Alexander's command, launched an offensive against the Bulgarians and sent them hurtling into a massive retreat. The Bulgarian government requested an armistice and on 29 September, in Salonika, Bulgarian peace delegates agreed to the cessation of all hostilities between Bulgaria and the Allies.

In October came the most wonderful news of all as reports reached London that Alexander had marched his troops once more into Belgrade.

In the chaotic, wonderful weeks that followed no news, not even the news of the German surrender, filled Natalie with as much joy and euphoria.

'And Julian will soon be home,' Diana said to her ecstatically as all over London – all over Britain – church bells rang.

Natalie forced a smile. She wanted Julian home with all her heart but her longing to see him again was mixed with unspeakable dread. When they were reunited she was going to have to tell him about Nicky. It was something she had never intended doing but she now had no choice. She had missed her period and was intuitively sure that she was carrying Nicky's child.

Chapter Seventeen

It seemed that every day there was momentous news. Royal crowns began to fall like confetti; the Kaiser abdicated; King Ferdinand of Bulgaria abdicated; Emperor Karl abdicated and with his abdication the Habsburg Empire, mighty for over a thousand years, finally disintegrated.

Nicky was ecstatic. 'Four new nations have been born,' he said to Natalie as they walked across a flag-bedecked Piccadilly Circus. 'Four! Just think of it, Natalie! Half of Europe is being given a completely fresh start. Austria has declared itself a republic, the Czechs and Slovaks have united, the Hungarians are now a separate nation and Croatia . . . Croatia is free!' Jubilantly he circled her waist with his hands lifting her off her feet, whirling her round and round.

Passers-by smiled indulgently. Young men were returning home from battle fronts in their droves and joyous public reunions were commonplace.

Despite all her inner anxieties, Natalie laughed back at him with sheer *joie de vivre*. Not only was Croatia free; so was her beloved homeland. Sometime over the next few weeks, perhaps even the next few days, Nicky would travel with other London-based supporters of the Yugoslav Committee to Belgrade in order to establish a National Assembly under Alexander's regency. When she had spoken with Julian she would either travel to Belgrade with Nicky or, if he was already there, join him.

'Now that Montenegro and Bosnia-Herzegovina have also voted for union with Serbia it's important the unions are ratified as soon as possible,' Nicky continued, setting her back down on the pavement and beginning to walk towards Regent Street again, one arm still securely around her waist.

At the mention of Montenegro a pensive expression entered Natalie's eyes. King Nikita had been one of the many kings to be forced into abdication and when she had read the news in *The Times* she had found herself thinking of Zorka, the aunt she had never known but to whom her mother had been so devoted. Zorka had been King Nikita's eldest daughter and she couldn't help but wonder what Zorka would have thought if she had known that one day her father would be dethroned in order that Montenegro could be united with Serbia and that her son, as Prince Regent, would rule over that union.

'Why is it important that the unions are ratified as soon as possible?' she asked, dragging her thoughts back to the present, her hip pressed close against his as they walked along the crowded street.

'So that we are in a strong position to prevent our Allies carving up our borders to suit themselves,' Nicky said dryly. 'Mercifully Prince Alexander is already in Belgrade and Ante Trumbich and other Yugoslav Committee members are already on their way there. They won't allow any time to be wasted . . .'

Natalie was no longer listening to him. She was wondering how long it would be before Julian returned home and she was wondering if her decision to speak to him about the baby, before she did so to Nicky, was quite as sensible as it had first seemed.

'Nicky . . .' she began hesitantly.

'. . . and before Christmas the Kingdom of Serbs,

Croats, and Slovenes will be official,' he concluded, grinning across at her.

She wanted to tell him about the baby but as his near-black eyes, brilliant with exultation, met hers she couldn't bring herself to do so. Julian was the one who must be told first. He was the one who was going to be devastated by the news and even more devastated by the decision she had made to return to Belgrade with Nicky.

A bus trundled past them bearing the mock sign 'To Berlin: Fare 1d.'

She had thought and thought about the situation she was in and she couldn't see any other solution. She had married Julian for no other reason than to save her parents the distress of being parted. Julian knew that and had happily accepted it. He had told her categorically that he didn't intend applying for a posting to Belgrade and, now that the war was over and there was nothing to stop her returning home, she knew his decision was one with which she couldn't possibly live.

She *had* to return home. All through her childhood she had lived as an exile and all through her childhood she had vowed that, when the day finally dawned when she stepped on the soil of her homeland, nothing would persuade her voluntarily to leave it. And she had *not* voluntarily left it. She had been forced to leave because of a whole series of unfortunate events, events that were now history.

She looked across at Nicky's profile, at his olive-toned skin and high Slavic cheekbones. They were both South Slavs; both Balkan. Nicky would be rewarded for his years of loyalty to the Yugoslav Committee members with a position in the new National Assembly. As his wife, and as a Karageorgevich, she would be actively involved in the organization and development of the new kingdom. Belgrade would be their home and the child she was carrying would be born there.

356

The happy drift of her thoughts came to a sudden and sickening halt as they always did when this point in her reverie of the future was reached. What of Stephen? She couldn't possibly leave him behind. For the hundredth time she tried to think as to what Julian's reaction to the problem would be. She was almost sure that he wouldn't try and deprive her of Stephen. He was too generous-hearted a man to behave in a manner that would cause not only intense suffering to her, but to their child also. Perhaps he would suggest that Stephen visit him once or twice a year?

As she considered the possibility she began to feel optimistic again. She might even be able to accompany Stephen on his visits to Julian. Though they wouldn't, of course, be able to be lovers any more, they could still be friends. She couldn't imagine not being friends with Julian. It was impossible. He had saved her from four tedious years of living in Geneva with her mother; he had been her comfort and her solace; he had never let her down and that he would do so now was unthinkable.

He came home the week that Alexander, as Prince Regent, officially announced that Serbia had ceased to exist as a separate and independent entity. His words when he had done so had been stiffly formal, as the occasion demanded, but emotive.

I am convinced that by this act of union I am fulfilling my duty as a ruler. I am carrying out that for which the best sons of our blood, of all three religions, all three names, on both sides of the Danube, Sava, and Drina began to work during the reign of my grandfather, that which corresponds to the desire and views of my people and so, in the name of His Majesty King Peter, I proclaim the unification of Serbia with the lands of the independent State of Slovenes, Croats, and Serbs in a single Kingdom of the Serbs, Croats, and Slovenes.

Natalie had read a report of his speech in *The Times*, tears running down her face. Everything so many hundreds of thousands of people had dreamed of for so long had finally come to pass. Sandro was no longer merely Prince Regent of a land-locked Serbia, he was Prince Regent of a country whose borders exceeded even those of Tsar Stephen's medieval empire. Though dynasties far mightier than the Karageorgevich dynasty had fallen as a result of the war, the Karageorgevich dynasty had not even tottered and now it was greater than it had ever been before.

She had looked at a newspaper photograph of Sandro and been proud. She had also been shocked. He was no longer the Sandro she remembered. Instead of the handsome young man who had laughed easily and often with her, he was prematurely middle-aged and sombre. She reminded herself that the photograph had been taken at a solemn moment, when laughter would have been grossly out of place, but looking down at his face she knew that wasn't the reason for his totally changed demeanour.

The Sandro who had been her friend before the war, no longer existed. The burden of seeing his country ravished by the enemy, the dreadful trek he had undertaken when ill, across the Albanian and Montenegrin mountains to the Adriatic, the pain he must have suffered on hearing of Olga's murder at the hands of the Bolsheviks, had all taken their toll. It was no wonder that he now looked sombre and grave. With terrible intuition she knew that for Sandro, the days of teasing and laughter were over and would never come again.

Though the war had also taken its toll on Julian, there was nothing sombre in either his demeanour or his expression when he walked into the Fielding town house, calling her name.

She had been in the nursery, kneeling on the floor and trying to piece together the rails of a train set while Stephen had his afternoon nap. At the sound of his voice she leapt to her feet, pieces of rail track scattering around her. With a disquieting sense of *déjà-vu* she raced along the corridor to the head of the stairs, just as she had done when he had arrived home on his last leave. Then, though, she had not been the mistress of another man. And she had not been pregnant. Pushing both thoughts to the back of her mind she ran down the stairs towards him, wings on her heels.

He hurtled up the stairs two at a time, meeting her on the first landing.

'Natalie! For Christ's sake! *Natalie!*'

His arms closed round her. She could feel his heart slamming against her own; smell the nearly forgotten odour of khaki and the faint, more dearly familiar smell of lemon cologne.

She tried to speak and couldn't. Now, and only now, she acknowledged how fearful she had been that this moment would never arrive and that, instead, a telegram would be delivered telling her that he was dead, as millions of others were dead.

With eyes shining she clung to him, seeing the liberal flecking of grey at his temples and not caring, caring only that he had returned safe and all in one piece.

'Natalie . . .' he said again thickly, almost reverently, and then, his face transfigured by joy, he lowered his head to hers and kissed her with all the released, pent-up passion of three long, lonely, crucifying years.

When she had realized that she was pregnant she had made up her mind that on Julian's return she would tell him the news immediately, before he even attempted to make love to her. That way she would be behaving as honourably as was possible, under the circumstances.

With his mouth hard and sweet on hers, and her arms hugging him tight, it no longer seemed quite as easy a plan of action as it had first appeared.

He lifted his head from hers, grinning down at her. 'You haven't changed,' he said, feasting his eyes on her heart-shaped face and the night-black curls springing free of her chignon and curling riotously at her temples. 'I told your father you wouldn't have changed.'

'Papa!' Gold-green eyes widened in stunned disbelief. 'You've spoken with Papa? Where? When?'

'In Salonika, before I boarded ship for home. He was also about to board ship, but for Corfu.'

'What did he say? Was he well? Has he been injured? Is he going to take Mama and Katerina straight back to Belgrade?' Questions tumbled from her. 'Did he ask after me? Did you tell him about Stephen? Did you tell him how much I missed him?'

'He was as well as can be expected after the ordeal he's been through,' Julian said gently.

She looked at him fearfully, aware for the first time of his own deep exhaustion, exhaustion his grin and passionate embrace had temporarily disguised. 'Has he been injured?' she asked again. 'Has the war made him old?'

Julian thought of Alexis, haggard and rake-thin. 'I don't think he's been injured in any way that is permanent,' he said truthfully. 'Like all of us, what he needs is plenty of good food and rest.'

With his arms still around her he looked down into the empty hall. 'Where is everyone? I expected a brass band at the very least.'

She giggled, feeling the years of separation sliding away into oblivion.

'If I'd known you were coming home today I would have arranged for one. Your father is probably asleep in his study. Your mother and Diana are out, I don't know where.'

She couldn't help satisfaction creeping into her voice. She was glad that they were out; glad there was no-one to intrude on their reunion.

'I must go down and see Pa,' he said, still keeping both arms firmly around her. 'But before I do, I have news for you.'

'Good news?' Her heart leapt. 'About Papa?'

His eyes laughed down into hers. She could see flecks of gold in the pupils; see her own face reflected back at her.

'Your father is arranging for your mother and Katerina to travel by sea to Nice. We are to meet them there.'

She gasped and if he had not been holding her so securely, would have fallen. 'When? How soon? Why is Papa arranging for a reunion in Nice? Why hasn't he asked us to travel to Belgrade and to meet with Mama and Katerina there?'

He said smoothly, 'Because Belgrade is still in chaos and will be for several months. Not only that, travelling overland through Europe is a virtual impossibility. There are no reliable rail services yet and the roads are thick with soldiers and refugees returning to their homes. If there is to be a speedy family reunion it's going to have to take place somewhere we can all reach comparatively easily.'

He tensed, waiting for her reaction. The last thing he wanted to do was to spoil their own reunion by being forced to tell her that no family reunion would ever take place in Belgrade, that she would never set foot in Belgrade again as long as she lived.

Alexis had left him in no doubt of it. 'Alexander's policy is to ensure the world is convinced of the Serbian government's innocence in the Sarajevo assassinations. A

361

little over a year ago Colonel Dimitrievich was court-martialled and executed. Officially the charge was plotting a mutiny in the army but Alexander let it be known that the chief reason for the court martial was Apis's known involvement with the Black Hand and the Black Hand's strongly rumoured involvement in the Archduke's assassination.'

Julian had sucked in his breath, both shocked and reluctantly admiring of Alexander's ruthlessness where his country's honour was concerned.

Alexis continued heavily, 'In all the investigations that will now take place into the event that triggered off the war, Alexander is determined he and his government will emerge blame-free. That being the case, and knowing that somewhere in the Habsburg archives there will be a copy of Natalie's extradition order and a statement from the officer who saw her with Princip, he can afford to take no chances.'

His face had been anguished and his voice had cracked as he had said, 'He has declared her to be *persona non grata*. She can never return home again.'

Natalie smiled sunnily up at him, accepting his explanation totally. 'When do we leave? Can we take Stephen with us? Will Katerina have Peter with her? Will Papa be there as well? What . . .'

The front door opened and Lady Fielding entered the house. She gasped as she saw the kitbag on the marbled floor and Julian kissed Natalie swiftly on the mouth, reluctantly released his hold of her and hurried downstairs.

Natalie remained on the landing, her thoughts in such confusion she could hardly sort one from the other. She was going to see Katerina and her mother again! They would be able to tell her in detail, and far more satisfactorily than they had been able to do in letters, everything that had happened to them during their four and a half years separation.

Hard on the heels of her joy came an agonizing dilemma. How could she now tell Julian about the baby she was carrying? He might not even accompany her to Nice once he knew. Even if he did accompany her, her mother would instantly realize that something was seriously wrong between them. And what if Julian told her what it was? Panic bubbled up in her throat. Her mother would have to know sometime, of course, but for her to know now would ruin their precious reunion.

As Julian accompanied his mother into his father's study, she frowned down into the again empty hall. For her mother's sake she couldn't allow their time in Nice together to be spoiled. Choice had, again, been taken away from her. Her confession to Julian would have to wait until their return from Nice. Which meant that despite all her good intentions her reunion with Julian would have to be a sexual one.

An emotion suspiciously like relief flooded through her to be followed almost immediately by fresh anxiety. What if he noticed the difference in her body? What if he guessed? She ran the palms of her hands down over her perfectly flat stomach. She wouldn't begin to show for months yet. When she had been carrying Stephen she hadn't begun to show until she was over four months pregnant.

With that anxiety taken care of her thoughts turned to Nicky. She wouldn't now be able to tell him about the baby until after she returned from Nice and had broken the news to Julian. She gave an exasperated sigh. All she wanted was for life to be trouble-free and, instead, it persisted in being infuriatingly complicated.

The front door opened and Diana entered, swathed in furs against the December chill. She stopped short, her eyes flying to the kitbag. As Natalie saw the joy flooding her friend's face she forgot all about the complications besetting her.

She began to run down the stairs, calling out euphorically, 'Julian's home, Diana! He's home and he's seen Papa and he's taking me to Nice for a reunion with Mama and Katerina! Isn't it wonderful? Isn't it unbelievably wonderful?'

They crossed from Dover to Boulogne, travelling by train via Montreuil and Abbeville to Paris, keeping as far west of war-ravaged Flanders and Picardy as was possible. On the long journey south to Nice Stephen amused himself by beating excitedly on the train windows every time he saw a cow or a horse in a field and Natalie rejoiced every time she glimpsed the French flag waving triumphantly from a farm or house window.

Her own excitement, as the train finally drew into Nice, was almost beyond bearing. She was on the verge of being reunited with her mother and Katerina and she knew that once she was, it would be as if the intervening years had never happened.

With a disconcerted nanny in tow holding tightly on to Stephen's chubby hand and Julian striding in amusement by her side, she practically ran from the station.

'Oh, hurry!' she exhorted Julian in a fever of impatience as he paused at the cab rank for the porters carrying their luggage to catch up with them. 'Do you think Mama and Katerina will already be at the Negresco? Do you think they will be waiting for us?'

'Will they recognize you if they are?' he said to her, his amusement deepening.

Her hand flew to her newly-shorn hair. The crown had been brushed into glossy submission and then at jawlength, below an embroidered headband worn rakishly

Indian-fashion, her ebony curls rioted untamed. The cherry-red dress and coat she was wearing were equally *avant-garde*, arrow-straight without even the slightest indentation at her waist, the vivid colour offset by the dramatically long black sable scarf that was thrown around her throat, the ends falling behind her back to her hemline.

She giggled, remembering all the old battles that had taken place over her clothes.

'I remember once I wanted to wear a devastatingly sophisticated mauve brocade ballgown and neither Katerina nor Helga would allow me to,' she said as the taxi was loaded with their luggage. 'Instead I had to wear demure white, decorated with pink rosebuds. It was the night of Mama's Summer Ball. The night you proposed to me.'

He felt his throat tighten with emotion at the memory and said as lightly as he was able, 'Thank heaven they talked you out of the mauve. If you had been wearing it I would probably have proposed to Vitza instead.'

Laughingly they stepped inside the taxi and Julian lifted Stephen on to his knee. Happiness, bone-deep, pervaded him. Though Natalie was still as oddly incapable of putting her love for him into words he hadn't the slightest doubt that she did, indeed, love him. The future stretched before him dazzlingly. He was demobilized; he had a brilliant career in the Foreign Office to which to look forward; there would be other children, maybe another boy, perhaps even a girl . . .

'The Negresco!' Natalie exclaimed joyously. 'We're there! Oh do look to see if you can see Mama at any of the windows!'

As they stepped out into the bright winter sunshine Stephen added his voice to hers, jumping up and down excitedly, shouting, 'The sea, Mama! The sea!'

For once Natalie paid no heed to him. If her narrow

skirt would have allowed her to run into the opulent foyer she would have done so.

'Oh, hurry!' she pleaded again to Julian. 'Hurry, hurry, *hurry!*'

They hurried. Leaving Nanny to placate Stephen and ignoring their luggage they entered the hotel. There were no familiar figures seated in the reception area and Natalie's heart began to beat in heavy, painful strokes. What if they were not there? What if they were not going to be able to be there? She already knew that her father wouldn't be at the hotel, for he had told Julian he was travelling direct from Corfu to Belgrade. What if Katerina and her mother had decided to join him and wait for her there? What if all her high hopes of being reunited within minutes, or at the most within a few days, were in vain?

Julian was at the reception desk and when he turned away from it she saw to her dizzying relief that he was grinning.

'Your mother and Katerina are taking afternoon tea in the sun lounge.'

She closed her eyes fleetingly in a silent prayer of thanks and then said urgently, 'Where is the sun lounge? Is it on this floor? Ask a bell-boy to take us there immediately! Please, Julian! *Please!*'

'There's no need for a bell-boy,' he said, tucking her arm in his. 'I used to stay here regularly with my grandparents when I was a small boy.'

As he was talking to her he was leading her across the reception lounge and towards a large, sunny room so green with giant potted palms and trailing vines that it looked more like a conservatory than a lounge. As they crossed the threshold she was aware of huge gold-framed mirrors lining the walls and the coolness of pink marble beneath her feet. Then she saw them.

They were sitting at a small round table in the far corner

of the room. Her mother was wearing a pale *eau-de-nil* silk day-dress, her dark hair swept elegantly into a Grecian knot. Katerina was wearing a long, toffee-coloured skirt and creamy silk open-necked shirt, the sleeves prettily flounced at the wrist. She looked so sophisticated that for a brief, heart-stopping second Natalie wondered if it was really her and then Katerina turned her head towards the door and their eyes met.

A sob of joy broke from Natalie's throat. Uncaring of the elegant figures at the other tables, uncaring of her narrow skirt and her dignity, she began to run.

Through the tears of happiness distorting her vision she saw Katerina and her mother rise to their feet, saw Katerina begin to run towards her and then, as waiters dodged apprehensively out of their way, Katerina's hands grasped hold of hers and all the intervening years went spinning into sun-shot oblivion, just as they had when Julian had come home and taken her again into his arms.

'Natalie! Natalie! Is it really you?' Katerina was saying, laughing and crying at the same time. 'Your hair! It looks *wonderful*! Oh, I've missed you so much! You'll never know how much! Never, never, never!'

The elderly couple at the table nearest to them prudently steadied their cake stand so that any further frenetic activity would not unbalance it completely and watched the encounter with interest.

From somewhere behind her Natalie could hear Stephen's toddling footsteps and a plaintive, 'Mummy! Mummy! Want to see the sea!'

Katerina dragged her eyes from Natalie's and towards her nephew and the tall, broad-shouldered figure about to scoop him up out of harm's way. Natalie's eyes, brilliant with tears, met those of her mother.

'Mama . . .' she said in a choked voice, releasing her

hold of Katerina and beginning to walk unsteadily towards her mother. 'Oh, Mama!'

At last her mother's arms closed around her. At last the long, painful separation was over.

'Champagne, I think,' Julian was saying as, Stephen high in his arms, he accompanied Katerina back to the table.

He turned to where Nanny was standing, her cheeks scarlet with the embarrassment she felt at being employed by a family who indulged in such ill-bred, Balkan displays of emotionalism.

'I think it might be a good idea if you asked to be shown to the suite into which we are booked and if you checked on the sleeping arrangements for Stephen,' he said pleasantly, aware of her discomfiture. 'Stephen has yet to be introduced to his grandmother and aunt and when he has been, and when the excitement becomes too much for him, I will bring him upstairs to you.'

She nodded assent, escaping from the room with vast relief, grateful he, at least, was British and conventional.

Natalie and Zita were now seated, their hands clasped, and Zita was looking towards Stephen.

'So you are Stephen,' she said gently, stretching her free hand out towards him. 'Are you going to come a little nearer and say hello to me? I've wanted to meet you for so long.'

Happy to make friends Stephen placed his chubby hand in hers. 'Want to see the sea,' he said confidingly. 'Want to see the waves.'

Zita smiled and for the first time Natalie became aware of the web of fine lines beneath her mother's carefully applied face-powder. She felt a pang of shock. The war had achieved what she had always thought impossible. It had aged her mother.

She looked swiftly towards Katerina. She was standing

368

next to Julian and suddenly she saw the strain beneath Katerina's outwardly serene radiance.

'It's all over,' she said to her impulsively. 'Nothing awful is ever going to happen to us again.'

Katerina smiled, but an expression very like pain still lingered at the back of her thick-lashed eyes.

A waiter arrived with champagne and as he did so Natalie said ebulliently, 'I always thought we would drink our reunion glass of champagne together in the *Konak*.'

No-one spoke. No-one was able to.

Natalie grinned, knowing they were all wishing they were in Belgrade rather than Nice. 'Never mind,' she said philosophically, bending down to Stephen in order to lift him on her knee, 'our next reunion will be in Belgrade and so we still have something absolutely wonderful to look forward to!'

Over the top of Natalie's bent head Zita's horrified eyes shot to Julian's. Reading the reason he still had not told Natalie about her permanent exile in his anguished eyes, she said a little unsteadily, 'I think it's about time Peter was woken from his afternoon nap and brought down to meet everyone. When he has been, I'm going to satisfy Stephen's craving to see the sea and it would be nice if Peter came as well.' She turned again to Julian. 'Would you like to join us?'

He nodded, grateful for the way she had created a situation where they could talk together out of Natalie's hearing.

Katerina fought down her horror at Natalie's ignorance as to what the future held for her and, understanding what was going on between her mother and Julian said, 'I'll go for Peter now. Do you want to come with me, Natalie?'

Natalie sprang to her feet. She most certainly did want to go with her. Not only was she impatient to meet her nephew, she wanted to question Katerina about her late husband. She wanted to know when she had met Major Zlarin and where, and she also wanted to know why they had married so precipitately.

'I met Ivan shortly after you left for Britain,' Katerina said as she lifted a still sleepy Peter from his bed. 'War was imminent and Papa had realized he would not be in Belgrade for much longer. As Ivan had been instructed to remain in the city and to defend it, Papa asked him if he would afford Mama and myself as much protection as was possible. Ivan said he would do so and Papa brought him to the house to meet us.'

'And you fell in love straight away?' Natalie asked, taking a bewildered Peter from Katerina and sitting him on her knee.

Katerina hesitated. She still felt so much guilt where Ivan was concerned that she found it almost impossible to speak about him.

'Not really . . . no . . .' she said awkwardly.

Natalie's eyes widened like saucers. 'Then why . . .'

Katerina didn't let her finish. Mindful that Peter was now fully awake and listening, she said hurriedly, 'I'll tell you later. When we're alone.' She began to ease Peter's legs into a pair of warm leggings. 'Do you know about Hélène's husband?' she asked, changing the subject. 'He was murdered by the Bolsheviks.'

Natalie sucked in her breath and Katerina added quickly, 'Hélène is safe. She and her little boy are now in Switzerland.'

'Is everyone else safe?' Natalie asked, pale-faced. 'Are Great-Aunt Eudocia and Vitza safe?'

Katerina nodded and Natalie said, 'And Max? Is Max still alive?'

A shadow crossed Katerina's face and Natalie was sure she was going to say that Max had been killed in action.

370

Instead she said, 'Max and his men were among the first troops to enter Belgrade. He's there now, with Sandro.' She hesitated for a moment and then said, an odd note in her voice, 'He's married. He met a Greek girl in Salonika and . . .'

'A Greek!' Natalie couldn't have been more astonished if Katerina had said Max had married a Turk. 'What on earth must Aunt Eudocia's reaction have been?'

Katerina had knelt down and begun to slide Peter's arms into the sleeves of his coat and Natalie could no longer see the expression on her face. 'Goodness knows,' she said as she began to fasten Peter's buttons and then, after another pause, 'They have a son. Xan.'

Natalie shook her head in disbelief. 'I can't imagine Max married. I wonder if he's still as moody and taciturn. I used to dread him marking my card at dances. He was always so clumsy and . . .'

'He's shy,' Katerina said unexpectedly, smoothing the deep-blue velvet nap on the collar of Peter's pastel-blue coat.

Natalie's jaw dropped. '*Shy?*' she said incredulously when she had recovered her powers of speech. 'How could such a giant of a man be *shy*? And he's a war hero! Heroes aren't shy!'

'Max is,' Katerina said in a voice of utter certainty. She leant back on her heels. 'Come on, let's take Peter downstairs to meet Stephen.'

Natalie remained where she was sitting. There was someone else whose welfare she needed to ask about; someone she didn't want to speak of in front of her mother and Julian.

'Have you heard any news of Gavrilo and Trifko and Nedjelko?' she asked, her eyes anxious. 'Do you know if they are in prison in Bosnia or Austria?'

At the expression on Katerina's face she felt fear clutch

her heart. 'What is it, Trina? What's the matter? Does no-one know where they are? Does . . .'

'Let me take Peter into my bedroom,' Katerina said, increasing her fear.

In an agony of apprehension Natalie waited as Katerina led Peter to the inter-connecting door, opening it for him and saying, 'I want you to wait for me in here, my love. You can play with my trinket-box. I shan't be long. I promise.'

When she re-crossed the thickly carpeted room her face was grave.

'What is it?' Natalie asked again, unsteadily. 'Is Gavrilo sick? Is he . . .'

Katerina sat down opposite her, taking her hand lovingly in hers. 'He's dead,' she said thickly, knowing there was no easy way for her to break the news.

Natalie tried to speak and couldn't. She felt as if she were being sucked into a swirling, bottomless pit. Gavrilo couldn't be dead, not now, when to so many millions freed of Habsburg tyranny he would be seen as a saviour, not a criminal.

'He died in Theresienstadt, a fortress somewhere between Prague and Dresden. A Czech doctor who befriended him there wrote to Sandro . . .'

'And Trifko and Nedjelko?' Natalie whispered. 'Are they dead too?'

Katerina nodded and Natalie gave a low moan, hugging her arms tight around her.

'I'm sorry, Natalie. Truly I am.' She hesitated for a moment and then said gently, 'They were all suffering with tuberculosis and the disease killed them.'

She didn't add that the conditions in which they had been imprisoned, in cold, damp, windowless cells, would have killed anyone. Nor did she add what she knew of Gavrilo's last, agonizing days on earth. '*He sustained a broken rib and a crushed arm when arrested,*' the doctor had written in small, meticulous handwriting. '*He received no proper medical attention and the arm began to suppurate and the infection to spread. In 1917 it was amputated and thereafter, handcuffs no longer being possible, he was shackled with leg irons, and in leg irons, barely conscious, coughed himself into eternity.*'

It was a hideous image and one with which she had no intention of burdening Natalie. 'Let's go downstairs,' she said gently. 'Let's introduce Peter to Stephen.'

Natalie's grief for her friends' deaths was deep but it was not a grief she could display publicly for she had the sense to know that her mother would not want reminding of the incident that had led to their long separation.

Later on in the afternoon, trying to distract herself with other thoughts until the time when she could be alone and could weep as she longed to weep, she noticed that although Peter was younger than Stephen, he was the same height. She wondered again about Major Zlarin. He had obviously been a tall man and, if Peter's silky-black hair was anything to go by, dark. She wondered if he had also been handsome; as handsome as Nicky.

At the thought of Nicky she was inevitably faced with the dilemma as to whether she dare tell Katerina about him. She wanted to. She wanted to be able to tell Katerina of the responsible position Nicky would soon hold in the National Assembly. Her head ached as she struggled to come to a decision, wishing that just for once life could be uncomplicated.

That night, with Stephen and Peter sleeping amicably together in a room nearby, Natalie sat at the end of Katerina's bed, nursing a cup of milky cocoa. Both she and Katerina were in their nightdresses and, apart from

373

the fact that Natalie wasn't going to remain in the room sleeping in a bed twin to Katerina's, it was just like old times.

'It was at night, just before I went to sleep, that I missed you most,' Natalie said with touching frankness. 'I missed exchanging confidences with you, giggling . . .'

A smile touched the corners of Katerina's generously curved mouth. 'What confidences?' she asked teasingly.

Natalie remembered the secrecy of her visits to the *Golden Sturgeon* and had the grace to blush. 'I would have confided in you about Gavrilo,' she said awkwardly, 'only I was so frightened of your disapproval.'

They fell silent for a moment, Katerina thinking how differently things might have turned out if Natalie had confided in her and Natalie mortified by the knowledge that yet again she was not confiding in Katerina as she longed to do, and again was not doing so because she feared her disapproval.

Instead of speaking to her about Nicky she hugged her knees to her chest, saying, 'Will you tell me about Ivan now? Were Mama and Papa approving? Did you marry in the cathedral? Why did you marry so quickly if you didn't fall in love at first sight?'

Katerina said slowly, 'Though I didn't fall in love with Ivan at first sight, I think he fell in love with me at first sight. After we were married he told me that he had done so.'

'But he must have told you he loved you before you were married!' Natalie protested, more intrigued than ever.

Katerina leaned forward a little, clasping her arms around her knees, her waist-length hair, free of its pins, tumbling silkily over her shoulders.

'It all began when Papa wrote Mama saying that Max wished to marry me and that . . .'

'*Max!*' Natalie nearly fell from the bed in shock. 'I

don't believe it! *Max?* He never ever gave the slightest indication of being in love with you. Do you remember when . . .'

Katerina said quickly, 'Papa was in favour of the match. In his letters, as the weeks went by and the fighting with the Austrians grew more intense, he became quite emphatic that it was a proposal I should accept. He had been so distressed by . . .' She hesitated awkwardly and Natalie's eyes clouded with remembered pain.

'By everything that led up to my marrying Julian?'

Katerina nodded, her throat tight. When she could trust herself to speak again, she said, 'All Papa wanted was to know that my future was secure and I knew that if I said I was in love elsewhere he wouldn't persist in his insistence that I marry Max.'

'But you weren't in love elsewhere!' Natalie could hardly believe what she was hearing. Surely Katerina, always so sedate and sensible and honourable, had not *lied*?

'In Papa's absence Ivan was scrupulous in offering Mama and myself all the protection possible. I grew to respect him very much and he was extremely hand-some . . .'

She paused again and for once Natalie didn't interrupt. Round-eyed, she waited with baited breath for the story to continue.

'When the Austrians first overran the borders and our troops fell back to the south to regroup, all the troops in Belgrade were ordered to join them. It was a terrible time, Natalie. The hospitals were crammed with wounded. I was working as a voluntary nurse with Mama and Cissie and Helga and we knew that the instant the troops left Belgrade, the city would be occupied. Ivan managed to see me before he evacuated his men. He pleaded with me to take Mama to Nish but I told him it was impossible. From

375

the first day of fighting Mama had made up her mind that she would not leave the city . . .'

Natalie gave a deep sigh of satisfaction. She had always known her mother was a heroine and now here was the proof.

'I told him that if he had asked anything else of me I would have complied without hesitation . . .'

'And?' Natalie prompted, hardly able to bear the suspense, 'And what did he say?'

'He asked me to marry him.'

'And you said yes? When you hardly knew him? You said yes rather than marry Max?'

Katerina's beautifully etched face was tortured. 'Yes,' she said in an agony of guilt. 'There wasn't time to think properly and I thought I would be able to learn to love him, whereas I was sure, then, that I would never be able to learn to love Max.'

Natalie let out a deep, shuddering sigh of amazement. 'I can hardly believe it of you, Trina. What if you'd been wrong? What if you hadn't learned to love him after you were married?'

Katerina remained silent, her eyes dark with emotions she still couldn't express. Some day she would tell Natalie about her wedding breakfast and the terrible moment of revelation when she had known that she would never love Ivan and that she could, very easily, have learned to love Max. Tonight, however, was not the time. It was already after midnight and she was sure that in their room further down the corridor, Julian was waiting up for Natalie.

Later, when Natalie had kissed her good night and gone to join Julian, Katerina had lain awake in the darkness, re-living the moment when he had greeted her.

In some ways it had not been half as terrible as she had feared. The war had changed him, as it had changed all of them, but there were no visible signs of the injuries he had sustained early on in the war, in Flanders. Though his dark-blond hair was streaked with silver at the temples it was still as thick and springy as a ram's fleece and he still wore it longer than any other Englishman she had ever met. Her relief at his well-being was deep, but hard on its heels had come another emotion, an emotion that was just as agonizing as she had anticipated it would be.

She still loved him. She had known the instant he took hold of her hand that she was still as emotionally bound to him as she had been the day she had discovered he was to marry Natalie.

Her heart physically hurt her. It was a burden she was going to have to bear life-long; a burden she could share with no-one, least of all Natalie.

Natalie, too, was tormented by the need to confess. Within days of their returning to London Nicky would be leaving for Belgrade and she and Stephen would either accompany him, or follow him as soon as was possible. When that moment arrived it would be impossible to keep their relationship secret and she wanted to tell Katerina about it now, to forewarn her.

Not until their penultimate day in Nice did she drum up the courage to do so. They were walking together in the high, hilly gardens that looked down over the port and that reminded Natalie of the Kalemegdan Gardens. Julian had taken Stephen and Peter to the Marine Aquarium. Zita was taking an afternoon nap.

'I can't bear the thought of saying goodbye tomorrow,' Katerina said to her suddenly, with fierce passion.

Though the January sky was a diamond-hard blue the temperature was low and her kid-gloved hands were tucked deep within a wolf muff.

Natalie pulled the collar of her wool, topaz-coloured coat, closer around her throat. It was fastened with smoky pearl buttons and on top of her dark curls she wore a matching hat jauntily decorated with a plume of jewel-coloured feathers.

'It won't be for long,' she said to Katerina comfortingly, 'there's something I've wanted to tell you ever since I arrived and now I'm going to.'

Katerina looked across at her in sudden apprehension. There was a hint of defiance in Natalie's voice. It was a tone she remembered well, a tone that had always presaged news of a scrape of some kind or another.

They had drawn abreast of a wooden bench, strategically placed so that those taking advantage of it could enjoy the magnificent view and she said, 'Let's sit down. You haven't done anything foolish again, have you?'

'I've fallen in love,' Natalie said, sitting down and deciding not to waste time in a preamble.

Katerina felt dizzy with relief. 'I'm glad,' she said sincerely. 'There was no need for you to tell me though. Seeing you and Julian together it's quite obvious . . .'

Natalie's sleek eyebrows rose until they were nearly lost in her hair. 'I'm not talking about Julian,' she said, amazed at Katerina's innocent assumption. 'Julian and I are *friends*. I've fallen in love with a Slav. A Croat. His name is Nikita Kechko and he's . . .'

Katerina stared at her, suddenly very still. 'You can't mean it,' she said at last, slowly, 'I don't believe you. How can you possibly have developed a crush on someone when Julian has only been home a matter of weeks?'

Natalie said patiently, 'I haven't developed a crush on Nicky. I'm *in love* with him, Trina. I've been in love with him for three years. He's an active supporter of the Yugoslav Committee and he's been promised a position in the new government. He'll be leaving London for Belgrade within days and I will probably leave with him. Even if I don't, I will follow him as soon as I can . . .'

'I don't believe you!' Katerina said again, her eyes wide and dark and full of an expression that Natalie had never seen there before; an expression she couldn't understand. 'I don't believe that even you could be so selfish and foolish and . . . and *wicked*!'

Every trace of colour had left Katerina's cheeks and now Natalie felt the blood drain from her own.

'Wicked?' she cried, mortified. 'How can you call me wicked? If it wasn't for my sacrifice in marrying Julian, Mama would have been separated from Papa for over four years!'

'They were separated anyway,' Katerina said with shocking, unexpected brutality, 'and there would have been no question of Mama leaving for Switzerland or anywhere else if it hadn't been for your heedless, irresponsible behaviour . . .'

'I wasn't heedless and irresponsible!' Natalie riposted indignantly. 'My seeing Gavrilo in Sarajevo was just an unfortunate accident . . .'

'An unfortunate accident?' As she thought of everything that the unfortunate accident had led to, a rage she had never believed herself capable of surged through Katerina. 'That "unfortunate accident" destroyed our family! Because of it, we'll never be a family again as we used to be! Never! Never! Never! All because you never troubled to think as to what the consequences of your friendship with student nationalists might lead to! And you're still not thinking about anyone but yourself! Julian loves you! How can you possibly consider leaving him after all he's done for you?'

It was the most terrible quarrel they had ever had and it had sprung up so quickly that Natalie could hardly believe it was happening.

'Julian knows I wasn't in love with him when we married,' she protested defensively, wanting Katerina to understand the way things really were more than she could ever remember wanting anything, except to return to Belgrade. 'Papa and Mama knew it and you knew it! You can't have expected me to live lovelessly all my life . . .'

'You haven't lived lovelessly! You aren't living lovelessly now!' Never, in all her life, had Katerina been so impassioned. 'Julian loves you with all his heart and it's obvious, just seeing the two of you together, how deeply happy you are with him. You can't possibly leave him . . . it would be an act of lunacy!'

A squirrel ran across the path a few inches from their feet and disappeared over the lip of the shrub-covered hillside. Neither of them paid it the slightest attention.

'It isn't an act of lunacy,' Natalie said, mortally offended. 'Under the circumstances it's the most sensible and honourable action I can take.'

'What circumstances?' Katerina's voice was very quiet, utterly implacable.

Natalie hesitated but Katerina's eyes were holding hers so fiercely she knew she had no alternative but to tell her the truth.

'I'm having a baby,' she said, defiance creeping back into her voice. 'It's Nicky's baby and I'm going to tell Julian about it immediately we leave for London. The only reason I haven't already told him is that I didn't want our family reunion to be spoiled . . .'

'Dear God,' Katerina whispered softly under her breath, her face chalk-white as she rose unsteadily to her feet. 'Dear, dear God.'

'. . . and I'm sure he's going to be far more understanding than you have been. We'll still remain friends and Stephen will visit him for holidays and perhaps Julian will visit Belgrade . . .'

'Belgrade?'

'Yes. I told you. Nicky is leaving London for Belgrade. He's going to be involved in the formation of the new government, though I don't know yet in what capacity . . .'

'And you think that you are going to join him there?'

There was an odd note in Katerina's voice. So odd that Natalie felt suddenly afraid.

'Yes, I told you. We may travel together or I may follow a few days later with Stephen . . .'

Katerina thought of all the anguish Natalie's past foolishness had occasioned and all the anguish her present foolishness was going to occasion. She thought of Julian and of his unselfishness and integrity and of how, if he hadn't so precipitately and gallantly married Natalie he might, eventually, have become her own much-loved husband.

Very slowly and very deliberately she said, 'You will never return to Belgrade, Natalie. Sandro has forbidden it.'

This time it was Natalie's turn to stare and to say in stupefied disbelief, 'I don't believe you! You're just trying to frighten me!'

Katerina shook her head and Natalie felt ice-cold waves of terror surging through her. 'What you are saying is impossible!' Her voice was cracked and scarcely recognizable. 'Sandro is even fonder of me than he is of Hélène! He would never do such a thing! Why should he? There's absolutely no possible reason . . .'

'Sandro will take any measure, no matter how painful to himself, to protect Serbia's honour. Even before you had left Belgrade the Austrians had requested your extradition. A copy will still be in the Austrian archives. If it ever comes to light it will link Archduke Franz Ferdinand's assassination to the House of Karageorgevich. Sandro is determined that if that situation ever arises he

381

will be able to show that you have been *persona non grata* in Serbia ever since the assassination took place. He told me of his decision long ago. He's since also told Papa and Papa has told Julian.'

'No!' Natalie could feel the ground tilting at her feet, shelving away into a great vast void. 'I don't believe you! If it was the truth Julian would have told me!'

'Perhaps he didn't want to hurt you.' Katerina's voice was terrifyingly steady. 'Perhaps he was just waiting for the right moment, just as you were waiting for the right moment to tell him about Nikita and the baby you are carrying.'

Natalie tried to speak and couldn't. The waves of terror surging through her were submerging her; drowning her. What would Nicky's reaction be when she told him she could never return to Belgrade? Would he be happy to remain in London? And if he wasn't, and if Julian's reaction was as unreasonable and as cruel as Katerina's had been, what then? What would she do? Where would she go?

Above all else, how could she possibly live the rest of her life without being allowed to return home? She couldn't even conceive of such a future. It was unimaginable. Impossible. As the enormity of the words *persona non grata* beat against her ears she whispered hoarsely, 'What am I to do, Trina? I can't bear the thought of living the rest of my life as an exile! I can't live with such pain! I can't survive it!'

For one long never-to-be-forgotten moment, Katerina's eyes held hers and in unspeakable horror Natalie finally recognized the expression in their grey-green depths. It was contempt.

She sucked in her breath, crying out yet again in protest and without speaking, without stretching a hand of comfort towards her, Katerina turned on her heel and began to walk away down the snowdrop-edged path.

382

Chapter Eighteen

Natalie was totally incapable of either movement or speech. She stared after Katerina barely able to comprehend the enormity of the nightmare that had engulfed her. How could Katerina have said such cruel things to her? How could she have been so uncaring? So pitiless?

Two small birds flew wrangling into a nearby shrub. The squirrel returned to the lip of the hillside and sat on its haunches, watching her with shiny-bright eyes. In the distance the winter sun gleamed on the red roofs of the houses clustered around the port and on the vast, shimmering, aquamarine surface of the sea.

Katerina had long since disappeared from view and Natalie suddenly became aware of how cold she was. The bench she was sitting on was hideously exposed and an insidious chill was beginning to seep through her body, bone by bone. Numbly she rose to her feet. She had to return to the Negresco. She had to speak to Julian.

The minute she entered their suite and he looked into her eyes he knew that Katerina had broken the news to her of her permanent exile.

'Oh, my love,' he said, his voice heavy with compassion as he walked swiftly towards her. 'I didn't want you to know until your reunion with your mother and Katerina was over. I didn't want these precious few days to be spoilt.'

He took her lovingly and comfortingly in his arms and she said in a tight, dry voice, 'It's true, then? Everything Katerina told me is true?'

He said gently, 'I don't know yet what Katerina has said to you but yes, anything she has said will be the truth.'

Her arms didn't encircle him in loving response. In a moment as horrendous as any she had just survived she knew that somewhere, deep inside, she had been cherishing the desperate hope that Katerina had been wrong and that Julian would tell her so and would put everything right.

Now, as she looked into his brandy-dark eyes and saw the pity there, the hope died and grief encompassed her. It was a grief too deep for tears. She felt as if she had died; as if she would never be able to give vent to any emotion ever again.

Her mother came and sat with her. A doctor came and gave her a sleeping tablet. Julian did his best to comfort her, holding her in his arms and telling her how the reunion in Nice would become an annual event and of how her parents and Katerina and Peter would be able to stay with them for long periods once they had a home of their own, whether that home was in London or some other European capital.

She had known that she should tell him about the baby but was as unable to do so as she was unable to weep. She would tell Nicky first, as she should have done weeks ago. And she would have to also tell him that they could never live together in Belgrade, that they would have to go instead to Zagreb or Sarajevo.

The next morning Katerina asked if she could say goodbye to Natalie in private instead of doing so on a railway platform. Neither Julian nor her mother thought the request odd, assuming she was simply too distressed to be able to cope with a public farewell.

When she entered the room Natalie was sitting on her dressing-table stool dressed in the narrow, ankle-length cherry-red dress and coat she had arrived in. Their eyes met in the dressing-table mirror.

'You haven't told him yet, have you?' Katerina asked starkly.

Natalie shook her head, still not turning to face her, mesmerized by the change that had come over Katerina, transforming her from a loving sister into an implacably cool, hostile stranger.

'Are you waiting until you have told Nicky first?' Katerina persisted in the same quiet, remorseless voice in which she had told her about Sandro's terrible decision. 'Are you thinking that if Nicky abandons you, you can pass the baby off as Julian's?'

With a choked cry Natalie spun round on the dressing-table stool. '*No!* That's a wicked thing to say! I'm telling Nicky first because it's his baby and he should be the first to know about it!'

It was true. She hadn't consciously thought that if Nicky let her down she would have the option of saying nothing at all to Julian. Now, looking into the muted-green depths of Katerina's eyes she knew that even if she had, Katerina would never have allowed her to get away with such a deception.

She said, truly not understanding, 'Why are you being so cruel to me over this, Trina? Why can't you understand how hard it's been for me, marrying someone who wasn't my choice . . .'

Katerina's eyes were darker than she had ever seen them and against the copper highlights in her mahogany hair her pale, creamy skin looked almost translucent. 'Then you shouldn't have married him,' she said inexorably. 'You should have gone to Switzerland with Mama and then maybe Julian would have fallen in love with someone else, someone who truly loves him.'

Natalie was growing more bewildered with every second. 'You're talking as if someone was in love with him when we were in Belgrade! They weren't. Not seriously. Vitza may well have had a crush on him but . . .'

'You're wrong,' Katerina said, pain flooding her eyes. 'Someone was in love with him when he was in Belgrade. And still is.'

'I don't understand,' Natalie said again, but this time with great uncertainty. 'How could you possibly know? Who could it possibly . . .' Her voice died away into stunned silence as she read the answer to her unfinished question in Katerina's eyes.

Behind Katerina the door opened and Julian entered, holding Stephen's hand.

'It's time to go, my love. The taxi has been waiting for over fifteen minutes.'

'Don't want to go!' Stephen said, a dangerous tremble in his voice. 'Want to stay with Grandmama and Auntie Trina. Want to stay with Peter.'

As Julian crossed the room towards her and, with his free hand, took hold of her arm, Natalie's eyes continued to hold Katerina's. Now, at last, she knew the reason for Katerina's harshness towards her. She knew also that Katerina would never have made such a confession to her if she had not intended the parting now taking place to be far more permanent than their previous parting in Belgrade station. There were going to be no more late night gossips over mugs of hot cocoa; no more long, companionable walks together.

The prospect of a future barren of Katerina's love and friendship filled her with a grief as great, if not greater, than the prospect of forever being barred from Serbia.

'Trina?' she said tremulously, desperate to put every-thing right between them before they finally parted. 'Trina?'

For a brief second Natalie saw suffering equal to her own in Katerina's eyes and then, for the second time in twenty-four hours, Katerina turned her back on her and walked away.

A miasma of despair suffused her as she left the hotel on Julian's arm. In a matter of hours she had lost all hope of a return home and she had lost Katerina. She remembered the dizzying elation with which she had arrived at the Negresco and the contrast smote her heart. Her only consolation now was Nicky.

As she entered the taxi that was to take them to the railway station a small gleam of hope lightened her darkness. Nicky wouldn't allow her to remain an exile for ever. He had powerful friends in the Yugoslav Com-mittee, friends about to play a large part in the formation of Sandro's new government. They wouldn't be content to see her an exile and Nicky a voluntary exile. Represen-tation would be made to Sandro on her behalf and when Sandro learned of her grief he would immediately give permission for her to return.

The small gleam of hope grew a little stronger. The more she thought about it, the more sure she was that the decision forbidding her to return home had not been taken by Sandro himself but by his prime minister, the elderly Nikola Pasich.

The bouncy optimism that was so integral a part of her personality began to reassert itself. Sandro had no doubt complied with his prime minister's request she be made *persona non grata* because he had been under the im-pression that she was happy and settled in Britain, just as Hélène was happy in Switzerland, and that exile would cause her no great grief. Once he knew differently, he would immediately give her permission to return.

The belief gave her the strength, when it came to saying goodbye to her mother on the station platform, to do so with commendable dignity. She could now, again, see a way ahead. She would soon be home in Belgrade and when she was, she would be able to talk to Katerina at length and make her understand about Nicky.

As their train began to ease its way out of the station and Julian took Stephen on his knee and dried his tears, promising him that he would see his grandmama and aunt and cousin again very soon, she looked across at him and wondered if he knew that Katerina was in love with him.

She remembered the unselfconscious and affectionate way he had greeted Katerina when they had arrived at the Negresco and knew that he did not.

The more she thought about Katerina's unspoken confession, the more incredible it seemed. *When* had Katerina fallen in love with Julian? And why hadn't Katerina told her she had done so? It was all very well Katerina saying that she, Natalie, had caused catastrophic problems by not confiding in her about her friends at the *Golden Sturgeon*, but what about the problems Katerina had caused by not sharing confidences? If Katerina had told her that she was in love with Julian she, Natalie, would never in a million years have considered marrying him.

But Katerina had not told her. They had both kept their secrets to themselves and the consequences had been monumental. As the train steamed northwards she resolved that once she had told Nicky and Julian about the baby she would never again live with any secret. The stress and strain were too great. In the future her life was going to be an open book, trouble-free and blissfully uncomplicated.

Fired with new resolve, confident that her present exile

from home was merely temporary, she looked down at her watch, counting the hours till she would be with Nicky again.

'. . . and so we leave for Belgrade at the end of the week!' Nicky said euphorically, pouring generous amounts of *slivovitz* into two glasses designed for water.

They were in his rented room in Camden and a large canvas bag was on the bed, already half-packed.

Natalie sat down beside it. Her news was going to devastate Nicky. All through the war years he had yearned to return home, just as she had yearned to return. As she looked across at him he swallowed his *slivovitz* in one gulp in a manner so typically Balkan that a lump came into her throat. She left her own glass untouched and said, 'I have something to tell you. Something important.'

His wide, dazzling smile vanished. 'About your husband? You're not going to leave him? Is that why you were away so long together in Nice?'

She shook her head, comforted by his fierce, jealous response.

'No. It's something political . . .'

She now had his absolute, undivided attention. He stood in the centre of the room, facing her, a frown on his high-cheekboned, olive-skinned face, his tangled black curls tumbling low over his brow. Not for the first time she thought he looked far more gypsy than he did Croat.

'About the Prince-Regent?' he asked sharply. 'You know of intentions he hasn't yet made public? Intentions about the internal organization of the new state?'

She shook her head, marvelling at his naïve belief that if Sandro had intentions for the new kingdom not yet made public, he would somehow have shared them with her. It was the same naïvety Gavrilo and Trifko and Nedjelko had displayed when she had met with them at the *Golden*

Sturgeon. They, too, had assumed she was in Sandro's confidence where political matters where concerned and they, too, had assumed wrongly.

She clasped her hands tightly together on her lap and said, 'It is to do with one of Alexander's decisions, but not about the new state.'

'Then what is it about?' His frown deepened. 'Did he write to you at Nice? Did he give you a message via your sister or your mother?'

'He gave me a message via my sister.' Her mouth had gone suddenly dry. 'I'm sure it's one we needn't worry about long-term. I'm sure that once the situation has been explained to Alexander he will . . .'

'What situation?' He had gone very tense and still.

She took a deep, unsteady breath. 'Because I was seen with Gavrilo in Sarajevo the day before the Archduke's assassination and because the Habsburg government requested my extradition . . .'

Nicky sucked in his breath, his eyes widening.

'. . . and because Alexander fears all this may come to light and implicate the House of Karageorgevich in the assassination plot he has forbidden me to return to Serbia.'

'Jesus God!'

Natalie ignored his stunned interruption saying quickly, 'That was the message Katerina gave me, but I don't believe it. It wouldn't have been Alexander's idea to make me *persona non grata*, it would have been his prime minister's. Alexander probably thinks I'm happy in Britain, just as his sister is happy in Switzerland, and so he agreed to it but once he learns how desperate I am to return home he will change his mind . . .'

'He's not going to change his mind before the end of the week!'

Natalie, painfully aware of the half-packed travelling

bag, said, 'Instead of going to Belgrade we could go to Zagreb and wait there until . . .'

'Zagreb?'

She nodded. 'I know Belgrade is where everything is happening at the moment but Zagreb is your real home and we can stay there until either my father or your friends in the new government explain to Alexander . . .'

'How can you go to Zagreb?' he said, interrupting her. 'Croatia and Serbia are now united. If you have been exiled from Serbia you have also been exiled from Croatia. You can no more go to Zagreb than you can return to Belgrade.'

She stared at him, her eyes widening, realization as to the full extent of her exile dawning at last. 'No . . .' she whispered protestingly. 'It can't mean that . . . it can't . . .'

Nicky hooked his thumbs down the leather belt slung attractively low on his hips and said, 'It does. It's only common sense. Have you told your sister to speak to Alexander when she returns home?'

She shook her head, still trying to come to terms with the new blow that had been dealt her. 'No. I didn't realize it would have been Pasich's decision, not Alexander's, until after I had left Nice.'

Nicky shrugged his shoulders, unhooked his thumbs from his belt and picked up a pile of clothing. 'Then the sooner you get in touch with her, the better,' he said, walking towards the bed and stuffing the clothes haphazardly into the travelling bag.

Dazedly she watched him, realizing that he still hadn't understood. 'You haven't understood,' she said bleakly as he re-crossed the room and began removing the last contents from a chest of drawers. 'If we can't go anywhere in the new kingdom we may as well stay in London until Alexander gives his permission for me to return to Belgrade.'

Nicky approached the bed again and crammed the clothes he was carrying into the now near-full bag. 'You're the one who is *persona non grata*,' he said reasonably. 'I'm not. And I'm not staying in this bloody country one day longer than necessary.'

'But it might be weeks before Alexander grants me permission to return! Prime Minister Pasich might be obdurate about it! There might be all kinds of complications!'

'Exactly. Which is why I can't possibly stay in London waiting for you to hear from him.'

He began to zip up the bag and with her heart beating lightly and rapidly somewhere up in her throat she said again, 'You don't understand, Nicky. I can't remain behind on my own in London because . . . because . . .'

'Because what?' He was grinning down at her as if nothing at all was amiss and she knew from the expression in his eyes that his thoughts had turned to lovemaking.

'Because I'm having a baby,' she said succinctly.

His grin faded. 'That is not a very funny joke.'

'It isn't a joke.'

As he continued to stare down at her, beginning to frown, she felt a surge of exasperation. Nothing was going the way she had anticipated. She had expected him to be far more stunned by her news that she couldn't return, as yet, to Belgrade. She certainly hadn't expected him to continue with his own travel plans nor had she anticipated telling him about the baby in such a stark, unromantic manner. She had envisaged them being in a loving embrace and Nicky being thrilled and delighted by the news.

His frown deepened. 'You're pregnant?'

She nodded. 'And so you see, I can't remain in London on my own. As soon as I receive permission to enter the country we can travel out there together and the baby will be born in Belgrade and . . .'

He was still frowning. 'Have you told your husband yet?'

'No. I'm going to tell him this evening when I go home.' She looked around the small, shabby room and said, 'We'll have to find somewhere else to live until we leave for Belgrade.'

'How do you know it's mine?'

The question was so unexpected, so dispassionate, that for a moment she thought she couldn't possibly have heard aright.

'How do you know it's mine?' he said again, making no move to take her in his arms. 'You've just come back after a family reunion with your husband. If you are pregnant, the baby is most likely his.'

'It is not!' Anger bubbled up in her throat. 'How dare you even suggest such a thing! I was pregnant before I went to Nice! I was pregnant even before Julian came home from Salonika!'

'That still doesn't mean to say the baby is mine.'

She hit him across the face with as much force as she could muster. Without a second's hesitation he hit her back, the force of his open-handed slap sending her half-falling against the bed.

'Bastard!' she hissed, regaining her balance, tears of pain glittering on her eyelashes.

He shrugged indifferently. 'If you're pregnant, it isn't mine,' he said again. 'Even if it were, it wouldn't make political sense for me to acknowledge it.'

'Political sense?' she stared at him as if he had taken leave of his reason. '*Political sense?* We're talking about a baby! *Our* baby! What do politics have to do with it?'

His thumbs were back in his belt as he said, 'There's going to be a God-Almighty battle when it comes to organizing the future state. Pasich and your precious cousin seem to think the Kingdom of the Serbs, Croats and Slovenes is simply another name for a Greater Serbia and it isn't. Now that the western powers have agreed to a federated South Slav state, there's nothing to prevent that state being a republic, not a monarchy.'

'What are you talking about?' She forgot all about the baby; all about his intention to return to Belgrade without her. 'It's in the new constitution that the new state is a monarchy! That's its *name*! The *Kingdom* of Serbs, Croats and Slovenes!'

'That's its name for the moment,' Nicky agreed dryly, 'because without an established monarchy fronting it, a united federated South Slav state might never have been born at all. Now it has, there's room for manoeuvre and the Croat Nationalist Party intends doing quite a lot of manoeuvring to ensure Croatia's interests don't come way behind Serbian interests.'

'The Croat Nationalist Party?' Natalie had never heard of it. 'Are you telling me that this Croat Nationalist Party will be working *against* Alexander?'

'Only if Alexander opposes our request for radical land reform. And I think he will. In those circumstances you can see how embarrassing it would be for me if it was rumoured I was linked to the Karageorgevichs, however distantly.'

Natalie's furious flare of anger began to ebb. The emotion she felt now was far worse than anger. She had been utterly deceived. Totally duped.

From the moment she had met Nicky she had been convinced she had found her soul-mate; convinced that they were both passionately ambitious for the same ends and that they were in perfect mental, as well as physical, harmony. Now she was face-to-face with the knowledge that it had never been so. Nicky's loyalties had never been in harmony with hers and no doubt no other members of the Yugoslav Committee and supporters had been either.

Just as when, friends with Gavrilo and Trifko and Nedjelko, she had never understood their true, terrorist intentions, so she had been blind to the fact that Nicky's loyalties were contrary to her own.

She stood facing him, the side of her face still burning from his slap, seeing him as she had never seen him before. He wasn't her twin soul. He wasn't even her friend. A friend would have expressed deep sympathy over the ban forbidding her entry to her homeland and would have vowed to do everything possible to have it rescinded. Nicky had done neither. Quite simply, he hadn't cared. She looked around the room, knowing she was doing so for the last time. It was exceedingly shabby. As shabby as their affair had been. Now, at last, she understood the contempt Katerina felt for her. It was contempt fully deserved.

She didn't say goodbye. Feeling as if she would choke unless she were able to breath in clean, fresh air, she turned on her heel and ran down the stairs and into the street. He didn't call after her and if he had, she would have taken no notice. Their affair was over. Finished. And never, as long as she lived, would she be so foolish again.

'It's over. Finished,' she said to Julian two hours later in their bedroom.

During her long, impassioned explanation of her affair with Nicky, Julian had not interrupted her once. When she had entered the room he had been about to go to the nursery to read a bedtime story to Stephen and Hans Andersen's *Fairy Stories* was still in his hand.

'I'll never be so foolish again,' she said sincerely as Bella settled herself comfortably at her feet, 'never.'

Still he didn't move; still he didn't speak.

'I'm sorry,' she said again. 'Truly I am. And I'm sorry about the baby. I know it will make things difficult . . .'

At last he found his voice. 'Sweet Christ!' he said, and his voice was the voice of a stranger. 'You've been having an affair for over three years and you're *sorry*!'

'Yes. I wish it had never happened. I wish I had never met him. I wish . . .'

'And you think the baby will make things *difficult*?'

As his eyes held hers she was filled with sudden uncertainty. Just as her disclosure to Nicky about the baby had not gone the way she had anticipated, so this conversation was not going the way she had anticipated either.

'We can't live together any longer,' he said harshly. 'You realize that, don't you?'

He could see by the expression on her face that she had realized no such thing.

'It would be easier, all things considered, if I moved into a *pied à terre*,' he continued, the skin tight across his cheekbones, his lips bloodless, 'that way it will be far less disruptive for Stephen . . .'

'I can't live here with your parents on my own! Not with them knowing you'd left me!' She felt faint at the very thought. 'Your mother *loathes* me! She thinks I'm not remotely good enough for you . . .'

Her voice tailed away.

He didn't trouble to state the obvious: that his mother had been absolutely right. He said instead, 'The scandal of a formal separation or a divorce would cause my mother even further distress and so, for her sake, I'm not going to instigate any such proceedings. I shall spend as much time with Stephen as possible and I shall accept the first posting abroad that I am offered. I shall then expect Stephen, in the care of his nanny, to visit me two or three times a year.'

His voice was cold and impersonal, the change in him as deep and catastrophic as the change that had taken place in Katerina.

She said unsteadily, 'I don't want us to live apart. I want us to be friends again . . .'

'Friends!' A spasm crossed his ravaged, grief-stricken face. 'I'm your husband, for Christ's sake! I knew you weren't in love with me when you married me, but our relationship since has been so . . . so . . .' He couldn't speak of their lovemaking, the pain was too great. When he could continue he said, 'I couldn't see how we could have been so happy, so compatible, unless you had fallen in love with me.'

Passion had again entered his voice and with a physical effort that was obvious he checked himself, exercising a control that totally unnerved her, saying in a hard, scarcely recognizable voice, 'Eventually, of course, you will have to move out of Cambridge Gate and I will find somewhere suitable for you. Eventually, too, when Stephen is older and at preparatory school, I shall expect him to spend his school vacations with me.'

Natalie felt beads of sweat break out on her forehead. Of all the nightmares she had endured; the news of her permanent banishment from Serbia; the loss of Katerina's love and friendship; the knowledge that her affair with Nicky was at an end, the one she was now enduring was the worst.

With Julian by her side she could have survived any of the previous hells she had been plunged into. Without him, nothing would be bearable. For the first time and far, far too late, she realized how truly necessary he was to her. From out of nowhere came the line in the Bible about Esau selling his birthright for a mess of potage. That was what she had done. She had forfeited the most precious thing she possessed or ever would possess, Julian's respect and love, for the dross of a cheap, shabby, sexual adventure.

Suddenly, as they continued to face each other, it was as

if scales literally fell from her eyes. He was the handsomest man she had ever seen, far handsomer than Nicky with his over-obvious, Byronic, gypsy attractiveness. He was also the kindest and most generous-hearted man she had ever met. Even now, when she least deserved it, he was being generous towards her in not insisting on a divorce.

Self-knowledge descended on her like a physical burden, making her gasp beneath its weight. She had always thought of him as her best and dearest friend and now she realized that he was much, much more. He was the man she loved. The man she had loved for years.

The ground seemed to shift beneath her feet as her world tilted on its axis and rearranged itself. How could she have been so criminally blind? So monumentally stupid? She remembered the passionate, unrestrained response he had aroused in her when they had consummated their marriage; the desperate eagerness with which she had greeted him at the station when he had returned from officer training; the agony she had suffered when she hadn't known if it had been him, or Edward, who had been massacred in Flanders. Of course she loved him. He was handsome and kind and honourable and no woman in her right senses could be anything else but in love with him. He made her laugh, he brought her joy in bed, and until now he had never failed to comfort her whatever her distress. And in return she had betrayed his trust in the most crucifying and terrible way possible.

With all her heart she wanted to put into words the love she felt for him and she knew, if she did so, he would not believe her. She had left it far too late and a protestation of love now would merely seem a tawdry attempt to avoid the future he had so starkly set out for her.

As she struggled to think of how she could narrow the chasm dividing them he said tightly, 'I don't think there is anything more we can possibly say to each other, is there?'

and without waiting for a reply, his eyes bloodshot with pain, he turned on his heel, walking away from her just as Katerina had walked away from her in Nice.

As the door closed behind him she sat down slowly on the edge of the bed. He had gone and she knew that he was never going to share the room with her ever again. Bella whimpered at her feet and Natalie picked her up, hugging her close.

Early evening merged into night and still she remained sitting on the bed, lost in a private hell of her own making, impaled by the past, paralysed by the present, unable to conceive of the future.

Three days later the downstairs maid approached her as she returned from taking Stephen for his morning walk.

'Mr Fielding is in the drawing-room and would like you to join him, Madam,' she said dutifully.

Asking her to take Stephen back to his nursery and nanny, Natalie apprehensively entered the drawing-room. To her vast relief it was empty save for Julian.

He had had his back towards her and had been looking out of the window towards the park when she had entered the room. Now, his shoulders tense, a pulse throbbing at his jawline, he turned to face her.

She wanted to ask him where he had been for the last three nights and what explanation he had given to his parents for his absence but was too nervous as to what it was he wished to say to her, to speak first.

He said tautly, 'I've been given a posting and will be leaving Britain at the end of the week.'

Shock stabbed through her. She hadn't doubted for a minute that he had been serious when he had said he was going to accept the first posting offered him but she had not expected it to be so soon. Now, as their eyes held, all her fierce hopes that somehow they would be reconciled before he left the country, and that consequently he might not leave at all, perished.

'Where are you going?' she asked, remembering how passionately determined she had been that she would never accompany him anywhere but Belgrade and ironically aware that if he were to ask her to accompany him now she would do so with a singing heart, even if the posting were to Timbuktu or deepest China.

He paused awkwardly for a moment, his hair burnished the colour of ripe wheat by the spring sunlight streaming through the window behind him and then, very reluctantly, he said simply, 'Belgrade.'

Chapter Nineteen

When Katerina walked out of Natalie's bedroom at the Negresco she did so feeling more bereft than she had ever done before in her life. Ever since she could remember Natalie had been not only her sister but her best friend, and now that friendship was at an end.

When she reached her own room she closed the door behind her and sat down on the edge of the bed. Not only was it at an end but she was the one who had ended it. Tears blinded her eyes. She had had no option. Natalie's betrayal of Julian's love and care for her was too gross an act for forgiveness. Even worse had been Natalie's complete blindness as to the enormity of her selfishness and stupidity.

She thought back to Natalie's happy belief that Gavrilo and his friends could plot and plan the downfall of the Habsburg empire without occasioning anyone any physical harm. Her blindness then had been stunning and even after all the catastrophic events which had followed in the wake of her friendship with Gavrilo, it was still stunning.

As she sat thinking back over their childhood she wondered if perhaps she and her parents were partly to blame for Natalie's inability to see events in any way other than the way she wanted them to be. Perhaps they should have been harsher with her whenever her dauntless optimism had led her far from the path of grim reality. She remembered Natalie's sparkling vivacity and knew that they couldn't have done so, that any attempt to crush her sunny buoyancy would have seemed unnecessarily cruel.

All through the long journey back to Belgrade the grief of her severed relationship with Natalie stayed with her. Her mother, unaware of its cause and assuming it to be the same grief she herself felt at the prospect of Natalie's long exile, did not distress her more by speaking about it.

Katerina was grateful. Not only was the journey long but, as their train entered Serbia, it was almost unbearably painful. Fields were devastated and denuded of crops, bridges were burned, towns had been reduced to shell-shattered ruins. As she looked out of the carriage window Katerina felt sick at heart. It was going to take years, perhaps even a decade, before her war-ravaged country was the country it had been before the war.

As they entered Belgrade it was hard to recognize it. Nearly every public building had been either destroyed or badly damaged.

'But it will all be rebuilt,' Zita said, reading her thoughts. 'And when it is, Belgrade will be as splendid as Geneva or Paris.'

Katerina was sure it would be but as the train began to slow down she had other thoughts on her mind.

'Will Papa be at the station to meet us?' she asked urgently, buttoning Peter's coat and smoothing his hair. 'Will he have received your telegram telling him when we left Nice?'

'Goodness knows,' Zita said, struggling to lower the carriage-window. 'I suspect the telegraph services are as war-ravaged as everything else and I rather doubt if my telegram will have travelled any further east than Geneva. However, if Papa has received it he will certainly be waiting for us.'

The window finally slid down and she leaned out, holding her hat on with a lilac-gloved hand.

'Is he there, Mama?' Katerina asked, squeezing next to her, holding her own hat on with both hands. 'Can you see him?'

'No . . . not yet . . .' The train began to slide into the station and suddenly she cried, '*Yes!* He's there, Katerina! He's there!'

For both of them it was a moment of sheer, unadulterated joy. The instant the train stopped they tumbled from the carriage, wings on their heels as they ran with an elated Peter down the crowded platform to where he was waiting for them.

They had all already been reunited once, in Corfu, but this reunion was no less special for now they were together again on Serbian soil.

'How is Natalie?' was the first question he asked of them when they had hugged and kissed and hugged again.

'She's very well,' Zita said, a tell-tale underlying tremor in her voice, 'but Julian hadn't told her of her exile. He hadn't wanted anything to spoil our reunion in Nice and had been going to tell her when they returned to London . . .'

'But she knows now?' Alexis interrupted anxiously, 'Julian has told her now?'

'It was Katerina who first told her.' Zita's gloved hands were still tightly clasped in his. 'Julian tried to cheer her by telling her that no matter where they might find themselves living, he would see to it that we all meet up as a family every year.'

'But not in Belgrade,' Alexis said heavily.

Her fingers tightened on his. 'No, my darling,' she said gently, 'not in Belgrade.'

As she watched her parents drawing comfort at the prospect of family reunions she knew would never take place, Katerina could hardly bear it. The war had taken its toll on both of them. The long arduous winter crossing of the mountains had prematurely aged her mother and her father's once upright figure was stooped with rheumatism after his years of living in water-logged trenches. They had suffered enough and they didn't deserve to suffer any further.

With a hurting heart Katerina wondered when Natalie would break the news to them that she was leaving Julian and that she would soon be giving birth to another man's child. An emotion she had never thought possible engulfed her. She was glad that Sandro had permanently exiled Natalie for if he hadn't done so, and if Natalie had returned to Belgrade with her lover, their parents' shame would have been so deep Katerina doubted if either of them would have survived it.

Her father put an end to her sombre reverie by throwing an arm lovingly around her shoulders and saying, 'Let's go home. The house is war-damaged and looted and, when I first returned, was filthy. Fortunately Laza came back a few weeks ago and immediately organized a massive clean-up operation.'

As they began to walk out of the station he said with a slight, disbelieving shake of his head, 'He lost an arm fighting the Bulgarians and was worried that I wouldn't re-employ him. Can you imagine that? I told him that he would have a home and employment with us for as long as he wanted and that I hoped that would be for the rest of his life.'

'And Cissie?' Katerina asked as she helped Peter step into a landau shabby from lack of use, the Vassilovich coat of arms barely discernible on its door. 'Is Cissie here as well?'

He nodded. 'She arrived five days ago after sailing from Corfu to Athens and then travelling through Greece and Montenegro. Why she chose to undertake such a journey when she could have travelled with you and Mama to Nice and then continued on to England with Natalie and Julian, I can't imagine.'

'Her parents are dead and she only has very distant relatives in England,' Katerina said as their coachman cracked his whip and the landau began to roll and bump over the cobbles. 'She thinks of Belgrade as her home and all the suffering she endured there during the occupation has bonded her even more closely to it.'

'Helga thought of Belgrade as her home, too,' Zita said quietly.

Alexis put his hand comfortingly over hers. 'The first thing I did on my return was to have Helga's body removed from the city cemetery and re-interred in the family mausoleum.'

She squeezed his hand gratefully. There had been times when she had wondered if bad memories would make her return home unendurable. Now, looking around at her ruined, shell-bombarded city, she knew that despite everything that had happened it was still the only place in the world she wanted to be.

Katerina, too, was profoundly grateful to be home. The Austrians, Hungarians, Germans and Bulgars might have destroyed ninety-five per cent of the public buildings but they had been powerless to destroy its magnificent setting. The Sava and Danube still curled magnificently around it, the Kalemegdan heights and ancient citadel still over-looked it. She held Peter's hand tightly, pointing out to him all the landmarks, wanting him always to remember the moment when he, too, returned home.

'Rumour has it that King Peter is not going to return to Belgrade, at least not in the foreseeable future,' Cissie said to her next day as together they began to white-wash the room that had once been Cissie's bedroom and that the Austrians had used as a storage room for munitions.

'But I thought he was here already!' Katerina exclaimed, putting down her brush and resting her aching arm. 'Where is he, if he isn't here?'

A strand of Cissie's mousy-brown hair had escaped from her protective dust-cap and she tucked it away before it got splashed with white-wash. 'He's in Greece and it's common gossip on the streets that he's going to remain there indefinitely.'

Katerina was stunned. It had never occurred to her that the king wasn't back in the city and in residence at the *Konak*.

'But why?' she asked, picking up her brush again, smudges of white-wash on her forehead and cheeks.

Cissie shrugged. 'Who knows? You might as well ask why Princess Hélène has chosen to remain in Switzerland.'

'There's no point. No-one knows,' Katerina said practically, beginning to once again apply white-wash to the walls. 'Prince Paul isn't in Greece as well, is he?'

Cissie shook her head. 'No, I've seen him in the city two or three times.' She paused for a moment, and then said, 'Max Karageorgevich entered the city with the Prince Regent, but there's gossip that he's no longer here.'

Katerina's brushstroke faltered slightly and then she said with apparent disinterest, 'He has a Greek wife now and has perhaps returned to Greece.'

'Perhaps,' Cissie said non-committally, wondering why Katerina always reacted so oddly whenever Max Karageorgevich's name was mentioned.

That evening after dinner Katerina said to her father, 'Papa, why hasn't Uncle Peter returned home? Cissie says there are rumours on the streets that he doesn't intend doing so.'

'I don't think he does,' her father replied equably, 'at least not for some time.'

'But why?' Katerina persisted. 'I thought there would have a been a glorious state entry and all sorts of celebrations.'

'Have you looked at the people in the streets?' Alexis asked gently. 'Have you seen the throngs of young men crippled and maimed? The number of women in mourning for sons and husbands and fathers? The war may be over but lavish celebrations are out of place. As for why Peter hasn't returned, I think the reason is that he doesn't feel like a king any more, nor does he want to be one. He handed all the responsibilities of kingship to Alexander long ago. He's an old man who has been made even older by his valiant participation in the fighting. What he needs now is rest and peace and he certainly won't find either in Belgrade at the moment.'

Katerina's eyes darkened slightly. She had known from the long hours her father was spending at the *Konak* that the proposed new constitution was already causing Sandro immense problems.

'Is that because there is still disagreement over the new borders?' she asked perceptively.

'No, the border issues are more or less resolved. The biggest problem facing the new parliament is the union with Croatia.'

They were alone in the drawing-room and he crossed to a sideboard and poured himself a glass of *slivovitz*. 'Croatia was left with three choices when the Habsburg empire disintegrated,' he said frankly. 'Absorption by Italy, union with ourselves, Slovenia, Bosnia-Herzegovina and Montenegro, or the prospect of going it alone as a new state, a republic on the lines of the new Czech republic.'

He walked back to the fireplace, placed his glass on the mantel shelf and stared down into the coal fire. 'Very few Croatians relished the idea of being absorbed by Italy and forced to become Italians. Not many, once free of the

Habsburgs and able to make a choice, relished the idea of being governed by ourselves. What the vast majority of Croats wanted was a new state, a Croat republic.'

'Then why didn't they hold out for one?' Katerina asked, mystified.

'Because they knew it would be pointless,' Alexis said dryly. 'They hadn't, through the war years, stated their case with the fervour with which the Czechs had done. I doubt if some western leaders even knew who the Croats were. Even if they did, the western powers were not in the mood to sanction another new state and Croatia knew it.'

'So they had no real choice?'

'None whatsoever. What is happening at the moment is that a commission, appointed by the Zagreb National Majority, is negotiating with Alexander and the Prime Minister in the hope that issues which cause them problems, such as Belgrade, and not Zagreb, being the seat of government, can be put to a free vote.'

'And will they be happy with the result of that vote, whatever it is?'

'I doubt it,' Alexis said heavily. 'They are Catholic. We are Orthodox. At heart they want a republic. We are monarchists through and through. It doesn't bode well for future harmony, does it?'

Katerina shook her head. She had never been passionate about Serbia becoming part of a united South Slav state and now she was even less so.

Alexis said gravely, affirming all her fears, 'The main problem is that the majority of our fellow countrymen, Prime Minister Pasich included, view Serbia as being the liberator of all those freed from Habsburg rule and the new kingdom as being not so much a united South Slav state as a Greater Serbia. Those with whom we have united, however, view it very differently. They see the new kingdom, quite rightly, as being a union of equals. What will happen when the gulf between these two viewpoints is exposed is anyone's guess.'

Katerina went to bed that night in a deeply reflective frame of mind. She knew very well that her father was speaking the truth when he said the new kingdom was being perceived very differently by vast numbers of its members. Natalie had most certainly perceived union with other South Slavs as being all to the greater glory of Serbia and no doubt still did so. The man with whom she had betrayed Julian was, however, a Croat.

As Katerina went quietly into Peter's room to make sure that he was still tucked snugly beneath his blankets and sleeping soundly she wondered what Nikita Kechko's perception of the new kingdom was. She also wondered if Natalie was going to be as unprepared for it as she had been when Gavrilo Princip had revealed his true colours to her and shot the Archduke and Duchess.

The next day, for the first time in nearly five years, she went with her mother to the *Konak*.

'Alexander wants to welcome us home,' Zita said as their landau rolled into the *Konak*'s courtyard. 'I doubt if he will be able to spare us much time, but it's a thoughtful gesture.'

It was obvious, almost immediately, that a major clean-up operation was in progress. As they entered the palace vestibule they did so against a tide of workmen, some of them ferrying away rubbish left by the Austrians, others painting and renovating.

Despite the mayhem there were some familiar and reassuring sights. The enormous brown bear reputedly shot by Karageorge himself still stood in a corner, stuffed and erect. Katerina smiled to herself, remembering how its uplifted claws had terrified Natalie and herself when they had been children.

The double-winged doors to the audience room stood wide open and Katerina could see her Great-Aunt Eudocia sitting stiffly on a silk-upholstered sofa and Vitza and Sandro standing nearby.

As soon as Sandro saw her mother and herself he excused himself from Vitza and strode towards them. He greeted her mother first and then herself and as she curtsied Katerina was instantly aware of the drastic change that had taken place in him. Whereas once he had exuded boyish good humour, now there was a reserve about him that was almost tangible.

'It's nice to see you back in Belgrade, Katerina,' he said, and though his voice was sincere there was no welcoming, familiar smile. 'I had thought you might have stayed in Nice longer. Early spring must be far pleasanter there than it is here.'

'I wanted to be home,' she said, feeling awkward with him for the first time in her life.

A shadow crossed his face and she wondered if she had inadvertently reminded him of Natalie. When he spoke she realized it had not been Natalie he had been thinking of, but the Russian grand-duchess he had hoped to marry.

'Those of us who are home are the lucky ones,' he said, pain in his clipped, curt tones. 'No Romanovs will be returning home to St Petersburg. Those who survived are scattered throughout Europe and even America. The Dowager Empress is in Britain, Prince Lvov is in France, Prince Youssoupov is in New York.'

Katerina said nothing. There was nothing she could possibly say. The last time they had met in the *Konak* it had been on the occasion of the announcement of his unofficial engagement to the Tsar's eldest daughter. In those far-off days that now seemed so idyllic, the

410

disintegration of the mighty Romanov dynasty had been as unthinkable as the disintegration of the Habsburg or Höhenzollern dynasties. Now no dynastic order existed in central Europe apart from their own. The Armageddon triggered off in Sarajevo had swept them all away. 'Hélène is in Switzerland,' he was saying. 'After the years she spent there as a child she thinks of it as home and is going to stay there.'

He didn't ask about Natalie and she was glad. It was going to be hard enough answering Vitza's queries about Natalie with white lies, without having to tell them to Sandro as well.

'When is Natalie returning home?' Vitza asked, blissfully ignorant that Natalie was forbidden to do so. 'Is she happy in London? Is her husband going to return to the British Legation in Belgrade?'

Katerina answered her questions as unprovocatively as possible, trying to turn the subject round to Vitza herself. It was the last thing Vitza wanted to talk about.

'What is there to say?' she asked bitterly. 'I'm twenty-six and unmarried. There isn't an eligible bachelor left from pre-war days. They're all either dead or maimed. My grandmother was certain that when the war ended everything would be as it was before. She imagined Sandro giving splendid balls in the *Konak* and all Belgrade's *haut monde* doing likewise. I tried to tell her she was living in a fool's paradise but it's taken today to make her realize I was right and she was wrong.'

Katerina looked across to her great-aunt. She was still sitting stiffly erect on a sofa, her jowls as heavy and her bosom as magnificent as ever.

'Five minutes with Sandro and she realized there were going to be no splendid balls,' Vitza continued caustically. 'He's thirty now and in my opinion he's turning into a crusty bachelor. Even if he weren't, you can't have balls when nearly every male member of the population is crippled in some way and unable to dance. You and Natalie were lucky. You married when there were still able-bodied men available.'

'I'm a widow, Vitza,' Katerina pointed out gently, 'and so are many others.'

Vitza had the grace to look ashamed. 'I know, and I'm sorry. I thought Major Zlarin very handsome. Alexander posthumously awarded him the Karageorge Black Star for gallantry, didn't he? You must be very proud.'

'Yes,' Katerina said, the familiar sensation of guilt settling on her shoulders. 'I am.'

'And you have Peter,' Vitza continued bleakly. 'I would have liked children.'

Katerina took hold of her hand and squeezed it comfortingly. 'There's no reason why you should give up hope of having children, Vitza. Every country in Europe is busy sending young diplomats to Belgrade. There may not be any lavish balls for them to attend but there will be afternoon parties and cocktail parties. You'll meet some-one soon and fall in love.'

'I wish I could fall in love as romantically and instantaneously as you and Natalie fell in love,' Vitza said wistfully, unconvinced. 'Do you remember the day at your home when we were having tea on the lawn and I first saw Major Zlarin? You must have been in love with him then, though I must say you never betrayed it by so much as a flicker of an eyelash. Was that why you refused to introduce him to me? Were you frightened I might steal him away from you?'

Looking into Vitza's sad, homely face, Katerina felt a great wave of pity and tenderness for her. 'Yes,' she lied, 'of course it was.'

A pleased flush touched Vitza's cheeks. 'That's nice.

I'm glad you told me. And you may be right about the diplomats. A new ambassador and his staff are due to arrive at the British Legation any day now. I've never really found Englishmen overly attractive but beggars can't be choosers, can they?'

At that very moment, in his study, Alexis Vassilovich was staring at one of the British Legation's new members of staff in stupefied disbelief. '*Belgrade?* You've been posted to *Belgrade?* But what about Natalie? Couldn't you have refused the posting? Couldn't you have explained that your wife is *persona non grata* in the new kingdom and that she couldn't accompany you?'

Julian shook his head. 'No,' he said heavily. 'Any other posting would have been just the same in that Natalie would not have accompanied me but would have remained behind in London.'

Alexis passed an unsteady hand across his eyes and sat down slowly behind his desk.

'I'm sorry, sir,' Julian said, wondering how little he could get away with telling him. 'We both know that my marriage to Natalie was a gamble. She wasn't in love with me and she was very young, still almost a child . . .'

'But I thought you were happy together! When Stephen was born both Zita and I thought . . .'

'I thought so too,' Julian interrupted tautly, 'but I was wrong. Though I was happy, Natalie was not. Consequently, despite the baby that will be born later this year, we have decided to live apart.'

'*Baby?* Natalie is having another baby and yet you've left her alone in London . . .' Behind his magnificently upturned moustaches, Alexis's face was even more disbelieving than it had been when Julian had walked into the room. 'Such a course of action is unforgivable! It's utterly dishonourable! It's . . .'

'It is what Natalie wants,' Julian said, his voice tauter than ever. It was a lie, but it was a lot more merciful than telling Alexis the truth and, in consequence, telling him the truth about the baby's paternity. 'And she isn't alone,' he added, trying to ease Alexis's anguish. 'She's living with my parents and sister.'

Alexis groaned and rested his head in his hands. The marriage between Julian and Natalie had been his idea and it had been taken for selfish purposes. For nearly five years he had been able to live with the guilt he felt because he had believed it was a marriage in which Natalie had learned to be happy. Now the knowledge that she had never done so weighed on his heart like a physical weight.

'I'm sorry, sir,' Julian said again, his own anguish glaringly obvious.

Slowly Alexis lowered his hands from his face and looked across at him. 'My suggestion that you marry Natalie has not only, apparently, made Natalie bitterly unhappy, it has quite obviously ruined your life as well. I owe you an apology, Julian. I hope you will accept it.'

'You have no need to apologize,' Julian said vehemently. 'You only suggested the marriage. I was the one who leapt at the suggestion and if I were faced with the same decision again I would, God help me, make the same decision.'

Alexis forced himself wearily to his feet and crossed the room to a glass-fronted drinks cabinet. 'Join me in a glass of *klekovacha*,' he said, reaching for a decanter of plum brandy distilled with juniper. 'Not for celebration this time, but for comfort.'

Alexis let out a heartfelt sigh of relief. The worst was over. His father-in-law now knew all he needed to know about his and Natalie's estrangement and would inform Zita and Katerina of it. Not for the first time he wondered if Natalie had confided in Katerina when they were in

Nice and if Katerina would know more about the circumstances leading up to their estrangement than he had told Alexis. If she did, he fervently hoped she would have the perception to keep her knowledge to herself.

'Zita and Katerina are at the *Konak*,' Alexis said, pouring the *klekovacha* into two crystal glasses. 'The Prince Regent is sparing precious time from his negotiations with the Zagreb National Majority to welcome formally all his female relatives back to the city.'

He handed a glass to Julian. 'It's a courteous action on his part,' he continued, glad of a non-controversial subject of mutual interest, 'but I think some of them are going to be disappointed by the change that has taken place in him.'

'In what way, sir?' Julian asked, as grateful as Alexis that personal matters had been temporarily set aside.

Alexis drained his glass in one swallow and said meditatively, 'The war has changed him, as it has changed all of us. He's become very monastic and spartan in his tastes and that won't suit the ladies.'

He sat down again stiffly, the changes the war had wrought in his health, obvious.

'Although he is having the *Konak* refurbished he isn't in residence there and doesn't intend taking up residence there,' he continued, disclosing a piece of information he hadn't yet had the courage to disclose to his wife and daughter. 'He's moved into a one-storey house within sight of the *Konak* and he's furnished it as if it were a military headquarters. Straightback chairs, solid tables, his old camp writing-table, a soldier's bed. His cousins and aunts are going to be appalled when they find out. After nearly five years of war and agonizing hardship they've been looking forward to the glitter of court life again and I'm afraid they're going to be denied it.'

Julian was just about to say that he thought the Prince Regent eminently sensible in organizing his life in a way that suited himself and not his relatives, when there came the distant sound of the front door being opened. Seconds later footsteps crossed the marbled hall and Zita's and Katerina's voices could be clearly heard.

Julian's and Alexis's eyes held in mutual horror.

'I had hoped you would be able to pre-warn them!' Julian said hoarsely.

The expression on Alexis's face told him Alexis had been hoping the very same thing.

'The problem was, I left England so suddenly it was pointless writing,' Julian continued, feeling some apology for what was now about to happen was called for. 'The letter would have arrived here no sooner than I did my-self . . .'

Zita's and Katerina's footsteps approached the study door, there was a token tap on one of the oak panels and then, without waiting for a reply, Zita opened the door and entered, Katerina close behind her.

At the sight of Julian she came to a halt so abruptly that Katerina stumbled into the back of her.

'Mama! What on earth . . .' she began, and then she, too, saw.

Alexis had risen to his feet as speedily as his rheumatism would allow.

'My dears! I'm afraid you've taken us completely by surprise . . .'

'Julian!' Zita was saying in stunned disbelief, disregarding her husband. 'Julian! What on earth are you doing in Belgrade?' She crossed the room towards him, pleasure at seeing him overcoming her shock. 'Are you *en route* for Athens?' she asked, kissing him warmly on the cheek. 'Is that to where you have been posted? Is Natalie waiting for you at the border?'

She had had to stand on tiptoe to give him her welcoming kiss and as she stepped away from him and he didn't flash her one of his heartwarming, down-slanting smiles, she realized at once that something was wrong.

'What is it?' she asked urgently, her own smile vanishing. 'Is it Natalie? Has there been an accident?'

Alexis walked heavily towards her and slid an arm around her shoulders. 'Natalie is perfectly safe,' he said, before Julian could answer her, 'and she is in London.'

'London?' Zita looked from her son-in-law to her husband uncomprehendingly. 'I don't understand . . .'

'Sit down, my dear,' Alexis said gently. 'Sit down and let me tell you what my selfishness has tragically led.'

Numbly she allowed him to lead her to a velvet-covered, button-back chair. In white-faced trepidation she waited for him to continue.

'Natalie married Julian for all our sakes,' he said, choosing his words carefully. 'We all know that. Julian was certainly aware that Natalie was not in love with him when they married but, like us, he believed that his love for her would be sufficient for their happiness and that Natalie would learn to love him.'

Knowing now what was to come Zita gave a low, anguished moan.

'Tragically we all assumed wrongly. Though there is to be another baby later this year, it is Natalie's wish that she and Julian live apart.' He rested a hand comfortingly on her shoulder. 'That being the case, when Julian was offered a posting in Belgrade there was no reason for him not to accept it.'

'Another baby?' Tears began to stream down Zita's exquisitely-boned face. 'How can she possibly have wanted an estrangement if she is to have another baby?' She looked up at Julian accusingly. 'Even if she wanted one, how could you have agreed to it? What if you're still here when the baby is born? What about Stephen? He's only just got used to having you home. How is Natalie going to explain to him that you've left him again, this time voluntarily?'

A spasm crossed Julian's haggard face and Katerina said in a choked voice, 'I think you need a drink of tea, Mama. I don't think we should discuss this any further until the shock has worn off and we can all think rationally.'

'Rationally? How can we be rational about Natalie living in exile without a husband by her side? How is it possible to be rational when I have a grandson who can never visit me and when I am to have another grandchild I shall seldom see?'

Never in her life had Katerina heard such bitterness in her mother's voice.

'If Julian had accepted a posting in Romania or Greece it would have been different,' Zita continued heart-brokenly. 'Natalie could have changed her mind about the estrangement and joined him. We could have visited them, perhaps been there when the baby is born . . .'

Her silent tears turned to sobs and she was unable to continue. Alexis said quietly. 'I think it would be best if you left us alone for a while.'

'Yes, sir. Of course,' Julian said wretchedly, a pulse beating furiously at the corner of his strong jaw line.

He turned and began to walk to where Katerina stood in the still open doorway. As their eyes met he saw with a rush of unspeakable relief that her eyes were not hostilely accusing, as Zita's had been. Instead there was a depth of understanding in them that almost rocked him on his heels.

As she turned with him and left the room and as the door closed behind them he said tautly, 'You know, don't you?'

She nodded, feeling so much love and compassion for him that she couldn't trust herself to speak.

'And about the baby as well?'

418

The corridor was deeply shadowed and she was grateful.

'Yes,' she said thickly, 'I know about the baby, too.'

He drew in a deep, shuddering breath. 'Thank God,' he said fervently. 'Thank God there's one person in the world to whom I don't have to lie!' And with a rush of the affection he had always felt for her, he took hold of her hand.

Chapter Twenty

Two days later, as they walked together in the spring sunshine in Kalemegdan Gardens, Peter scampering ahead of them bowling a hoop, Julian said, 'Perhaps it would be more politic if I told you of Natalie's confession to me, before I ask what she said to you.'

Katerina nodded. It was the first time they had met since the traumatic moment when her mother had collapsed in floods of tears, weeping not only for the present but for things long past.

'Yes,' she said quietly, grateful he had realized Natalie might have told her things he still did not know and that she might not want inadvertently to reveal to him. 'Perhaps that would be best.'

They walked another dozen yards in silence and then he said starkly, 'She told me she had been having an affair with a fellow Slav, a Croat, and that she was expecting his child.'

With great difficulty Katerina kept her eyes straight ahead, on Peter in his pastel-blue coat, on the wobbling hoop, on the distant view across the Sava.

'I take it you were told the same?' he asked, his pain so obvious that she winced.

'Yes.' She didn't trust herself to look across at him. 'She told me his name was Nikita Kechko, that he was shortly leaving Britain for Belgrade and that she was going to come with him.'

'And was that when you told her she couldn't do so? That she was *persona non grata*?'

Katerina nodded.

Julian dug his hands deeper in his overcoat pockets. 'When we returned to London and she told Kechko of her inability to return to Belgrade, he refused to alter his plans for her. For all I know he's here now and I'm just praying to God that I don't run into him, because if I do . . .'

The pulse at his jaw line began to beat again and inside his pockets his hands clenched into fists.

Katerina stood stock-still on the gravelled pathway, her eyes wide with shock. 'He's abandoned her?'

Now a few feet ahead of her Julian halted and turned to face her. 'Yes. He apparently disclaimed all paternity for the child into the bargain.'

Katerina's eyes widened even further. 'Then when you led Mama and Papa into thinking that the baby was yours, you weren't doing so because you felt it was Natalie's responsibility to tell them the truth about the baby's paternity? You did so because you don't intend them ever knowing the truth? Because you intend acknowledging it as your child?'

His gold-flecked eyes were darker than she had ever seen them. 'Yes,' he said, turning his velvet coat collar up against a light breeze that had begun to blow from the river. 'Unless I do so, Natalie will be publicly seen to be an adulteress. For Stephen's sake that's the last thing I want.'

Slowly Katerina began to walk again, her mind racing at all the implications of his decision. As he fell into step beside her she said, her soft smoky voice cracking slightly, 'That means that your parents will be deceived into thinking Kechko's child their grandchild! That the child will grow up believing you to be its father!'

'I'm well aware of all it will mean,' he said tautly. 'I only wish I believed Natalie was half as well aware.'

For a few more moments they walked together in

silence, both thinking of Natalie, both knowing she would never appreciate the terrible depths of the deceit that, for her sake, he was going to live with for the rest of his life.

For the next few months, as Belgrade became a hotbed of political and diplomatic activity, she saw little of him. When they did meet, however, they did so in deep, unconditional friendship.

Very few questions were asked as to why Natalie had not returned to Belgrade with her husband. An extended family was the basic social unit in Serbia and no-one thought it odd that Natalie should be living with her husband's family, especially as it was now known that she was having another child.

When Zita told Alexander that she was to be a grandmother again he responded with relief, believing it meant that Natalie was happy in her hurriedly arranged marriage and happy in London.

In early May, on one of the rare occasions when Katerina found herself able to talk to Alexander without half a dozen people listening to every word, she said as casually as possible, 'Do you know of anyone by the name of Nikita Kechko?'

Alexander frowned slightly. 'No. Should I?'

'He was a loyal supporter of the Yugoslav Committee and I believe he thought he would be given a position of some kind in the new parliament.'

'The name means nothing to me,' Alexander said again, 'but if it's someone you are anxious to trace the best person to speak to would be Prime Minister Pasich.'

Katerina didn't follow his advice. If the name meant nothing to Sandro then she doubted it would mean anything to his aged prime minister. Natalie had been wrong in thinking that Nikita Kechko was heading for a brilliant political future in Belgrade, just as she had been wrong about so many other things.

Her reaction had been one of vast relief. It meant there was little likelihood of Kechko and Julian meeting and it meant that her father, too, was unlikely to make his acquaintance.

At the end of the month Zita announced she was going to give a ball.

'It won't be as grand as the balls I used to give,' she said as she sat in the Italian room, drawing up an invitation list. 'It will, however, make a lot of people happy. Not least Eudocia and Vitza.'

Alexis grunted disparagingly and burrowed himself even deeper behind the *Serbian Literary Herald*.

Failing to elicit the response she desired from her husband she looked across to where Katerina was embroidering a waistcoat for Peter.

'I wonder if I will be able to persuade Sandro to make an appearance?' she asked meditatively. 'It would do him good to relax a little more.'

'I doubt if Sandro will attend anything frivolous while the Versailles talks are still being conducted,' Katerina said, regret in her voice.

Alexis lowered his newspaper. 'He's not in France all the time and he just might be persuaded to attend. If he does, can I ask both of you not to make the true reason for the ball embarrassingly obvious?'

'What true reason?' The waistcoat Katerina was embroidering was a traditional one and she snipped off rose-pink embroidery thread and began to re-thread her needle with moss-green thread, genuinely perplexed.

Zita kept her eyes judiciously on her invitation list.

'That Alexander is being given an excellent opportunity

to survey the prettiest girls and to turn his thoughts towards marriage?'

Katerina's eyes flew towards her mother. 'Is that true, Mama? Is that the real reason you are having a ball?'

Zita laid down her pen, saying with an air of great patience, 'Sandro is now thirty. If he doesn't marry soon he's going to turn into a confirmed bachelor. It's important for the dynasty, as well as for his own happiness, that he doesn't do so.'

'At thirty, a man has plenty of time in which to find himself a wife and obtain an heir,' Alexis said, mild amusement in his voice.

'For some men, maybe,' Zita said placatingly, 'but not, I think, for Sandro.'

Alexis's amusement vanished. 'I hope to God you're not insinuating . . .'

'Of course not!' There was loving ridicule in her voice. 'If I thought that I certainly wouldn't be encouraging him to marry! Sandro's problem is that he is serious-minded by nature and the problems he now faces as Prince Regent are making him even more so. He needs the comfort and companionship of a wife and finding a wife is quite obviously not one of his present priorities. The only people being received in that ghastly house in which he has chosen to live are politicians, generals and delegates.'

'And you would like to see a few women being received?'

'I would like to see some feminine interest in his life,' Zita retorted, unabashed. She picked up her pen again but before she returned her attention to her invitation list she looked across at Katerina, adding gently, 'And I would like to see some masculine interest in your life, Trina. You've been a widow long enough, my dear. It's time you made us all happy and provided Peter with a loving stepfather.'

★   ★   ★

424

The announcement of the Vassilovich ball sent a *frisson* of excited expectation through the city. Even for those with no hope of being on the guest list it was a welcome indication that life was returning to normal.

'What a pity it's still a month too early for roses,' Zita said to Katerina, casting a satisfied look around her refurbished ballroom. 'Another month and we could have filled the house with them.'

'The house looks wonderful,' Katerina said truthfully. 'I never thought I'd see the ballroom so beautiful again.'

'No,' Zita agreed quietly, remembering the mayhem when hundreds of terrified Belgraders had taken shelter there and then the later horror, when their home had been occupied and vandalized by the enemy. 'Neither did I.'

They fell silent, thinking of all the terrible events that had taken place since the last Vassilovich ball; the occupation of the city, the typhoid epidemic, the deaths of dear friends.

Alexis strode up behind them, resplendent in white tie and tails. 'Why the deep introspection?' he asked, putting his arms around their shoulders. 'The house looks wonderful. The ballroom is a vision of splendour. Alexander is to be guest of honour. What more could you both want?'

'Nothing,' Zita said with a wide smile, banishing the wave of melancholy that had swept over her. 'Prince Paul is coming too. Ever since Sandro returned to Belgrade Paul has been his constant companion and closest adviser. I'm not sure whether Prime Minister Pasich approves. I rather think he would like Sandro relying on him alone for political advice, but Sandro and Paul have always been as close as brothers and it is a situation with which Mr Pasich is going to have to learn to live.'

'Prince Paul's presence will undoubtedly set a few feminine hearts beating faster,' Alexis said, guiding them both gently out of the ballroom and towards the head of the grand staircase. 'And talking of hearts beating faster, I've just seen Cissie and could hardly believe my eyes. She's wearing a ball dress of scarlet chiffon and is looking very Mata Hari and not at all sensible and British.'

'Good,' Zita said, unperturbed. 'Cissie has been sensible for far too long. Perhaps tonight she will make a conquest.'

Vitza, too, was dressed to make a conquest. Her gown was of embossed indigo brocade, the neckline swoopingly low, the skirt as stiff and regal as a coronation gown.

Later, when everyone had been formally received, she said casually to Katerina, 'Is it true that King Peter and your father once discussed the possibility of a match between Sandro and Natalie?'

Katerina's eyebrows rose slightly. 'Yes,' she said, wondering where on earth the conversation was leading, 'a long time ago.'

Vitza's eyes gleamed. 'Then if Natalie was once considered as a possible bride, there's no reason why I shouldn't be considered as well.'

'Except that there has never been any special relationship between the two of you,' Katerina said cautiously. 'I also think it likely that Sandro will do as he did before when choosing a bride. I think he will choose the daughter of a ruling house. Princess Marie of Romania perhaps or . . .'

'Don't be ridiculous, Katerina. Princess Marie isn't even Slav! She's all Höhenzollern and Saxe-Coburg.'

'She's part Slav,' Katerina corrected gently. 'On her mother's side she's descended from Tsar Alexander II as well as Queen Victoria.'

'A smidgeon of Russian blood doesn't make her a Slav,' Vitza said obdurately.

Katerina sighed. She liked Vitza and didn't want her to be hideously disappointed, and disappointment was most certainly lying in wait for her if she continued to believe that Sandro might ask her to be his future queen.

The band began to play the 'The Blue Danube' and as her father took her mother in his arms and began to dance with her Katerina had the dizzying sensation of having been transported back in time. It was 1914 again and she could smell Natalie's light, flowery perfume; hear her infectious giggle. At any moment Julian would dance past, Princess Militza in his arms; Max would ask if he could mark her dance-card; Great-Aunt Eudocia would be heard, making disparaging remarks about the Tsarina.

'Prime Minister Pasich *certainly* won't want Sandro marrying a non-Slav,' Vitza continued, shattering the heart-aching illusion. 'I think perhaps I should engage him in conversation this evening. I think I shall say that . . .'

Katerina never did learn what Vitza intended saying to the prime minister. At that moment Cissie danced past in the arms of one of Alexander's equerries and Vitza's jaw dropped.

'Great heavens! Is that Natalie's ex-governess?'

'In the scarlet chiffon?' Katerina asked, keeping amusement out of her voice only with the greatest difficulty. 'Yes. She looks wonderful, doesn't she?'

'She looks nothing of the kind! She looks . . .' Vitza sought vainly for a suitable adjective. 'She looks *fast*! It's the kind of dress a Russian ballerina might wear! And why is she still in Belgrade? Even more to the point, why is a governess at such an occasion as a guest? I know your mother is eccentrically radical but . . .'

'Cissie is in Belgrade because she has chosen to make Belgrade her home,' Katerina said equably, 'and she's a governess no longer. She's Papa's secretary and Mama bought her the dress for her birthday.'

'Then I don't think Aunt Zita showed her usual impeccable taste when she did so,' Vitza said frostily, trying to keep the envy she felt from her voice. 'A gown like that can't help but draw attention. She must be feeling acutely uncomfortable.'

As the music changed from Strauss to Lehár and as Katerina danced with Sandro, she caught several glimpses of Cissie. With her mousy-brown hair brushed to a burnished bronze and swept into an elegant knot in the nape of her neck, she looked anything but uncomfortable. She looked serene and quietly composed and very, very feminine.

'Do you remember asking me if I knew of anyone by the name of Kechko?' Sandro asked her suddenly.

Katerina returned her attention to him. 'Yes. I wondered if he was a member of the new parliament or perhaps even a junior minister.'

'He's very far from being either,' Sandro said grimly. 'He's Dr Josip Frank's chief henchman.'

'I'm sorry, I don't know Dr Frank . . .'

Sandro waltzed her past the band. Out of the corner of her eye she could see Vitza dancing with a junior aide from the French Embassy.

'Josip Frank is leader of an extreme Croat nationalist party known as the Party of Croat Rights and is militantly anti-Serb. I'm curious as to how you know him. He's not the kind of man with which any Karageorgevich should have dealings.'

'I don't have dealings with him,' Katerina said, trying to keep the shock she felt out of her voice. 'Someone I met in Nice asked me if I knew him. They said he had been a supporter of the Yugoslav Committee and that he expected to have a position in the new government and so obviously I thought him loyal to yourself . . .'

Sandro made a disparaging sound and then said,

'Whoever your informant was, they didn't know their man very well. Kechko might very well have been a loyal supporter of the Committee and its aims of uniting all South Slavs into one state, but now those aims have been achieved he, and a handful of other extremists like him, want more. They want Croatian dominance within that state and they want a republic, not a monarchy.'

Katerina remembered Natalie's sunny conviction that her lover was as ardent a supporter of the monarchy as she was herself and felt a stab of pity for her. Did Natalie now know the truth? Had Kechko revealed his true political colours to her when he had revealed his true character, refusing to share her exile with her and disowning any responsibility for the child she was carrying? Since Nice, no letters had passed between them and she had no way of knowing.

As Sandro continued to waltz her around the room she reflected that even if Natalie did know Nikita Kechko's true political aims she would in all likelihood reason them away, as all her life she had always reasoned everything unpleasant away.

All the complex turbulent emotions Natalie aroused in her rose to the surface until she felt as if she were going to choke with them. How could Natalie have agreed to marry Julian, in the circumstances in which she did so, without giving him her unconditional loyalty? How could she possibly have imagined that her family would view her action in taking a lover as being reasonable and justifiable? When Katerina remembered how Natalie had intended accompanying Kechko to Belgrade, and the distress and shame her parents would have suffered if she had done so, the stab of pity she had felt earlier for her disappeared. Whatever anguish and disillusionment Natalie might now be suffering was anguish and disillusionment well deserved.

The dance came to an end and as Sandro returned her to

her father's side her heart leapt. Julian was standing next to him, resplendent in white tie and tails.

There had been times, over the last few days, when she had doubted if he would be in attendance at all. Her mother had been adamant that she was not going to invite him. In her eyes, despite the explanation he had given her, she saw him as having abandoned Natalie when Natalie most needed him. It had been her father who had tactfully pointed out that so far no-one in Belgrade thought it odd that Julian, a diplomat, should be in Belgrade while Natalie remained with her parents-in-law in London.

'Rumours about their relationship will only start to fly if we are seen to be behaving oddly towards him,' he had said reasonably. 'And having a grand ball with the world and his brother in attendance and our son-in-law conspicuously not in attendance, will most certainly be perceived as being odd.'

Katerina knew that her father felt deeply responsible not only for Natalie's unhappiness, but for Julian's unhappiness also. Their marriage had taken place at his suggestion and his motives had been selfish. For that reason, the relationship that now existed between himself and Julian was as close as the relationship between Julian and her mother was cool.

He said to her now, 'Julian has claimed your next dance, my dear. I'm promised to Vitza and must set about finding her.'

Behind them, in one of the giant mirrors lining the room, Katerina could see their reflections clearly. In the months since the war had ended her father had regained a lot of his old vigour and in evening dress, with his moustaches magnificently waxed and curled, he looked almost as fine a figure of a man as he had in 1914.

Over the last few weeks Julian, too, had recovered much of his old élan. Strain was still visible in the tiny lines at the corners of his well-shaped mouth but his inner unhappiness was no longer nakedly visible. In a room dominated by stockily-built Slavs his tall, broad-shouldered physique and Anglo-Saxon blondness set him noticeably apart. He looked very northern, very English. Even though his married marital status was common knowledge Katerina could see many interested feminine eyes looking covertly towards him. As her own eyes returned to his reflection the love she felt for him flooded through her so that she could hardly bear it.

Terrified that her emotions were showing on her face she met her own eyes in the mirror. Her fear was groundless. She looked cool and calm, her hair swept high in cloudy waves, her skin creamily pale against its mahogany darkness. At twenty-five she was no longer a young girl and she had not dressed as one. Her ballgown was of black tulle over moonlight-blue and it emphasized her natural elegance and sophistication. She looked a young woman who had never entertained a carnal thought in her life and at the disparity between her inward emotions and her outer demeanour an expression of wry disbelief touched her mouth.

'It's a long time since we danced together,' Julian was saying to her as he led her out on to the dance floor. 'It seems strange to think how little we realized then how near we were to war. I don't believe the possibility was even discussed that evening.'

'Our thoughts were on other things,' Katerina said, a shiver of pleasure running down her spine as he took her lightly in his arms and they began to dance to a melody by Schubert.

He was silent for a little while, remembering how his head and heart had been full of Natalie and his determination to make a proposal of marriage to her.

After a little while, as an elderly gentleman swept past

them, an impressive array of orders and decorations on his chest a stately Eudocia in his arms, he said wryly, 'I still can't regret everything. If I hadn't married Natalie, Stephen wouldn't have been born and it's impossible for me to imagine a world without Stephen.'

It was her turn to be silent for a little while. She knew the pain it must have cost him to leave his son, with whom he had only just become acquainted, two thousand miles away. She knew also that he hadn't had to do so. He could have engaged a nanny for Stephen and brought Stephen with him to Belgrade, but if he had done so it would have been quite obvious that his marriage was no longer viable and rumours as to the paternity of Natalie's coming child would have been rife.

She wondered what would happen when Nikita Kechko's child was born and if Julian would keep to his decision about publicly and privately accepting it as his own. She wondered, too, if she should tell Julian of Nikita Kechko's present whereabouts and loyalties or if the mention of Kechko would cause him too much unnecessary pain.

As if reading her thoughts he said suddenly, 'Don't you find it strange that Kechko hasn't surfaced here yet? It's just possible, of course, that he might have changed his mind. That he's not in Belgrade at all but in London and that he's going to accept paternity for the child . . .'

'No,' she said firmly, knowing that no matter what the consequences she couldn't possibly let him continue to hope for such an eventuality. 'Kechko isn't in London. He's in Zagreb.'

The orchestra was blazing into a new coda and as he whirled her past the orchestra dais conversation of the kind they were now conducting was impossible.

'Let's go outside,' he said tautly, waltzing her towards the nearest of the french windows. 'I want to know every single damn thing about Kechko. And I want to know

432

why, if you know his whereabouts, you haven't told me of them before.'

It was too early in the year for the night air to be warm and only a few couples were enjoying the relative privacy of the moonlit terrace. With his hand beneath her elbow he steered her across it and down the steps on to the gravelled path that skirted the lawns and led towards the rose-garden.

Not until the music from the ballroom was muted by distance and no-one else was within sight did he come to a halt. His face was grim as at last he turned to face her, saying again, 'If you know of Kechko's whereabouts, why haven't you told me of them?'

'I've been told of them only this evening and . . .' she hesitated and then said awkwardly, 'and I didn't know if you would want to know. I thought perhaps you might never want to hear Kechko's name again.'

A pulse began to beat at the corner of his jaw. 'I wish to God I didn't need to,' he said tersely, 'but for professional, as well as personal reasons, I do.'

In the chill late spring air Katerina shivered and he took off his tail-coat, slipping it around her shoulders. 'Well?' he said, his voice softening slightly. 'How long has Kechko been in Zagreb and what is he doing there?'

They were only inches apart. She could smell the familiar fragrance of his cologne and feel the warmth of his breath on her cheek. If she lifted her hand only slightly she would touch him.

Remaining perfectly still she said as steadily as she was able, 'I asked Prince Alexander some time ago if he knew the name Nikita Kechko and he said that he didn't. Tonight, however, he asked me why I had wanted to know.'

The slight frown furrowing his brows deepened. 'You didn't tell him?'

She shook her head. 'No. I said that someone I had met in Nice had been asking about him and that they were under the impression Kechko was destined to be a junior minister in the new parliament.'

Faintly the strains of Strauss's 'Emperor Waltz' lapped around them.

'And tonight?' Julian prompted. 'What did the Prince Regent say to you tonight?'

She pulled his tail-coat closer around her shoulders, knowing how bitterly he would receive the news that the man with whom Natalie had betrayed him was a man who wasn't even loyal to the Karageorgevich dynasty.

She said reluctantly, 'He said that Kechko was very far from being a member of his government. He described him as being Dr Josip Frank's chief henchman. Dr Frank is the leader of an extreme Croat nationalist party and is virulently anti-Serb.'

Julian, well aware of Dr Frank's political beliefs, gave a short, mirthless laugh. 'Natalie really surpassed herself this time, didn't she? She might just as well have allied herself with a Habsburg as with a crony of Josip Frank's.' The bitterness she had known he would feel was naked in his voice. 'I wonder if Kechko told her of his true political allegiance when he told her he was leaving London without her?'

It was a question Katerina had asked herself only half an hour earlier and which she had been unable to answer.

As she remained silent he shrugged his shoulders, dismissing Nikita Kechko temporarily from his thoughts, wanting to change the subject entirely and to say something to her that he had wanted to say for a long time. With brotherly affection he took her hands in his.

'I want to thank you for your friendship, Katerina,' he said with deep sincerity. 'Without it, these last few months would have been unbearable.'

434

She tried to make a suitable response and failed. Though they had danced together and often spoken together, there had never before been such intimate contact between them and it was almost more than she could bear.

A tremor ran through her and mistaking it for a shiver of cold he said wryly, 'It was a little warmer the last time we talked here. I remember intending to ask if you thought Natalie would accept my proposal of marriage and Max Karageorgevich joined us before I could do so.' He gave her a crooked smile. 'What would you have said to me if he hadn't done so? Would you have told me I would be rejected? That I shouldn't persist? If I hadn't your father would never in a million years have suggested I marry Natalie and take her to London. She would have gone to Geneva with your mother and would no doubt still be there.'

In the distant chandelier-lit ballroom the orchestra had played the last notes of the 'Emperor Waltz' and were taking a few moments rest. There was very little scent in the air for only a few early-flowering roses were in bloom. A few yards from them a gallant *Gloire de France* boasted pale pink blossoms and a little further away a *Princesse de Lamballe* gleamed milkily in the darkness.

She said quietly, 'I doubt if I would have said any of those things. I would have been too shocked.'

It was not what she had intended saying. She had intended saying something inconsequential; that it was impossible for her to know what she might, or might not have said, five and a half years ago or that Natalie might have settled happily in Geneva now that Hélène was also living there.

Their eyes held; his surprised, hers dazed with disbelief.

'Shocked?' It was not the answer he had expected and

his eyebrows quirked quizzically. 'Why? Because Natalie was only seventeen?'

It would have been easy to agree with him; easy to step back from the precipice her words had brought her to. She didn't do so. Inadvertently she had spoken to him from her heart and she knew, no matter what the cost, that she had no option but to continue.

As the orchestra began to play again and the muted, melodic notes of 'Roses From the South' drifted towards them she said with devastating simplicity, 'No. Not because of that. Because I had foolishly believed it was me you wanted to marry. That it was me to whom you were about to propose.'

He sucked in his breath as though she had dealt him a blow to his chest and she was swamped by instant, bitter regret. A moment ago he had been completely at ease in her company. Now he would never be so again.

'I'm sorry,' she said hoarsely, trying to disengage her hands from his. 'That was supremely foolish of me. I didn't mean to embarrass you . . .'

He held her hands fast. 'You haven't embarrassed me.' The implication in her words had been searingly clear and there was stunned incredulity in his voice. 'You haven't embarrassed me in the slightest, Katerina. It's just that I hadn't realized . . . It had never crossed my mind . . .'

'No,' she said with so much emotion she shocked even herself. 'I know that it hadn't.'

His eyes continued to hold hers, his mind racing back to the spring and early summer of 1914. He remembered how he had always looked forward to meeting her at a *Konak* tea party or garden party; the friendly ease of the chats in which they had always indulged; his realization that she, and not the kitten-faced witch he was in love with, was the true beauty of the Vassilovich family.

He remembered more recent things too. He remembered Nice and the overwhelming pleasure he had felt at meeting her again. He remembered the hell of explaining to Alexis and Zita why he had accepted a posting in a city Natalie was forbidden to travel to and his overwhelming relief that there was one person in the world he didn't have to deceive. He remembered how deep his affection for her had always been and how highly he had always valued her courage and integrity.

He said slowly, almost as unbelieving of the road his thoughts were taking him down as he had been when he had first realized what her confession implied, 'And if I had proposed to you? Would you have accepted me, Katerina?'

Time seemed to waver and halt. The night air was cool on her cheeks. Beneath the cover of the nearby rose bushes a small nocturnal animal scurried about its business.

'Yes,' she said quietly, over the precipice and heedless of the consequences.

For a long moment he neither moved nor spoke. He wasn't naturally introspective but at that moment he faced a great inner truth. Though it was Natalie with whom he had fallen hopelessly in love, it was Katerina he should have married. His character and hers were deeply compatible. How could he, all these years, have been so blind to something so obvious? Another realization followed swiftly and with utter certainty. It wasn't mere affection he felt for her. It was far, far more. He was on the very edge of being in love with her.

Katerina was aware only of his silence and the unreadable expression in his eyes, an expression she was certain was going to change at any moment to one of pity. The band had once again ceased to play and in a desperate attempt to free them both from the agonizingly embarrassing situation she had plunged them into, she said stiltedly, 'It must be the supper break. Your partner must be wondering where you are.'

'I didn't promise to partner anyone into supper.'

There was a new note in his voice. A note she didn't understand, but one that was certainly not pity.

He made no attempt to begin walking back to the house and no attempt to release her hands. In the moonlight the upswept waves of her hair had the sheen of satin and her lips were as softly inviting as the petals of a flower. Desire pulsed through him. He wanted to feel the unpinned weight of her hair sliding down over the backs of his hands and to crush the sweetness of her mouth beneath his.

It occurred to him that he had grossly underestimated the depths of his new-found feelings for her. He wasn't on the edge of being in love. He was in love. Not in the way he had been with Natalie. That thunderclap of unreasoning, instant infatuation had been a once in a lifetime experience and would not come again. What he was experiencing now was love of a different kind. Love that would be fully and loyally returned.

Gently, and very firmly, he drew her closer towards him.

'I made a very great mistake the last time we were in this garden in the moonlight together,' he said thickly. 'And it's a mistake I have no intention of making a second time.'

There was no misunderstanding now the vibrations of tenderness in his voice, or his intentions, and her heart began to slam so hard that it hurt.

As his arms encircled her waist she knew a hair's breadth of hesitancy and then she remembered Nice and Natalie's terrible confession and all hesitancy vanished. Natalie did not love him and never had loved him. No-one was being betrayed. Guiltless and in utter certainty of the love she felt for him her hands slid up around his neck, her lips parting willingly beneath his as his mouth closed at last on hers.

*   *   *

A week later, in Kalemegdan Gardens, he said tenderly, 'I've moved out of my apartment adjoining the Legation and into a small house in one of the little cobbled streets behind Terazije Square. It's Hungarian in style and drowning beneath lilac and jasmine blossom. We should be able to meet there without attracting comment from my neighbours.'

They were walking a very proper foot or so apart and she longed to close the distance and slip her hand into his.

'I shall only be able to visit you there on an afternoon,' she said, a touch of apprehension in her voice in case he had not realized how difficult it would be for her to spend time unaccounted for away from home. 'Peter has music lessons on Monday and Friday afternoons and French lessons on Thursday afternoons. Usually I while away his lesson time by walking here or down by the river, but now . . .'

A faint flush of colour touched her cheeks and he grinned across at her, marvelling at the power of the emotion he now felt for her.

'But now you'll spend that time with me,' he said, and uncaring of who might see his action he took her pale-gloved hand in his.

Their fingers interlocked tightly. Ahead of them, within sight but out of earshot, Peter was running towards the ruined fortress, a Dalmatian puppy at his heels. The puppy had been a present from Julian and Katerina was heart-achingly aware that it was exactly the kind of present he would have bought for Stephen.

'I wish we could be a proper family!' she said with sudden passion. 'I wish we didn't have to lie and pretend to people! I wish the three of us could live together openly in the little house behind Terazije Square!'

A couple had turned on to the shrub-shaded pathway

439

some way ahead of them and in mutual anguish they released hands.

'Dear Christ! You think I don't long for that too?' he said, his voice so raw with pain she sucked in her breath, appalled at the hurt she had unleashed. 'If there was any way it was possible I would take it. But there isn't. You're my sister-in-law and even if I get a divorce from Natalie, marriage between us is impossible.'

'I know,' she said contritely, wishing she could take hold of his hand again, wishing she could show him how sorry she was for having spoken her hopeless thoughts out loud. 'And I know that there is nothing that can be done to change the situation. It was foolish of me to have spoken as I did. I didn't mean to and I won't do so again.'

'You've every right to do so,' he said thickly. 'You were born to be a wife and mother, not a mistress.'

He turned his head towards her, his throat tightening. She was wearing a mauve voile dress and a matching wide-brimmed hat. Her stockings and shoes were ivory and there was a heavy rope of creamy pearls around her neck. She looked timelessly beautiful, exquisitely fragile. At the thought of all she was risking in embarking on an affair with him he was overcome by agonizing doubt. Was he asking too much of her? Was his new-found, selfish need of her going to ruin her life?

The couple passed them. Ahead of them Peter disappeared from view round the far side of the fortress.

Once again he reached out for her hand. Standing still he turned her to face him. 'I love you,' he said fiercely, wishing to God he could draw her into his arms and physically impress on her how much. 'I want to live with you for the rest of my life, but it isn't possible, not legally, and any other way would cause your parents and Peter crucifying hurt. All we can ever hope for are snatched meetings and there will always be the chance that the

440

wrong person will see you entering or leaving the house or will begin to think that, as Peter's uncle, I spend too much time taking him on outings and that your attendance when I do so is unnecessary and a little suspect.'

At the expression in his eyes she felt her stomach muscles tighten in a sickening spasm. 'What are you trying to say, Julian?' There was a hint of unsteadiness in her voice that, try as she might, she couldn't control. 'Are you saying that the risks are too great for you? That exposure would compromise your career?'

If their affair really were a threat to his career then she would have no option but to relinquish him. She wouldn't be able to live with herself if, for selfish motives, she caused him professional ruin.

He shook his head, the sun glinting on his hair. 'I wasn't thinking of me,' he said sombrely. 'I was thinking of you and the risks you are running. They are very great, my love. Perhaps too great. For your sake, and for Peter's and your parents' sake, it might be better if . . .'

'No!' She pressed her gloved fingers against his lips, her pupils wide. 'Don't ever say it! Don't ever even think it! I should never have spoken as I did! What we have now is more than I ever dreamed of having! It's all I shall ever need!'

His relief at her reaction was overwhelming. Hardly able to speak he lovingly took her hand away from his mouth and kissed the back of it. 'I love you,' he said huskily. 'Never doubt it.'

Though her eyes were still brimming with tears her smile was radiant. Their misunderstanding was over. Though they would never be able to live together in the way they both longed to, they would love each other with utter commitment, causing hurt to no-one.

As Peter began to run down the pathway towards them Julian reluctantly released hold of her hand. He, too, was determined that their affair would be life-long and even though marriage was out of the question he wanted to become morally free as soon as possible. With a stab of bitterness he wondered how Natalie would react when she learned of his intention.

The only correspondence that had passed between them since he had been in Belgrade had been a brief letter from himself asking for frequent news of Stephen and the subsquent notelets she had written, complying with his request. All of them had been frigidly stilted and in none of them had she made even the briefest of references to her own welfare, to the coming baby, or to the hideous situation that now existed between them.

As Peter seized hold of his hand, asking him if he would take him into the ruined fortress, he decided he would write to his solicitor the instant he returned to his Legation.

All through the summer the political situation was turbulent. More and more Croatians made their discontent at being ruled from Belgrade, and not Zagreb, obvious and only immediate occupation of Croatia by the army prevented a setting up of a peasant Communist state.

Julian's workload was heavy and he spent long hours at the Legation, returning late each night to the white-walled house behind Terazije Square.

On Monday, Thursday and Friday afternoons he escaped from the Legation on the pretext of meeting with one of the many politicians with whom it was his business to keep in contact and Katerina would hurry to meet him after taking Peter to his music or French lesson.

Their lovemaking had been a revelation to her. During the brief period of her marriage to Ivan Zlarin she had submitted dutifully in bed, with all the gentle tenderness of her nature, but she had never felt any reciprocating passion. Her body had remained always within her control, curiously inviolate.

Now, in Julian's arms, it was inviolate no longer. Skilfully and tenderly he had carried her through an invisible barrier into a country she hadn't dreamed existed, a country in which she lost all sense of self. As she had experienced the convulsion of true sexual fusion for the first time the depths of her abandoned, primeval response had shocked and almost frightened her. Lovingly, with hands and lips as well as with words, he had reassured her, treating her as if she were a bride and not a widow with a child.

In August Julian received a brief notelet from Natalie. Her baby had been born. It was a little girl and though she had weighed only five pounds at birth she was healthy. 'Your parents have assumed she was premature and I haven't disabused them,' Natalie had written bluntly. 'I've named her Zorka after my mother's girlhood friend, Princess Zorka.'

'I suppose I should be grateful my mother can at least assume the child to be mine,' he said savagely when he had broken the news to Katerina, 'though God knows how she'll come to terms with the name. She detests all things foreign and there's no way it can be pretended Zorka is an English name.'

He screwed the note with its large emerald-inked handwriting into a tight ball, his knuckles white. 'I wonder if she has an address for Kechko?' he demanded, his pain nakedly obvious. 'I wonder if he'll appreciate having his daughter named after a Montenegrin?'

They were questions to which he obviously expected no answer and she remained silent, deeply shocked at the realization that his hurt was still so raw and deep.

At the end of the month Cissie became engaged to the equerry she had captivated on the night of the ball and a week later Max returned to Belgrade with his small son, but minus his Greek wife.

'He's widowed,' Vitza said to her starkly. 'She had consumption and though Max was making arrangements to take her to Switzerland in the hope she would recover there, the deprivations of the war years were too much for her. She died a month ago. What Max's feelings are it's hard to know. He was always impossible to communicate with and the war has made him even worse.'

Katerina was sure she knew what Max's feelings were. He wasn't a man to have fallen in love lightly and beneath his taciturn exterior he would be suffering great grief, grief he would be unable to express. She wanted, very much, to be able to offer him her sympathy but he made no family visits and she was reluctant to intrude on his self-imposed isolation.

At the end of September Julian received notification from London that he was to leave Belgrade and report to the British Embassy in Paris. It was a notification he had known would come eventually and he had long ago made up his mind that when it did, rather than be separated from Katerina, he would decline the posting and resign from the diplomatic service. Or he could leave the diplomatic service and, on the recommendation of Alexis, remain in Belgrade as an adviser to the Prince Regent.

For the first time in a long while he visited the Vassilovich house to speak to his father-in-law and without any intention of catching a glimpse of Katerina. Then, late that night, after asking Alexis if he would recommend him as an adviser to Prince Regent Alexander, he wrote to Natalie, appraising her of the decision he had made.

444

For the next week or so Katerina remained in ignorance of his plans. Then she received a letter from Natalie. In vivid green ink on mauve paper it had obviously been written with intense emotion. On a number of occasions the fountain pen had scored the paper and as well as Natalie's customary blots there were suspicious marks indicating that she had been crying while writing it.

Dearest, dearest Trina, I can't bear this silence between us any longer. I know now how utterly wicked I have been and I don't blame you in the slightest for not wanting anything else to do with me. I don't want anything else to do with me but I can't escape from myself and I do so wish I could. I never knew it was possible to be so miserable and lonely. Diana is engaged now and I hardly ever see her. My father-in-law is sweet but Julian's mother is hateful. I loathe her as much as I loathe London and I loathe, loathe, LOATHE, London! If it wasn't for Stephen and the new baby I swear I would kill myself.

How could I have been so stupid? Even now I don't understand it. I simply thought of Julian as being my very best friend and because I hadn't CHOSEN to marry him it never occurred to me that I would have married him of my own accord once I realized how truly wonderful he was. I felt so CHEATED, you see. I'd always expected to fall madly in love with a prince or a count and that I would have a splendid wedding in the cathedral with Uncle Peter and Sandro in attendance and perhaps even Hélène and members of the Russian imperial family there was well (oh God, when I think of what happened to the Romanovs I can't bear it!) and I felt in some peculiar way that I was OWED something. I thought that something was Nicky and I was so, so wrong. I see now that it was homesickness for everything Slav that I loved, not Nicky himself.

The person I love for himself is Julian. Will you tell him that for me, Trina? I can't tell him in a letter. His letters to me are so stiffly formal they terrify me and I'm certain he would put any letter from me that wasn't about Stephen straight into a waste basket. Will you tell him I do truly love him and that if only he will love me again I'll never do anything stupid again my whole life long? Tell him that Stephen cries for him at night and that the new baby is the prettiest most placid baby in the whole world and that her existence isn't her fault and that I know he wouldn't be able to stop himself caring for her if only he were to see her.

Tell him I had been waiting for him to be transferred to an embassy where I could visit him and say all this for myself but that now he has decided to leave the diplomatic service and stay in Belgrade I won't be able to do so. Please, please tell him that I don't want to be divorced from him and that his solicitor is horrid and speaks to me as if I were a criminal. Tell him I love him and that more than anything in the world I want to be able to tell him so.

There was a large smudge on the unusually restrained signature.

Katerina put the letter down on her dressing-table with an unsteady hand. She hadn't known of Julian's decision to leave the diplomatic service and to remain in Belgrade. Even more devastatingly, she had never even suspected Natalie's true feelings for Julian or the anguish she had been suffering ever since he had left her.

As she looked out of the window, across the lawns and towards the chestnut trees, she felt curiously calm. Her affair with Julian was at an end, of course. She had known that the instant she had read Natalie's first tear-stained reference to him. She remembered his pain when he had received news of Zorka's birth and knew that despite the sincerity of his love for herself, he was still bound to Natalie by bonds that only Natalie could break. And Natalie did not wish to break them. She loved him and she wanted a reunion. She wanted them to be a family again.

Slowly she picked up Natalie's letter and put it into her purse, then she rose to her feet and, unable to see very clearly, put on a straw hat with a large posy of poppies pinned to the brim.

Julian had said himself that he was a family man and she knew that he would be as wonderful a stepfather to Zorka as he would have been to Peter. With his generous, compassionate nature it would be impossible for him not to be.

Picking up a pair of lace gloves she left the room and for the last time set out towards the little white-walled house behind Terazije Square.

'A letter? What kind of a letter?' he asked, his eyes darkening, sensing instantly that some profound change had come over her.

She handed him the distinctive sheets of thick mauve notepaper. 'It arrived this morning,' she said quietly. 'Natalie wanted me to tell you its contents but I think you should read them.'

His eyes held hers for a long moment and then, unwillingly, he looked down at the heart-achingly familiar handwriting.

She turned away from him, not wanting to see the expression on his face as he read. They were in a downstairs room that served as a salon. There were two low divans upholstered in peasant needlework and on the walls were decorative homespun rugs and a framed photograph of the king.

She remained standing, still wearing her hat and gloves, her cream silk dress cool in the late summer heat.

After what seemed to be an eternity of time he said

thickly, 'This letter doesn't change anything. I've already made up my mind to resign from the diplomatic service and remain in Belgrade in order that nothing, not even my career, will separate us . . .'

She turned to face him. 'You're wrong,' she said quietly, her heart aching with love for him. 'Natalie's letter changes everything. Before, I truly believed that no-one was being hurt. Now I know differently and nothing can ever be the same.'

'Do you truly think Natalie would be claiming to be in love with me if Kechko was still around?' he asked tautly.

He was wearing a silver-grey three piece suit, a gold fob-watch chain looped across his chest. In the nape of his neck his sun-bronzed hair curled over his high, waxed shirt-collar and he looked as handsome as he had the day she had first realized she was in love with him.

'I don't know,' she said truthfully, her voice very steady. 'I don't think that it matters. What matters is that his desertion has made her face reality and you are her reality, just as she and Stephen are your realities.'

A lock of hair had tumbled low over his brow and he pushed it away, his eyes avoiding hers. 'And what about the realities of the last few months?' he asked brusquely. 'What about the peace and contentment we've known?'

Her throat hurt and it was a moment or two before she could speak. When she could, she said, 'Neither of us will ever forget it. It will always remain a precious memory.'

He remained silent and with a hurting heart she knew he was going to protest no further. Sincerely as he loved her he was not in love with her in the way he was in love with Natalie, and that he was still in love with Natalie she had known ever since she had seen his reaction to the news of Zorka's birth.

She said quietly, 'I didn't know about your decision to leave the diplomatic service. Did you make it because you

448

had been asked to leave Belgrade and serve somewhere else?'

He nodded. 'I'd been asked to transfer to Paris. I haven't yet replied to the request that I reconsider my letter of resignation and so I assume the offer is still open.'

Katerina thought of the glamour of Paris and despite all her heartache a shadow of a smile touched the corners of her mouth. Paris was Natalie's spiritual home. In Paris Natalie would be happy.

All the time they had been talking they had been several feet apart and now, knowing that if he moved towards her, her precarious self-composure would vanish, knowing that there was nothing more to say, she walked with all the will power she possessed towards the door.

'Will you come with me to the station when I leave?' he asked, his voice so charged with emotion it was all she could do not to turn and run into his arms.

'Yes,' she said, not trusting herself to look at him, reaching for the door handle, her eyes blinded by tears. 'Yes, of course I will.'

Until the day she did so, she did not meet him again, alone. To have done so would have been to have exposed herself to a hurt too deep to be borne. With an outer composure that betrayed no hint of her grief she explained to Peter that Julian would soon be leaving Belgrade and that they mustn't be upset, but must remember how happy Stephen would be at being reunited with his papa.

When the day for goodbyes arrived Julian came to the house. There was no longer any chilliness between himself and Zita. Radiant with happiness at the knowledge that Natalie and Stephen would soon be with him in Paris, she kissed him warmly on the cheek, making him promise to send a photograph of the new baby at the very first opportunity.

Alexis was visibly happier than he had been for months, vastly relieved that the marriage for which he was so responsible, was again viable. Shaking Julian warmly by the hand he promised that in the very near future he would bring Zita and Katerina and Peter to Paris in order that they could all make Zorka's acquaintance.

Katerina was paler than usual and very quiet. This was not her goodbye to Julian. Her goodbye would be said in another hour or so, at the train station.

When he had gone, bearing gifts from Zita for Natalie and the baby, she discreetly left the house on the pretext of visiting her dressmaker.

She walked to the station, grateful that it lay in the opposite direction to Terazije Square and the maze of cobbled streets behind it. There were rumours that King Peter was, at last, about to make his return to the city and the streets were more crowded than normal, a buzz of expectation emanating from the cafés.

Alexis had said that when Peter did return to the city, he had no intention of taking up residence in the palace Sandro had so carefully renovated for him and she wondered where he would live and if, rather than leaving the palace unoccupied, Sandro would move back into it.

Although her apple-green dress was elegantly plain and unadorned her head-turning grace drew many admiring glances and she lowered her parasol discreetly, not wanting to be recognized and waylaid by a relative or a friend.

Hundreds of times over the last few days she had asked herself if going to the station to say goodbye to him was in her best interests and the answer had always been the same. It wasn't. It was going to tear her apart. The alternative, however, was unthinkable. She couldn't say goodbye to him in public, as though they had never been more to each other than loving friends.

As she entered the station's cave-like coolness she

remembered the evening she had entered it in order to say goodbye to Natalie and knew that, terrible as that leave-taking had been, the one that lay ahead of her was going to be far, far worse.

'The king is coming!' she heard on every side of her as she squeezed through the crowds towards the platform for the departure to Budapest and the connection onwards to Paris. 'His train is due in at any moment! The king is coming and is hoping not to be noticed!'

Katerina, too, did not want to be noticed. With her face no longer shielded by her parasol she neared the platform and saw him waiting for her at the barrier.

'I thought you weren't going to come!' he said tautly, and uncaring of the crowds around them, uncaring of the physical distance they had so scrupulously maintained ever since their last meeting in the little house behind Terazije Square, his arms went around her and his mouth came down hard on hers.

There was pandemonium around them as amid a cacophony of whistles, cries of *'The king's train is here!'* erupted jubilantly. There were other shouts, too. Shouts warning all departing passengers that the train for Budapest was about to leave.

At last, in agonizing reluctance he raised his head from hers. 'It isn't too late,' he said hoarsely. 'We could leave together!'

She pressed a finger gently against his mouth. 'Good-bye,' she said thickly. 'God bless.'

White clouds of steam were belching towards them. A porter had already carried his bags on to the train. Releasing his hold of her he said harshly, 'I love you. I shall always love you. You were never second best,' and then he turned on his heel and strode down the platform.

As he boarded the train it was already moving. Within seconds he slammed a window down and leant out, his eyes holding hers until the train emerged into bright sunshine and he could see her no longer.

She stood, as she had once stood before, until the train was out of sight. Once again a part of her life was over. It was a part of her life she would never forget. A part of her life she would treasure for always.

At last, numbly, she turned away from the barrier. The crowds had all moved to the far side of the concourse where a red carpet had been hastily unrolled and only one large, looming figure stood between her and the station's cavern-like exit. Her eyes focused on him in disbelief.

He walked towards her, ignoring the eruption of cheers that indicated King Peter had at last re-entered his capital.

'You look as though you're in need of comfort,' he said bluntly.

She remembered his recent bereavement and knew that grief would be the last thing she could ever hide from him.

'Yes,' she said, knowing that he had seen everything and had understood everything and wondering how she could ever have thought him insensitive. 'I am.'

He said simply, as farouche in manner as ever, 'So am I.'

As he lifted her hand and slipped it into the crook of his arm she knew that her future was no longer inconceivable but very, very obvious. She knew also that nothing would happen quickly; that everything would take its time; that the relationship she and Max were about to build together would be built slowly and carefully and on foundations nothing would ever shake.

Together, the only people on the concourse not thronging in welcome around the newly returned king, they stepped out of the station's gloom and into the brilliantly sunlit square beyond.

May 1943 – June 1945

Chapter Twenty-One

The office in Baker Street looked out towards Regent's Park and as Stephen Fielding faced a massive desk fronting a top floor window he could glimpse nannies wheeling prams and small children carrying bags of bread to feed to the ducks.

'Take a pew,' the civilian-suited figure behind the desk said affably. 'This is likely to take some time.'

'Thank you, sir.'

Stephen, parachute wings on his uniformed arm, sat down in the cracked leather armchair facing the desk.

'You've been serving in the Canal Zone I believe?' his silver-haired interviewer asked pleasantly.

'Yes, sir.'

'And you have languages? French, German and Serbo-Croat?'

'Yes, sir,' Stephen said, already certain of where the conversation was heading. 'I have a degree in Modern Languages and my mother is Serbian.'

The gentleman he was facing, and whose name he did not know, swung his swivel-chair to the left so that he, too, could look down over the park. Without any eye contact at all with Stephen he said musingly, 'And you know Yugoslavia? You've visited it with your mother?'

'I know the country and have visited it often, though not with my mother.'

His interviewer did not pursue the curiosity of his last statement. 'Good,' he said succinctly. 'First let me fill you in on the present situation in Yugoslavia and then I'll tell you why you're here.' He steepled his fingers together. 'Ever since the Germans invaded the country in 1941 the Allies have been giving logistical support to General Dräza Mihailovich. General Mihailovich is, as you no doubt know, a former Royal Army officer and the acknowledged leader of Yugoslav Resistance. He and his men go by the name Chetniks, which can be a bit confusing as in Serbo-Croat Chetnik merely means any kind of irregular guerilla organization and there are other, not so disciplined groups which also go by that name. To differentiate Milhailovich's men from other Chetnik groups we generally refer to them as Loyalist Chetniks. Recently, however, we have received information that much of the sabotage being carried out against the Germans is, in fact, not being carried out by Mihailovich and his Loyalists but by a rival resistance organization known as the Partisans. If this is true, it leaves us with a problem. Is Tito, the leader of the Partisans, more worthy of our support than Mihailovich?'

Stephen frowned slightly. 'Why does there have to be a choice, sir? Surely both groups can liaise?'

The man behind the desk swung his chair around, facing him again, saying dryly, 'In a simple situation that would be the most obvious and satisfactory solution. However, in the Balkans nothing is simple.'

He crossed one leg over the other, revealing a surprisingly louche purple sock. 'Mihailovich and his Loyalist Chetniks are monarchists. Tito and his followers are communists. Though their short-term aim, resistance to the Germans, is the same, their ambitions for a post-war Yugoslavia are so vastly different that no co-operation can possibly exist between them. Consequently it is a question of supporting one or the other of them, but not both.'

He leaned back in his chair, swinging his foot. 'Which is where you come in, Fielding. Before such a decision can be reached we need to know if the information we have received is true or propaganda. The outfit for which I am responsible, Special Operations Executive, parachuted a three-man military mission into the country some time ago, their brief being to make contact with Mihailovich. The outcome wasn't successful. Two members of the mission were British with only a small understanding of Serbo-Croat and to compensate for this deficiency the third member of the mission was a Canadian of Croat descent. Tito is also a Croat and when Mihailovich learned a Croat was with the mission he was immediately mistrustful and refused to rendezvous with it.

'I'm hoping that, if you agree to leave your present unit and join SOE, you will lead a similar, and this time successful, mission into Yugoslavia. You've got all the necessary qualifications. You've already served with a Parachute battalion, you know the country, speak the language, and your family connections are such that Mihailovich is sure to trust you.'

'My mother was only a distant cousin of the late king, not a first cousin,' Stephen said, not wanting there to be any misunderstanding.

His interviewer patted one of the buff folders on his desk. 'Her mother was a Karageorgevich,' he said, unperturbed. 'That will be testimonial enough for Mihailovich.' He heaved himself from his chair, signalling that the interview was at an end. 'Cairo is the centre of operations where the Balkans are concerned and I want you to fly out there immediately.'

His acceptance of the offer made to him having been taken for granted, Stephen rose to his feet. 'What about the men who are to accompany me, sir? Will they be flying out with me?'

'No. Your team are already in Cairo. And don't worry about your reception committee when you hit Yugoslav soil. The leader of the Loyalist group who will take you to Mihailovich is someone well known to you.'

Stephen stood very still, hoping with all his might, mind and strength that the assumption he had leapt to was going to be correct.

'All Mihailovich's officers are former Royal Army officers and Peter Zlarin is no exception,' his interviewer said, a glimmer of dry amusement entering his voice. 'On this mission, no matter what the other difficulties, I think it can be guaranteed suspicion and mistrust will not be among them.'

'Yugoslavia?' Julian said, not remotely surprised. 'I wondered how long it would take before SOE recognized you would be of use there.'

'And to meet up with Peter,' Stephen said with deep satisfaction.

Julian moved towards the fireplace and knocked his pipe out. 'Your relationship to Peter would have been the clincher as far as SOE were concerned,' he said, wondering which arm of the intelligence service had first realized that Loyalist guerilla leader Major Peter Zlarin was first cousin to Captain Stephen Fielding of the 156th Parachute Battalion. 'Once the connection was realized and once they knew how familiar you were with the country and the language they couldn't have done anything else but ask you to join them.' He grinned, looking far younger than his fifty-five years. 'Your mother will be pleased. Dear God, your mother is going to be ecstatic!'

'Yugoslavia!' Natalie said in stunned wonder. 'Are you truly going to be fighting for freedom in Yugoslavia?' Eyes shining like a girl's she turned to face Julian. 'Was this your doing, darling? Did you arrange it all?'

Julian shook his head, amused as always by her belief

that as an ex-ambassador he had only to say the word and the whole of Whitehall would leap to his bidding. 'No. Now that the German position in Italy is crumbling it's only sense that Allied attention should begin to be focused on the other side of the Adriatic and I imagine every Serbo-Croat and Greek speaker in the army will be transferred there.'

With all his heart he wished he could tell her the true nature of Stephen's mission and that he was going to rendezvous with Peter. Unable to do so he changed the subject, saying, 'As Stephen leaves for Cairo tomorrow, let's have dinner at the Dorchester tonight. Do you think we can persuade Zorka's new young man to join us?'

'He isn't her young man,' Natalie admonished, a shadow crossing her face. 'Xan is Zorka's young man. Her present friend is a work colleague, nothing more.'

Her change of mood was shared by Alexis and Stephen. Since the Germans had invaded Yugoslavia two years ago there had been no news of Katerina and Max, or of Max's son, Xan.

Stephen said tentatively, trying to offer his mother what comfort he could, 'I imagine Xan is with the Loyalists. Zorka believes so. She says if he were dead she would know.'

Natalie drew in a sharp breath, empathizing with her daughter utterly. When Julian had been in Flanders she, too, had been certain that instinct would tell her if harm came to him. She said a little unsteadily, 'I wish they'd married when we were last all together. I wish we knew if Mama and Papa and Max and Katerina are still alive. I wish Hitler was in his grave and this bloody, bloody war was over.'

'So do we all,' Julian said gently, drawing her towards him and sliding his arms comfortingly around her.

Stephen turned away. He was quite accustomed to

459

displays of love and comfort between his parents and it wasn't their embrace that made him feel uncomfortable. It was his knowledge that at least one member of their family in Yugoslavia was still alive and that for security reasons he could not tell her so.

Natalie continued to rest her head against Julian's shoulder. Ever since Stephen had been old enough to tell stories to, she had told him of Tsar Stephen Dushan and of the Slav heroes who had freed her homeland of Turkish domination, wanting him to be as familiar with his Slav heritage as his schooling would make him familiar with his British heritage. Now, in fighting on Yugoslav soil to free the country from an invader, Stephen would be emulating the heroes so familiar to them both and though she was deeply proud, hard on the heels of her pride had come fears for his safety.

'Does the Dorchester manage to rise above rationing?' Stephen asked, aware of the direction his mother's thoughts had taken and wanting to distract her. 'Or are we going to be faced with a ghastly meat-alternative such as whale?'

Natalie shuddered. 'If we are, I shall stick to pink gins.'

'Pink gins,' Julian said to Stephen, a smile tugging at the corners of his mouth, 'have enabled your mother to sleep through the most horrendous of air raids in her own bed and to be high-handedly contemptuous of public shelters. Fine for her, but nerve-wracking for those of us who are not similarly anaesthetized.'

Stephen grinned. In the early days of the war his father had done everything possible to persuade his Aunt Diana and his mother and Zorka to move to their family home in Northumberland. Diana, more for her children's sake than her own, had done so. His mother and sister had not. Natalie had declared that in the last war, neither her mother nor sister had fled Belgrade until they had done so in the company of the king and the army and that she had not the slightest intention of leaving London, especially as King George and Queen Elizabeth were not doing so. Zorka had merely said that her position as secretary to a high-ranking civil servant made it impossible for her to leave and that even if it didn't, she wouldn't do so.

As his parents exchanged loving, complicit glances he said, 'As it's the last time I'll be able to do so for a long time I'm going to take Rosie for a run in the park.'

Hearing her name, his mother's aged black spaniel waddled hopefully towards him.

'I think you mean a walk, Stephen,' Julian said wryly. 'It's been quite some time since Rosie ran.'

Stephen fondled the top of Rosie's silky head. 'A walk then,' he said, sadly aware that Rosie might not be alive when he next returned home and wondering how his mother would cope with her loss.

One of his first memories had been of Rosie's predecessor, Bella, romping playfully around his ankles. When Bella had died at the ripe old age of fourteen, his mother had been distraught. It had been as if a member of the family had died. She had vowed she would never have another dog, that no other dog could ever replace Bella. His father had sensibly ignored her protestations and had brought Rosie home and Stephen knew he would never forget the look of gratitude his mother had given his father when he had placed the tiny black bundle in her arms.

With Rosie on a lead he left the house and crossed Cheyne Walk, heading for Battersea Bridge and the park on the far side of it. When he had been a small boy, living in his grandparents' house at Cambridge Gate, the park his mother had always taken him into had been Regent's Park. He could never remember his father accompanying them there but later, when they moved to Paris, he had very clear memories of his father walking hand-in-hand with him along the banks of the Seine and of their flying kites together in a small park behind their home on the Avenue du Bois.

Five idyllic years in Paris had been followed by three years in Madrid and then they had moved to London again and his parents had bought the house in Chelsea that was still their home. It had been a happy, privileged childhood. Every year, at least once a year and sometimes twice, there had been family reunions with his mother's Yugoslav relations. Their favourite rendezvous was the Hotel Negresco in Nice and some of the happiest days of his life had been spent with his sister and his cousin and stepcousin on the pebbly beach fronting the hotel.

As he crossed the bridge in the bright May sunshine he wondered just when Xan and Zorka, friends since babyhood, had realized they were in love. Everyone, apart from his mother, had been staggered when they had made their announcement.

'Xan is not Zorka's first cousin,' his mother had said practically. 'His mother was neither a Karageorgevich nor a Vassilovich. She was a Greek. I think their falling in love is absolutely wonderful.'

Later, Zorka had said to him, 'Mummy wants me to have a splendid wedding to compensate for the fact that her wedding to Daddy was apparently pretty makeshift. It's the last thing Xan and I want but I haven't the heart to tell her so.'

He turned left into Parkgate Road, keeping his pace leisurely out of consideration for Rosie. Whether the eventual wedding was sumptuous or simple one thing was certain. It wouldn't take place in Belgrade.

Not until he was fifteen had his father explained the reason why Natalie never accompanied them on visits to Yugoslavia. Only then had he realized the pain she must have suffered when his aunt had married Max Karageorge-vich and his father had taken both himself and Zorka to the wedding in Belgrade. There had been other celebrations too, which she had been unable to attend. Alexander's marriage to Princess Marie of Romania; her cousin Vitza's marriage to a White Russian old enough to be her grandfather. He had been too young to remember King Peter but he remembered his mother's tears when news came that he had died, and he remembered her telling him that the king's body would be taken to Openlats in Shumadia, the traditional burial place for all direct descendants of Karageorge.

He stepped into Battersea Park and let Rosie off her leash. Even now, nine years later, there were times when he could scarcely believe the story his father had told him. To him, Gavrilo Princip was a name from a history book. It seemed beyond belief that his still ravishingly pretty, warm-hearted, vibrant mother could have been one of Princip's personal friends. It was even harder to believe that anyone could have thought her capable of being involved in the plot to kill Archduke Ferdinand.

When King Alexander had been assassinated by Croat nationalists in Marseilles in 1934 his first reaction, when he had recovered from his outrage and shock, had been to wonder whether his mother's long banishment from Yugoslavia might at last be at an end.

Both he and his father had attended the funeral in Belgrade. Accompanied by their Karageorgevich relations they had walked with bare heads behind the bier. It had been an emotional experience. Alexander had been only forty-six years old and the manner of his death had been hideously violent. His cousin and closest friend, Prince Paul, led the mourners. King Carol of Romania and the Duke of Kent, representing King George V, walked beside him followed by a score of other statesmen and minor royals.

Afterwards, Alexander's body had been taken by train to Openlats and Prince Paul had been declared Regent for the duration of eleven-year-old Prince Peter's minority.

'Will Prince Paul allow Mummy to visit Belgrade?' Stephen had asked his father while they had been seated at the dinner table with his grandparents and aunt and uncle.

The tension around the table had been palpable and then his father had said quietly, 'I hope so, Stephen. I've already asked for an interview with him so that I can request she be allowed to do so. Grandpa and Uncle Max are going to accompany me.'

His grandmother had excused herself from the table and Stephen had fervently regretted asking his question in front of her for he knew she was going to her room to cry.

All their hopes came to nothing. Prince Paul was deeply unhappy at becoming regent. He had never been a politician, never even been a soldier, and he was profoundly unsure of his ability to govern. In an effort to make no wrong decisions he chose to make as few decisions as possible and he adamantly declined to overrule any decision Alexander had ever taken.

As Stephen made his way towards the boating lake, Rosie gallantly keeping pace with him, he marvelled at his mother's lack of bitterness. Though she had been devastated with disappointment she had not uttered one word against Paul, just as she had never uttered a word of criticism against Alexander.

He took a ball out of his pocket and threw it a short distance across the grass, hoping to lure Rosie into a little exercise. She wagged her tail and ignored it. Realizing he had been expecting too much of her he walked across and picked it up, still thinking of his mother.

Ever since he could remember she had been the centre of his life and he had adored her, and still did. As a small boy he had been aware that his friends' mothers were all

464

tediously elegant, tediously conventional and tediously dull. Natalie was never dull. She possessed a fizzing, magical quality that made the most mundane of activities seem full of fun. Zorka possessed the same bouncy effervescence. Whenever he had brought girl friends home, no matter how wonderful he had initially thought them, he had quickly realized that in comparison to his mother and sister they were grey and uninteresting and not special at all.

He began to walk towards the north-west exit from the park. Although Zorka had inherited Natalie's innate gaiety and reckless impulsiveness he was well aware that he had not done so. Like his father he was quiet in manner and though his hair was darker than his father's, he was still unmistakably English. Zorka did not look at all English. Her hair was so glossily dark as to be almost black and she wore it shoulder-length, held away from her face by heavy tortoiseshell combs. It wasn't only her colouring that was so startlingly different from their father's. Her high cheekboned face was unmistakably Slav, as was her outgoing, animated temperament. Ever since she had been a teenager there had been a constant stream of admirers in her wake and he was sure the young man his mother had earlier referred to as being merely a work colleague would have preferred it if the description had been different.

His assumption was confirmed that night when they all dined together at the Dorchester and he saw the expression in the young man's eyes whenever he looked towards Zorka, which was often. Zorka was as obviously uninterested as he was interested and Stephen wondered whether it wouldn't be a kindness to take the young man aside and have a few frank words with him.

Just as he was making up his mind whether or not to do so the young man turned to Julian, saying in genuine puzzlement, 'What I don't understand, sir, is why Yugoslavs have always been so at odds with each other, with Croats at the throats of the Serbs and vice versa.'

Natalie's eyes flashed fire and before she could launch into a heated, subjective explanation Julian said, 'To be able to understand the divisions that cleave Yugoslavs you have to understand a little of their history.'

He laid down his knife and fork, raising his voice slightly so that it could be heard above the band music and the distant boom of the Hyde Park guns. 'The problem goes back to the Middle Ages when the entire peninsula came under alien domination, the south and east being occupied by Moslem Turks, the north and west being occupied by Austrians and Hungarians. Slavs under Turkish rule looked culturally and spiritually towards Constantinople and were Eastern Orthodox in religion. Those under the Habsburgs looked westwards, towards Vienna, and like their rulers were fiercely Roman Catholic. This cultural, political and spiritual divide went very deep and it's a divide more recent history has done nothing to resolve.'

He leaned back in his chair, pushing his plate away from him. 'The first Slavs to achieve freedom from alien rule were the Montenegrins and Serbs, but even when the peninsula was free of Turks, Habsburg rule in the north and west remained. The majority of Slavs under Habsburg rule wished to be free of it and they looked to Serbia to help her. When Gavrilo Princip, a Bosnian Serb who fiercely resented the Austrian misrule of Bosnia, assassinated the heir to the Habsburg throne and precipitated the First World War, Serbia fought with the Allies, her aim being to free her fellow Slavs and to create a united kingdom of all South Slavs.'

He paused, looking towards Natalie. At the mention of Princip she had gone very still. Sitting next to her,

Stephen instinctively covered her hand with his.

'But when they finally achieved unity, they still scrapped and squabbled,' Zorka's friend pointed out, spearing a Brussels sprout with his fork. 'Instead of living under a European democracy, King Alexander ended up as a royal dictator.'

'Think of the problems he had,' Julian said dryly. 'Serbs who had fought with the Allies were deeply resentful of being joined in union with Croats who had taken the side of Austria-Hungary. The Croats in their turn regarded the Serbs as being their cultural and spiritual inferiors and resented being ruled not from Zagreb, but from Belgrade, a city they viewed as being little more than an Oriental fortress. Given a choice they would have preferred to form their own separate state and if they had done so it wouldn't have been a monarchy, but a republic. The western powers, however, felt that the end of the war had brought enough new states into being and refused to support the idea, leaving Croatia with a choice. Union with Italy, Roman Catholic like themselves but racially very different, or union with fellow Slavs of a different religion. They chose union but they didn't do so whole-heartedly. The political unrest that followed made democratic rule impossible and it was only after a Croat politician was shot dead by a political opponent during a parliamentary debate that Alexander dissolved parliament and began to rule without it.'

'And you think his decision was wise, sir?'

'I think it was understandable. Unfortunately what it did, of course, was to drive opposition groups underground. One such group, a Croat nationalist group, re-christened themselves Ustasha, became openly terrorist and were responsible for King Alexander's assassination.'

Julian took another sip of his wine. 'In March 1941 Nazi Germany presented the Yugoslav government with an ultimatum demanding the incorporation of the country in the Nazi New Order. It was a question of either complying or being annihilated and the Regent, Prince Paul, complied. As soon as news of the deal became public knowledge there was a huge outcry of protest. A *coup d'état* by the army deposed Paul, put eighteen-year-old Prince Peter on the throne and denounced the agreement with Germany.'

'And the Germans attacked?'

Julian nodded. 'It was, as Prince Paul had known it would be, annihilation. King Peter and his government left for Cairo; the remnants of the army headed into the hills to form a national resistance movement, and Germany occupied and dismembered the country.'

'And it was then that the Ustasha came into its own,' Zorka said, the lovely triangle of her face very pale. 'They were allowed to form an independent Fascist state and if the rumours coming out of Yugoslavia are true, they're vying with the Germans in acts of actrocity against non-Croat Slavs.'

'Add to that the differences in ideology between communists and monarchists, with the communists determined on bringing about a complete social revolution in the country, once the war is over, and you can see why unity in Yugoslavia is in such short supply,' Julian concluded, bringing his potted history lesson to a close.

Looking across at him, Stephen could see that he was regretting ever having embarked on it. The mood of light-hearted gaiety had been entirely dissipated. The expression in his mother's eyes was abstracted and it was obvious that Zorka was thinking of Xan and wishing her present companion a million miles away.

'Let's dance,' he said to her as the band began to play a quickstep. 'It will be ages before we get the chance again and I want to put a suggestion to you.'

'Yes?' she said queryingly the instant they were out of hearing distance of her parents and her friend.

'There's just a chance, a very faint chance, that I might run across Xan some time in the next few months. If you want me to act as a mailman I'll be happy to oblige.'

Later, when they had returned home and he was in bed, reading, his mother knocked on his door as he had known she would.

She was wearing a heavily flounced and totally impractical rose chiffon nightdress and negligée and her hair was loose, making her look years younger than forty-six.

She sat down on the edge of his bed, saying as if he were still a small child, 'You won't let anything awful happen to you in Yugoslavia, will you, darling? Promise me you will be careful.'

He took her hand comfortingly in his. 'Nothing is going to happen to me. Only the good die young, remember?'

She smiled, but the smile didn't reach her eyes. They were still troubled and anxious. 'It's just that I know you won't be able to keep in regular touch any more and it's bad enough not knowing if Mama and Papa and Katerina and Max are safe, or where Peter and Xan are. I couldn't bear it if anything happened to you.'

'Peter and Xan will be fighting with the Loyalists,' he said reassuringly, wishing he could breach security and tell her he knew categorically that Peter was doing so.

'If there's any chance at all of you getting to Belgrade . . . of making contact with your grandparents or Aunt Katerina, you will do so, won't you?'

'You know I will,' he said gently.

She squeezed his hand tightly and then said, 'There's something else I would like you to do for me if you can. If you find yourself in Sarajevo, will you visit the cemetery for me? Gavrilo and Nedjelko and Trifko are all buried there and I would like you to put some flowers on their graves.'

As she saw the rather startled expression on his face, she said defensively, 'I know your father and Aunt Katerina don't think they were true friends to me, but they're wrong, Stephen. Gavrilo must have been questioned about being seen with me and he obviously denied doing so. In shielding me he must have suffered, for it's common knowledge now that all three of them were tortured during questioning.' Her voice had become unsteady. 'So you do understand, don't you, why I still regard them as friends, especially Gavrilo? And if you can, you will take flowers to their graves for me, won't you?'

He nodded, his throat tight.

She leaned over and kissed him on the forehead. 'Always remember how much I love you and how proud I am of you,' she said huskily. 'Good night, darling. God bless.'

When she had gone he had lain awake for a long time, doubting that any other British officer parachuting into Yugoslavia would be doing so entrusted with such an odd extra-curricular assignment. Then, fiercely looking forward to his reunion with Peter, he turned off his bedside light and tried to sleep.

Chapter Twenty-Two

Stephen had plenty to think about on the flight out to Cairo. For the past two years he had listened assiduously to every BBC news report concerning General Mihailovich, certain that Peter and Xan would be fighting with him. Now he was being asked to verify or disprove the rumour that much of the sabotage being carried out in Yugoslavia was not, in fact, being carried out by Mihailovich and his men but by the communists.

If it were true, it would be a very hard pill to swallow. His mother's loyalty to the monarchy was such that she would view British support of the Partisans as unforgivable treason and, out of respect for her feelings, he had no desire to be partly responsible for the British government deciding on such a course of action.

The problem was, of course, that his mother could never be objective where her homeland was concerned. She had always been totally uncritical of King Alexander's royal dictatorship seeing it not only as understandable, as his father had done, but as being also morally acceptable, which his father had most certainly not done. Where Prince Paul was concerned she had been equally blinkered.

'Paul isn't a leader,' his father had said to him heavily after Alexander's funeral. 'He isn't going to be able to command respect in the way Alexander commanded it. Things aren't going to improve in Yugoslavia. They're going to get worse.'

They had. Though Paul valiantly struggled to bring about a reconciliation between Serbs and Croats, he failed miserably. His capitulation to the Germans, though made out of concern for his country's welfare, finished him utterly in the eyes of his subjects. Even those who had been critical of King Alexander knew that he would never have done such a thing. And the thought of old King Peter capitulating to anyone without a fight was unimaginable.

It was as if all real hopes of unity in Yugoslavia had died with Alexander in Marseilles. Despite striving to do so, Paul had not advanced them and at eighteen and head of a government in exile, King Peter was too young and in no position to do so.

'And even if he were, I doubt he has the ability,' Stephen could remember his father saying to him after he had visited Peter when he first arrived with his ministers in London. 'His head is full of cars and girls, not politics.'

Peter's immaturity certainly didn't bode well for Yugoslavia's future and as the plane droned eastwards Stephen wondered, not for the first time, if his mother's homeland wouldn't be better off as a republic.

His briefing in Cairo did nothing to reassure him. 'It all boils down to one thing,' his superior officer said brutally. 'Who is killing most Germans? If it's Tito and his Partisans then we're going to have to overlook their political persuasion and give them whatever logistical and air support they need. Your task is to evaluate Mihailovich's effectiveness. You'll be going in alone, not as part of a three-man team as was first planned. We don't want your credentials marred by your having companions Mihailovich might not trust. You can operate a wireless transmitter, can't you?'

★   ★   ★

Five days later, accompanied by portable wireless transmitting and receiving sets, batteries and charging engines as well as a dizzying array of equipment ranging from explosives to louse powder, he left Cairo by train for the SOE airfield at Derna, Tunisia.

The train was slow and once again he had plenty of time for thought. This time he didn't reflect on the murderous complexities of Yugoslav politics, but on the very special nature of his relationship with Peter.

Nice, 1919; though he had only been three and a half years old he could remember it clearly. The excitement his mother's excitement had engendered in him, even though he didn't fully understand the reasons for it. His wonderful, miraculous first glimpse of the sea and then, after he had been petted and fussed by his aunt and grandmother, his meeting with Peter.

His mother had told him that his cousin was younger than himself and, at an age when seniority made a signficant difference, he had anticipated that Peter would be smaller than himself and malleable.

He smiled to himself at the recollection. Not only was Peter far from being smaller it was obvious, even then, that he would never be malleable. With his jet-black hair and strong straight mouth, he was as forceful in looks as he was in personality. Within five minutes they were friends. Before the day was out they regarded themselves not as cousins, but as brothers.

At subsequent family reunions he had also made friends with Xan and later all three of them had had to endure Zorka toddling after them wherever they went. Soon, as she became less of a nuisance, they had become a firm foursome but within that foursome, whenever they had split into pairs for games, the split had always been himself and Peter, Zorka and Xan.

He shifted his pack against the train window, leaning

against it more comfortably. As they had grown up the balance had never shifted. In retrospect, he couldn't think why he had been even faintly surprised when Zorka had told him that she and Xan were in love and were going to marry. They had always been a pair and it was impossible to think of them as being anything else.

The train crawled into Derna and an hour later, as night fell, he was bundled with all his baggage aboard a Halifax bomber.

As he waited for take-off he found himself still thinking about his cousins. Where Peter possessed the wide, high cheekboned face of a Slav and was, like his stepfather, well over six feet tall and as broad-chested and dark as a pantomime demon-king, Xan was an inch or so under six feet and slenderly built. People meeting them as a family for the first time always assumed that Peter was Max's natural son and that Xan, with his grey long-lashed eyes and classically handsome bone-structure, was his stepson.

'Xan's mother must have been an extraordinarily beautiful young woman,' he once overheard his grandmother say to his mother. 'In physical appearance he's obviously all his mother's son while Peter is just as clearly all his father's.'

'I never met Ivan Zlarin,' his mother had reminded her, 'though I must admit I've always been curious about him.'

'Major Zlarin was very . . .' his grandmother had begun and then she had become aware that he was listening and annoyingly, instead of finishing her sentence and allowing him to learn a little more about Peter's war-hero father, she had begun to talk of something else.

An RAF sergeant brought him back to the present, fitting his parachute and easing the webbing into position over his shoulders, saying reassuringly as he did so, 'You've got a good night for it, sir. Nice and clear with no forecast of low hanging cloud.'

Stephen grinned, not remotely apprehensive about the jump he was to make. All he was apprehensive about was Peter's reaction when he told him the purpose of his mission. The area into which he was parachuting was south-west Serbia, on the border with Bulgarian-held Macedonia. As the aircraft began to lose height he readjusted his parachute harness. He had always looked forward to reunions with Peter, but had never arrived at one in such a spectacular manner before.

As the hatch was lifted and a blast of icy wind tore at his face and hair he could see small fires on the ground, indicating his landing position.

'Despatching your supplies now!' the flight sergeant shouted to him, rolling containers holding his own supplies and supplies for Peter and his men to the edge of the hatch. 'Be ready to follow them!'

The plane banked into a stiff turn. The containers were ejected. He placed himself in position at the open hatch and then, as the flight sergeant brought his hand down in a sharp cutting action, jumped.

He had always enjoyed the danger and exhilaration of night-time drops and this one was no exception. He was in mountainous country and he was thankful for the fires indicating he was heading for a relatively smooth piece of ground and not a ravine.

He could hear jubilant shouts as the containers hit the earth and he tensed himself against the shock of his own landing. Seconds later he was down, rolling with practised ease over damp, sweet-smelling grass. As he slipped out of his harness he saw that he had landed a little way from the ring of bonfires. He began to gather up his parachute, grinning to himself in elated anticipation as booted feet thundered towards him.

'Stephen! Stephen, my brother!' a familiar voice shouted out in typically Slav manner, racing towards him. 'I was told we were to rendezvous with a Captain Fielding but I hardly dared believe it would be you!'

The piratical figure that flung arms around him, hugging him in a vice-like grip, was barely recognizable. When they had last said goodbye, four years ago, Peter had been an ultra-smart Royal Yugoslav Army officer. Now a fierce black moustache decorated his face and he was wearing a black woolly cap, sheepskin bolero and breeches tucked into what looked to be German field boots. A bandolier crossed his chest, stuffed with ammunition, a revolver and a murderous-looking knife were jammed through his broad leather belt and a rifle was slung over one shoulder.

Stephen returned the bear-like hug and then, as Peter's companions ran welcomingly up to him, he looked around at the jagged black peaks of mountains etched against the night-sky, saying with laughter in his voice, 'It's not the Negresco, is it? Where do we lay our heads, Peter? A cave?'

'You should be so lucky!' Peter's grin nearly split his face. 'Caves are for generals! Come on, let me introduce you to my men and then we'll ferry the supplies you've brought back to our headquarters and down some *slivovitz*. This is Marko and this is Vlada.'

Marko and Vlada hugged him exuberantly saying almost in unison, 'Bravo! Well met, Captain Fielding!'

'And this is Tomas, Tomas is our cook. You need to keep on the right side of him! And Vlatko, my second-in-command, and Milos, my adjutant.'

'Welcome, Captain Fielding!' Vlatko said warmly, thumping him on the back. 'I hope you're only the first of many British officers who are going to come and join us!'

'And this is Peko and this is Joshko.'

Shouts of welcome almost deafened him and he couldn't hear the names of the remaining handful of men. One hand that grasped his, though its grip was as firm as all the rest, was disconcertingly small-boned and later, as he helped seach for the containers and load them on to sturdy peasant carts, he saw that it belonged to a slim-hipped, extremely effeminate looking youth, his Serbian army breeches and German jackboots set off by a RAF flying jacket and a RAF cap worn at a jaunty angle.

As they put out the fires and left the landing-zones he was bemused. A homosexual Slav was a rarity and he certainly hadn't expected to encounter one among Mihailovich's guerilla fighters.

'You will want news of my mother and our grand-parents,' Peter said as they began to descend from what Stephen now saw was a plateau, into a ravine. 'I've had no personal contact with them for eighteen months but I received news from a courier a week ago that they were all alive and still in Belgrade, though living under terrible conditions.'

They were both silent for a few moments, thinking of their grandparents, knowing that neither of them had the physical strength necessary for such an ordeal. Alexis was seventy-six and troubled with rheumatism and though Zita was younger, she had never been robust since her winter trek across the Albanian mountains.

'And Max and Xan?' Stephen asked, hopeful that where they were concerned the news would be more cheerful. 'Are they both in the resistance as well?'

'It could be said that Xan is,' Peter said dryly. The track they were following was now running along the banks of a rushing stream and he raised his voice to be heard above it. 'As for Max, he was one of the generals who instigated the *coup d'état* against Paul,' he continued, not elaborating further on Xan's whereabouts. 'Even though he and Paul were not close, he was deeply distressed at having to take such action. He had no choice though, not if Yugoslavia was to retain a remnant of honour, even my mother realized that.'

'And where is he now?' Stephen asked as Peko and Joshko hauled one of the peasant carts past them.

Peter grinned, his teeth flashing white in the darkness. He both loved and respected the bear of a man who was his stepfather and was proud that even though Max was now in his mid-fifties he was still a soldier and still a force to be reckoned with.

'Last I heard of him he was commanding Bosnian resistance forces. Wherever he is, he'll be thrashing the Germans and enjoying himself hugely.'

Ahead of them in the moonlight was the indistinct shape of a farmhouse. 'Home,' Peter said with satisfaction. 'I hope to God when we open the supplies we find some weapons in good working order.'

Looking at the men around him Stephen didn't think weapons were in any short supply. Apart from knives and revolvers jammed through belts, every shoulder boasted a rifle and there were captured enemy Schmeissers and sten guns in plenty.

The men trundled the handcarts up to the farm and immediately began unloading them. Peter led the way inside, having to bend his head as he did so to clear the doorway.

'Bring out the *slivovitz*, Olga,' he said to an unseen girl, throwing his rifle down on to the nearest chair and then, turning again to Stephen he said, 'Well, what do you think of my headquarters? Cosy, aren't they?'

The low-ceilinged room was lit by an oil lamp and there was a wood-burning fire in the grate over which a huge cooking pot was hung. The only furnishings were a large table and a miscellaneous assortment of wooden chairs and stools and a ladder leading up to the open door of a loft in which Stephen could glimpse pallets piled with straw and covered by rough blankets.

'The Negresco is a slum in comparison,' he said with a grin, looking around for Olga and the *slivovitz*.

There was no farmer's wife or daughter to be seen. Instead, the slim figure that had so attracted his attention earlier, placed a bottle and glass on the table.

As he saw the expression on Stephen's face, Peter chuckled. 'Don't worry. I'm not commanding a troop of Amazons. Everyone else is male.'

There was no flicker of amusement on the girl's face. She merely said, 'I'll help unload the supplies now, Major,' and with the peaked RAF cap emphasizing her delicate bone-structure, left the room.

'There are quite a few girls among General Mihailovich's forces,' Peter said, reaching out for the *slivovitz*. 'They fight like demons and that's what they are; fighters not camp followers.' He poured the fiery home-brewed alcohol into the glass they were to share, saying with another chuckle, 'Don't try your luck there, Stephen. Not unless you want to find yourself facing the wrong end of a sten gun!'

Later, as they all sat around the huge table and the contents of the steaming cooking pot had been ladled into bowls, Stephen found himself looking constantly in Olga's direction. She was very young, scarcely out of her teens, and it seemed incredible to him that she could live in such close intimacy with hardened soldiers and not be plagued by unwelcome sexual overtures. That she did so, however, was immediately obvious from the men's attitude towards her. There was nothing sexual in it, nothing patronizing. She was, like them, a soldier of the resistance.

Toasts were beginning to be drunk and with great difficulty he dragged his eyes away from her, drinking to the success of the Allied cause; to young King Peter's health; to General Mihailovich's health; even to the memory of his and Peter's mutual great-great grandfather, the legendary Karageorge.

Later still, as the evening grew progressively noisier, Peter said to him, 'Let's go outside. I want to know why you're here. I don't believe for one moment it's simply to act as a straightforward liaison officer.'

Rather reluctantly Stephen rose to his feet and followed him from the room. He wasn't looking forward to explaining why he had been sent to Yugoslavia. Peter and his men had been fighting the Germans for nearly two years under the harshest possible conditions. The news that the Allies were considering switching support from them to their communist enemies would be far from welcome.

Once outside the single-storey farmhouse Peter walked a little distance to where the land dipped steeply. Sitting down on the lip of the hill he took a cigarette from his breast pocket and said, 'Well? Spill the beans as you and Uncle Julian would say.'

Stephen sat beside him. The night sky had lightened and on the horizon there was a faint rim of gold, presaging dawn. 'It isn't good,' he said bluntly. 'Rumours have reached London that Loyalist resistance to the enemy is not all it's been made out to be and that the Partisans are being far more effective. My mission is to meet with General Mihailovich and to verify whether the rumours are true or false.'

'Christ!' Peter ran a hand through his sleek-dark hair.

Stephen felt a sickening lurch in the pit of his stomach. He had anticipated a reaction of stunned incredulity and there had been none in Peter's savagely utterly blasphemy.

'Christ!' Peter said again, this time with even more ferocity. 'Bloody, bloody *Christ*!'

Stephen waited. Down in the valley an early rising cock crowed lustily.

Peter drew heavily on his cigarette and at last said, 'The

hell of it is, there's foundation for such rumours, Stephen. Not because we aren't eager to fight, but because of the consequences when we do.'

Stephen remained silent. On the horizon the rim of gold had become an apricot haze.

'In the early days, in late 1941 and early 1942, we inflicted huge damage on the Germans. Unable to retaliate successfully against us, they began retaliating on the civilian population.' He paused for a moment and then continued harshly, 'I was with Mihailovich when he booted the Germans out of a small town called Kragujevac. It was recaptured. The instant the Germans were again in possession they shot five thousand men, women and children in reprisal. It wasn't an isolated incident. In October 1941 Hitler ordered that a hundred Yugoslav civilians be executed for every German killed by resistance forces, and that fifty Yugoslavs die for every German wounded. What would British troops do if they knew that for every German killed a hundred British civilians, many of them women and children, would be slaughtered?'

Stephen didn't look at him or answer. He was staring down at the grass between his feet, thinking again of his aunt and grandparents in German-occupied Belgrade.

'What General Mihailovich did was to revise his strategy,' Peter continued. 'Instead of engaging in acts of resistance that carried too high a price he decided we should build up our strength numerically and concentrate on preparing for the day when the entire country, supported by an Allied landing, rises up against the Germans. Until then, although we still carry out acts of sabotage, we do so mainly to disrupt German transport systems.'

'And the Partisans?' Stephen asked, already knowing the answer.

'The Partisans don't have our scruples,' Peter said

481

bitterly. 'To them, war is war and civilians have to take the consequences.'

Stephen stared down into the distant valley. In the rosy glow of morning it was spectacularly beautiful. The slopes were thick with oak and beech trees and every now and then there was a glimpse of the stream they had followed the previous evening.

He knew what opinion would be taken in London. It would be the same opinion the Partisans held. 'I'm afraid London is going to agree with them,' he said heavily. 'The argument is going to be that a resistance force has to engage the enemy, no matter what the cost.'

Peter ground his cigarette into ashes and rose to his feet. 'That's Xan's viewpoint too,' he said tersely. 'He's been fighting with the Partisans ever since Mihailovich issued his directive that sabotage must be carried out without Germans being killed in the process.' He dug his hands deep into his breeches pockets. 'It's hard to blame him. Sitting on a mountain, doing nothing more than blow up an occasional bridge or making a raid on an armaments depot is a hard test of endurance. Like many others who have joined the Partisans he hasn't turned communist. He just can't stand the relative inactivity into which we've been plunged.'

Sounds of movement were now coming from the farmhouse and Stephen also rose to his feet. 'I need to speak with Mihailovich as soon as possible,' he said unhappily. 'However valid his reason for not engaging with the enemy he has to know what the consequences will be if he continues with it.'

Peter turned and began to walk back to the farmhouse. 'It will take us a good five days to reach him. I need to take one of the horses down into the village to be reshod. It will only take an hour or so. We'll have breakfast, ride down to the village and then be on our way.'

Breakfast was blackbread and *slivovitz*. It was a drink Stephen's grandfather had introduced him to at an early age but Belgrade *slivovitz* wasn't as raw as home-brewed mountain *slivovitz* and Alexis had certainly never encouraged him to drink it at breakfast. With his eyes watering and his throat burning he downed it in a traditional single swallow, longing for a civilizing cup of English tea.

In daylight Peter's men looked even more fearsome than they had the previous night on the dark mountainside. Even though it was still only early morning they were armed to the teeth, knives jammed through belts and thrust down boots, handguns hanging nonchalantly at their hips. All of them were heavily moustached, the majority of them having beards as well. Coherent uniforms were non-existent. Royal Yugoslav army jackets topped German breeches. British battledress was enlivened by Bulgarian boots. Sleeveless sheepskin jackets proliferated.

Across the breakfast table a noisy argument began as to who was going to accompany Peter and himself down into the village.

Peter grinned at him. 'Don't be flattered, Stephen. You aren't the attraction. The village girls are.'

It was settled that Marko, Vlada and Milos would ride with them.

'The villagers always inundate us with gifts of food,' Peter said to Stephen as they saddled up. 'It would be a shame not to be able to transport back everything offered.'

Stephen swung himself on to the back of the fit-looking horse Peter had allocated to him and as the men around him urged their mounts into movement he did likewise.

At the first bend in the track some instinct made him rein in and look behind him. Olga was sitting on a bench outside the farmhouse door, cleaning her rifle. She wasn't wearing her RAF cap and in the sunlight her hair, fastened

483

in a loose knot in the nape of her neck, was so fair as to be almost blonde.

Sensing his gaze she raised her head and their eyes met. Impulsively he waved goodbye. There was no response. She merely returned her attention to the rifle lying across her lap and, curiously deflated, he turned away, urging his horse down the dust-blown track.

The village was hardly deserving of the name. It consisted of a single street of white-washed, red-roofed houses, a church and a communal water pump.

Every person they passed called out a greeting and by the time they reached the forge Stephen could see why Peter had thought it sense that Marko, Vlada and Milos accompany them.

Black-garbed village women thrust baskets of fruit and vegetables into their grateful hands. There were presents of butter and eggs, even presents of home-brewed *slivovitz*.

The warm-hearted generosity put Stephen into such good spirits that he felt almost in a holiday mood as he followed Peter into the forge. It was a mood swiftly dispelled.

'A Bulgarian patrol has been reported heading in this direction,' the blacksmith said succinctly. 'My boy set off to tell you a half hour ago and returned when he saw you on your way here. He's a lazy little bastard. Won't exert himself if there's no need.'

Marko, Vlada and Milos turned immediately on their heels.

'Where were they coming from?' Peter demanded. 'The south-east?'

The blacksmith nodded.

'I'll collect the horse later,' Peter said tersely. 'Come on, Stephen. We need to warn the others.'

Marko, Vlada and Milos were already re-mounting their horses, much to the disappointment of the village girls clustering hopefully around the village pump.

Peter strode across to his own horse, saying to Stephen, 'It may only be a routine patrol, in which case all we have to do is keep our heads down. On the other hand it could be a clean-up operation. If it is, and they're looking for us specifically, we're going to have to give them the slip and find another base.' He swung up into his saddle. 'Either way, our jaunt to Mihailovich is going to be a little delayed.'

They heard the distant, furious exchange of gunfire even before they were out of the village street.

'*The Bulgars!*' Vlada shouted frantically. '*They've by-passed the village! They're attacking the farm!*'

Like men demented they urged their horses onward at breakneck speed.

Stephen could feel perspiration trickling down the back of his neck. How many men had been at the farmhouse? Eight? Nine? And how many men would be in the Bulgar patrol? He thought of Olga, sitting in the sunshine, cleaning her rifle. To anyone approaching the farm she would have made a completely unprotected target.

'*Faster, God damn you!*' he swore at his lathering horse. '*Faster!*'

As they neared the farm it became obvious that the regular volleys of gunfire were now some distance from it, higher on the mountainside.

'*They must be chasing them off!*' Peter shouted across to Stephen.

Stephen nodded, hoping to God that Peter was right. He wondered from which direction the Bulgars had attacked the farm. If they had attacked from the rear there was a chance that Olga had had plenty of warning. If they

485

hadn't . . . Fear gripped him. She hadn't exchanged a single civil word with him but he knew in utter certainty that if she were to die it would affect the entire course of his life.

The steep track levelled off just before the farm and as they careened around the last bend a blood-stained figure ran towards them.

'*Don't rein in!*' Peko shouted to them as from further up the track another outburst of rifle fire cracked the air. '*Vlatko has got them pinned down in the wood but he needs all the help he can get!*'

As they galloped headlong past him he shouted after them, '*Joshko is dead! Tomas and Olga are wounded!*'

There was nothing Stephen could do. It was impossible to swerve around and return to the farm. Praying to God she hadn't been too badly wounded he urged his horse up the track towards the wood.

On its perimeter Peter signalled to them to rein in.

'Spread out and keep down!' he instructed tersely, springing from his saddle. 'And for Christ's sake don't shoot any of our own!'

At a low run they entered the wood, giving Vlatko and the others the back-up they so desperately needed. The battle was short and sharp and, from the Bulgarians' point of view, ugly. When the last rifle-shot cracked the air only one Chetnik, Lieutenant Vlatko, had been injured. All the Bulgarians were dead.

Peter wiped the sweat from his face. 'Strip the bodies of weapons and ammunition,' he said to Milos and Vlada and then, to Stephen, 'did Peko say that Joshko was dead?'

'Yes, and that Tomas and Olga were wounded.'

'Then get back there. See what you can do for them.'

Even before Peter had finished speaking Stephen had turned on his heel and broken into a sprint. Cairo had sent medical supplies but they hadn't been opened yet and he had no idea what was in them. He hoped to God there was some morphine, and he hoped even more fervently that it wouldn't be needed.

He didn't waste time searching for his horse. Running and leaping he crashed down the mountainside, entering the farm from the rear. She was slumped against one of the inner doors, blood pouring from her shoulder. His first reaction was one of vast relief that it wasn't an abdominal wound and then he saw the colour of her face.

Swiftly he crossed the room towards her, yanking his shirt over his head and folding it into a pad to staunch the bleeding.

'Can you hold it in place?' he asked, pressing it against her shoulder.

She nodded. 'You need to attend to Tomas first,' she said, white-lipped. 'He's more seriously injured than I am.'

There were faint groans from outside the front doorway and reluctantly he turned away from her, grabbing one of the medical packs, ripping his way into it.

Later, when he had done everything he could for Tomas and when he had removed the bullet from Olga's shoulder and was cleaning the wound, he said to Peter, 'What happens now? Are you going to be able to stay here?'

'No. We'll have to leave. We have a back-up base deeper in the mountains. I'm afraid the injured are going to find it a rough journey.'

Stephen looked down at Olga. Her face was ashen, the skin taut across her cheekbones.

'Perhaps, for Olga, the village would be a better bet,' he suggested, feeling sick at the thought of her having to climb over treacherous terrain. 'As a woman, her presence can easily be explained away. She can pass as someone's

487

visiting sister or cousin without enemy suspicions being aroused.'

Peter nodded, seeing the sense of the suggestion. It was Olga who rejected it.

'No,' she said, her speech slightly slurred by the morphine Stephen had given her. 'I'm not as badly hurt as Tomas and Vlatko. If they can make it up to the cave, so can I.'

'Tomas and Vlatko have no choice,' Stephen said gently. 'Their presence in the village would immediately excite attention. Yours won't.'

She shook her head and the knot at the nape of her neck came loose. 'No,' she said again, her near-blonde hair slithering down past her shoulders. 'You're an Englishman. You don't understand how tough Slav women are.'

Stephen thought of his grandmother and aunt toiling over the icy wastes of the Albanian mountains. 'I'm an Englishman who happens to be half-Slav,' he said dryly, 'and I'm well aware of how tough Slav women are.'

Despite the horrors they had just endured Peter chuckled. 'I take it you're thinking of our mutual grandmother?' he said, vastly amused.

Stephen merely grinned in answer and Olga looked from him to Stephen and then back again.

'Oh,' she said dazedly, understanding dawning. 'Are you cousins? No-one told me,' and then, after a little pause, 'It doesn't make any difference though. I'm not going down to the village!'

Later in the day, as a grave was being dug for Joshko, Stephen established wireless contact with Cairo. When he had laboriously tapped out his message he stood by to receive an incoming signal. When it finally came and when he had decoded it, he stared down at it for a long, long time. Then, almost as ashen-faced as Olga had been, he went in search of Peter.

He found him on the lip of the hill, looking out across the valley, deep in thought. The sun was beginning to set and the sky was flushed with warm, amber light.

'This has just come through from Cairo,' he said to him starkly, handing him the decoded message. 'It looks as if we won't be jaunting off to see Mihailovich after all.'

Their eyes met and then, with deep reluctance, Peter looked down at the flimsy piece of paper. The message was brief and to the point. '*It has been decided to discontinue all support of Mihailovich and his forces. You are to make your way south and join with Partisans. Further instructions will follow.*'

He remained silent for a long time and then he said bitterly, 'That's it, then. The British have deserted us and we're on our own.'

Stephen said only, 'When do you plan moving the wounded up to the cave?'

'Tonight. And you? When are you going to leave for the south?'

'Tonight.'

Over the distant mountain tops the amber sky was turning a blood red.

'Then it's goodbye,' Peter said, his deep voice oddly brittle. 'Perhaps when you're with the Partisans you'll meet up with Xan. Whether you do or not, we'll all meet up again when this bloody war is over. Alexis and Zita. Xan and Zorka. Max and your father. Your mother and mine. You and me.'

'You've missed someone out,' Stephen said, wanting Peter to watch over her like a hawk.

Peter's black eyebrows flew high. 'Who? Aunt Vitza?'

'No,' Stephen said with prophetic certainty. 'Olga.'

Chapter Twenty-Three

He left with two horses, the stallion Peter had allocated to him when they had ridden down to the village and a pack horse for his supplies and bulky radio equipment. The nearest Partisan activity was to the north-west, in Montenegro, and with a map heavily marked for him by Peter and in the knowledge that he would, no doubt, be receiving further and more detailed instructions from Cairo, he set off alone into the darkness.

As a boy he had often accompanied his Uncle Max and Xan and Peter on camping holidays in the Yugoslav mountains and the rough terrain held no terrors for him. Among his supplies were American K-rations which needed only boiling water to be reconstituted into meals and he relied on them heavily, avoiding all contact with German-riddled towns and villages.

By the end of the first week radio signals from Cairo had supplied him with precise map references for where he was to make and had also added the laconic warning that German activity in the area was heavy.

As he continued to ride westwards in lonely isolation he pondered long and hard on the politics of the situation in which he was embroiled. By switching support from General Mihailovich to the communists, the British government was effectively ensuring that the communists would be in a strong enough position, when the war was over, to take over control of the country. The consequences of such a take-over would be the end of Karageorgevich rule in Yugoslavia and the establishing of a socialist republic.

He was riding uphill through a thick forest and he ducked low on his horse to avoid a rain-sodden, overhanging branch. If King Peter was exiled permanently from Yugoslavia his mother would be heart-broken. His mother, however, was no longer a citizen of Yugoslavia. Unlike his grandparents, aunt, uncle and cousins, she hadn't had to endure a quarter of a century of Croat and Serb hatred and strife.

Peter had told him that the deciding factor for Xan, when Xan had been making his decision as to whether or not to join forces with the Partisans, had been the fact that in Partisan ranks Croats and Serbs were fighting together against a common enemy. If, under communist rule, that sense of unity could be maintained, surely the price paid would be worth it?

He wondered what his grandfather would think. As a Vassilovich, Alexis had never been starry-eyed about Karageorgevich rule. 'Old King Peter and King Alexander were both fine men and scrupulously conscientious kings,' he had told him at their last family reunion, 'but they didn't come from a long line of such kings. Earlier Karageorgevichs were so hotheaded as to be menally unstable and though young King Peter isn't unstable, he certainly doesn't possess the same strength of character as his father or grandfather.'

The way had become so steep that he slid from the saddle to make the going easier on his horse. As he trudged upwards between birch and pine trees he wondered how long it would be before he was able to enter Belgrade and again enjoy a lively, challenging discussion with his grandfather.

That night, crouching beside his camp fire, he pored over his much-creased map. He was moving further and further away from Belgrade, not nearer to it, but he was moving marginally closer to Sarajevo. It lay some fifty miles to the north-east and it wasn't beyond the realms of possibility that some time in the near future he would be able to enter it and fulfil the promise he had made to his mother.

He folded the map and put it away. Sarajevo could wait. A more immediate priority was making contact with the Partisans. According to radio signals from Cairo he was within days, perhaps even hours, of doing so. He took a billy-can of boiling water off the fire and emptied a packet of dried soup from his K-rations into it. He hoped that once he was with the Partisans, not only would his diet become a little more interesting, but also that he would see some action against the enemy.

When he settled into his sleeping bag he lay awake for a long time, thinking of the battles that were to come; of his parents and sister in London; his family in Belgrade; and last but no means least, of Olga.

He was woken by a brutal kick to his legs and a savage enquiry as to his identity. The enquiry was mercifully in Serbo-Croat and not German or Bulgarian but he was appalled at not having woken instinctively minutes earlier. Three men were standing over him, their rifles pointed at his chest. They were dressed in a mixture of civilian and captured enemy clothing, the only item common to all of them being grey side caps embossed with a red star.

'I'm a British officer,' he said succinctly, scrambling to his feet as the rifles were lowered. He repeated the phrase in English to make his point and then, reverting to Serbo-Croat he asked, 'Are you Partisans?'

There were wide grins and the rifles were slung back over their shoulders.

'We are,' one of them said. 'And are you the British liaison officer we have been told to expect?'

'Most likely,' Stephen said with an answering grin, grateful for Cairo's efficiency.

'We've been told that when you arrive you will arrange with your headquarters that supplies are sent to us,' the self-appointed spokesman of the group said as his companions began to peer beneath the tarpaulin covering the transmission and receiving sets. 'Our commanding officer, Major Kechko, has been anxious for your safety. My name is Lieutenant Stefanovich. I am a Croat. My companions' names are Yelich and Velebit. They are Serbs.'

'I'm Captain Fielding,' Stephen said, shaking his hand. 'How near are we to your headquarters, Lieutenant?'

'Four miles, five,' Lieutenant Stefanovich said with a shrug of his shoulders and then, reading Stephen's mind, 'We have time for coffee. Do you have coffee?'

'I have ersatz coffee.'

Lieutenant Stefanovich looked puzzled.

'It's a substitute for coffee. It's not very good but it's better than nothing.'

Lieutenant Stefanovich grinned. 'Then we'll have ersatz, Captain Fielding. It will be a luxury.'

The Partisans were all on foot and later, walking alongside them, his horse and pack-horse following on a leading-rein, he asked curiously, 'Are you seeing much fighting? I've hardly been able to move these last few days for enemy patrols.'

'The Germans are trying to encircle the area,' Lieutenant Stefanovich said grimly. 'It is Major Kechko's intention, now that you have joined us, to make a break northwards over Mount Durmitor and into Bosnia. The main body of our army are already on the mountain. We will meet up with it and, as soon as conditions allow, the Allies will send us weapons and arms.'

Stephen didn't demur. His orders from Cairo were to liaise fully with the Partisans and to arrange landing-grounds where supplies could be dropped to them.

'You will not need to speak in Serbo-Croat to Major Kechko,' Lieutenant Stefanovich said with undisguised pride. 'Many years ago Major Kechko lived in London and he speaks English fluently. He is looking forward to meeting you very much, Captain Fielding.'

Stephen was intrigued. His parents had always kept open house for Yugoslavs visiting London and though the name Kechko meant nothing to him it wasn't beyond the realms of possibility that the major had once been a guest at his parents' Chelsea home.

Once out of the forest they had magnificent views of a spectacular mountain range. The peaks rose like dragon's teeth their barren flanks, silver in the morning sunshine, gashed by cruel-looking ravines.

'The mountain in the middle is Mount Durmitor,' the young man who had been introduced to him as Yelich, said a little shyly. 'Mount Durmitor is one of Yugoslavia's highest mountains.'

'It's also where Tito and the main body of our army are at the present moment,' Lieutenant Stefanovich said informatively, adding with dry humour, 'I hope you have a good head for heights, Captain Fielding!'

Their way continued over level open ground and then dipped suddenly into a copse of trees. Hidden from aerial view by the foliage a handful of tents surrounded a stone-built shepherd's bothy. At first glance Stephen estimated that there were twenty or so men clustered either in or around the tents, some cleaning equipment, others smoking and talking. Certainly there were more men in the camp than there had been at Peter's headquarters.

'The British officer has arrived!' Lieutenant Stefanovich called out a little unnecessarily as they dropped down the steep incline towards the first of the tents.

Rifles and rags were hastily put down, conversations brought to an abrupt end. As the men began to converge on him, demanding to know if he could speak Serbo-Croat, asking where he had come from, when supplies would be arriving, the door of the bothy flew open and an authoritative, athletic figure strode towards them.

'So! You have arrived, Englishman!' Nikita Kechko said in heavily accented English. 'What took you so long?'

Even though his orders were now to liaise fully with the Partisans Stephen had no intention of revealing any Loyalist positions, especially Peter's, and he said merely, 'I ran across a lot of German patrols, Major. They slowed my progress considerably.'

Nicky stood, his hands on his hips, taking his measure of Stephen with dark, fiery eyes.

Unlike his men, he wasn't wearing a side-cap and Stephen could well understand why. His night-black hair was such a tangle of curls that it was hard to imagine a cap remaining in position. The thin line of an old scar ran through his left eyebrow and though he was in his early forties, perhaps even a little older, he was obviously extremely fit.

Stephen's second impression was one that, under other circumstances, would have made him chuckle. With his mass of unruly dark curls and equally dark smouldering eyes, Major Kechko bore a startling resemblance to Natalie.

'Captain Stephen Fielding,' he said, proffering his hand, 'and just for your information, Major, I speak fluent Serbo-Croat.'

If he had said his name was Adolf Hitler and that he

495

spoke fluent Japanese he couldn't have met with a more stunned reaction.

'Fielding?' Nicky said at last, staring at him as if at a ghost. 'Fielding? Is that a common English name, Captain?'

'Fairly common,' Stephen said, slightly bemused.

'How come you speak fluent Serbo-Croat, Captain Fielding?'

It was a reasonable enough question and Stephen said obligingly, 'It is my mother's language. She is Serbian.'

The skin had become very tight across Nicky's cheekbones. 'Do you have a younger brother, Captain Fielding?' he asked tautly.

'No, but I have a sister. Do you know my family, Major Kechko? I understand you lived for a time in London and . . .'

'No,' Nicky lied abruptly. 'No, I do not know your family, Captain Fielding. Tell me, is your sister younger than you?'

'Zorka is four years my junior,' Stephen said, bemusement turning to curiosity. 'Why do you ask, Major Kechko?'

Making a lightning calculation that left him with only one conclusion Nicky said with a wide grin. 'I am interested. I am interested in the family details of all my men.' He chuckled, vastly amused at fate's perversity and draping his arm around Stephen's shoulders in a typical gesture of male Slav friendliness, he said, 'Let's eat, Captain Fielding. And while we eat you can tell me what kind of help the Partisans can now expect from the Allies.'

He led the way towards a scattering of rough-hewn tree stumps and fallen branches, the men who had been clustering around them following hard on their heels. From the bothy a couple of young boys emerged, carrying a heavy steaming cooking-pot and tin-plates.

'Zorka is a strange name for an English girl,' Nicky said

musingly as they sat down, wanting to know more about the girl who was his daughter. 'It is a very Slav name. Is your sister perhaps very Slav, Captain Fielding? Is she more Slav than English?'

Amused by Kechko's continuing interest in his family Stephen took the plate proffered him, saying truthfully, 'My sister is very Slav in both looks and temperament.' He remembered that Xan was with the Partisans and that Kechko might know him and added, 'So much so that she's engaged to a Yugoslav.'

Nicky's grin almost split his face. 'A Yugoslav? Your sister is engaged to a Yugoslav?'

Stephen nodded, amused by the major's almost childish delight, knowing he was going to increase it even further. 'His name is Xan Karageorgevich,' he said, as a helping of beans was spooned on to his plate. 'You may know him. He's a Partisan.'

'But of course I know Major Karageorgevich!' Nicky's elation knew no bounds. 'He is one of Tito's most trusted aides and is with him now on Mount Durmitor.'

There was uproar from the men clustering around him.

'Karageorgevich!' Lieutenant Stefanovich shouted for the benefit of those who had perhaps not heard. 'The British officer's sister is engaged to Major Karageorgevich!'

Stephen was receiving so many slaps on his back that he could barely keep his plate on his knees. 'Major Karageorgevich is my distant cousin,' he said, and this time the uproar was total.

From all sides he was told that he wasn't just a fellow officer, that he wasn't even merely a comrade and friend, but that he was a fellow South Slav. A Partisan. A blood brother.

'Soon you will meet up with your cousin,' Nicky promised, utterly enthralled at the prospect of his unknown daughter marrying a man who was one of Tito's most trusted aides. 'As soon as we have eaten we will strike camp and set off towards Mount Durmitor.'

Five days later they still weren't at Durmitor and Stephen was beginning to suspect they never would be. German patrols were as thick on the ground as daisies in an English field. Twice, sometimes three times a day, enemy planes flew overhead necessitating a mad scramble for the nearest ravine or gully. When, under cover of darkness, they finally climbed into Durmitor's rocky foothills they did so knowing that the Germans were hard on their heels.

It soon became obvious to Stephen that the mountain's night-black slopes were alive with men, all of them snaking upwards in long thin columns. When his own party made contact with a party of stragglers and wounded he realized that there were entire battalions of Partisans on the mountain and that they were all trying to cross its perilous ridges before dawn exposed them to German air attack.

It began to rain and the ground became muddy and treacherous underfoot. Short, inadequate stops for rest were made. As the way became steeper Stephen grew increasingly anxious for the safety of his horse and pack-horse and, as it became apparent that Yelich had the eyes of a cat and the sure footing of a mountain-goat, he handed the wireless-laden pack-horse into his care.

Just before dawn a complex of deep caves were reached and exhausted men, horses and mules stumbled gratefully into them.

'Can you contact Cairo on your transmitter?' Nicky asked him. 'Can you tell them that Tito and nearly all his men are trapped on the Durmitor ridge? Perhaps Cairo could send planes to keep the Germans at bay?'

Stephen shook his head. 'It's impossible to make contact from a cave. Even if I could, Cairo doesn't possess enough bombers to come to our aid. Sorry, Major Kechko.'

'Nicky,' Nicky said, slumping down on to the dry but freezing cave floor. 'Call me Nicky and I will call you Stephen. Have you photographs of your family, Stephen? Have you a photograph of your mother and your sister?'

With raw, rain-lashed fingers Stephen undid his greatcoat and the jacket beneath it. Then he reached into his inner pocket for his wallet. From outside the cave came the sound of enemy planes approaching.

'This photograph is of my mother,' he said, withdrawing a small black and white photograph that had been taken on the beach in front of the Negresco and handing it to Nicky. 'This one is of my mother with Zorka. It was taken in the summer of 1939, just before the beginning of the war. And this one is of my father.'

As the planes dropped their small ten and twenty kilogram bombs the cave walls shuddered and an avalanche of shale reigned down on them. Nicky was oblivious. Ignoring the photograph of Julian he stared down at Natalie's face, and at the face of his daughter.

His daughter was very beautiful; dark-haired and dark-eyed with a wide, generous, smiling mouth. He wondered how anyone could ever believe that the fair-haired Julian Fielding had fathered her. He wondered, also, what it would have been like to have reared her; to have had her love and respect. He smiled wryly. That he could ever have done so was a crazy notion. He had never stayed with one woman, or in one place, long enough to call anywhere home. His daughter was much better off believing the caring and respectable Julian Fielding to be her father than she would have been in a strife-torn Croatia, trailing in his own wake.

His smile deepened as he looked down at the photograph of Natalie. It had been taken on a breezy day on the Promenade des Anglais. She was wearing a long, narrow, white summer dress and there was the gleam of what looked to be gold at her ears and wrist. She was smiling radiantly at whoever was taking the photograph, pushing her wind-blown hair away from her face, her vibrancy and vitality almost tangible.

His throat tightened. Until a short time ago he had not thought of her in years. Now, looking down at the photograph, he was again enraptured by the sheer voluptuousness of her smile. She had been the most excitingly unpredictable, intensely passionate woman he had ever known and he marvelled at how he had so nearly forgotten her.

He thought back to their last meeting. For months prior to it he had anticipated that when he returned to his homeland, she would return with him. Then her husband had returned from Salonika; there had been the family reunion in Nice; and there had been her incredible announcement that she could never return to Belgrade, that King Alexander would not allow her to do so. For a few brief moments he pondered on how different his life might have been if that veto had never existed and then, reluctantly, he handed the photographs back to Stephen.

'You are a lucky man,' he said to him as Stephen put the photographs back in his wallet. 'Your mother and your sister are both very beautiful. Are they happy, too?'

'My mother's parents and sister are in Belgrade and they're not happy about that situation,' Stephen said dryly. 'But the war apart? Yes, they're happy. Both of them have happy natures and both possess the precious gift of making those around them happy as well.'

Nicky nodded, understanding very well the quality about Natalie that Stephen was describing, pleased that their daughter had inherited it. Another thought occurred to him, one that filled him with delighted speculation. 'Zorka was the name of a Montenegrin princess,' he said, in case Stephen was not aware of the fact. 'Her father was called Nikita, like me.' Then, grinning to himself, he settled himself comfortably against the cave wall and within minutes was asleep.

The next day, shielded from air attack by dense cloud and mist the arduous march continued. Stephen thought of his aunt and grandmother making a similar trek across the Albanian mountains with a young baby to care for and marvelled again at their stamina and endurance.

'Once we've crossed the heights we have to drop down to the Piva gorge and cross the river,' Nicky said to him as dusk began to fall. 'The Germans will be trying to get there first to destroy the bridge. If they do, we stand no chance. We'll simply be rats caught in a God-Almighty trap.'

On the second day on the mountain Stephen managed to make brief radio contact with Cairo. He was told he wasn't the only British officer on Durmitor. A six-man mission had been parachuted in four days earlier and had established immediate contact with Tito.

'They must be in the forward columns,' Nicky said to him as they trudged upwards through knee high, melting snow. 'Have you any more chocolate left in your rations? I feel hungry enough to eat one of the horses.'

They crossed the Piva on a swaying suspension bridge and then watched, appalled, as Stuka dive-bombers decimated it, trapping columns of wounded on the other side. Moving by day was now impossible. Only at night could they make any progress. In front of them, the forward columns were engaged in heavy fighting, clearing a route for those coming behind. Stephen wondered if Xan was with them. If Xan was still alive.

As German attacks became even more ferocious a message was passed down through the columns to all units. No more central orders would be issued. From now on tactical decisions would be made by the commanders of each unit. Only in small, mobile groups was it going to be possible for any of them to survive.

'I hate mountains,' Lieutenant Stefanovich said savagely as they rested in one of the innumerable caves. 'I come from the Vojvodina. In the Vojvodina we have meadows and woodland but we have no mountains, thank God. Never again, as long as I live, do I want to see another mountain!'

There was a flurry of stones as a figure Stephen assumed to be a courier slid down the steep approach and entered the cave.

'Major Karageorgevich!' Lieutenant Stefanovich said in stunned wonder, recognizing him first.

In the cramped confine of the cave Major Kechko's men scrambled hastily to their feet.

'I understand you have a British liaison officer in your unit,' Xan said to Nicky and then, before Nicky could reply, he saw Stephen standing at the rear of the cave, grinning at him.

'Stephen! *Stephen!*' he exploded striding towards him, hugging him tight. 'Why the devil didn't you try and get a message through to me? How long have you been with Kechko? Have you any letters for me from Zorka?'

'I'd have got a message through to you if I could,' Stephen said, noting with amusement that Xan's grey uniform wasn't the usual hotch-potch of peasant and captured enemy clothing and that the jacket was enviably well-cut, 'but I've barely been able to establish contact

502

with Cairo and I knew they would do the job for me. As for how long I've been with Major Kechko, it feels like a lifetime but is probably only a week.'

'And a letter from Zorka?' Xan asked urgently, his handsome face taut with tension. 'Have you got a letter for me?'

'I might have,' Stephen said, his grin deepening. 'Is there anywhere we can talk in private on this God-damned mountain without being cut to pieces by German bombs or guns?'

'We can talk in English,' Xan said and then, interpreting correctly the slight lift of Stephen's eyebrows he added, 'on the other hand we can risk life and limb and go outside for a few minutes.'

Once outside Stephen said, 'Major Kechko lived in London some years ago. His English is pretty good.'

'And you want to ask me about Peter?'

'I don't need to ask you. I was with him until the message came through that it had been decided to discontinue all support of Mihailovich and his forces. According to Major Kechko, you're one of Tito's right-hand men. What's going to happen to the Loyalists now? Is Tito going to wage war on the Loyalists as well as the Germans?'

The ledge outside the cave was narrow and beyond it the ground fell steeply away, sweeping down to a tributary of the Piva. On the far side of the valley was yet another mountain and Stephen knew that if he looked through his field-glasses he would see German troops massing on its slopes.

Xan said heavily, 'The brutal answer is yes. A large proportion of Loyalist Chetniks have begun collaborating with the enemy and taking part in German actions against us. When that occurs the Partisans have no option but to fight back.'

'And what about Loyalist Chetniks who would sooner kill themselves than collaborate. Chetniks like Peter and his men?'

'They'll do what I have done. Join the Partisans.' Seeing Stephen's deep frown he added reassuringly, 'Peter understands why I did so, Stephen. There's no division between us. I still love him and admire him just as much as I've always done.'

The unselfconscious ease with which his Slav cousins were able verbally to express their feelings had always been a source of envy to Stephen. He, too, loved and admired Peter but English reticence would never have allowed him to say so in such a direct manner.

He reached into the inside pocket of his bomber jacket and withdrew the letter that had been there ever since he had left London. 'Here,' he said, his throat tight. 'Is this what you've been waiting for?'

Xan snatched the letter from his grasp. 'You devil!' he said, his face ablaze with joy, 'Why didn't you give me it earlier? I was beginning to think you hadn't brought one!'

Without waiting for a reply to his questions he ripped the envelope open, feasting his eyes on the contents.

Stephen looked away and at the German infested mountain on the far side of the valley, marvelling as he always did at how different in physique Xan was to his father. Only the dark hair and high cheekbones were similar and even then they were not the same. Xan's hair was silky, not coarse, and there was a faint hollow under the cheekbones that emphasized the Greek classicism of the rest of his features, robbing them of any hint of Slav heaviness.

'What happens now?' he said to Xan when he had finished reading, referring to their military position. 'We were told a short while ago there would be no more central orders issued. Is it going to become a case of every man for himself?'

Xan folded Zorka's letter and put it securely in an inner pocket of his tunic. 'No,' he said emphatically. 'But the German ring is so complete that the only way of breaking out of it is in small groups. Tito wants you to stay with Major Kechko. He already has two British officers and four other ranks with him, one of them a wireless operator. It's a pity, because it means I don't know when I'll see you again.'

'I'll see you in Belgrade,' Stephen said, his throat tighter than ever.

Xan nodded, not trusting himself to speak and then, as enemy aircraft approached, he embraced Stephen hard and turned on his heel, sprinting back to his waiting horse.

That night, led by Nicky Kechko, Stephen and his companions slipped through the German lines. Two days later, shortly after they crossed the border into Bosnia, Stephen established radio contact with Cairo and the order he had received from Tito, via Xan, was confirmed. He was to stay with Major Kechko until further notice.

'And we're to carry out sabotage operations on all rail lines leading to Sarajevo,' he said to Nicky. 'Cairo will drop us supplies. All we have to arrange is a suitable dropping-zone.'

All through the summer they arranged dropping-zones and all through the summer they conducted a relentless onslaught on all possible lines of German communication. In September the Italians surrendered and huge quantities of captured weapons and ammunition boosted the vital supplies being parachuted in to them.

By the end of the year it was obvious that the Germans were beginning to lose the war and it was also obvious that when they did so, the future government of Yugoslavia would be dominated by the communists.

'Is that a future you can stomach?' Nicky asked Stephen as together with the rest of the unit they crouched around a roaring wood fire in a shepherd's hut while a snowstorm raged outside.

'If it means an end to Serbs and Croats constantly being at each other's throats and Moslems, Catholics and Orthodox finally welding together in a united country then yes, I can probably stomach it.'

Nicky grinned. He enjoyed trying to bait Stephen politically and it amused him vastly that Stephen never rose to the bait and never became heatedly contentious as one of his own fellow-countrymen would have done.

By the time spring came, Stephen found it hard to imagine any other way of life than the one he was now leading. The spartan simplicity and male camaraderie suited him. He enjoyed living for the most part out in the open; marching in the early morning across mountain slopes; resting in orchards thick with plum and almond blossom; eating around a camp fire and then, at night, setting off on adrenalin-packed sabotage missions.

As month after month passed and the Germans were pushed gradually further and further northwards, Stephen was aware that more and more Loyalists were throwing in their lot with the Partisans. At the end of the summer a BBC broadcast ensured that even greater numbers began to do so.

'I don't believe it!' Nicky gasped as the voice of young King Peter, speaking from London, called on all Yugoslav patriots to abandon their support of General Mihailovich and to rally behind Tito and his Partisans. 'King Peter will be joining us himself, next!'

'If he still has hopes of returning to Yugoslavia as king that is exactly what he should do,' Mitja Stefanovich said dryly. 'Why should any Yugoslav welcome a king back who hasn't fought with them and for them?'

Though in full agreement with him, Stephen kept silent. He was wondering what his mother's reaction to King Peter's broadcast would be. It was a betrayal of General Mihailovich and all those, Peter and Max included, who were fighting with him and she was bound to be distressed and bewildered by it.

In midsummer Mitja Stefanovich was promoted to the rank of major and Nicky was ordered to report to Staff Headquarters, leaving Mitja in command of the unit.

'It doesn't look as if we'll be entering Belgrade together after all,' Nicky said in deep dudgeon to Stephen as he loaded his few possessions on to his horse. 'Why the devil I've to be given a Staff appointment just when things are coming to a military conclusion, I can't begin to imagine.'

'If the conclusion is going to be soon, it will be easy enough for us to meet up after it, in Belgrade,' Stephen said, as disappointed as Nicky that there now seemed no likelihood of their fighting their way into the city side by side.

Nicky finished strapping his pack on to his horse. 'Don't take any nonsense from Mitja,' he said gruffly.

Stephen grinned. Mitja Stefanovich was the most easygoing and reasonable of men and as unlikely to dish out 'nonsense' as he was to fly to the moon.

Nicky turned towards him, his eyes overly bright. 'Goodbye, my friend,' he said, embracing him. 'Promise me one thing. Promise me you'll always take good care of that sister of yours.'

'I promise,' Stephen said thickly.

Nicky mounted his horse. All the men he had led for so

long, under such difficult conditions, were gathered to see him go. He raised his hand to them in a clenched fist salute and then, reluctantly, he pressed his heels lightly against his horse's flanks and minutes later was only an indistinct figure in the distance.

Chapter Twenty-Four

In the weeks and months that followed, Stephen missed Nicky greatly. They had lived together and fought together as blood brothers for well over a year and though Nicky's mercurial temperament had often exasperated him, it had also ensured that when there had been long gaps in military activity, life had never been dull.

Hard on the heel of Nicky's departure came news from Cairo that the Russians were storming through Romania and would shortly be entering Yugoslavia from the east and joining forces with the Partisan Army in the fight for Belgrade. Everywhere, on all fronts, the Germans were under pressure and Stephen decided that the time had come for him to visit Sarajevo.

'Sarajevo?' Mitja said to him, puzzled. 'Why do you want to enter Sarajevo? Orders from both my command and yours are that we should be making our way towards Belgrade.'

'I have a visit to make in Sarajevo,' Stephen said, wondering what on earth Mitja would say if he knew what the purpose of his visit was. 'I'll leave the wireless transmitter and receiver in your care and catch up with you as soon as possible.'

'You'll be court-martialled if anyone finds out!'

'Very likely,' Stephen said dryly. 'To avoid complications let the wireless batteries run down. Twenty-four hours of not being able to establish contact won't harm Cairo and it won't harm us.'

'It's a woman, isn't it?' Mitja said with a sudden grin. 'You're going to see a woman?'

'No, but I'm going to do a favour for one,' Stephen said, beginning to strip his sten gun down so that the magazine and short body and barrel could be carried in the inside pockets of his sleeveless sheepskin jacket.

'You must love her very much.' Beneath his forbidding, bearded exterior, Mitja had a tender heart. 'She must be very special.'

Stephen stowed the separate parts of his gun away, satisfied that together with his hand gun he carried enough firepower to get himself out of any trouble into which he might get himself.

'I do,' he said wryly, 'and she is.'

He had little trouble entering Sarajevo and walking through its streets. The Germans had far too much on their minds to worry about a young peasant in mud-stained clothing, especially a peasant carrying an incongruous bunch of late flowering wild white roses.

Asking for directions in fluent Serbo-Croat from elderly ladies he made his way on foot, up through the dusty streets towards the cemetery.

Though there was no distinctive monument, the graves were easy to find. They lay near the cemetery palings, three stone slabs, the area around them neglected and untended.

The central slab, under which Gavrilo Princip was buried, was slightly raised and Stephen laid his posy of white roses on top of it.

He stood silently for a long time, thinking of the nineteen-year-old whose patriotic, criminal action had brought such cataclysmic consequences in its wake. Because of what had happened in Sarajevo on that sunny June afternoon thirty-one years ago the world had been plunged into war. Even now, in the midst of a second world war, the reverberations of that action continued. He thought of his mother, exiled for all of her adult life from the country she so passionately loved and he marvelled again at her lack of bitterness. In her eyes, Gavrilo Princip had been her friend.

He pondered on what might have happened if Gavrilo had admitted to speaking to her in the Oriental bazaar; of having met regularly with her in Belgrade at the *Golden Sturgeon*. In all likelihood she would have stood trial accused of being an accomplice in the plot to assassinate the Archduke. And she might have died in prison, as Gavrilo and his friends had died, and been buried alongside them.

It was an eerie thought and he knew that she was right in thinking that Princip had been a true friend to her. Wishing him eternal rest he made the sign of the cross on brow and breast and then, his mission completed, he made his way back to the cemetery gates and the narrow, busy street beyond them.

It took him a day and a half to catch up with Mitja and his men. Though they were camped in thick woodland he had no trouble in finding them. It was a camp site they had used before, earlier in the year, convenient not only because of the cover it gave from enemy aircraft but also because a nearby stream boasted a deep sandy bank warrened with man-sized hiding holes.

Giving the low whistle that was his unit's call sign, he made a cautious approach.

'We have visitors,' Yelich, who was on sentry duty, said to him. 'They say they know you.' There was curiosity in his eyes. 'Major Stefanovich thinks one of them could be the reason you went to Sarajevo.'

Stephen's heartbeats began to slam against his

breast-bone. Mitja had assumed the reason to be a woman and the only woman he knew who could possibly be a visitor to a Partisan guerilla camp, was Olga.

There was no sign of a raffish RAF cap among the grey side-caps worn by the men sitting and talking on the banks of the stream. Then he saw the burly, unmistakable figure of Marko.

'Marko!' he shouted joyously, hurrying towards him. 'What the devil are you doing here? Is Peter with you? Is Olga?'

Marko strode to meet him, looking oddly alien in Partisan uniform. 'I'm here for the same reason as you are,' he said with a face-splitting grin. 'To fight the Germans. Where our other friends are, I'm not sure. Apart from Olga of course. Olga is making her report to Major Stefanovich.'

'Then I'd better join them,' Stephen said, breaking free of Marko's bear-like embrace. 'Does she know I'm with Stefanovich's unit? Is that why you came here?'

Marko's grin grew even wider. 'Aren't you taking rather a lot on yourself, my English friend?' he asked, vastly amused. 'Why should Olga want to join up with Stefanovich just because you're his liaison officer? And why the devil would either Olga or Major Stefanovich want you with them while she makes her report? It would be far more sensible of you to stay here with me and to listen while I tell you of the Russian troops with whom we made contact four days ago. They were part of the Soviet Fourth Mechanized Corps and had enough trucks and tanks with them to storm Berlin, let alone Belgrade.'

Despite his fevered impatience to see Olga again, Stephen's attention was hooked. 'What strength were they?' he asked with urgent interest. 'A platoon? A brigade? A company?'

'A division,' Marko said, enjoying the expression of

512

incredulity on Stephen's face. 'An entire division, my English friend. The battle for Belgrade is imminent.'

Stephen's elation turned to sudden horror. 'Christ Almighty!' he said, staring at Marko appalled. 'And I asked Mitja to let the battery on the receiving set run down!' He turned on his heel and began running in the direction of the felled tree that customarily acted as Mitja's desk. He had to make sure if Mitja had done as he had asked and, if he had, he had to begin cranking the stiff handle of the battery's generator immediately.

At his approach Mitja looked up from the slenderly built figure he was talking to; an expression of vast relief crossing his face.

'Stephen! Thank God you're back!' he exclaimed, rising to his feet. 'The entire First Army Group is bearing down on Belgrade. Our orders are to remain as a sabotage unit and to keep up heavy pressure on the Belgrade to Sarajevo line. We have two additions to our ranks to help us do so. Lieutenant Marko Tomosevich and Lieutenant Olga Marinko. I believe you're acquainted with them both?'

Olga had been standing, facing Mitja and now she turned around. The pale oval of her face was as impassive as it had been when he had first seen her, putting the bottle of *slivovitz* and glass on the table in Peter's headquarters. Then he saw the expression at the back of her eyes and he knew that her impassiveness was nothing more than a defensive shield for uncertainty and shyness.

He could only think of one reason for the uncertainty and elation sang through him. 'Yes,' he said, suddenly sure that she knew what his feelings for her were; that Peter had spoken to her. 'We're acquainted. How is the shoulder, Lieutenant Marinko?'

She shrugged, as if proving that it was no trouble whatsoever, her eyes not leaving his.

Mitja said briskly: 'Both Lieutenant Tomosevich and

Lieutenant Marinko are explosives experts. We're going to leave at dusk and blow the Belgrade–Sarajevo line at its nearest point to us. Can you discuss the plan with me now?'

'I have to make contact with Cairo first and if you let the battery expire, as I suggested, I'm going to need help cranking the generator.'

'Lieutenant Marinko will help you. We need to divide ourselves into three separate groups for tonight's action. Two groups to cover the line left and right and one to lay the charges. If you and Lieutenant Marinko fix the charges, I'll command one of the protecting groups and Lieutenant Tomosevich can command the other. I'll go and speak to him now.'

When he had gone and when Stephen had ensured there was no-one else within hearing distance, he said, 'What's happened to the others, Olga? Have they joined Partisan units as well? Where is Peter?'

She said carefully, as if filing a formal report, 'After you left, and we went up to the cave, we saw very little action. Every sabotage act Major Zlarin wished to carry out had to be sanctioned by General Mihailovich. This meant long delays while couriers informed the general of the plans and then, nearly always, the general vetoed them. Everyone grew exasperated and one or two of the younger ones, Peko and Tomas, followed you north-west to join Partisan units.'

'And then?' He took a packet of cigarettes out of his shirt pocket and offered her one.

She shook her head, saying a little unsteadily, 'And then we received confirmation that some of our units were collaborating with the Germans. Major Zlarin said they weren't doing so with General Mihailovich's sanction and that we shouldn't let it deter us from continuing to give the general our loyalty, but it was hard to stomach. Lieutenant Vlatko said he'd rather fight with the communists than have people assume that as a Chetnik he was a collaborator and after a terrible argument with Major Zlarin he left, taking Milos with him.'

In sudden weariness she sat down on the tree trunk. 'After that we weren't viable as a unit any longer. Major Zlarin said he was going to join General Mihailovich and asked Marko and me if we wished to go with him.'

For the first time there was undisguised, anguished emotion in her eyes. 'Marko said that by not quelling the traitors in his ranks immediately, General Mihailovich had lost all credibility as a resistance leader. He said he had joined the resistance to fight the Germans and if the only way he could so was by throwing in his lot with the Partisans, then that was what he was going to do.'

'And you left with him?'

She nodded. 'We've been with a unit about twenty miles to the south of Sarajevo. Two days ago orders were received to join with the main body of the army ready for the assault on Belgrade. We asked if, as our experience was in sabotage, we could join with Major Stefanovich's unit instead.'

'I'm glad you did,' he said, resting a booted foot on the tree trunk a few inches away from her and looking down at her intently. 'I've thought of you often.'

Her hands were folded on her lap and she averted her gaze from his, looking down at them, the merest suspicion of colour heightening her cheeks. Her hands were long and narrow with beautiful almond-shaped nails. He wondered how, handling gelignite as she did, she managed to keep them so smooth and unstained. He wondered also if he was about to make a God-awful fool of himself. He remembered his father telling him how he had fallen in love with his mother almost instantly and without hardly knowing her. He couldn't remember his mother telling him that she had fallen in love equally precipitately, but considering the circumstances under which they had married she must have done so. It was a marriage blatantly happy and successful and it had been founded on little more than instinct.

Following family tradition and trusting to instinct himself, he said huskily, 'I missed you, Olga. We had too little time together.'

'Yes.' She lifted her head, her eyes meeting his, her face impassive no longer. 'I missed you, too. When you had gone I realized that I had not thanked you for the medical care you gave me and I realized something else, too. I realized that because I had not known you were part Slav, I had been very impolite.'

The laugh-lines edging his mouth deepened. 'Why did realizing I was part Slav change anything?'

She said gravely, 'In the weeks prior to you joining us there had been several BBC reports of sabotage action being carried out by Partisans when it had, in fact, been carried out by Loyalists. It was obvious to me that the British were preparing to abandon General Mihailovich and switch their support to Tito and so I felt hostile towards the British. And because you are British I felt hostile towards you, too.'

'And now?' he asked, his amusement deepening.

There was a glimmer of an answering smile in the dark depths of her eyes. 'And now I realize that though you are British, you are not typically British. That you care very much what happens to Yugoslavia.'

'I do,' he said sincerely, remembering the urgent need to make radio contact with Cairo. He tossed his cigarette stub away. The present conversation could be continued later, under more suitable conditions. What was important now was that they began cranking the generator and that enough life was restored to the battery to enable him to send a signal that evening.

'Come on,' he said, stretching a hand down to her and helping her to her feet, knowing that a totally different and far more intimate relationship had been forged between them. 'We have work to do.'

Just before dusk he tapped out his message about Russian activity in the area and stood by to receive an incoming signal. Its contents were totally unexpected. He was to stay with his present unit until Belgrade had been taken. He was then to make his way to Belgrade and the British Legation where he would meet with other SOE officers who had been acting, as he had, as liaison officers with the Partisans. From there they would be flown to northern Italy where they would continue liaison work, this time with the Ligurian partisans.

He realized, the instant he read it, that he had been a fool not to have expected such an order. It had been obvious for months that the guerilla phase of the war in Yugoslavia was coming to an end and that once Belgrade was taken, small sabotage units such as the one in which he was operating, would be defunct.

As he set off at dusk on what was possibly going to be one of his last sabotage missions in Yugoslavia, he pondered the problem he now faced. Was he again going to part from Olga without there being a satisfactory understanding between them, or was he going to ask her to marry him?

The unit was moving down a hillside swiftly in a double column. She was a little ahead of him, marching alongside Marko, a pack on her bag, a rifle slung nonchalantly over one shoulder. He knew that the pack was stuffed with sticks of gelignite and he grinned, remembering how insignificant his London girlfriends had always appeared when seen alongside his mother or Zorka. Insignificant was certainly not a word that could ever be used to describe Olga.

Sensing his eyes on her, she turned her head, looking back towards him. For a brief moment their eyes met and she flashed him a quick wide smile.

He returned it, knowing with a slam of utter certainty that he wanted to marry her, aware of only one possible obstacle. Had she become a communist? If she had, the political gulf between them would make mental affinity a near impossibility and their future life together would be fraught with difficulties. He wondered when he could possibly ask her such a question, for if her answer was the one he was hoping for, it would have to be when no-one else was within hearing distance.

Darkness fell and under the light of a pale moon, avoiding all paths and villages, they made directly for their objective.

At last Mitja, at the head of the column, halted. In front of him, about two hundred yards distant, lay the main railway line between Sarajevo and Belgrade.

Everyone knew the part they were to play. Marko and the men detailed to him found a commanding position from which they could offer Stephen and Olga covering fire from the sentries who regularly patrolled the line. Mitja did likewise.

'Are you ready?' Stephen whispered to Olga as, in the distance, a train carrying German arms and ammunition could be heard approaching.

She nodded, her face taut.

'Right then,' he said, adrenalin pumping along his veins. 'Let's go!'

In perfect accord they sprinted across night-wet grass to the railway embankment, scrambling up it as the train steamed into view. Though they had never worked as a team before both knew down to a split-second what their tasks were.

As Stephen fixed the charge and she knelt beside him,

clamping the fog signal, he knew there would never be a more perfect moment to speak to her without being overheard.

'There's something I need to ask you,' he said urgently, sweat beading his forehead as he wedged the explosive under the line. 'Are you a communist?'

She sucked in her breath and then, trusting him completely, said succinctly, 'No.'

With swift expertise he fixed the fuse. The train was bearing down on them at high speed and they had only seconds in which to put as much distance between it and them as was humanly possible. With a last look at the charge he grabbed hold of her hand, diving with her down the side of the embankment.

The train wheels were almost on top of the detonator and as they regained their balance and began running, he yelled over the roar of the engine, '*Will you marry me?*'

In a cacophany of screaming rending metal the night erupted around them. The train catapulted off the buckled rails and over the embankment, goods carriages telescoping into each other, debris rocketing over their heads. As he threw himself to the ground for cover, dragging her with him, she shouted back one word. '*Yes!*'

Romantic liaisons were deeply disapproved of between comrades in Partisan units and both of them knew they couldn't display any sign of their new-found relationship. On the return march back to their base Olga strode alongside Marko. Stephen, several yards behind her, kept Yelich company.

The entire unit was in high spirits. Not only had their mission been successful, everyone knew that the battle for Belgrade was imminent and might even have started.

It was early morning when they entered the wood

sheltering their camp site and the general mood was one of euphoria. It was dispelled almost instantly.

Velebit had remained behind on sentry duty and he came hurrying to meet them, his face ashen. 'A courier came only seconds after you left,' he said to Mitja. 'We're to begin moving forward to Belgrade.'

'What else?' Mitja demanded, knowing that such an order couldn't possibly account for Velebit's obvious distress.

A spasm crossed Velebit's bearded face. 'He said that Major Kechko had been killed in a bomb explosion. He said that there hadn't been a burial, as there hadn't been enough left of Major Kechko to warrant one.'

Every man stood in appalled silence. Violent death was commonplace among them but Nicky Kechko had been special. He had been their commanding officer when they had been trapped on Mount Durmitor and it had been every unit for itself. Under his leadership they had been one of the units to survive.

'Shit,' Yelich said, tears trickling down his face. 'Hell, bollocks, *shit*!'

Stephen felt as if a fist had been slammed into his stomach. In the many months they had been together Nicky had been like an older brother to him. An irresponsible, irrepressible older brother; but an older brother all the same.

Turning away from the others he walked down to the stream, standing on its banks, his hands deep in his breeches pockets. He had never understood why his family life should have been of such absorbing interest to Nicky but he had known, right from the first, that Nicky's interest had been deeply sincere. He remembered the last thing Nicky had asked of him and his throat tightened. Behind him a twig cracked and he turned, facing Olga.

'I didn't know if you wanted to be left alone or if you

wanted some company,' she said hesitantly.

'I want your company,' he said truthfully. 'Let's walk further along the bank and I'll tell you about my friend, Nicky Kechko.'

Three weeks later they were in Belgrade. Olga's home town was Zagreb and she had never been to Belgrade before.

'It's a bit hard to recognize,' Stephen said to her grimly as they made their way through the bomb-blasted streets to the British Legation. 'That ruined building over there was the *Konak*. No-one ever lived in it after old King Peter. King Alexander never cared for it and Prince Regent Paul built himself a palace of his own, on the outskirts of the city. I imagine Tito will have made his headquarters in it.'

'And your grandparents' home? Where is that?'

'Not far,' Stephen said white-lipped, icy fingers of fear gripping his heart. 'The minute I've reported to the Legation we'll go there.'

Everywhere they looked there were traces of savage fighting. Burnt-out tanks littered the streets and in every square and on every scrap of waste ground there were wooden crosses marking graves.

As they approached the British Legation Stephen was relieved to see that it was still standing. It indicated that despite the damage done to the *Konak*, other solidly-built buildings, such as his grandparents' home, might also have escaped unscathed.

When he entered it, he did so alone, leaving Olga waiting for him outside its very English, mock Queen Anne frontage.

'You've got eight hours, that's all,' he was told bluntly by a kilted brigadier. 'Report to the aerodrome at 1800 hours.'

Vastly relieved that no time was to be wasted in an official debriefing he strode back outside, breaking the news to Olga as gently as he could.

'It isn't long, is it?' she said a little unsteadily as he held her close.

His lips brushed the satin-sheen of her hair. 'No,' he said tenderly, 'but the Germans aren't just on the run in Yugoslavia. They're on the run everywhere. In another few months the war will be over and we'll be together for the rest of our lives.'

He was speaking the truth and she knew it. Comforted, her fingers intertwined with his. 'Let's go to your grandparents' house,' she said, knowing that the moment of truth he was so fearing could be put off no longer. 'If they've been bombed out of it, it might take all of your eight hours to find them.'

Unsaid was that they might not find them. That they might never find them or ever know what had happened to them.

With hands tightly clasped they walked through the cratered streets. Everywhere there were Russians, so many it was as if Belgrade had been turned overnight into a Russian town. Occasionally they caught sight of an American or a British flag hanging from a window, but it was the Russians who had fought with the Partisan First Army and liberated the city, and it was the Russians who were the heroes of the hour.

With his heart in his mouth Stephen turned into Prince Milan Street and approached the familiar, ornate iron gates of the Vassilovich *konak*. His relief, as he saw beyond them, was seismic.

The white-walled house was still standing. In the courtyard there was a jeep bearing a Russian pendant and nearby, on the ground, lay a torn and muddied German flag.

As they walked up the stone steps towards the heavy oak door it swung open and Stephen saw a sight he knew he would never forget; a sight he would treasure in his memory as long as he lived. Laza, emaciatingly thin, shabbily dressed, was beaming at him with blackened teeth.

'I saw you coming, Mr Stephen,' he said as Stephen stepped over the threshold. 'I saw you coming from the window in the general's study.'

'The general?' Stephen said, embracing him.

'General Zerdlov,' Laza said, beaming welcomingly at Olga. 'Throughout the war the house was a German headquarters. Now it is a Russian headquarters. When it was a German headquarters your grandparents and aunt moved in with my parents in their little house down near the river. Now the Russians are in temporary residence they are allowing your grandparents and aunt the use of some of the rooms.'

'They're here now?' Stephen's voice cracked under the weight of his relief. 'All of them?'

Laza nodded, his eyes suspiciously bright. 'They are in the Italian room, Mr Stephen. Mr Xan is with them. He told them you would be here soon.'

Stephen passed his hand across his eyes. That both his grandparents and his aunt were still alive after living for more than three years under German occupation was more than he had dared hope for. He turned to Olga, knowing that the next few moments were going to be the most emotionally charged of his life. 'Come on, my love,' he said a little unsteadily, taking hold of her hand. 'I want you to meet my family.'

Laza walked ahead of them across the marble-floored hallway and one-handedly opened the double doors of the small, south-facing drawing-room. 'Mr Stephen,' he announced, a tremor in his voice. 'And a young lady.'

Dimly Stephen was reminded of the moment when, as a small boy he had walked into the Negresco's sun lounge and been introduced to his grandmother and aunt for the first time. Then, as now, they had been sitting together taking afternoon tea and he had thought them both exquisitely beautiful. His grandmother had been dressed in a gown of soft turquoise and his aunt had been wearing cream and brown and burnt umber, the colours emphasizing the titian highlights in her mahogany-dark hair. With a catch in his throat he realized that by a freak coincidence his grandmother was again wearing turquoise and his aunt was wearing an ivory blouse and a deep caramel-coloured skirt very similar in shade to the skirt and blouse she had been wearing all those years ago. There was only one major difference. Instead of being highly fashionable the clothes they were now wearing were much-mended and heart-achingly shabby.

As his grandmother gave a small cry and rose to her feet, opening her arms welcomingly, he saw that though the suffering she had undergone had altered the quality of her beauty it had not eradicated it. Her snow-white hair was piled high on her head in lush, deep waves and though her face was now webbed by tiny fine lines her wonderful bone structure and wide radiant smile made them insignificant.

'Stephen!' she said joyously, her arms closing around him, 'Oh, Stephen! I can hardly believe it's you! Xan is here as well! He arrived an hour ago and he said you would soon be here, but I didn't dare believe him!'

From a window-seat overlooking the courtyard Xan grinned, highly pleased at having beaten his English cousin in the race to the family home.

'And Xan has brought us news of Peter and Max,' his grandfather said gruffly from his position in front of the fireplace. 'A temporary amnesty has been extended by Tito to officers serving with General Mihailovich. Xan has

524

persuaded both Peter and Max to take advantage of it.'

Very gently Stephen extricated himself from his grandmother's embrace. Before talk turned to other family matters there was an important introduction and announcement to be made.

'I want to introduce you to Olga,' he said to the room at large, taking hold of Olga's hand. 'She was a member of Peter's unit when he was in Montenegro. For the past few weeks we have been in the same unit and she's been helping me sabotage the Sarajevo–Belgrade railway line. She's also the girl I'm going to marry.'

Katerina gave a cry of delight, walking swiftly towards them both. 'You were with my son?' she said to Olga, her eyes shining as she embraced her. 'You were with Peter?'

It was hard for Olga to answer her and make her voice heard. Xan was giving an exultant whistle. Alexis was saying buoyantly, 'Congratulations! Congratulations! We need to make a toast! Where is Laza? Where the devil is that bottle of *klekovacha* I hid away?'

Zita was saying, 'I can't believe it! I truly can't believe all the wonderful things that are happening today!'

'When are you going to get married?' Xan asked Stephen practically when the din had died down and Laza had hurried in with the precious bottle of *klekovacha*. 'Immediately, or when the war ends?'

'When it ends. It's impossible to do it any sooner. I leave for Italy tonight.'

'Then we could have a double wedding,' Xan said, crossing the room and kissing Olga warmly on both cheeks, thoroughly approving of his cousin's choice of a bride. 'What better way could there be of celebrating the peace?'

Zita gave a gasp of incredulity. 'But that's a *wonderful* idea,' she said as Alexis pressed a glass of *klekovacha* into her hand. 'The Russians will have gone by then and we can clean up the ballroom and hold the reception there. It will be just like old times! Cissie and her husband can come and stay with us and Vitza can come and stay and . . .'

A shadow crossed Katerina's face. 'You're forgetting something, Mama,' she said gently. 'You're forgetting that if the wedding is in Belgrade, Natalie won't be able to attend it.'

Zita stared at her. For a brief, beautiful moment she had forgotten all about the ban on Natalie ever returning home and now all her happiness drained out of her and she turned to Alexis, seeking for his hand, saying brokenly, 'I forgot, Alexis. How could I have done so? How could I possibly have forgotten?'

Olga looked towards Stephen, mystified.

He said quickly, hating to see his grandmother robbed so cruelly of her dream of a wonderful double wedding, 'Perhaps we could have the weddings at the Orthodox church in Nice. Nice has always been second home to us all and . . .'

'No,' Xan said peremptorily, back in the window-seat, sitting longways with an arm hooked loosely around his knees.

As all eyes flew to him in dazed disbelief he said again, 'No. I've no intention of marrying Zorka anywhere else but in Belgrade.'

Katerina sucked in her breath sharply.

Alexis said, 'I don't think that's being very sensitive, Xan. Natalie will want to see her daughter married . . .'

'If Xan feels so strongly about marrying Zorka in Belgrade, I'm sure my mother will understand,' Stephen said, a shutter coming down over his face. 'But I shan't be marrying here. My mother's suffered enough heartache over the years by not being able to attend family

526

celebrations in Belgrade without being unable to attend my wedding as well.'

A lock of silky-dark hair had fallen low over Xan's brow and he pushed it away with an impatient gesture. 'For goodness sake, Stephen! What do you take me for? Of course I'm not suggesting a ceremony Aunt Natalie won't be able to attend!'

'Then what are you suggesting?'

Xan grinned. 'I'm suggesting a double wedding in Belgrade,' he said again, enjoying Stephen's incomprehension.

Stephen waited, knowing that though Xan was teasing him, he wouldn't be doing so purposelessly.

With the easy grace which characterized all his movements Xan swung his legs from the window-seat and stood up, saying in exaggerated exasperation, 'It's so obvious I can't believe that you can't see it.'

He looked around at his family. Only his grandfather had a gleam of understanding in his eyes. He put his hands in his trouser pockets and said, 'When the war ends, and it will end within the next few months, the man wielding power in Yugoslavia is not going to be a Karageorgevich. It's going to be Tito.'

Stephen drew in his breath sharply.

Xan grinned, knowing that Stephen had mentally leapt ahead of him and now understood fully, knowing also that he would be cursing himself as a fool for not having understood long ago.

For the sake of Zita and Katerina he continued patiently, 'Tito isn't going to care if Aunt Natalie returns to Belgrade. The veto King Alexander put on her ever returning home is now as dead as Alexander himself. It was Prince Paul who senselessly perpetuated it and Prince Paul is now history. Times have changed. The *world* has

527

changed. No-one *cares* any more about the whys and wherefores of the First World War. The subject is as obsolete as the dodo.'

Katerina drew in a deep, shuddering breath. Only Zita was still bewildered. Lovingly Xan crossed the room towards her, taking her hands in his. 'The time has come for Aunt Natalie to return home,' he said to her gently. 'The time has come for the best family reunion ever.'

Chapter Twenty-Five

Natalie stared at Stephen, as bewildered as her mother had been. 'I can go home?' she said dazedly, 'I can return to Belgrade?'

'Yes,' he said patiently for the second time, Rosie sprawling welcomingly across his feet.

As realization flooded through her she put a hand out to the mantelpiece to steady herself. Through the drawing-room window she could see two youths strolling on the tree-lined Embankment looking almost as incongruous in their ill-fitting demob suits as Stephen did in his.

She wondered what kind of demob suits Yugoslav soldiers would now be wearing and smiled at the very idea of Yugoslavs squeezing themselves into any kind of a suit. Her fellow countrymen would be wearing knee high boots and breeches and sheepskin waistcoats.

'Just as soon as it's safe for you to travel across Europe,' Stephen was saying, 'Xan will arrange the weddings and . . .'

She looked at him in disbelief. 'But it's safe now! Returning refugees are criss-crossing Europe in their thousands! It says so in the newspapers!'

'Conditions are still chaotic,' Stephen said dryly, remembering the horrors of his own journey across Italy only days previously. He looked towards his father for support. 'Perhaps by the end of the month Father will be able to arrange suitable travel arrangements with the Foreign Office.'

'End of the month!' Natalie's eyes were wide with incredulity. '*End of the month?*' she said again, regarding her beloved son as if he was an escapee from a lunatic asylum. 'I've waited over thirty years to return home and now that I can do so, you suggest I wait another month! Never! I'm going now! Today! This very minute!'

Like a human whirlwind she made a dash towards the door. Julian stepped restrainingly in front of it. 'I understand your impatience, sweetheart,' he said gently, 'but Stephen is right. Europe is still in chaos and . . .'

Natalie spun around. 'When are you going to return to Olga?' she demanded, her cheeks flushed, a note of hysteria in her voice. 'Are you going to wait until the end of the month? Is Zorka going to wait until the end of the month before being reunited with Xan?'

'No,' Stephen said uncomfortably, 'but that's different. We're accustomed to the difficulties of wartime transport . . .'

Natalie drew in a deep, quivering breath. 'For the last six years I have lived in a city that has taken everything Hitler was able to throw at it. How can you possibly imagine I am going to fall to pieces at the sight of an overcrowded train? I don't care if I have to stand every inch of the way through France and Italy. I don't care if I have to sit on the roof! I'm travelling with you and Zorka to Belgrade and I'm going upstairs to pack a bag now!'

She meant every word and Julian knew it. 'Give me a few hours on the telephone,' he said persuasively. 'I might be able to pull a few strings where the travel arrangements are concerned and it will give you time to find a suitable present for Olga.'

'We'll leave by this evening? You promise?'

'Yes,' he said, his throat tight. 'I promise.'

With tears of joy brimming her eyes she stood tiptoe in her perilously high wedged-sandals and kissed him on the mouth. He had never let her down once in all the years they had been married and she knew that he wouldn't let her down now. Thirty-one years and two world wars after leaving home she was, at last, about to return.

Despite all Julian's best efforts it was an horrendously uncomfortable, exhausting journey. Food had to be bought on the hop at whatever station the train decided to stop and the little available was rarely fresh. There wasn't enough money in the world to buy wagon-lit accommodation and as their train trundled from France into Italy nights were spent huddled cheek by jowl with their fellow passengers in crowded, ill-ventilated carriages. Neither Natalie or Zorka or Stephen cared. All had loved ones waiting for them. All were counting the minutes until the train edged into Yugoslavia.

When it did so, Natalie burst into tears. 'I can't believe it,' she kept saying to Julian time and time again as they stood in the cramped, swaying corridor and she feasted her eyes on hills and rivers and distant mountains. 'Despite everything that has happened, the landscape is still the same! Lakes are still where they used to be! Forests are still where they used to be!'

As they began the final approach to Belgrade, on a railway line Stephen claimed he and Mitja had once bombed, she said, 'Will you all excuse me for a few moments? I'm going to change.'

'Change?' Zorka stared at her in bewilderment. 'Change into what? Change *where*?'

Natalie hugged a bulky brown paper parcel to her breast. 'You'll see,' she said, her eyes feverishly bright. 'As to where, in the water-closet if necessary.'

Side-stepping a small child on a chamber-pot and a family of Moslems eating lunch off their knees she squeezed out of the carriage and into the corridor.

531

Thirty-one years ago she had made a vow to herself and it was one she intended keeping, no matter what the difficulties. As she pushed and shoved her way towards the tiny and inadequate water-closet she knew that the difficulties were going to be considerable.

When she had removed her blue, peplum-waisted costume from its layers of tissue-paper and mothballs not even Diana had been able to help her squeeze into it. 'It's no use,' she had said despairingly, 'you were *seventeen* when you last wore this, for the Lord's sake! You'll need a shoe-horn to get into it and even then it won't button up!'

In the tiny, vile smelling water-closet Natalie cursed her pleasingly plump curves and breathed in as deeply as she was able. She had let out the ankle-length skirt seams herself and she held her breath as she nudged the skirt up over her thighs. The material strained and then miracu-lously accommodated itself to the difficult task being asked of it. With a sigh of relief she fastened the hooks and eyes on the waistband. At least the skirt was on, though it was so narrow at her ankles that she wondered how she had ever managed to walk in it.

She stepped into the pearl-grey, Louis-heeled shoes she had originally worn with it and turned her attention to the nip-waisted jacket. With its sable collar and cuffs it was as pretty now as it had been when she had first worn it to a *Konak* tea party. It was also still as small.

Wondering how and where her extra inches had come from, she squeezed herself into it and began to fasten the long line of tiny covered buttons. The top one burst from its anchorage seconds after being fastened but the others held. Triumphantly she secured the little nonsense of a hat to her hair with a hat-pin and looked in the cracked mirror at the result.

In all due modesty she had to admit that she looked

sensational. The blue was still as singing and vibrant as ever and the flaring peplum flattered her hips and accentuated her waist. The jacket was tight across her bosom but it was voluptuously tight, the burst button looking exceedingly provocative. As for the hat crowning her riot of shoulder-length waves and curls, with its vivid yellow feather it was still as jaunty, still as heart-stoppingly defiant as ever.

As she stepped triumphantly out into the crowded corridor she saw through the grubby windows that countryside had given way to bomb-damaged houses and streets. Her breath caught in her throat. They were entering Belgrade. She saw an onion-shaped dome she recognized and caught a glimpse of one of the bridges across the Sava.

As the train began to slow down and more and more people with bags and bundles began to throng the corridor she saw Julian pushing his way through the crush towards her.

'Stay where you are!' he shouted over a sea of heads. 'Stephen and Zorka are getting out down here. We'll get out at the door nearest you.'

As he squeezed past the last of the people separating them and he saw what she was wearing his eyes widened and his jaw dropped.

Despite her almost paralysing nervous anticipation she giggled. 'Do you recognize it?' she asked unnecessarily. 'I had a little bit of a struggle getting into it. Do you think these buttons are going to hold?'

Julian looked down to where the tiny buttons were straining over her magnificent breasts. 'They may do for a little while,' he said, keeping loving laughter out of his voice only with the greatest difficulty, 'but I don't think they will for long.'

The train begun to shudder to a halt. She put her hand

in his. 'This is the happiest moment of my life,' she said simply.

Quite unable to speak he squeezed her hand tightly and then opened the train door. 'This is it.' His voice was raw with emotion. 'You're home.'

As she stepped out on to the platform she saw that the station was just as large and cavernous as she remembered it being. Ahead of her she could see Stephen and Zorka running towards the crowd of faces waiting at the barrier. She saw a fair-haired girl begin to run towards Stephen, her eyes shining, her face radiant. She saw Stephen's arms close around her, saw his mouth come down hard on hers. She saw Zorka hurtle into Xan's arms and saw Xan exultantly swing her round, lifting her bodily off her feet.

Despite her long narrow skirt she began to run also. Through a blur of tears she recognized the faces waiting for her; her mother and father, Katerina and Max, Peter, Cissie and Vitza. Everyone had come to meet her. Everyone she loved was there to welcome her home.

She saw Katerina burst past the barrier; saw her running towards her.

'Oh, Trina!' she gasped, flying into her welcoming arms, tears streaming down her cheeks, 'Oh, Trina! I'm home! I'm *home*!'

From the moment Katerina had first glimpsed the defiant, jaunty, vibrant yellow feather she had felt as if her heart was going to burst. Knowing the chaotic conditions that still existed in Europe no-one, not even Xan, had expected Natalie to return to Belgrade so soon. When the telegram announcing her impending arrival had been delivered, Katerina had felt almost disorientated with joy. It just didn't seem possible that after so many years the Kara-georgevich, Vassilovich and Fielding families were at last going to enjoy a *zadruga*-style reunion.

Even now, as she released Natalie from her embrace in order that their mother could give her the hug she had looked forward to giving her for so many, many years, she could scarcely believe that as a family they were all at last truly united.

Understanding how deeply emotional the moment was for her, Max slipped his arm around her shoulders. She raised her hand to his, pressing it lovingly against her lips, deeply grateful for his instinctive sensitivity.

Stephen was introducing Julian to Olga and a smile touched the corners of Katerina's mouth. Over the last few weeks she had become very well acquainted with Olga and she knew that Julian was going to be delighted with his new daughter-in-law.

As he turned away from Olga and accepted an affectionate kiss on the cheek from Cissie, their eyes met. What they silently conveyed was more than anyone around them, apart from Max, could ever imagine. That they were both idyllically happy; that they had no regrets about the past; that they would always be each other's dearest friend.

'It's good to see you again, Julian,' Max was saying to him sincerely, giving him a typically masculine Slav bear-hug. 'Will you be having a few words with Tito on behalf of the British government while you're here?'

'Quite possibly,' Julian said, amused as always by Max's perspicacity. 'Though the person I really want to speak with to get a true picture of what is happening politically, is yourself.'

'We'll do that tonight,' Max said agreeably, 'over a bottle of Alexis's best *klekovacha*.'

Katerina slid her hand once more into her husband's. He knew about her affair with Julian for it had been one of the first things she had told him when they had embarked on their own love affair. He hadn't been remotely surprised or disturbed about it. Right from the very beginning he had known about her feelings for Julian and he knew what her feelings for Julian were now. He knew that she regarded him as a deeply loved friend and nothing more; that he, Max, was the real love of her life and always would be.

Over the hubbub of Natalie and Olga's emotional introduction, Peter and Stephen's exuberant reunion, Zita's loving exclamations as to how Zorka had become even more beautiful since she had last seen her, Vitza's voice rose in pained disbelief, 'Why on *earth* are you wearing such an outmoded costume, Natalie? It looks as if it's come from a museum. Surely even the war hasn't reduced London women to such desperate straits?'

Peter shouted with laughter. Natalie rounded on Vitza in high indignation. Alexis began to shepherd them all out to the two waiting cars.

'Cissie and Vitza can go with Xan and Zorka in Peter's car,' he said, judiciously separating Vitza and Natalie as Natalie began to remind Vitza of a particularly hideous blue brocade dress Vitza had once worn to a Vassilovich ball.

'It was ruched and draped like a lampshade,' Natalie said to Olga as Peter handed Vitza and Cissie into a battered, open-top car. 'Vitza has never had the slightest dress sense, not ever, and marriage to a Russian hasn't improved it.'

'Natalie, you come with your mother and Katerina and Olga in my car,' Alexis instructed. 'Stephen and Max and Julian can walk.'

The Vassilovich car was so ancient that Natalie marvelled at its being mobile. The hood was down and as it rolled away from the station she took hold of Katerina's hand, suddenly silent. This was the moment she had waited thirty-one years for; this was the moment when she could look around at her city and know that she was truly home.

Both Julian and Stephen had warned her of the changes and devastation she would find. 'It's not just been one world war since you were last home,' Julian had pointed out to her gently, 'it's been two. Very little will be the same as when you left in 1914, perhaps nothing.'

As the car trundled across the cobbled square fronting the station she steeled herself for the worst and the worst was terrible. Shattered buildings. Cratered streets. She knew that Katerina was watching her, fearful of her reaction, terrified it was going to be one of crushing disappointment. She squeezed her hand and said quietly, 'It's what I expected, Trina. London is a half-wrecked city, too.'

She looked around her and saw beyond the destruction and dereliction. High on its hill overlooking the Sava, the ancient fort in the Kalemegdan Gardens could still be seen, peeping over the tops of the trees surrounding it. Tram lines still ran down the middle of the streets. Ochre-stoned houses still boasted little rickety verandahs. Acacia trees still sprouted in the tiniest of gardens.

They turned into a chestnut-tree lined street named after Marshal Tito. Seeing her bewilderment Katerina said with amusement in her voice, 'You always wanted Prince Milan Street to be renamed and now it has been.'

'I didn't expect it to be renamed after a Croat!' Natalie said indignantly and then, as their eyes met, she began to giggle and by the time Alexis drove between the high ornate gates of their family home and into the dearly familiar little courtyard they were both helpless with deliriously happy laughter.

For everyone in the family the next few days were days to treasure. Katerina and Natalie walked together in

Kalemegdan Gardens, giggling and chattering as if they were seventeen and nineteen again.

Peter, Xan, Max and Julian discussed politics far into the night and though Peter and Max's views were far more to the right than Xan's, they were agreed on one thing. If under Tito, Croats, Serbs, Catholics, Orthodox and Moslems could live in something approaching harmony, then they were prepared to accommodate Tito's nationalistic brand of communism.

Cissie and Vitza sat sewing Zorka and Olga's wedding gowns, Vitza discussing at long, interminable length what she would wear on the great day.

On one memorable evening as they all sat down to dinner together, Zorka spoke enthusiastically of the little house she and Xan had found in which to live.

'It's absolutely exquisite, Aunt Trina,' she said as Julian passed a dish of peas across to Max, and Alexis topped up Stephen's glass of *slivovitz*. 'It's a little Hungarian-style house half-hidden away in a tiny cobbled street behind Terazije Square. There's a lilac tree in the garden and roses climbing up the walls and . . .'

The dish of peas dropped clumsily to the table.

'. . . the most wonderful portrait of old King Peter still hanging on one of the downstairs walls.'

Katerina choked on her wine.

'. . . and two ancient Turkish divans upholstered in peasant needlework,' Zorka continued, pouring her aunt a glass of water. 'I know we're going to be unutterably happy there. Does Uncle Max still want those peas or are they going begging?'

When it came to a decision about what she was to wear for the weddings, Natalie hadn't a shred of doubt. 'I've taken my blue costume to the most wonderful tailor and he says he can make it look as if it were made to measure for me.'

'It was made to measure for you,' Katerina pointed out, her voice thick with loving laughter. 'The only problem was it was made to measure for you thirty-one years ago!'

Natalie threw a cushion at her head and said: 'We're lucky, aren't we? We're gaining two wonderful daughters-in-law. You've loved Zorka ever since you first set eyes on her and Olga is the most amazing girl. She looks so quiet and gentle and yet she has the courage of a lion.'

'Yes,' Katerina said quietly, thinking of Max and her much-loved son and stepson, 'we're very lucky.'

They were alone in the Italian drawing-room and as Natalie looked around at its familiar blue and yellow upholstered furniture and its sunny, lemon walls, she said with a note of wonder in her voice, 'It's strange, I've never thought of anywhere as home but this house and Belgrade, yet since I've been back I've realized that neither the house nor the city is truly my home and hasn't been for years. My home is wherever Julian is.'

'I'm sure Julian realized that a long time ago,' Katerina said gently. 'But you must tell him all the same. It will make him happy.'

In the incense-filled cathedral, as she sat with Max on one side of her and Natalie on the other, Katerina knew that her own happiness was absolute. At the altar Xan and Zorka, Stephen and Olga, stood hand-in-hand. Peter and three of his friends held golden nuptial crowns over their heads and as the service ran its long, solemn course, lit by hundreds of candles and underscored by the sublime singing of an all-male choir, Katerina knew it was the wedding her mother had so longed for, the wedding both she and Natalie had denied her.

With her hand in Max's she looked across to where her mother was sitting and saw the tears glistening on her cheeks. There was a suspicious gleam of tears in Cissie's eyes too. The yellow feather on Natalie's hat partially obscured Vitza from her vision but she had a shrewd suspicion that even Vitza, resplendent in royal purple, was dabbing at her eyes with a handkerchief.

'I never thought I'd see the day when I became father-in-law to Natalie's daughter,' Max said in an undertone to her as a little later they followed the two happy couples down the aisle and out into brilliant sunlight. 'Thank goodness she isn't as volatile and hotheaded as her mother.'

'I think you may be wrong there,' Katerina said in amusement, looking across to where Xan and Zorka were gazing rapturously into each other's eyes. 'But if you are, I don't think Xan is going to mind.'

Xan had managed to procure a small fleet of army cars to take them back to the *konak* and as Max helped Katerina into the nearest one he said dryly, 'Something else I never expected was to be on the receiving-end of communist largesse. Did you know Tito has sent half a dozen crates of champagne for the wedding breakfast?'

'Just be grateful he didn't insist on being a wedding guest!' A faint shadow darkened her eyes. 'Do you think Mama was wise in insisting that we celebrate with a family ball? She so wants it to be like the old days, yet in the old days the guest list was always over two hundred and tonight there will only be thirty or so of us. I'm afraid the ballroom is going to seem very empty and that she's going to be disappointed.'

'Nonsense,' he squeezed his huge frame into the seat beside her. 'Tonight's celebration is going to be in the very best *zadruga* tradition. A gathering of extended family, with second cousins and stepcousins married to each other and no-one able to tell where one particular side of the family ends and the other begins.' His heavy featured face creased in a fond smile of remembrance. 'Do you

540

remember the ball in 1914? You didn't want to dance with me and when you did, you didn't pay me the slightest attention.'

'I shall tonight,' she said, lovingly slipping her hand into his. 'I shall dance with you all night long.'

All through the last occupation of the city the German military had used the ballroom for receptions and high-ranking soirées and it showed very little signs of neglect or decay. Laza and a team of helpers had polished the giant mirrors until they glittered and armfuls of Zita's favourite roses filled the gold-coffered alcoves in vase after vase.

Katerina stood inside the open double doors, gazing around the vast, marble-floored room, knowing that her mother had been right in wanting to evoke old memories and to intertwine them with the memories of her grand-children's wedding day.

The gypsy band had just finished playing a wedding *kolo* and Natalie was still in Julian's arms, laughing breathlessly up at him. In her shot-silk, emerald green ballgown she looked far too young to be Stephen and Zorka's mother. Her eyes were dancing with happiness, her hair piled high in a riot of glossy-dark waves and curls, decorated by a full-blown, lush white rose.

Her father, who had joined in the dance for the last few steps, was smiling lovingly down at her mother. Cissie was standing with her Yugoslav husband, her arm resting lightly in his. Vitza was sipping at a glass of Marshal Tito's champagne, her elderly husband sitting on a gilt-edged chair by her side.

As the band began to play again she saw Peter approach one of Olga's girl friends and ask her to dance with him and maternal hope burned in her heart. Perhaps another romance was blossoming; perhaps Peter would soon be married as well.

The lilting strains of 'The Blue Danube' filled the ballroom and both Olga and Zorka, ravishing in their sumptuous, hand-sewn wedding gowns, stepped out on to the marble floor with their husbands.

Tears burned at the back of Katerina's eyes. Though there were no tiaras in the room, no royal princes and princesses, the scene was far more wonderful than it had been in the dim and distant summer of 1914. Nearly every couple now waltzing together were deeply in love. Her mother and father. Cissie and her husband. Vitza and her husband. Olga and Stephen. Xan and Zorka. Natalie and Julian. And the only couple dancing who were not in love, Peter and his partner, looked as if they were on the brink of being so.

From behind her a deep voice said, 'I know you complain that I dance like a hippopotamus, but if I promise to try very hard not to tread on your toes, will you have this waltz with me?'

She turned towards the bear of a man she loved with all her heart; the man who was her fortress and her peace. 'Yes, Max,' she said, slipping into the circle of his arms as the lyrical notes of Strauss's magical, incomparable masterpiece lapped around them. 'Of course I will dance with you. Only you. For ever.'

THE END